IMPLOSION

"The hands of every clock are shears, trimming us away scrap by scrap, and every timepiece with a digital readout blinks us towards implosion." -Dean Koontz

By
Fran Riedemann

PUBLISHED BY

Consider the Source Publishing, a division of

Consider the Source, LLC

ISBN: 9781466445437

Implosion copyright © 2011 by Fran Riedemann

Implode: Function: verb: to burst inward: to undergo violent compression <massive stars which implode> to collapse inward as if from external pressure; also: to become greatly reduced as if from collapsing, to break down or fall apart from within: self-destruct

Implosion: Function: noun: the inrush of air in forming a suction stop, the action of imploding , the act or action of bringing to or as if to a center; also: integration <this implosion of cultures makes realistic for the first time the age-old vision of a world culture> — Kenneth Keniston

∼∼∼

The sun will become dark, and the moon will become as red as blood before the terrifying day of the LORD comes. Joel 2:31

∼∼∼

Watch therefore, for you do not know what hour your Lord is coming. But know this that if the master of the house had known what hour the thief would come, he would have watched and not allowed his house to be broken into. Therefore you also be ready, for the Son of Man is coming at an hour you do not expect. Matthew 24:42-44

CHAPTER 1

Jeremy removed his Burberry sunglasses, slipping them inside his shirt pocket. In their place, he donned a baseball cap conspicuously embroidered with his company's logo, looking above him where large cotton candy clouds seemed to be hanging motionless in the sky—the humidity was high. Perfect! The day was unfolding as though scripted.

Jeremy searched the crowd in vain, trying to locate his wife, Lenette. The crowd was larger than predicted, and parking was nonexistent; even with her VIP pass she would have a hard time making it through security, much less finding a place to park. He regretted not sending someone to pick her up.

Jeremy Dobson was the no nonsense, second generation owner of Dobson Detonations Inc., a company sought around the globe for the purpose of bringing down structures that had outlived their usefulness. Their job description was to eliminate no longer useful properties by the method of implosion, thereby making way for what was implied to be newer and better. It might be said the buildings weren't simply destroyed, but instead pulverized—or more technically, collapsed inward violently.

He was the son of Dan Dobson, known to most as Dusty, except notably his mother who refused to call him by anything but his given name with the futile hope that might distance her from any association with her son's slovenliness. It could be said that Dusty wore his work home.

Dusty passed away far too early, ultimately succumbing to the ravages of cigarettes, cigars, and Mesothelioma; the culmination of decades of exposure to asbestos, and other toxic debris. The harmful micro biotic particles were a well-known risk of the implosion business, but if Dusty knew about the hazards he ignored them.

While the risks of smoking were well documented, Dusty started smoking at thirteen and, unfortunately, the habit won. He was a self-described maverick, bragging to anyone who would listen how risk was what he lived for. His favorite quote was, "I'm too bad to go to Heaven, and too good to go to Hell, so it looks as though I'll be sticking around for a long time." His final quote was, "I'm counting on the Good Lord winning this one." His family retained the comfort that, in the end, it was God's grace that led him home.

The maverick gene skipped over Jeremy entirely. He was as careful an individual as ever walked the planet. Jeremy, unlike his father, was fastidious, and found the idea of being covered in grit repulsive. Even as a child he remained a safe distance from the nitty-gritty that his father was a magnet for. It was a pretty safe bet Jeremy would never be called Dusty.

He viewed things from a technical perspective, preferring to pour over plans and blueprints, while assigning the dirty work for someone else, unlike his dad who was hands on throughout the process. When he was a kid, his father got a kick out of introducing him to people as "the milk man's son." At the time, Jeremy thought it was a compliment, finding his mother's reaction of abject disgust perplexing.

It perplexed his father to have a son with none of his penchant for adventure, but he gradually, howbeit begrudgingly, grew to respect the anal way Jeremy approached their livelihood. Dusty had grown the business in a haphazard way—having no technique, but pressing forward because of the times he got it right.

When Dusty started the company his method was to set the explosives randomly throughout the doomed building, the removal of the building being the goal, except the clean-ups afterward were, at best, challenging. A newspaper article once stated, "Dusty Dobson is writing the textbook for how not to learn from one's mistakes." In spite of Dusty, the business prospered.

Early on he could get away with his cavalier approach, since most of his business was rural. However, after taking on an urban implosion, whose end was quite the opposite, Dusty was given some compelling incentive to rethink his methods. Thankfully, that was before the world became overly litigious, or the aftermath might have included the implosion of his business. The temporary loss of profit, along with the threat of a lawsuit, took some of the swagger out of Dusty's step compelling him to give way to what one of his foreman called, "method over madness."

Jeremy spent much of his youth tagging along behind his dad, doing so as a bored and seemingly reluctant observer. However, contrary to his bored demeanor he was taking in more than appeared on the surface. One night at dinner Jeremy spoke up, boldly announcing that he'd figured out what Dusty was doing wrong.

After a few days of Dusty giving him the silent treatment, Jeremy tried again. This time his dad's response was, "Okay, smart boy. Let's see if you're as smart as you think you are." While still annoyed, Dusty was curious to see what he had come up with, so Jeremy finally got his chance to explain what he had figured out.

To Dan Dobson's amazement, Jeremy was that smart. He explained to his dad how a structure could be summarily weakened if the explosives were placed expeditiously—even a massive building could be taken down with minimum risk to the buildings around it, and with fewer explosives needed to achieve the infrastructure's demise.

Over time, Jeremy perfected every preliminary facet up to and including the precise placement of the explosives, all complimented by the synchronized timing of the detonations; setting the dynamite to go off in millisecond fractions of time apart. The lower levels of a structure detonated split seconds before each subsequent level followed suit—moving from the bottom of the building upward.

Ironically, it was the vacuum created by the sequence of exponentially arranged explosions that caused the building to collapse inward, or implode, rather than it blowing up and outward, thereby leaving behind far less debris and with minimal risk to man and property. Thus, out of carefully orchestrated violence, a building would all but disappear in one graceful collapse.

For the inexperienced, it seemed to happen all at once. The structures appeared to self-destruct as if with no effort; the casual observer having little clue to the level of preparation that preceded the moment. Buildings that stood within a few feet of each other would gracefully collapse without damage to the adjoining buildings—if done with the appropriate finesse.

It was a given Jeremy would run the company one day. How could he not? Dusty said he would die a happy man if he thought his life's work might bless his son as much as it had him. Although Dusty's sheer love of danger birthed the business, it was Jeremy's natural acuity in engineering that catapulted it into what was now a world-class business. Before Dusty's illness, he and Jeremy traveled the world, signing contracts amounting to millions of dollars to have the privilege to do what they had loved to do—blowing things in—and in the process meeting everyone from the rich and famous to royalty.

Dusty's last, and most meaningful work, was a book he co-authored with Jeremy called *Dusty Dobson's Journey of Deconstruction*; a collaboration of their implosion adventures with pithy journal entries and photographs taken from their most noteworthy trips. The book was published in May 2007, and in September of that year, Dusty noticed some bumps on his chest that wouldn't go away, followed by chills and a cough. It was Mesothelioma.

~~~

Six men comprised the Detonation Team. Their unit's responsibility was to make sure the explosives weren't defective and were placed exactly where the plans indicated. The second crew was the Sweep Team; it was their job was to go through the entire building, floor by floor and room by room, to insure neither man nor beast remained inside.

Having completed the list of checks, and double-checks, the last two crews exited the building in full view of the spectators, calling out the "All clear!" Their announcement resounded like a series of echoes, when it was shouted from one man to the next before the last man raised his walkie-talkie to let Jeremy know it was safe to proceed.

Jeremy counted his men...ten, eleven, twelve, thirteen, fourteen...all accounted for.

Unexpectedly, a person in military uniform appeared on the roof of the building where an American flag was still hanging from a pole. Jeremy raised his right hand to touch his forehead in salute to the flag.

From somewhere behind the crowd, the lonely strains of a trumpet sounded out "Taps" while the flag was lowered. Jeremy's hand automatically went to his heart, reminded of his father, who started this tradition as a tribute to the rising and falling, and the raising again that symbolized the opportunities his beloved country offered the ambitious. Jeremy's father fought in the Korean War; and the experience impacted him mightily. He had seen virtuous men fall there, fighting in a war that seemed futile and unwinnable. Dusty returned home, but his time in the service made it impossible for him to take his freedoms lightly. What only Jeremy could appreciate was that the flag used in the ceremony was the same flag that was handed to his mother after Dusty's funeral.

Many of the observers wiped tears away at the unexpected reverence, watching while the flag was reverently folded into a triangle. The practice was Jeremy's tribute to both his father and his country.

~~~

This particular event had drawn additional media attention because it was taking place in Jeremy's home town, adding a personal element to the implosion. Jeremy was used to both the media, and the large crowd's, events like this drew. An implosion had a similar effect as a circus coming to town; it was impossible not to draw a crowd of curious spectators.

He glanced around; making sure everyone was safely behind the barriers. The relentless persistence of the media to get up close and personal made him react like a nervous parent, who was attempting to keep his children away from fireworks on the Fourth of July; if he looked away for even a second one of the children would be back in harm's way.

It wasn't the drama of the last few moments of an implosion that was Jeremy's rush; for him, that part was anticlimactic. His satisfaction was the passage; every minute detail that had taken place during the long months of planning, strategizing, and detailing—the extensive foreplay that made the climax possible. The big-bang the onlookers witnessed belied the weeks and months of effort that had gone on before—the symphony of overlapping details that were orchestrated in concert over long hours of painstaking planning—that would culminate in one exquisite, even graceful, occurrence that, by design, was intended to look effortless.

Every consecutive layer of the doomed edifice, starting with the substructure, would be compromised before this moment could take place. This was the appointed time; the last single detail remaining was for Jeremy to push a button.

CHAPTER 2

Lenette Dobson stood at her kitchen sink, peeling the speckled brown and yellow skin from a ripe banana. She, too, was appreciating the windless and sunny day, aware it was precisely what Jeremy ordered.

The sun was streaming in through the south facing windows that overlooked the swimming pool, and carefully chosen view. The morning the plots in their development were released Jeremy's car was parked, and waiting, outside the developer's office at dawn to insure he got the lot he wanted. *How is it possible that was three years ago?* She asked herself. Jeremy's meticulous attention to detail had nearly cost them their contractor more than once, but his efforts resulted in a home where no detail was overlooked. When they finally moved into the house before the holidays, every agonizing delay was worth it.

She glanced over her right shoulder at their five month old baby boy, Caleb, who was waiting for his lunch in his Baby Bjorn bouncer chair, and vigorously kicking his feet in anticipation of his lunch.

She and Jeremy were often mistaken for sister and brother—they shared an uncanny resemblance. They were both naturally blonde, although her hair was straight, while his was curly, and both had blue eyes and small features; what distinguished them was Jeremy's ruddy complexion that acted as a bellwether, indicating his moods. It was a dice roll who the baby looked like, other than, thankfully, having his mom's peaches and cream coloring.

Jeremy and Lenette had almost given up on being able to conceive when she learned she was pregnant. Neither of them cared about whose gene pool won; Caleb was a miracle.

~~~

Lenette quickly replaced her displeasure with the nanny's failure to show up with contentment to have the unexpected time with her little son, despite having to put off a meeting she'd arranged for later that afternoon. There was no back-up plan because of the nature of the meeting.

Lenette had been relentless in her pursuit of today's contact, and after some decidedly dogged persistence she ultimately established direct contact, convincing her source into taking her seriously. It was, as a spy novel might describe it, a clandestine meeting. She had not met her contact in person, nor did she know who would be sent to meet with her. Between them they had set up an elaborate series of checks and balances, being extraordinarily diligent not to leave a trail. Somehow, she would have to reconstruct her credibility and arrange another meeting. Lenette hadn't dared tell Jeremy what she was up to, or he would have forbidden it. And, now, after all her efforts, her contact would think she was a no-show. On top of it, she couldn't find her cell phone, and that was where she had stored the phone number.

"Melissa, you are in big trouble this time." She spoke it out loud, with the baby squealing his agreement. This was not the first time Melissa had failed to report for duty.

Lenette shed her linen jacket and matching blouse. *What was I thinking, buying another linen suit?* She scolded herself. Every time she bought anything linen she made a resolution to buy anything but. She looked with dismay at her crumpled garments—there went another $15.00 wasted at the dry cleaners!

Folded on top of the washing machine was one of Jeremy's crew-neck shirts, the working uniform for his employees. The red, white, and blue logo of "Dobson Detonations, Inc." was embroidered on the pocket on the left side of the white T-shirt. She slipped it over her head, patting the logo for good luck—sending Jeremy a telepathic message that at the very least she was with him in spirit. *Of all days to have misplaced my cell phone!* By now Jeremy would be missing her.

She was in the process of transforming chunks of banana into a glue-like pulp when it occurred to her the event was being televised on a local channel. Reaching for the remote, she turned toward the small television mounted beneath the kitchen cabinets to her right.

It was in that split second the bullet that was intended to strike her between her eyes, struck her left temple instead. Lenette's body lurched backwards, her right temple smashing against the edge of the granite counter on the island behind her, causing an arc of blood to spray across the counter where her baby sat waiting for his lunch.

She dropped to the floor without making a sound. Mercifully, it was determined later that her death was instantaneous—she felt no pain.

~~~

At precisely that moment, Jeremy was concluding an interview with a member of the media, having reduced the technical details of the demolition into layman's terms for her audience. Reporters from all over the Midwest crowded around him, holding out their microphones to catch what he was saying with their camera men jostling each other to get the best angle for each network. Annoyed, Jeremy tersely announced the interview was over, impatiently pushing his way through them toward the platform.

That was the only part of his job he hated, and he hated that it showed. It was impossible to avoid the pandering, but on the bright side, when the interview was aired later it would garnish a ton of free advertising, and once the Associated Press picked it up the story would be looped repeatedly all over the country and beyond. By the time the story ran that evening, Jeremy would be at home in his favorite chair with his feet up, enjoying a beer. And, the next morning, his office would be inundated with incoming calls and emails from potential clients asking for information about his firm.

He glanced at his watch—it was precisely one-thirty P.M. He lifted the detonating device from off the make-shift podium and held it up for the cameras and crowd to see before pushing the necessarily red button.

What followed was the rotation of blasts from the dynamite detonating, followed by a whooshing noise, and the subsequent chorus of convulsing steel, glass, wood, and concrete; all together creating the crescendo that signaled a successful ending to the months of exhaustive attention to detail. A plume of dust and smoke hung in the air like a final curtain.

Jeremy saw implosion as a necessary part of the evolution of the progressive fittest. After all, nothing lasts forever.

~~~

By disposition, Jeremy was a rule follower—his only exception was his car. He glanced down at the speedometer of his gas guzzling, politically and environmentally incorrect, deliberately un-green, black Escalade and ironically checked his speedometer to be sure he wasn't going more than five miles over the limit. He was vaguely concerned that he hadn't heard from Lenette—not that they spoke to each other often during the day, but it wasn't like her not to have checked in with him by now.

He and Lenette met when they were both attending Georgetown University where Jeremy was concluding his senior year in the college of engineering; Lenette was a junior studying political science. Their first encounter happened one afternoon when Jeremy observed a trail of fluttering yellow fliers on the windshields of a row of parked cars. He followed the trail to see who the polluter was and observed an attractive blonde leaning over the hood of a red Mercedes, putting one under its windshield wiper.

Such activity happened to be a particular pet peeve of Jeremy's, and whenever he found similar unwanted solicitations stuck on his own car, it provoked the thought of what kind of people made it their calling to put them there. The young woman leaning over the car in front of him answered his question—it was cute people who put them there—at least from his current vantage point; and from that vantage point he couldn't help but think she might be the cutest thing he'd ever laid eyes on. Her outstretched torso had caused her short T-shirt to ride up above some extremely tight hip-hugging jeans exposing a particularly cheerful looking daisy tattoo. It was a favorable first impression, and he had yet to see her face.

She turned around to find Jeremy standing immobilized on the sidewalk, gawking at her. Lenette leaned back against the hood of the Mercedes waiting for him to say something. Jeremy's limbs felt like rubber, and his vocal chords weren't cooperating, but he retained enough presence of mind to realize any attempt at a cool first impression was long gone.

She returned his gaze, observing that while he appeared a bit nerdy, the man standing in front of her produced the kind of reaction that might occur were she to look into a mirror, and it dawn on her that she was a man after thinking she was a woman her whole life up until now. It was uncanny, for sure. She wondered if she'd seen something like that on the Dr. Phil show.

Is this crazy, or what? Jeremy was also noticing the remarkable resemblance. It felt surreal, adding to his sense of inertia. Later, both would acknowledge Lenette was, by far, the cooler of the two of them.

However long the moment lasted, she appeared to be thoroughly enjoying his obvious discomfort. She was the first one to speak. "Coffee?" she asked. His brain managed to get a signal to his neck to nod yes. Ten minutes later they were seated in two overstuffed arm chairs at a coffee shop near the campus. He would later insist that she had cast a spell over him; her response was that rather than a spell it was overwhelming compassion because she thought he was mute. For both, falling in love was instant and involuntary, improbable, and undeniable.

~~~

Jeremy drove leisurely through the familiar countryside that led to his home. He and Lenette lived in the extended suburbs, just far enough outside the limits of the city to pretend they'd escaped it, the distance justified by close proximity to a super market, a dry cleaner, and, most crucial for Lenette, a highly rated nail salon.

He spoke her name into his iPhone, "Lenette,"...waiting while it obediently dialed hers. No answer.

He glanced at the clock on his dashboard; it was just after three o'clock. Normally he wouldn't arrive home until after six; perhaps today he would be the one who sent the sitter home and took the baby into the swimming pool.

He slowed the car, turning onto the Bradford Pear lined drive that led into their gated community, speeding up to tailgate behind one of his neighbor's cars, wondering why no one had complained about the obvious breech in security. When choosing where they would live he'd insisted on as much privacy as money could buy, and got it. The land parcels in the neighborhood were in the range of three acres, but with the curved streets and cul-de-sacs, they seemed much larger.

The Dobson's property was located at the farthest end of the neighborhood. Their lot was wide and fairly shallow, but it backed up to a preserve, creating the illusion of a much vaster space. The view behind the house was forested, and immediately behind their property was a several acre pond that was stocked with an assortment of game fish. There was no contest that Jeremy had snagged the best lot in the development. When he was in his back yard, there were no visible reminders of human habitation whatsoever. The sun rose over the landscape behind the house, and Jeremy rarely failed to wake up in time to appreciate it.

From entering the front gate to pulling in his driveway took Jeremy four minutes based on the twenty five miles an hour speed limit and for him it was the best four minutes of the drive. The layout of the neighborhood incorporated winding streets, heavily planted berms, and several small lakes with water features; there were riding trails for residents who kept horses. The project's density was one house to every five acres, so the resulting green space made the area luxurious and unique—and pricey.

He turned down his street and waved at his neighbor, Alex Perry. Once they had moved in the Perry's seemed like the one glitch in Jeremy's carefully crafted privacy barrier, but Lenette enjoyed Alex's wife and the couple made it their mission to look after Lenette and the baby when Jeremy went out of town on business. He had decided that one could put up with a lot of personality quirks with that kind of unsolicited generosity.

He eased the car into his driveway, impatiently tapping his fingers on the steering wheel while waiting for the garage door to open. Their nanny's car was gone; he was relieved knowing Lenette would be home. Her car was in its place with her briefcase leaning against the driver's door—he pushed the thought aside that he'd noticed it there when he left before dawn that morning. When he walked by her car, he noticed her iPhone lying on the passenger seat explaining why she hadn't answered his calls. He reached in and grabbed it for her, putting it in his pocket.

"Lenette." He called her name when he entered the house.

No answer.

"Lenette!"

He tried to shake off the feeling that something was terribly wrong. Just when he was about to shout her name for the third time he noticed the infant seat on the kitchen counter with Caleb's little head rolled to one side, asleep. But, before he could reach him Jeremy was assaulted by an odor. He smelled blood.

Instinctively he reached for the infant seat, pulling the baby towards him, noticing his little face was splattered with dried droplets of something brown, and his breathing was rapid and shallow. Jeremy stared at him, looking around the kitchen, confused and suddenly very afraid.

But again, the smell commanded his attention. It was then that his eyes locked on Lenette's hand, lying open and pale against the dark wood floor on the other side of the island.

CHAPTER 3

Eleanor Crosby uncrossed her long legs, stretching them out in front of her while smoothing the fabric of her black silk suit with both hands. One of her pet peeves was to be kept waiting, and she was agitated that no one had called to advise her that her car was running late.

Being pragmatic, she was using the time to collect her thoughts. Today she would be interviewed by the popular and controversial television commentator, Rod Larson. His persistence in pursuing her had paid off. Normally Eleanor shied away from anything politically charged, mainly because she felt any association with politics might confuse the prophetic message of her own ministry. But, after doing some detective work, and evaluating what made him controversial, she made her one and only exception. Now, if she could just rein in her thoughts...

Eleanor Crosby was often referred to as an attractive woman, followed by the humbling disclaimer of "for her age," but, she accepted it as genuine. It had been awhile, but, in her youth, she had been stunning. Her sixty-seventh birthday had been a few weeks prior, celebrated with her niece and a few close friends. Eleanor always insisted on no fussing, but this year her niece decided otherwise. Although the gathering wasn't a complete surprise, the surprise was where they dined. Her friends used all their collective bargaining chips to secure a reservation at her favorite restaurant which typically required a long lead time to get in. Of course, the winning chip was dropping her name, because whether Eleanor Crosby liked it or not, she was a celebrity.

The essence of her renown began with a disciplined concept of Bible Studies. She had developed a specific method for studying scripture that had been accepted by Christians worldwide; she had long since lost track of how many languages her studies were printed in.

The lessons were detailed and comprehensive, but their success spoke for itself by virtue of millions of students that crossed over every denominational line—a following who was eager for stick to the ribs teaching. Each course was accompanied by a series of DVD's that added her own verbal commentary to the study. Her personal expositions made the hours of homework worth the effort. She was not afraid to stand up against tired traditions or dogmas that she believed had paralyzed the Body of Christ.

Eleanor's books contained persuasive and strong messages accompanied by warnings that Christian people must become prepared to defend their faith and compelling them to return to the inerrancy of the scriptures; a not subtle hint to church leaders who she saw as disarming God's word of its power by watering it down. The books were instant best sellers in spite of the grumbling from social gospel oriented denominations who could cooperate for the purpose of denouncing her steadfast defense of God's word as absolute, and were doing so with increasing vigor.

It was the controversial nature of her books that propelled her into being a frequent guest on many popular Christian and secular television programs. Her passionate and unapologetic looking to the Bible for the answers for the world's woes and changing culture made her a popular and highly sought personality. Even Larry King had enjoyed sparring with her regularly—Eleanor Crosby never shied away from a good debate. Today would be the end of such interviews. Her goal, going forward, would be to devote herself to sounding the alarm through the venues she was most gifted in.

She felt an increasing urgency to speak out about what the scriptures had to say about the ticking clock of the prophetic calendar, and in particular drawing attention to the increase in cultural clashes and natural disasters worldwide, paralleling them with biblical precedents.

By design, her mass gatherings were kept to only a few a year, with each one drawing a larger audience than the last. The weeks before an event she spent studying, fasting, and in prayer. Something she didn't do, was specifically prepare for her message, relying instead on the Holy Spirit to communicate the message through her.

The gimmicks some evangelists used to fill an auditorium flabbergasted her. Her philosophy was, "If a rock band can fill a stadium and the Holy Spirit can't, I'm in the wrong business." Her seminars were always filled to capacity, therefore her seminars didn't require a fleet of semis nor were there gaudy props or fancy lighting. Each program began with a breathtaking rendition of "We shall behold Him" sung acapelia. When the vocalist exited the stage one direction Eleanor simultaneously appeared from the other, dressed in her trademark black silk suit, pearl earrings, and carrying a black Bible embossed with a gold cross.

Her only prop at her meetings was an unpretentious wood lectern with a cross carved on the front panel. She opened and closed each session with the sobering words, "The time is short"—words that while anticipated had the desired effect on those assembled by setting the stage for the serious message to follow. Often she would speak for two hours with no notes.

She called the media a "necessary evil." There was no way to keep them away from her events, as much as she might wish it possible. Her security team was instructed to confiscate any cell phones or cameras they saw being used during the event; but, regardless, news outlets managed to get enough material to edit her talks and broadcast out of context edits that were intended to accentuate the stereotype of her being extreme.

Eleanor's messages paralleled the warnings of the Old Testament Prophets; warnings for God's people to resist identifying with the decaying culture around them. It was her detractors who dubbed her with the label "The Prophetess". To their chagrin, it stuck—seized upon by her large following and the increasingly curious public.

While she was ripped by some and dismissed by others she earned a begrudged respect from her detractors because of her unmoving reliance on the scriptures for answers. She left out her own personal opinions; she held some but kept them private, aware of how often human err discredited even the most honorable spokesmen for God. Eleanor Crosby was well aware of her humanity. It was her goal to awaken the Church to be vigilant and ready...for anything!

~~~

Eleanor was never married, although she had come close twice—at least it seemed so at the time. Looking backward, hindsight offered the clarity to see that she was never close at all. Her first serious relationship was with a college professor who she believed to be divorced. Their relationship ended abruptly when his wife confronted them exiting a restaurant one night after dinner. Eleanor promptly quit showing up in his class and magically, at the end of the semester, she got an A. It had not been earned in class.

It took a year before she would allow herself to say more than a quick "Hello" to anyone of the opposite gender, vowing she'd learned her lesson. It turned out she was a slow learner, requiring her to endure yet another painful lesson; the next time with an unmarried co-worker that she met shortly after accepting her first job.

After graduating she accepted a position with an agency that had a reputation for exposing companies that were suspected of water or air pollution due to the irresponsible disposal of toxic waste—they were a glorified detective agency, only not seedy. Her heart hurt still to recall the abuses she had witnessed firsthand that were brought about by industries that knowingly compromised the health and welfare of the very workers who were making them wealthy.

The years as an environmentalist turned her into a hardcore cynic. Because of those experiences she'd formed idealistic beliefs that all capitalism was evil, and white men were historically guilty of environmental rape. Blinded by youthful zeal she failed to notice that her firm, on the corporate level, was owned by a variety of Waspish white men who wore suits and ties, had excessive profit margins, and hired lobbyists to wine and dine legislators to forward their agendas.

Gil Norris, alias Lesson Number Two, was handsome, dashing, sarcastic, and, if possible, more cynical than Eleanor. They were teamed up to work together on several projects that were under investigation in various parts of the country. She credited Gil with teaching her how to get the most out of her expense account, among some other things that were only slightly less ethical.

In spite of vowing not to fall in love again, she did fall—and hard. Once he perceived their relationship had progressed to where she had expectations his exit was so hasty that she would still wince when she thought about it. After it ended she was devastated, humiliated, and if possible, more cynical and hardened than before. Eleanor never loved again, at least not carnally. Instead, she put her dreams for a family of her own into her emotional recycle bin and married the environment.

She had earned her Master's Degree from Wheaton College, with a double-major in world history and literature. While her studies' focus might have appeared light years away from what she found herself doing after college, both courses proved more than enlightening when she was discovered to have a natural talent for public speaking.

Her natural acuity in public speaking resulted in her employer designing programs for the express purpose of recruiting students into what later would become "The Green Movement". Her seminars were eloquent and compelling, inciting mostly young activists by expounding on stunning examples of man's raping of the planet throughout history—punctuated by graphic slide shows.

Eleanor's reputation as a motivational speaker for the cause earned her large fees and endorsements by Influential environmental groups. One lingering reminder of the decidedly different Eleanor Crosby from those days still haunted her—how she had once told a reporter she pictured her audiences naked "just for the fun of it". It continued to be a favorite quote with the media.

~~~

Eleanor heard her niece, Candy Porter, clearing her throat and interrupting her musing. Candy was Eleanor's emotional right arm and personal assistant who, at the moment, was holding out a mug that contained a concoction made up of two tablespoons of organic cider vinegar, organic honey, with emulsified wheat grass, an immune booster, combined with green tea all steeped together in hot water. In her other hand was a small paper cup filled with an assortment of nutritional pills and capsules; it was Eleanor's twice daily regimen she religiously took to maintain her stamina. She swore by the concoction—to look at her one might agree there was something to it.

Candy was five foot two inches tall, fine boned, hazel eyes, and every bit as sweet as her name. Her hair was naturally ash brown, made blonder with added highlights, which her aunt pronounced as "utterly ridiculous." Eleanor found it incomprehensible anyone would willingly pay over one hundred dollars to spend an afternoon, sitting in a salon, to emerge later looking like, as she descriptively put it, "an animal print". Candy dismissed the critique, insisting her aunt was "a hoot", letting her know she wasn't going to allow her aunt's bias to ruin it for her. Eleanor further stressed her point by reminding Candy how she colored her own hair and used L'Oreal because she was worth it. Candy's comeback was, "Yes, but I definitely think you could use some highlights!" Once every two months the topic was revisited.

Candy was the daughter of Eleanor's older sister, Phyllis. From Candy's birth, a unique bond had formed between she and Eleanor that defied explanation; the attraction was mutual and time proved the relationship beneficial for both. In the beginning, Phyllis was threatened by Candy's preference for her aunt, but was also wise enough to realize it was God-given. That released Phyllis to be blessed by how Candy filled the void in Eleanor reserved for a child.

Every six weeks Eleanor made the trip from Maryland to Seattle to spend time with her little niece. From the onset, Eleanor began to set aside money in a secret college fund for Candy. Over the years her brother-in-law mercilessly teased Eleanor for living a frumpish life, because she allowed herself few frills; later he would be forced to eat those words.

Although Candy was a decent student, she wasn't scholarship material, and it became clear she would be going to a state college because out-of-state tuition couldn't be justified. Candy didn't deny her part in her less than stellar grades, but she confided to Eleanor her desire to have the opportunity to study away from home and live on her own.

The summer before Candy's senior year of high school Eleanor disclosed the fund she had set aside for Candy, challenging her to make her senior year count. Candy did work hard, ending up with a 3.8 grade average for the year, and while it wasn't enough to pull her overall GPA up to the scholarship level she was accepted into Wheaton College; her aunt's Alma Mater. Neither Candy, nor her family, would ever know that Eleanor, early the year before, had sent the college her personal letter of recommendation, accompanied with a large contribution in Candy's behalf.

~~~

Over time, Eleanor had become increasingly disillusioned with the hypocrisy in the environmental movement that she originally had believed was driven by a pure devotion to protecting the environment, for the environment's sake. While she had uncovered bona fide abuses so horrendous it was breathtaking, there was also a constant and relentless pressure for her to doctor her reports to create exaggerated worst case scenarios, intended to engage the public's sympathy.

If Eleanor turned on her TV at all, it was for the white noise that helped distract her from the noisy neighbors that lived in the apartment above her. One night, when she was putting on her pajamas, she glanced at the TV and recognized some people being interviewed in an expose that one of the networks was doing on toxic waste.

The people were from a community in western Pennsylvania where Eleanor had spent six months for the purpose of exposing industrial abuses that were purportedly perpetuated by Bower Industries who employed much of the community. One of the women, Joyce Sills, was one of her case studies. In spite of Eleanor's repeated attempts to get Joyce to open up, Joyce never budged in her defense of her employer. A remarkably different Joyce Sills was describing to the EPA, through tears, a myriad of symptoms she and her family were experiencing; blaming Bower Industries.

There was only one explanation possible; Eleanor had been removed from the case without notice and Joyce had been persuaded to change her testimony. Everything the woman was now claiming was the polar opposite of what she had said to Eleanor only months before.

While Joyce voiced some concern about future health issues, neither she, nor her family, was concerned enough to quit their jobs. She had gone so far as apologizing to Eleanor because she couldn't be more helpful, defending her employer as conscientious. The adage that 'everyone has their price' became the final straw in Eleanor's growing disrespect for her firm's agenda. What saddened her most was how, in the beginning, she had respected Joyce Sill's ethics.

The following morning, an indignant Eleanor, marched into her supervisor's office, demanding an explanation. Her unblinking superior informed her how it had become obvious that Eleanor was not adequately doing her research, and that she needed to be replaced. Eleanor was outraged. After reflecting on their meeting later, she was convinced her supervisor was expecting her.

In an attempt to justify herself, Eleanor returned to the scene of the crime. To her amazement nearly every person she'd interviewed moved away or declined to meet with her. The monies involved in the legal settlements had to be calculated to be significant to justify paying off a third of the town to pervert their testimonies. Joyce's case was settled out of court for an undisclosed amount of money, further punctuating Eleanor's righteous indignation.

One month later Eleanor tendered her resignation and was offered a substantial severance package if she would agree not to talk about any of her field cases after she left. She accepted their terms, wishing later she'd shown more backbone. But, her goal at the time was to put as much distance from her third disillusioning lesson in Truth & Ethics as she was able. She wisely decided that becoming a whistle-blower might be a slippery slope.

~~~

After some serious therapy, Eleanor could peer around her anger issues and acknowledge how her own choices aided her current disillusionment. The next phase was to direct the anger back at herself for being so naïve, but after more painful introspection, she admitted her naiveté also was a choice. When the emotional dust settled she believed it was divine destiny that had protected her from continuing down a path where she could have lost her way entirely.

Her passion toward the environment never abated. She still considered any plundering of the planet environmental rape, taking pride in having been a pioneer for her generation in shedding light on how man failed to steward the earth.

Initially, she succumbed to an emotional apathy that left her feeling rudderless and emotionally spent. The numbness was replaced by a vacuum that she would later describe as a "spiritual hole". She'd become so immersed and cause driven, that she'd exchanged her belief in God for concern about the environment, allowing it to supplant her faith. The end result was how it became a complete misappropriation of what she was raised to believe. In her quest to protect the planet, she'd left behind its Creator.

The environmental cause's loss became Heaven's gain. Eleanor did a spiritual one-eighty, vowing to the Almighty that she would use the rest of her life addressing the insidious pollution of a culture where its moral plumb line had ceased to guide the people. Her first book was titled, "Toxic Waste—The Pollution of our Youth's Minds by Hollywood". It was an expose of how Hollywood used their influence to support politically correct causes. She had never been timid when she believed in something.

It was her spiritual convictions that compelled her, replacing her zeal. Once she'd inserted herself into the Christian culture, she unhesitatingly took on the Christian apologists, giving them a run for their money. She learned quickly that apologists rarely apologize.

But, because she had been forced to get tough, she stood

immovable and unapologetic, fully persuaded that mankind was living out the last hours of God's tolerance. In spite of being relentlessly taken to task by members of the larger church, who took a more moderate approach to prophecy than hers, she chose to not to name names when pointing out the differences in their spiritual philosophies—retaliation was tempting, but non-productive to the Kingdom's cause.

Her quest to educate her fellow man to divide rightly between truth and error was her calling. Eleanor had little doubt that the battle would be fierce; her second most valuable weapon was having experienced how the other side worked. So, the happier ending for Eleanor was that she did fall in love again.

~~~

They were startled by a loud knock at the door; their escorts had arrived.

After a rather inglorious climb into the waiting limo, Eleanor remarked to Candy that she was glad there were no Paparazzi present, or she would be forced to bribe them to keep any photographs from being published. A limousine was something she could never justify herself, but once they were settled inside she admitted to Candy that it was a spoiler.

Over the years, Eleanor visited New York City often, usually for the promotional value of availing herself to the media. Her meetings gained added notoriety with the help of the teasers the various talk shows used to entice viewers to their programs. This particular time, however, she had been asked to come incognito.

Her host, Rod Larson, was the outspoken and relentless voice, who daily warned the American public to wake up and smell the roses, before the winds of change moved them too far along to find their way back—warning that the United States and Europe were being herded towards a New World Order and world government. Now, his avid fan, Eleanor wondered if he might be one of the last voices to cry out with a warning before the tentacles of the promised "hope and change" wrapped themselves inextricably around those refusing to acknowledge what was happening right under their noses. It would be impossible to turn back the no longer hidden agenda that was compelling the country toward a globally centered government, without alerting the masses.

Eleanor compared Rod Larson to the Prophet Malachi, the Old Testament's last voice to warn God's people about the dangerous reprisals for having wandered far from his Covenant promises to them. The prophet's message to God's chosen was how, if they would repent and turn back to God, grace would preempt his judgment. But, rather than repent, for the last time, they ignored yet another prophet's warnings, after which God remained silent for four hundred and forty years.

~~~

The term "New World Order" could no longer be dismissed as a conspiracy theory. The term no longer retained the shock value for the listener, and with each subsequent sunrise, it's not being a theory had more legitimacy for the watchful. Rather, the concept was now openly being moved along by world governments and their leaders who could lay aside their differences to unite for a singular purpose—to control the earth's population.

Eleanor recalled a quote from C.S. Lewis's book, *The Screwtape Letters*, "The greatest evil is not done now in those sordid 'dens of crime' that Dickens loved to paint. It is not even done in concentration camps and labor camps. In those, we see its final result. But it is conceived and ordered (moved, seconded, carried and minuted) in clean, carpeted, warmed, and well-lighted offices, by quiet men with white collars and cut fingernails and smooth-shaven cheeks who do no need to raise their voice."

She shuddered involuntarily, thinking, *Is it possible one of those offices is oval?*

CHAPTER 4

Having been questioned, and summarily dismissed, Jeremy retreated from the kitchen, shutting himself inside his office. The kitchen had been confiscated by law enforcement—he felt like an intruder in his own home. Nearly every room on the lower level of his house had been overwhelmed by police, homicide and forensic units, along with people from the DA's office—each jockeying for control of the crime scene. That didn't account for the FBI, who he'd been told were being called in.

Some members of the press had managed to get through the gates—*Probably tailgating,* Jeremy thought. They and a growing crowd of neighbors were gathering in the street outside, representing both the curious and concerned.

Jeremy was shutting the blinds when he observed someone being escorted down the driveway in handcuffs—protesting loudly that his rights were being violated. He represented the first of the vultures who made their voyeuristic living by taking salacious pictures to sell to the highest bidder in the tabloid industry; caught attempting to get off a shot of Lenette's body through the broken kitchen window. Even while the intruder was being shoved into the back of a police car, another officer was stretching yellow tape across the driveway to keep the uninvited away.

Lenette's body remained where she had fallen, now outlined in white chalk. Jeremy was told there was nothing to indicate she had as much as twitched after she fell; that her death was instantaneous. Apparently that was supposed to make him feel better.

Outside, the coroner's van idled, waiting to take the body to the morgue.

~~~

When he found her body Jeremy's initial reactions, while robotic, were instinctively good. After dialing 911, with the exception of tending to the baby, he'd left everything precisely the way found it. He'd looked at her one time only, and that was when he crouched down beside her to feel for a pulse. She'd fallen backwards and was lying on her back with her eyes half-open, staring upward. He looked away when he noticed them; their bright blueness dulled, and opaque, staring up at nothing.

Gone—just like that—she was gone! Her vibrant energy was gone...

His own needs came second to the baby's, who had begun whimpering as if upon awakening, he'd returned to where he left off fussing before falling asleep. Relieved to have something to do, Jeremy lifted him and hugged him close, ignoring the soggy diaper that was soaking through his shirt. He talked to him, soothing him, trying to fill the terrible silence, hearing his own voice and barely recognizing it.

Jeremy carried him into the bathroom and wet a washrag—what he wasn't going to do was leave the baby covered in his mother's blood. He tenderly wiped away the now brown droplets from Caleb's face, his nose, and eyelids. Caleb stared up at him, cautious and unsmiling, as if he sensed something had changed.

A bottle of Lenette's breast milk was saved in the freezer, stored for an emergency—this qualified. He went through the motions of thawing it out in a bowl of warm water, aware this would be his beautiful wife's final gift to their son. He carried him upstairs to the nursery to change him into something clean; the silence shattered by the eerie wail of sirens in the distance, growing louder, and louder, until suddenly the house was overtaken by people and confusion.

After feeding the baby his bottle, Jeremy gently laid him in his crib, waiting at the foot of it until he fell asleep, feeling the need to act out being his protector. Caleb looked up and smiled before accepting the offered pacifier, already having forgiven Jeremy the long afternoon of unintended neglect.

He walked across the hall and stood outside the door of their bedroom; waiting for several minutes before he could will himself to enter. He wondered how he could sleep in their bedroom again; to be reminded of the intimacy they'd shared there; or would he instead go to a bedroom down the hall and sleep alone?

Lying, like a puddle on the floor outside their closet, was Lenette's blue nightgown. Seeing it forced yet another realization on him; of how she would never wear it again and his knowing that disturbing it wasn't something he could do. He grabbed a clean shirt off a hanger and went down the hall to the guest room to change.

So this is what it feels like, he thought. In that instant, he pictured the admired towers that once stood tall and proud, teaming with life and purpose, and at someone's whim were reduced to rubble...

So this is what it feels like, he thought again, *my life has imploded.*

~~~

Jeremy waited in his office, feeling disassociated and displaced. He opened the door a crack, trying to eavesdrop on the conversations in the kitchen. When he heard the word computer, it grabbed his attention. It was at that moment he remembered that her briefcase was in the garage.

Reacting to another rush of adrenalin, he dashed down the hall and into the garage, grabbing the briefcase and thrusting it through the open front window of his SUV, where it dropped to the floor with a thud. He slipped inside the house, easing the door shut behind him. On the chance that someone was wondering where he was, he wet his hands in the hall bath as a ruse, nonchalantly sauntering into the kitchen. No one gave him as much as a glance, satisfying him that his sense of invisibility wasn't entirely purposeless. He mentally calculated his errand took him less than two minutes.

The kitchen counter was littered with various sizes of zip-lock bags and plastic containers, where anything considered a clue was being stored and labeled. Nearly every drawer and cabinet was hanging open and in disarray.

Her cell phone vibrated in his pocket—another reminder that he had managed to confiscate the two pieces of evidence that could provide clues for why she was murdered. What he hadn't considered was how having retained them put him in the sights of whoever was behind it.

On Lenette's planning desk, he noticed an open container of latex gloves. He inched his way along the wall until he was standing directly in front of it, and casually reached behind him with one hand to grab a handful of the gloves. He quickly stuffed them in his back pocket. Another arbitrary line had been crossed, with the potential of propelling him further into the unknown.

~~~

It was concluded Lenette had not left the house that day, making the whereabouts of the babysitter part of the mystery, and implicating her as a suspect. That possibility had not crossed Jeremy's mind.

Their babysitter, Melissa Riley, was twenty-one years old, a college drop-out turned nanny, and a fairly lazy nanny at that. But, she was clean, with no obvious tattoo's, didn't have a ring in her nose or her tongue, presented herself well, and adored Caleb, that being the criteria that mattered most. Caleb's immediate smile and outstretched arms when he saw her were her job security.

After repeated attempts to reach her by phone, the officer in charge called the station requesting that officers be sent to her home—

simultaneously putting out an APB on her car on the chance she had fled. *Wow*, Jeremy thought. He couldn't imagine Melissa could hurt a fly, much less pull off a killing; not to mention how any kind of criminal activity would take premeditation; her planning ahead seemed unlikely even under the best of circumstances.

~~~

The Dobson's were recognized as celebrity by their community, who had followed Jeremy's father's success with immense pride. Jeremy expected that once the crime became public the media would be swarming every nook, and cranny, trying to get a different slant on the story—the murder had the potential of a colossal news event. He was glad his neighborhood was gated. The risk of the story getting out emphasized the urgency he felt to contact Lenette's family. It would be about this time, on most days, that Lenette, or Lindsay, would be calling each other.

The combination of exhaustion and lack of food were making him shaky. He wondered what it would be like to experience a police interrogation with low blood sugar and high adrenalin. In his mind, he pictured himself cast in a scene, like in the cop shows, sitting at a table in a windowless room. He was facing a mirror where he suspects a gaggle of people are watching his every move, diagnosing every nuance of his body language and eye-contact, for clues that would be dissected later on the news ad nauseam. He accepts endless cups of coffee from the interrogating officer who promises that if he will write down his confession he can take a nap.

What a system, He thought. He wondered how many guilty people walked because some poor innocent slob drank the offered coffee, wasn't allowed to sleep, and was coerced into a confession on the promise he could take a nap after he confessed.

Jeremy was sure he'd confess.

CHAPTER 5

Nelson Saunders sat at his desk, wishing there was a way out. The problem was that he truly loved his wife, although he doubted she believed it, but, he knew full well that Lindsay was the best thing that ever happened to him. Other couples, couples who married for convenience, for lust, for money—right now he envied them those reasons. He and Lindsay had married for love, with neither of them considering it could ever morph into something different.

Nelson stood up, pausing at the wall of windows across from his desk to look outside. Far below he could see people going about their day, mostly preoccupied with getting home in time to avoid the Friday rush. He leaned over to open a door in the vintage Herman Miller credenza across from his desk—the credenza the antique dealer assured him was once owned by Katherine Hepburn. Every piece of furniture in his office had a better provenance than he did. He rummaged through his collection of Scotch's, choosing a bottle of Delphinine and a cut-glass tumbler. There was no water or ice, but today's drink was about needing a drink, not wanting one; warm and neat would do.

He glanced down at his Rolex. Lindsay should be arriving home about now after visiting the nursing home. On Friday's she tended to his mother who'd had a stroke. She'd adopted two other inmates (as he called them) who she said didn't get visitors. Lindsay let them glom onto to her; she shopped for them, ate lunch with them, and gave them all manicures. Ugh! The idea of doing some old ladies fingernails made him shudder, but his wife did it every Friday, and returned home saying what a blessed day she'd had. Whatever motivated her was a mystery to him. What made her stay married to him was another credit to her benevolent nature. *Face it Nelson, you're a worm compared to her*. He knew it was true.

Nelson had concluded long ago their relationship had become so complicated they both should both get some therapy—group therapy might also prove enlightening for anyone who lived with a twin. One day they could be furious with each other, and then, without addressing the issue, and sans any apology, shake it off as though nothing had happened. His wife and her sister still looked enough alike to confuse people who didn't see them often, but were polar opposite in personality. Living with one was confusing enough. Their overly close relationship and need to share everything was what he blamed for the dilemma that surfaced some months before. He tried to ignore the incident, but it stubbornly refused to go away.

Lenette was easily excitable, compulsive, and had a penchant for digging into things that we none of her business. Lindsay's temperament was peaceful and optimistic; she chose to see the world through a rosy lens and didn't seem to care particularly about what went on outside it. That was how Nelson liked it. She loved domesticity; the cooking and decorating channels were all the stimulation she needed and their home reflected it. Well, at least until recently.

~~~

The twins were both devout Christians, although they wore their faith decidedly differently. Their childhoods were shaped around their family's involvement in church related activities—church camps, mission trips, youth group, and what Nelson's mother referred to as "familial indoctrination"; Ethel Saunders was unable to relate to Lindsay's personal faith experience.

Nelson's family's roots were in the Episcopalian Church. Their attendance was sporadic, with the exception of the High Holidays, and his parent's obligatory appearances at congregational meetings and fundraisers—just enough to maintain their social resume. Nelson's concepts of faith and religion were biased by their hypocrisy. It would seem ironic later that it was Lindsay's passion for her faith that was part of what attracted him to her.

Lindsay was working on an internship at an interior design firm in Georgetown, and Nelson was in his graduate program at Georgetown University. They'd met through a persistent friend, and when Nelson finally agreed to ask Lindsay out his only goal was to get his friend off his back. Lindsay agreed to go but seemed equally hesitant. They met at The Tombs Restaurant on Thirty Sixth Street late one Friday afternoon.

Rarely was Nelson surprised by anything or anyone, always insisting on him being the one in control; anything he involved himself in would be thoroughly researched beforehand and only then would he allow himself to move forward—for him, it was all about strategy. His philosophy was that one could only be blindsided if they were unprepared, and preparation put him in the position to do the blindsiding.

His time on the debate team during his undergraduate years at Yale, further crafted his intended persona of being intimidating. Whoever dared engage him in a discussion, unless they were on the same side of the issue, did it one time only. Nelson had the remarkable talent to be totally wrong, win the argument, leaving his opponent shaking his head in bewilderment over what just happened. For sport, even if he was in agreement in a conversation, take the adversarial position with the same result. That was not the case when he met Lindsay Kennedy. It was Lindsay who left him shaking his head, wondering what happened.

The bar was so noisy he surprised himself by asking Lindsay if she would enjoy having dinner somewhere quiet, to which she unhesitatingly answered yes. Simultaneously, she stood up, grabbed her purse, heading for the door with him in tow. She led the way to a little French restaurant on M Street—four hours later they emerged holding hands. He clearly never knew what hit him.

It wasn't long before he was accompanying her to church on Sunday's, and to a Wednesday night Bible study. Whatever built-in arguments he'd previously used for not believing were totally blotted from his mind. Lindsay's enthusiastic faith in a personal God, who left Heaven to involve himself with his fallen creation, was both compelling and convincing. Despite every rationalization he once used to deny God's existence, Nelson believed.

Exactly one year later he and Lindsay were married in a quiet ceremony in the New Beginnings Church, in Georgetown. Lindsay didn't want a large wedding, and Nelson didn't care. He was sure his mother would have guaranteed their wedding would be hell, and this would keep her out of it. Not surprisingly, she declined their invitation to attend.

They promised each other the rest of their lives would be their Honeymoon...until death parted them.

~~~

A venomous and irrational dislike for Lindsay seized his mother from the day they met, and as time went on it would not be a well-kept secret that she also despised her twin, Lenette, who was cause driven. She was not only opinionated, but she "took it to the streets", as Nelson's mother complained to Albert. She hoped Lenette's misguided involvements would not attach themselves to Nelson, or tarnish the family's reputation. Nelson's carefully guided career path might be jeopardized were Lenette's extremist viewpoints to become associated with him. Thankfully, Lenette married someone who moved her halfway across the country, and convinced their mother to move with her.

When Nelson first met Lindsay's sister, she had taken on the National Education Association. At the time, Nelson convinced himself she was as loony as a Loony Tune, howbeit harmless—nevertheless, he was thankful for the distance separating them, relieved that Lindsay could not be overly influenced by her, and inevitably drawn into her involvements. But, that was not a cause for concern; Lindsay's preference was to remain in the background, content to stay home, and create a beautifully designed nest for them. His career would not tolerate him having an activist wife, and he hoped Lenette's causes would remain her own. And, for the most part, until recently they had...

~~~

The tumbler of scotch was empty. Nelson thought about pouring another drink, but his priority had to be keeping his wits about him. He opened his desk drawer, fully extending it, and slid his fingers along the left side, in search of a small lever, which he tripped. There was a click, and a panel across the back of the drawer collapsed, exposing a secret compartment. He felt around, shoving several other things out of the way, making sure his gun was still there, waiting for him. He pulled it out to check it was loaded. Satisfied, he returned it to its hiding place and closed the panel.

The phone interrupted him. It was his brother-in-law, Jeremy, calling to inform him of the murder. They concluded that Nelson should be the one to tell Lindsay—and quickly. "Oh, God...please let this be over." He realized it was the first prayer he'd said in a long time.

CHAPTER 6

Jeremy was nursing a full blown migraine from not having eaten, not to mention being awake since well before dawn. He assumed his symptoms stemmed from the combination of caffeine, and boosts of adrenalin; causing him to disconnect from what was going on around him. He presumed himself to be in shock.

My wife is dead. My wife is dead. My wife is dead. The mantra in his brain was relentless.

Jeremy avoided the kitchen, distancing from when they would remove Lenette's body. He was startled by the sound of a zipper, realizing, too late, that her body was being zipped inside a body bag. Queasy, he rushed toward the bathroom, almost colliding with the gurney. Hunger was no longer an issue.

Occasionally family members would comment about how devastating it would be for a twin to lose their other half. Lenette and Lindsay were so close, it was impossible to contemplate the loss. He thought of Lindsay, and what her reaction to the news would be; they had been companions from conception.

Once again, Jeremy's thoughts were interrupted, only this time it was the intrusive sound of two squad cars arriving with sirens blaring. Jeremy felt like shouting that everyone leave, and cut out the unnecessary drama. But, it would be Jeremy who would be asked to leave, not them. The house would remain a crime scene until he was further notified.

~~~

Jeremy's neighbor, Alex Perry, was being questioned in the kitchen. His recollections were helpful with establishing a time line, having seen a car leaving their street about an hour before Jeremy arrived home. He believed the car was Jeremy's, but other than that it seemed odd to him that Jeremy had parked it at the far end of the cul-de-sac, nothing else seemed out of order.

Alex's wife, Jenny, was in the dining room, also being questioned. At the time of the shooting, she was in the back of their house on her computer, totally preoccupied, and wished she had seen something. Jeremy overheard one of the detectives asking her if she had room for a guest. Moments later, Jeremy was sent upstairs to pack a few things for him and the baby. When he backed his car out of the garage, a police officer surprised him by tapping on the window.

His manner was blunt and to the point. "Sir, I'm sorry, but I have more bad news." He paused, giving Jeremy just enough time to recognize the now familiar adrenalin rush that accompanied fear. The officer continued, "We found your babysitter." He cleared his throat before continuing, "Ah, she's dead, too. She was shot in the head like your wife."

Jeremy felt the blood rushing to his head. This was big; bigger than he wanted to think about. What did Lenette know that put her, and those around her, in so much danger? Just in time, he managed to fling the car door open. Only this time he threw up—on the officer's shoes.

CHAPTER 7

Because Eleanor didn't watch much television, until recently she was unaware of the brash young man she and Candy were sitting across from. His rise to fame, she'd been informed, was like a rocket being launched. He was loved, or he was scorned, and by Rod Larson's own design, the viewer was left with little room to remain ambivalent. His direct approach of exposing what he believed were the real agendas behind the progressing cultural issues targeted those watching who had been content to dwell in self-protected, mental gray areas that provoked little, or no, response—he relentlessly pushed for them to get off their proverbial couches, and engage in the debate in a public way.

Day after day, he made one compelling case after the other about governmental and political issues, hidden agendas, and anything else that threatened to comprise the constitution and individual liberties of the citizenry. His arguments were crafted from a combination of history, statistics, and documented incidents, all pulled together to lay out his case. History appeared to be repeating itself, only this time it was heading down an unfamiliar highway at breakneck speed. The mathematical probabilities of the current, overlapping events as being pure coincidence would be astronomical. And, he didn't stop there; he was also exposing international schemes and agendas that overlapped what was happening in the United States.

Rod Lawson had taken the world by storm. If you were standing next to him at Starbucks you might not notice him at all; his appearance was average and boyish. He was audacious, entertaining, and extremely controversial—at times irreverent, but then again, so were a lot of other television personalities. The fuel that propelled this relatively young man to his conspicuous Rocket Launch Career was how he could ferret out an arsenal of dovetailing current events that, by the law of averages, defied being cast aside as coincidental. He backed his findings up with similar occurrences throughout history, drawing direct parallels between the evolving current events, and backing them up with a history of what could happen if they weren't stopped.

Once he appeared on her radar, Eleanor began to watch his program on a daily basis, with a mixture of both curiosity and amusement. She thoroughly enjoyed brash people, so it tickled her to see this fellow's obvious enjoyment at sticking it to his detractors; and, for his following, that was part of the fun. She described his humor as "the spoonful of sugar" that made the heavy doses of bitter medicine palatable. She knew, from having championed both worldly, and unworldly, causes, the odds weren't with him for mass appeal; like ostrich's, the majority preferred sand in their eyes.

He'd struck a nerve with the mainstream media, who used every opportunity to discredit him, both professionally and personally. By doing so, they thought they could divert attention away from their own inability to bring his message down with facts, but, as a result, his ratings soared. The irony was how the attacks from the left had become so irrational they ceased to have credibility with the mainstream, which was leaving the networks for cable in droves. The increasing frequency of negative assaults would substantially increase the odds of his family being in real danger, deliberately inciting those who could be manipulated to act out.

Although she wasn't an expert on American political history, she was aware of how many significant facts about America's spiritual roots in particular, were in the process of being summarily hidden—deep-sixed by those with extreme leftist views, and while it wasn't anything new, the overt way it had been accomplished in the open—was.

An exorcising of American History had been taking place in textbooks; museums, movies, and documentaries—like, for example, the recent one done on John Adams life that, while well done, had left out his deep faith. *How many generations will it take before no one remembers what is factual?* She wondered. What made it breathtaking to watch was that it was happening on so many levels at once...

On the other hand, Rod had known who Eleanor Crosby was for some time. His wife attended one of her Bible studies, and her enthusiasm about what she was learning overflowed into their household.

~~~

From the time they began dating, Jenna and Rod attended church. But, it wasn't until after they lost a baby daughter they realized they were, as they viewed it in hindsight, *tepid* in their beliefs. They believed in Jesus, and had each accepted Him as Lord, but it wasn't until their faith was tested that they discovered how being lukewarm was a frightening place for the believer to exist.

The baby's death brought with it a boatload of conflicting emotions for Rod, although his core Christian beliefs weren't threatened. If anything, he believed their little girl was in Heaven with Christ; that fact wasn't negotiable. But, for the first time since they married, both were questioning if they were spiritually equipped to take on life's challenges.

Their baby's funeral was tear-jerking, tender, and on the surface, it was comforting. However, when they reflected back on it afterward, and had begun asking themselves the hard questions, they could see how superficial their church experience had been—eternity had intruded into their daily lives, and they needed more than platitudes. Even their small children were seeking more substantial answers than scriptures offered out of context, and "everything happens for a reason" pats on their shoulders. Rod and Jenna acknowledged that they had shopped for a church that fit their faith philosophies, and now saw the danger of rarely being challenged to grow, question, or to be held accountable.

Their spiritual lifeline became the couple next door to them, neighbors they'd made little effort to get to know. Rick and Diane Simmons were the first people to appear at their door after hearing of their loss—with food, offer's to watch their children, and a willingness to simply *be there* when Rod and Jenna needed company, while expecting nothing in return. It was because of their unconditional generosity that Jenna and Rod saw how the Gospel message was supposed to work; the Simmons exampled the living faith they were seeking. Soon Jenna was drawn into Diane's circle of Christian women, and Rod found himself surrounded by men that not only knew in depth what they believed, but lived it.

The only time they had given the word prophecy any credence was when the History Channel did a special feature on Nostradamus. Ironically, while their pastor dissuaded his congregation from pursuing the study of biblical prophecy, he encouraged them to watch the History Channel special. Because of his endorsement, Jenna and Rod watched, but his inconsistency caused them to question his credibility.

For Rod, the topic of prophecy was a turn-off from the beginning, so he'd required little urging to remain skeptical. For Jenna, it was confusing. Thus, by mutual agreement, they avoided anything that smacked of doomsday religion. Jenna now understood God's foreknowledge was not necessarily his will, and how his people historically tested his long-suffering. As Eleanor Crosby put it, "If his people taken the command to be good stewards of the earth to heart the it wouldn't be in the mess it's in today."

Rod's men's group was related to current events; analyzing the spiraling crescendo of cultural changes and scrutinizing how that correlated with what the scriptures taught, after which they would compare their findings to what the Founding Fathers intended when birthing the country. The full circle was scrutinizing how the nations falling away from those core principles had influenced the current events of the moment.

The core group started with twenty-five men, who on their own time, would search for, and dig through out-of-print books, historical literature, trails that evolved from internet searches, and their own family journals and letters, each trying to meld what they were learning individually into what the larger group was coming up with. Ultimately, they decided to have a bi-monthly gathering, so they could bring in speakers, opening the door to inviting family and friends, hoping their efforts would spawn other groups like theirs.

Their first speaker was so enlightening the attendees' enthusiasm spread throughout the community. Unbelievably, by word of mouth alone, the next bi-monthly meeting drew nearly ninety people, making it apparent they would need a different facility. After one year, the attendance for the bi-monthly speaker events had an average attendance of three hundred people.

The wives pressed the men to write a letter to Eleanor Crosby, to ask if she would speak at one of their meetings. She declined, but sent the group a complementary set of DVD's of her soon-to-be-released study on the Book of Revelations, encouraging them to press forward with what they were doing for the Lord. The DVD's changed the course of Rod's career.

After listening to the DVD's with his group, he ordered a set for him and Jenna. They piqued his curiosity about the imminence of Christ's return being sooner rather than later, and the need for believers to be ready. Rod became her devotee from then on. So, it was the series of events after the loss of their baby that inadvertently brought them together for the present moment.

Eleanor recalled the men's letter. At the time it stood out to her, because of how the wives' involvement in her studies had affected their husbands. And, now, to think Rod Larson had been a member of the group that wrote her—their paths were indeed destined to cross. It humbled her how God had used one of her studies to help birth this prophet, making the grueling chore of research, preparation, and endless edits worth it.

Rod Larsen leaned back in the comfortable, overstuffed lounge chair across from Eleanor, also overwhelmed with the sense of destiny that brought them together. She asked him if she could pray and he nodded his acceptance; her prayer was short, and to the point. "Your will be done, oh Lord." That was it. There was nothing else that needed to be said.

Rod intention was to use the time prior to the taping to prep her for it, but the two found it hard to stay on topic, relishing the opportunity to hear each other's opinions, and theories about how the events happening around the globe possibly related to the scriptures, and the bible's prophetic calendar.

Rod leaned forward, smiling, but dead serious, "We're both marked men, Eleanor—you do know that, don't you?"

She didn't need the reminder. She already knew.

CHAPTER 8

Aura arranged her yoga mat on the floor of her apartment, sat down, and assumed the lotus position. It was time for her morning ritual to connect with her center.

The shades in her apartment were drawn, and the air was permeated with the cloying, sweet scent of Jasmine incense. Personally, Aura despised the smell of incense, but since she taught inner consciousness classes, and sold incense to her students, she felt like a hypocrite if she didn't use it. *Funny that should bother me*, she thought, annoyed that she had allowed her mind to wander. *Get back here*, she scolded herself.

Recently a lot of things had begun to bother her. Like, for example, how of late she'd begun feeling guilty for charging people to do readings for them. The woman who cut her hair pointed out to her (in one of their in-depth conversations), how Jesus Christ didn't charge people when he helped them. *Good point*—not that her beautician was the best role model for what she said she believed. But, still, the thought stuck.

Didn't I hear somewhere that "money was the root of all evil"? Or is it "the love of money"? Well, whatever! Either way, she felt guilty, because if she was honest she had to admit how she often thought about the money even before she thought about who was coming to see her—or why.

But, more than that was troubling her. Another example was how, until recently, she'd lived her life on the principle "To thine own self be true". She had truly believed it, lived it, and quoted the phrase like it was scripture, to her customers who counted on her for insights into their problems. After a reading her parting words would be, "But in the end, 'to thine own self, be true...'". It was her philosophical benediction, of sorts.

One afternoon a client mentioned that it was Shakespeare who wrote it. Aura wasn't convinced that was true, so the following morning she went to the library to check it out. It was, indeed, from Shakespeare's "Hamlet".

Yet here, Laertes! Aboard, aboard for shame!
The wind sits in the shoulder of your sail,
And you are stayed for.
There ... my blessing with thee!
And these few precepts in thy memory
Look thou character, give thy thoughts no tongue.
Nor any unproportion'd thought his act.
Be thou familiar, but by no means vulgar.
Those friends thou hast, and their adoption tried,
Grapple them to thy soul with hoops of steel;
But do not dull thy palm with entertainment
Of each new-hatched, unfledged comrade.
Beware of entrance to a quarrel but, being in,
Bear it that the opposed may beware of thee.
Give every man thy ear, but few thy voice;
Take each man's censure, but reserve thy judgment.
Costly thy habit as thy purse can buy,
But not expressed in fancy; rich, not gaudy;
For the apparel, oft proclaims the man;
And they in France of the best rank and station
Are of a most select and generous chief in that.
Neither a borrower, nor a lender be;
For loan oft loses both itself and friend,
And borrowing dulls the edge of husbandry.
This above all: to thine own self be true,
And it must follow, as the night the day,
Thou canst not then be false to any man.
Farewell; my blessings season this in thee!

Crud! In its context, what she thought it meant didn't at all resemble the trite advice she'd been handing out for years, and took people's money for. *Oh, for Pete's sake, I didn't even know who the author was!* She thought, kicking herself some more.

If possible she would retrace her steps, take her clients by the shoulders, and inform them, "I hope you didn't listen to me; I have no credibility; my own life's a mess! To thine own selves be true!" That's what she would do—if she didn't need the money. But, in her mind her life was a mess, although not that it showed outwardly. In her true to herself fashion, she was a walking advertisement for the benefits of daily meditation, yoga, deep breathing, and whatever eating no meat or dairy was supposed to do for a person. Her hair was bright, candy-apple, out-of-a-bottle red, that she wore straight and blunt. It hung just below her ears; her bangs were also straight and blunt, ending just above her eyebrows. Her eyes were green and she wore no makeup, other than an occasional swipe of red lip gloss.

Aura's wardrobe consisted of leotards, form fitting leggings, with some jeans thrown in, tank tops, and sweat shirts. She wore no jewelry, although she sold birthstones, along with various stones, rocks, and crystals, all with so-called healing powers.

By all appearances, she had her psychic act together. Well, as long as no one looked at her hands, because she'd chewed on her fingernails so long that she barely had any left. To make matters worse, she would often chew on her fingernails while she meditated! *What a sham you are*, she thought.

She didn't take a newspaper or watch television, other than occasionally watching old movies that were aired in the wee hours when she couldn't sleep. She avoided watching the news, or otherwise exposing herself to negativity that she believed might depress, or affect her spirit, in a negative way. She read a lot, but what she read pertained to her holistic persuasions; so she only read books and magazines that pertained to the New Age Movement, spiritual evolution, channeling, or biographies of people like Emma Hardinge Britten, Florence Cook, or more contemporary teachers like Barbara Brennan or Shirley McLain. She had also read many of L. Ron Hubbard's works, although she wasn't a Scientologist.

For all of her self-disciplines, and questing for truth, she was not a fulfilled person. Over the years, she'd pursued numerous mentors, only she'd paid to be mentored, and that, she was now convinced, detracted from it. She was licensed in massage, tattooing, and piercing, although, in practice, she never got beyond piercing ears, because piercing other body parts repulsed her.

Aura recycled everything and neither ate, or wore, anything synthetic. The only dairy she allowed herself was fertilized eggs. Everything else was organic; therefore, she avoided anything containing growth hormones, gluten, or that was high in sodium. She attempted to stop her brain from listing her fetishes, because the list scared her. She had, however, found and retained her inner child.

Such convictions came with a price, and despite the seeming frugality of her lifestyle; everything that was left for her to eat or do was costly. Money! It would be terribly difficult to live out her lifestyle without it, and by observation, her clients were anything but poor in spite of the camouflage of dressing and living as though they were.

Her livelihood was deliberate, although when she chose it, she had no other career options to pick from; nor did she now. She had a true gift of insight that she communicated to her clients, and she believed that part of her job was convincing people to be "true to themselves". Now, she was convinced if she read Shakespeare's poem to them in its entirety they would want their money back. The thought disturbed her; she began chewing on her thumbnail.

~~~

It was a hamburger that changed her destiny.

One Friday afternoon, a frustrated Aura, decided that what she needed was a break—a holiday. She lived in Petaluma, California, and considering how she relied on public transportation, all she could come up with to do were two options; either she could go north into Wine Country, or the opposite direction, towards San Francisco Bay. Drinking alone didn't sound like much fun, and when she visualized the bay she was certain her spirit was telling her that she needed to be near water. So, she boarded a bus headed towards San Francisco, with Sausalito her destination.

The bus ride lifted her spirits. When she got off the bus in Sausalito she wandered aimlessly toward the water, and that was when she found herself behind a group of people who were waiting in line for something. Curious, she walked around them to the front of the line, wanting to see what the attraction was.

The crowd-pleasing attraction was a hole-in-the-wall diner. The kitchen was visible through the front window, where a carousal of sizzling meat was circling over a bed of hot coals. Inside were maybe a dozen people, sitting at tiny tables lined up along the wall; outside there was nowhere to sit, but that didn't seem to matter—apparently what they served was worth waiting for.

Fascinated, she watched the hamburger groupies paying for their bags of decadence, making their way across the street to picnic on park benches, or munch on their food while they walked—well; it looked and smelled magical. For the first time in over eleven years, Aura was hungry for MEAT.

Aura made her way to the back of the line to wait her turn. What happened next was just as remarkable; she began openly eavesdropping on the conversations of her unexpected peers, making her wonder what it was in her psyche that had caused her to avoid being around people. She couldn't explain it, but she was sure the interactions were making her spirit feel brighter.

This is fun! She thought. *I'm having fun!* She was preparing to break a rule, and it felt wonderful—like her life might be turning a new corner. For the first time in a long time, Aura felt hopeful.

When she heard her name called she stepped forward to accept her paper bag of delicacies, clutching it as if it were full of gold coins. Following the sidewalk downhill toward the Bay, she recalled a place where she could eat and be near the water. The moment was meant to be—when she got to her spot, no one else was there but some waiting birds, so she sat down, deliciously alone, on top of the cement retaining wall that rose above the waterline.

Seated with her legs dangling over the seawall, she opened the bag, lowering her head over it to inhale the tantalizing aroma, while at the same time chiding herself that there was still time to stop. She couldn't believe it was her.

With extreme care, she peeled the wrapping away from the hamburger, opening her mouth wide, and sinking her teeth into her first bite of hormone-laced, charcoal charred beef, in nearly a decade, followed by a chaser of French-fried potato. For some unimaginable reason, and for the first time in years, she allowed herself no guilt.

The crowd of pigeons quickly formed a semi-circle behind her, soon joined by some obnoxious sea gulls circling and diving above, all accustomed to tourists less protective of their meals than she was. But, on this particular Friday afternoon, eating lunch by the bay in Sausalito, she had no compunction whatever to share even one morsel of her meal with the birds.

To prolong the unexpected pleasure she ate slowly, savoring every bite, down to the grains of salt that she licked off her fingertips—having been totally true to herself. She gathered up the remnants of her meal and stuffed them into the bag.

It was when she stood up and turned around she saw him.

~~~

His name was Maxwell Zimmerman—"Lawyer by day and Artist by night," as stated on his website. His reason for being in Sausalito was a showing of his paintings in a gallery up the street. A sudden urge for a cigarette was what compelled him to take a walk, ending up by the water.

His acclaimed oil paintings were studies of people; ordinary people that he captured unawares, inviting the viewer be a voyeur of an unguarded and luxurious moment of abandon, the kind that after childhood happen seldom, if at all. Max had just happened upon one of those moments.

He tossed his cigarette aside, slowly reaching into his pocket for his cell phone, careful not to move too quickly. Stealthily, he began taking pictures, wondering how what he was doing could be legal. But, he'd done it before, and he knew he'd do it again, given the opportunity. Max had the sensitivity to recognize the true wonder of such a moment, and for him, the sin would be to waste it.

His inspiration was the elegant back of a red-headed woman, dressed in blue jeans and a tank top, who was savoring a hamburger as if it were Foie Gras & Caviar. Spread out in front of her was a view of the hills of Tiburon, replete with several dozen sailboats that bobbed atop the sparkling, choppy waters of San Francisco Bay at mid-day.

Cautiously, he inched his way forward, guardedly moving from side to side, as if he were line dancing in slow motion, trying to capture every possible angle of her seemingly unobserved moment; even managing to catch her tongue while it licked a few grains of salt from her fingertips.

Max believed such moments were ordained. *Yes,* he thought. *That will be the title; Ordained to find her thus.*

For some reason, such moments of intrusion, for Max, seemed less so when done through the lens of a camera. He continued to view her, snapping pictures, while she neatly folded the used wrappers, putting them inside the paper bag. She rose to her feet in one graceful motion; a by-product of years of Yoga.

Before she could catch him spying on her he shoved his phone back into his pocket, but remained where he was—mesmerized. There was no way he could leave before seeing her face.

~~~

The woman who faced him was older than what he was expecting, perhaps in her late thirties. She was beautiful, but Max immediately noticed that her face exhibited the complex beauty that life's palate knife sculpts into it over time—a softness, and sensuality, with a trace of sadness around the eyes. Her red hair and green eyes were striking.

Later she would say that had she walked away and never saw Max Zimmerman again after that day she would have remembered him—having seen someone full of light, whose spirit was strong, kind, and honest.

She took him home with her that night.

CHAPTER 9

Nelson was trying to pay attention, attempting to focus while Jeremy haltingly described the details of his wife's execution—he was unable able to feel anything. In his innermost being, Nelson believed he'd sold his soul. *But, surely*, he thought, *I've known that for some time.* His complete lack of empathy, while listening to Jeremy, was his final proof—he felt nothing. His conclusion was that he'd been dead for some time, but no one had noticed but him.

Jeremy was right in pressing him to tell Lindsay. If possible, he would have passed it off, but were she to find out another way, and discovered later that he'd known, would only add to her devastation. By the time he'd walked halfway to the train station, he was kicking himself for not having called for a car. On Fridays, when the weather permitted, he enjoyed the walk to Grand Central. It symbolized shedding the dirtiness of what he did during the week, before going home for the weekend. As crazy as it might seem to people who thought they knew him, he thoroughly enjoyed the commute, and the comradeship of the other passengers as well; who were all going to and fro, each narcissistically preoccupied. He fit right in, but, he knew he wasn't like them; well, other than being narcissistically preoccupied—that couldn't be argued.

While it wasn't rational, he blamed the death of his soul on his mother, Ethel; whose relentless pursuit of her ambitions for him made him feel like he'd been raised by a stalker. His father, Albert S. Saunders, was the brains behind Saunders Enterprises—a consortium of retail business's. It was the chain of high-end department stores that were credited for the family's wealth, and prestige. Albert was the second generation retail giant, and he had also inherited the Midas touch.

According to legend, the pert and beautiful debutante, Ethel Stewart, allowed Albert Saunders to enjoy the thrill of chasing her until she very skillfully caught him. Once married, Albert found himself in second place to her undisclosed career path that marrying him made possible; which was Ethel making sure she was seen in the right circles, known by the right people, and positioned to elbow her way into every photo-op with the potential to put her front and center, of the social pages. She was shrewd, ruthless, and soulless; but pleasant if you didn't live with her. While Nelson wasn't born with them, over time he adopted those attributes. The single emotion he was still able to identify was his hatred of her.

His father's notoriety served as his armor, helping him to keep Ethel from dominating him totally; her lack of success would have never been for lack of trying. No one in Albert's family had ever divorced, and it was his choice not to be the first to lay that stigma on his family, nor would he abandon his two sons to her. That was his justification for the extra marital liaisons he enjoyed, and managed to keep hidden—few mistresses were better kept than his were.

As a boy, Nelson remembered the relief he and his brother, Ned, would feel when their father was home—when Ethel's attentions were temporarily diverted away from them. But, whenever their dad left, which he did often, her attention would refocus back toward the two unfortunate boys; devoting herself, again, to micro-managing every possible detail of their hapless lives.

Nelson credited going to boarding school for having saved him, convinced that he might have been suicidal left to his mother's obsessive control. Thankfully, his father went to Salisbury School, as had his father before him, and, that he and Ned would attend might as well have been written on their birth certificates next to their names; it was nonnegotiable.

Nelson was a stellar academic, earning him a scholarship to Yale. His resume of social status, high marks, extra-curricular achievements, and athleticism, insured him an invitation into the exclusive, and well-known, secret fraternity, The Skull & Bones Society. The association indoctrinated him into an amoral world of secrecy—a far cry from his strict Episcopalian education at Salisbury, whose motto was "helping young men find their moral compasses". How Nelson eventually rationalized the loss of his own moral compass was "You find things, you lose things, or you trade things; then you trade those things for other things…"

Nelson doubted that he would recognize a moral compass if he saw one. His associations at Yale had worked to feed his dark side. His decision to work on his graduate degree at Georgetown offered him a respite, permitting him to walk into the light that Lindsay brought into his life. But, over time new associations took him in the other direction. But, if anything, Lindsay's light grew even brighter. Nelson was sure if he were to locate his moral compass, it would point down.

A few months after they met, Lindsay invited Nelson to a Sunday afternoon barbecue at her parent's lake cottage to meet her family. The afternoon was casual, unpretentious and far different than anything Nelson had ever experienced. The entire family participated in preparing the food and the clean-up afterward, still finding time for canoeing, a long walk in the woods, followed by an unforgettable group examination of each other for ticks.

Nelson liked her family—a lot, although he had reservations about her sister. While the girls looked alike, their personalities could not have been more different. Had he been fixed up with Lenette instead of Lindsay, he concluded he would have left the bar after one drink. When Ethel learned through his brother that Nelson had met Lindsay's family, she insisted he bring Lindsay home to meet his. Lindsay's last name was Kennedy, and Ethel was ecstatic, thinking how he seemed to be planning ahead, for once.

Nelson procrastinated telling Lindsay about the invitation (synonym: summons) until his mother's relentless nagging resigned him to accept the fact it had to happen sometime. The invitation/summons was issued and accepted.

Nelson had deliberately neglected describing what his mother was like to Lindsay; partly because he didn't have appropriate adjectives, along with the inevitability of Ethel being the deal-breaker. He further neglected to mention the afternoon would have the trappings of meeting the Queen of Scots, since his mother thought she was meeting one of The Kennedys'. After that day, he understood what denial was; his definition of denial could be defined as being between a rock and a hard place, made more difficult by immobility.

When he picked Lindsay up at the train station, his heart sank. His definition of casual was a far cry from hers. She was wearing a loose-fitting sweater and jeans—the trendy kind, with frayed holes, and deliberately faded in places—Nelson foresaw that his mother would think she looked like a bag lady.

Ned was conveniently away, visiting friends upstate that weekend; also prepared for the worst, and thrilled not to witness it, leaving Nelson with no moral support. It was doomed to become one of those afternoons, to put it mildly.

When they drove through the gate, Lindsay looked up at the grand house looming ahead, and then down at her jean-clad legs, reactively covering two of the holes with her hands. She looked helplessly at Nelson, whispering "Oh no." under her breath, to which he replied, "No kidding."

He assured her the worst thing that could happen would be that his mother might faint, making it possible for the best thing to happen, which would be that they could eat dinner without her. Lindsay giggled, thinking he was joking. He wasn't. His fantasy was actually his best case scenario; he was in unchartered territory.

"It's my fault, Lindsay. I should have warned you..." He offered lamely, amazed that she wasn't asking him to drive her back to the train.

The afternoon was a disaster of historic proportions. It was Ethel's meeting, and she took full advantage of the opportunity to go after Lindsay with a battering ram of questions, firing them at her like cannon balls; questions about where was she born, what schools she had attended, her sorority, what was her father's occupation, her coming out, etc.

Nelson and his father both sat in silence, watching Lindsay, who was nervously pulling loose threads out of the frayed holes in her jeans and dropping them on the floor under her chair. All three of them avoided making eye-contact with Ethel lest they encourage yet another round of questions. The girl's passivity made no difference—Ethel was determined to lay all of her cards on the table. Lindsay didn't cry, but Nelson came close.

When the day was mercifully over, on the way to the train station Lindsay asked Nelson if his mother thought she was gay, not having a clue what Ethel meant by "coming out". At any other time, he would have laughed, but he was preoccupied, thinking ahead to the interrogation he knew would be waiting when he returned. Lindsay had ceased to tremble by the time he kissed her good-bye; he hadn't, and he was dumbstruck she kissed him back.

During his absence, Ethel did an internet search of Lindsay's family; there was precious little to find; their only commonality with "The Kennedy's" was that they were also once Irish Catholic.

Nelson's attempt to avoid his mother by sneaking up the back stairs failed—she was waiting on the landing with legs splayed, and her arms crossed over a manila folder that contained the printed off pages from her internet search. Her stance reminded him of a female Gestapo guard in a Grade-B movie.

Nelson resolved then and there that Lindsay was the best thing that had ever happened to him, and he was not going to allow his mother to ruin it for him. In the short term, he succeeded, but over time the grim reality became how in much the same way his mother sucked the life out of him growing up, he would do, in turn, to Lindsay; the mantle of generationally gifted control would prove irresistible.

The couple's decision to wed far away from the social pages sealed Ethel's resentment of her new daughter-in-law. Ethel spent most of her married life sowing towards her social paybacks, and in her mind their decision to have a small wedding was premeditated, and intended to humiliate her in front of her friends. Having Lindsay killed, and her body disposed of, in pieces, was an idea she toyed with. The girl had actually managed to steal her son, but Ethel would not allow her to ruin his future.

~~~

Lindsay's grief was so palpable it could have been bottled; her unchecked wailing so terrifying, that neighbors who stopped by to console her, instead rescued their three children, taking them home with them. Her wailing lasted a day and a half, with virtually no respite. She would neither eat nor drink, saying over and over again, "How can I still live...?"

Nelson wanted to know what the news media was reporting, but Lindsay's unchecked grieving made it impossible to turn on the television without upsetting her further. He could finally leave the house after she had locked herself in their bedroom.

There was a vintage 1950's motel, one he had passed hundreds of times on his way to the train, not far from their home. He checked himself in, sprinting past the turquoise seahorse fountain in the courtyard, to find his room. He turned on the television, realizing, with a sigh of relief, they had cable—he hadn't thought to ask. He flipped from one channel to the other for over an hour, listening to the endless speculations about what the motive might be for killing Lenette Dobson and their babysitter—there were few clues. He was relieved to know she hadn't suffered.

The reports stated the killer used a long range M150 sniper's rifle, hiding himself in the brush behind the property, where the grass was freshly trampled; there were no casings left behind and clues were few. A neighbor reportedly saw a car matching Jeremy Dobson's parked on the end of the cul-de-sac, suggesting the killer may have had an accomplice. Nelson decided someone was leaking too much information.

After it was clear there was no breaking news he left, neglecting to check out. *Oh, well*, he thought, *they have my credit card; the worst that can happen is they sock me for an extra day*. He couldn't believe he was that calloused.

A memory verses from one of his religion classes at Salisbury came to mind. "*The heart is deceitful above all things and beyond cure. Who can understand it? I the Lord search the heart and examine the mind, to reward a man according to his conduct, according to what his deeds deserve.*"

CHAPTER 10

Jeremy lay on his back in bed, staring up at the ceiling in his neighbor's guest bedroom. He felt wasted, yet sleep was eluding him. His consolation was that by being forced to leave his home had spared him the decision of where to spend his first night without Lenette.

He got up to look out the window at his house that was still ablaze with lights. The police were still inside collecting evidence. He lay back down, soothed by the sound of Caleb's baby snores coming from the porta-crib next to his bed. *How will I possibly raise this little boy by myself?* He wondered, trying to imagine what lay ahead for them.

The last several days' events had been a roller-coaster of stress levels, heightened with the implosion that morning. More than anything else, right now he missed his dad; he sure could use him now. But, his dad was where Lenette was. He wondered if she knew what he was going through—he hoped not.

He had been up since 3:30 that morning and on the implosion site by 5:00; it was now 2:00 a.m. He'd been awake for twenty-three hours, although it seemed much longer. How was it possible that in less than a day his life had been turned upside down, and inside out, both.

The importance of the owner's physical presence on the job was something he'd learned from working with his dad, whose work ethic remained a legacy for anyone who was fortunate enough to have been employed by him. Jeremy had grown up with the philosophy, "Work the way you expect the men who work for you to, and they will do anything for you, because they did it with you." Dusty Dobson had his own brand of wisdom, but wisdom it was. With rare exception, the employees of Dobson Detonations had a work ethic that was humbling.

"Dad, I need you," he whispered. As clearly as if his dad were sitting beside him, he heard the whispered words, "Son, I need you, too. I know how much you need me." But, he realized that the voice wasn't his dad's voice; it was his Father's—the one he hadn't talked to in a while.

It was then that he began to weep. He turned over onto his

stomach, and buried his face in the pillow, allowing the bottled tears to be expressed. It felt as though the shoulder he needed had suddenly presented itself. He wasn't alone, and he never had been. And, he knew he wouldn't be alone to raise his son. What was it his pastor had called it, "The peace that passes understanding...?"

The tears fell, accompanied by the memories; her face, her smile, her husky voice, the scent of her breath, the soft fuzz on her neck; all parts of the remarkable woman she was. He would sleep in their room; he wanted to be reminded of what was contained within those walls.

"Lenette," He spoke her name out loud, but softly, into the quiet space, "how can I possibly live without you?"

It was as if the air stirred above him. Comfort...he felt comforted.

Finally, he slept.

CHAPTER 11

With another dawn came the suns intrusive streaming through the windows, and with it, like a laser, came the awful knowing that part of her was missing. Her life had ended—it wasn't over, but as sure as the sun rose in the sky, Lindsay was convinced it had ended. Half of her had been cut away, amputated, callously disposed of—and what remained seemed irrelevant without her other half.

Worst of all, she believed she was responsible. If she had tried harder to dissuade Lenette's radical persuasions, perhaps she would have abandoned them, but instead she'd allowed herself to become involved with her, in spite of the fact that up until a few weeks ago, Lindsay refused to involve herself in anything that was even remotely controversial.

Lindsay wondered how long it would take before someone found her dead, too. It was him; somehow he must have found out. *I must have been careless*, she thought. And, her carelessness had cost Lenette her life.

The wailing began again; a pitiful, mournful, involuntary sound that forced its way out of her; a volcano of grief erupting unsolicited from a source she had no control over. *When will the pain end—will it end? I can't bear it. God, please take me, too. It should have been me.* She thought. *Yes, I will welcome death. So be it.*

Finally, she fell asleep from sheer exhaustion, with her arms flailing about, as if she were warding off some demon, which, like some obnoxious insect, relentlessly pursued her. Awake or asleep the terrible wailing continued, making those who gathered to comfort her, chill at the obvious distress it represented. The only exception was Nelson, who would leave, return, and then leave again, not able to face what it all could mean, never having expected the extent of what was happening. Her grief was too deep for him to fathom.

Their three children remained in the care of their neighbors, and while young, they understood their aunt died, and how something was broken that couldn't be fixed—their three solemn faces testified to the uninvited intrusion of mortality into their young lives.

Nelson's sporadic absences came as no surprise to Lindsay's friends, who remained at the house. For years, those who knew her well wondered what she got out of the marriage, admiring her because she exhibited a love with few conditions. None of them could remember ever hearing her complain.

Nelson had never been a relationship person. He had few friends— no, he had no friends—he had acquaintances. Intimacy of soul was something he experienced once, and that was because of Lindsay; maintaining intimacy was something else entirely.

His father was a social animal; a dynamic businessman as well as a sportsman, games man, and ladies' man. Nelson resembled his father it was in appearance only; he was less than charming, unsociable, unlikeable, and self-indulgent.

~~~

Lawrence Edwards was the upperclassman the fraternity assigned to mentor the new pledge Nelson Albert Saunders. His father was Lawrence Edwards III. His friends called him Larry. Larry Edwards typified the spoiled indulgence that went with several generations of inherited wealth, and the assumed gratifications that accompanied it. While some might see some similarities in Nelson, he did not relate, finding Larry superficial and shallow. But, as could be expected, Nelson's mother was ecstatic when she learned who Nelson's Big Brother was, and wasted no time bragging to her circle that Lawrence's father was the CEO of Levy and Sinclair Investments, Inc.—a global investment banking and securities firm; the second largest bank in the country.

The firm's main offices were located in Lower Manhattan, and they were, by their own websites front-page description, the best positioned firm "for the reshaping of the world's changing economy". Their self-proclaimed world mission wasn't subtle; but neither was Ethel's. Nelson's acquaintance with the Edwards, in her mind, was destiny. She was on a mission, and failure wasn't an option; the Edwards became her new best friends.

According to Ethel, one of Albert's failures was having remained in an industry that was failing—never mind that his timing to sell before the retail bubble burst had preserved their fortune, and the public humiliation other's not so fortunate were enduring. He had friends in high places who warned him when it was time to sell. Two years later, similar retail giants sold off their inventories for pennies on the dollar, retreating into obscurity. Ethel's hindsight observation was how Albert should have had the foresight to diversify, giving him no credit whatever for The Pennies on the Dollar Stores that continued to bring in enormous profits.

Ethel took pride in not having allowed her sons to work in the stores, an insult aimed at Albert whose philosophy was to "work up from the bottom". For his sons, that philosophy was something like viewing a mockup of dinosaur bones in the Smithsonian.

Despite Nelson's antisocial personality, in business he had value for that same reason; he was unscrupulous and his loyalties were purchased, not personal. His rise to the top in Sinclair and Levy wasn't because of any strings pulled by his mother, although no one would convince Ethel that could be true. It was because Lawrence P. Edwards II recognized, after spending time with Nelson, how he would be capable of making merciless decisions without any hesitation. He concluded "Nelson has a bullet proof brain", meaning no matter how loud the whining, how awful the press, or who might get in his way, Nelson would be worth his weight in securities. Lawrence Edwards used people, and Nelson gave him permission him do it.

While industries, fortunes, and families were imploding around him on every side, until Lenette's death, Nelson Saunders could sleep at night because it simply hadn't mattered to him who got hurt.

CHAPTER 12

Maxwell Zimmerman was employed by a small, but very prestigious consulting firm located in Beaverton, Oregon; a suburb of Portland. Bob Murphy, the firm's founder, picked the Portland area as the location for Murphy's Law, preferring for it to maintain a low profile—both personally and corporately. He gambled on the fact, were his firm less known, rather than well known, and could avoid unnecessary notoriety; it would be more desirable for those clients who needed their expertise, while desiring little or no attention drawn to them.

His premise was genius. Few people could come up with the name of his firm if asked, but somehow, by word of mouth alone, Murphy's Law would be called upon, and paid handsomely, to pull together the special witness research for their client's high powered attorneys to use in court.

Occasionally, one of Bob's hand-picked, very bright, young associates would approach him to ask if he would mind if they accepted an interview with some media outlet. Bob would listen intently; feigning interest, and then pausing for a few very pregnant seconds, before asking, "I assume this has something to do with your exit interview?" It never ceased to amuse him, watching them process his response, and subsequently backing out of his office, stammering something like, "Sorry to have interrupted you, Bob...I assure you, it won't happen again."

Max was one of his protégé's. Bob had an instinct for spotting talent, and whenever he discovered someone, he would spare no expense mentoring, and molding their specific gifts to bring them to their potential, paying them handsomely when they reached it.

Bob and Max met at a community wine festival & art show. Normally going to festivals wasn't his thing, but Martha had fallen in love with one of Max's paintings and begged Bob to look at it before she bought, since it was pricey. She knew from experience he would second guess her later, inquiring why she hadn't "talked the artist down"—something she hated doing.

Bob tried, and failed. Max refused to budge on his price, but offered instead to deliver the painting and hang it for them. The next thing Bob knew, he was filling out a check, and listening while his wife invited Max to join them for dinner the following evening.

By the time the meal ended, Bob had learned that besides being an artist, Max was also an attorney; he liked his style and immediately zeroed in on his expertise. When Max left their home later that evening, he had been offered an invitation to join Murphy's Law. Martha took full credit for having found him.

Max's job description was to act as, in Bob's words, the firm's 'built-in, back-up, legal responder', on the chance they were ever the target of a lawsuit; his official title was Corporate Attorney; more important, he had the expertise to be able to anticipate weakness's that might invite one. Max's name and job description were promptly displayed on the front page of their website, eliminating, for Bob, the aggravation of having to educate off-site attorneys whenever they needed legal assistance. Bob personally groomed Max, who would also use his specific talents in the cases where Murphy's Law would be asked to testify in court in behalf of their client. Max found it amusing how Bob had named the firm Murphy's Law, when he had never had an attorney on staff.

Max never took his job for granted. He met interesting people, travelled, and got to read the very pricey research their clients paid the other part of the hand-picked staff to do for them. He testified in behalf of very elite clients, always flew first class or by private plane, stayed in the best hotels, and got to keep his points for both. He learned a lot in the process, and considered that as one of his perks.

What he appreciated most was, while other members of the firm spent long days and even evenings doing research when cramming to meet a deadline, he could go home and paint. Either no one he worked with had noticed, or it was politely never mentioned, that, most afternoons, he was out of the office by five o'clock. The reality was that Max's expertise made everyone else's appear better; he was a real asset to the team.

Max made a lot of money for what he did; less than what Bob's research team made, but his relaxed schedule allowed him to pursue his painting. Plus, the hourly billing, the bane of so many of his attorney colleagues, was no longer an ethical issue for him.

He was good in the witness stand; a by-product of his training in trial law. And, that talent quickly became his job security, because, in reality, he didn't do a whole lot else. He was a quick study, and could quickly digest the specifics of each case, along with having impeccable timing on the stand for when to drop the proverbial bomb. Needless to say, he was a great conversationalist.

He used his vacation time for scheduling his art shows; he had more vacation time than he could use. To make use of it, after the show ended he would stay on afterward if the area interested him. Sausalito was one of those places. The galleries hosting him covered his expenses. Since his previous show in Sausalito, California, was successful, he had a following, and because of it, the gallery's owner suggested he stay on an additional couple of days to meet with some clients who were considering commissions.

Max hated commissions. His artwork was able to emotionally grab the viewer, because of the objectivity he achieved when he didn't know his client. It was a royal pain in the rear to have to play mind games with someone about what they thought they wanted, and retained the right to critique, when he was finished. Because of it, he up-charged his commissions an additional twenty percent from the price of a piece on the wall, just for the aggravation, and would have charged more if possible.

Commissions were lucrative in other ways than money, because it was often the rich and famous that wanted them, and, as his galleries reminded him, wasn't that what an artist dreamed of on their resume?

After enduring several meetings for the purpose of prescreening potential commissions, he ended up signing one, leaving him with an extra day to check out the area. That was when he found Aura. Suddenly, sightseeing was no longer his priority.

~~~

Surreal might best describe how Max felt the next morning after meeting Aura, and waking up beside her. It was well over a year since he'd dated anyone; his work and painting left him little time to socialize and he'd learned the hard way that he painted best when he wasn't in a relationship. Three dates with anyone led to expectations, and although Max was no prude, his upbringing was something like having Jiminy Cricket residing on his shoulder. That reminder of Jiminy caused him to sit up in bed, wondering where he'd had gone off to the night before. He probably left in shock.

He looked over at the stranger sleeping beside him, taken by surprise at how protective he felt of her. He imagined when she woke up, she would feel as tentative as he did; their encounter was an unexpected turn of events for both of them. He'd wasted a night's lodging at the Sausalito Hotel, which no doubt also caused Jiminy some angst. *I hope the cricket's using it*, Max mused.

He slipped out of bed, and wandered around her tiny apartment, trying to absorb what it was Aura did for a living. On a table in the main room, was a deck of weird-looking playing cards, along with a book about Nostradamus. Her appointment book was lying open; it appeared, from the entries, that business was good. There were books and magazines stacked in piles everywhere—on the coffee table, end tables, on the floor, and even in the bathroom; there wasn't one he was familiar with. Spread across the window sills were a dozen or so small boxes, displaying various kinds of stones, and on the window sill was a large piece of amethyst quartz.

The kitchen was only an L-shaped counter. He looked around for some coffee, realizing she must only drink tea—green tea, black tea, and a blend he didn't recognize. Her tiny refrigerator was well stocked with fresh fruits and vegetables, soy milk, and some kind of egg substitute. Next to the sink was a Vega-matic; otherwise, the counter was empty, other than a turntable filled with a variety of vitamins and food supplements. He didn't see any cookbooks. Max decided, after looking around, the hamburger might as well have been manna.

He returned to the bedroom; coffee could wait. Jiminy would no doubt be returning soon, but until he showed up, Max was going to enjoy the moment. He would hear from Jiminy again, but not before he and Aura realized that what happened between them was unexpected and wonderful. As Aura explained it to Max, "In this world nothing happens to a person he does not, for some reason or other, deserve. Therefore, we must accept that Karma has put us together."

Neither questioned that, in some way, it was destiny that introduced them—nor could either imagine a future without the other.

Max knew it wasn't Karma.

CHAPTER 13

If the description of a clue is "something that serves to guide or direct in the solution of a problem or a mystery" then "clueless" would be "the absence of a clue". Jeremy concluded the police appeared to be clueless. Incompetence on any level frustrated Jeremy, and it frustrated him now—until he retraced the details of the crime, and the retracing put him inside his own garage, tampering with evidence. He had usurped the key clues, and in the fog of dealing with the aftermath, he'd totally blown it off. His frustration was replaced by disbelief—he was the reason the case bogged down.

It seemed as though weeks had passed since Friday, rather than days. It was now Thursday, and the memorial service should have been over, except that Lenette's body had not been released from the morgue. Feeling settled was not something that was going to happen any time soon.

With the help of Lenette's mother, all of the arrangements had been made for the service, but the lack of closure was closing over him again. He knew any perceived sense of his having control over his emotional state was an illusion, because he'd proved incapable of protecting what was most valuable in his life.

The local police had some holes in their investigating, as the other agencies did, as well. Jeremy might have described it as mayhem, but he shoved those judgments aside because one thought would turn itself into another and the speculating propelled him further down a path leading to nowhere. Jeremy had no idea who had jurisdiction of the case, but due to the confusion between the agencies some things were overlooked; luxury of time was never on the side of an investigation.

~~~

When Jeremy looked out the window the Thursday morning after the murder, the yellow crime scene tape had been removed. He could go home. He didn't question why he wasn't contacted, nor did he waste a minute gathering up his and the baby's things, looking forward to some privacy. What he hadn't considered was that when the investigation was over they would simply walk away. When he returned to his home it was in shambles.

The sight of the chalk outline of Lenette's body in the kitchen, surrounded by broken glass, blood, and hard blackened bits of banana was so utterly unexpected Jeremy barely made it to the bathroom before regurgitating the coffee and bagel he'd forced down an hour earlier.

He dialed 911, venting to the poor slob on the other end, graphically describing the mess he'd returned to. The unfortunate call-taker put Jeremy on hold, attempting to find a cleaning service that cleaned up crime scenes for him. While Jeremy was on hold, he couldn't help thinking how it took a different breed to want that as a job description. Jeremy was informed there were two such services; one was there within the hour.

It didn't take long for word to get out that he and Caleb had moved home. Immediately, a steady stream of people began arriving with food, flowers, and toys. As it is with shared grieving, the entire community expressed their grief by becoming part of Jeremy's. His secretary called to tell him the office was overrun with people, also dropping off food and flowers because they couldn't get past the gate guard in his neighborhood.

Jeremy was humbled; particularly because before this experience, he doubted he would have thought to have made even one of the gestures himself.

The following evening, after putting the baby to bed, he brought Lenette's briefcase inside, setting it on the kitchen counter. He was jumpy; pretty sure that his heightened sense of jumpiness was indicative of someone who had a legitimate reason to be jumpy. While staring at the briefcase, he concluded he could remove "commit a felony" from his bucket list.

He once read a quote credited to Pope Alexander, "An excuse is worse than a lie, for an excuse is a lie, guarded." He was living it out in real time; yet, deep inside he believed he was following a prompting that wasn't of himself. Only time would tell.

He already knew the briefcase wouldn't be locked; he and Lenette had an unspoken respect for each other's space. It would have never occurred to him to look inside it for something or to rummage through her purse without asking her first. Up until last Friday his fingerprints wouldn't have been on it. *Funny I'm thinking about fingerprints*, he thought; he was getting accustomed to Freudian Slips.

He remembered that he'd hidden the latex gloves in his glove box. Looking around the kitchen, he spotted a partially burned candle on the counter, sitting by itself under the boarded up window. The candle was green, with a metal label imbedded in the side that read "Sage". Lenette loved candles. "Light my way, Baby" he whispered when he lit it, adding, "God, please guide me." It would be folly to go where he was heading alone.

He looked around the room again, feeling creepy. He couldn't put his finger on whether what he was feeling was guilt, apprehension, or a combination of both. The possible discovery of what may have caused his wife's death was a click away; he might also be a click away from joining her.

He scolded himself for being paranoid, but the voice inside his head was reminding him that Lenette died because something she knew, or had, made her dangerous to someone.

Cautiously, he undid the latch—the snap making him jump. He recognized the feeling; it wasn't apprehension—it was fear.

He sat down on a bar stool and found himself staring at the briefcase some more. After two beers he finally got up enough courage to open it. *No more excuses*, he told himself. He spoke it out loud to himself again, his own voice urging him forward.

CHAPTER 14

Lindsay's wailing ceased and, mercifully, exhaustion took over. Her best friend, Maryellen Sifford, refused to leave the house, waiting for Lindsay to ask for her. By the end of the second day, it became obvious someone would need to intervene, and there was no one to do it, but her; Lindsay couldn't remain locked in her room. Finally, after repeated pleas from Maryellen to be allowed to come in, Lindsay unlocked the door.

Like a ministering angel, Maryellen stayed with Lindsay, who accepted her friend's tender ministrations without shame. Maryellen undressed her, bathed her, put clean sheets on the bed, and helped her dress, leaving only long enough to get something for her to eat. It was after Lindsay had eaten that she asked for her children.

Lindsay was finally coming out of it. It was the most terrifying thing Maryellen had ever witnessed.

~~~

The Thursday after the murder, when the dust was finally beginning to settle, Nelson announced he would be staying in the city until the following Friday; his excuse was to catch up at work. Lindsay, while annoyed, was relieved she would be spared having to process his moods. With the children back at home, Lindsay had little time left over to think about anything outside their immediate needs. They were almost as inconsolable as she had been, and that required her to put aside her own grieving to help them work through theirs; and, predictably, she had to do it with no help from Nelson.

To learn what Nelson knew about Lenette, she would have to set the stage for him to open up. The Friday he was due home, she phoned their favorite restaurant, asking if they would do take-out for her—something they normally didn't offer. Like everyone else, they were aware of Lindsay's overwhelming loss, and grateful for a tangible way to extend themselves to her.

On Friday afternoon, she picked up their dinner, and set a table for two in the sunroom, praying he would come home relaxed, so they could have a productive conversation. His mood was worse than she could have imagined; he was sour, petulant, and less than enthusiastic about a quiet dinner, having sensed that Lindsay was pumped about something—all of his defensive hackles were standing on end.

Before dinner, Nelson poured himself a scotch, filling another glass with ice. After starting for the sunroom, he turned back to the bar, grabbing the scotch bottle and putting it under his arm. When Lindsay saw him, her look of dismay added to his defensiveness. He remarked, "You remind me of my mother"; he wasn't going to play her game.

Nelson started eating before Lindsay could sit down, and continued eating with his head down and eyes lowered, with the only exception being to look up and reach for his drink. Finally, unable to resist any longer, she asked, "Nelson, can I ask you about..."

Abruptly, Nelson stood to his feet, throwing his napkin on the floor. He grabbed the bottle of Scotch and stormed out of the room. A few minutes later she heard his car start, and watched the headlights pointing down their driveway, away from the house.

His behavior was stunning—even for him. She'd absorbed his seeming insensitivity for years, allowing him breaks for his upbringing, and lack of positive role models, but this time he'd backed her against a wall. At one time, she truly believed she could love him enough. But, in reality, she had loved him more than enough, and for her own mental health's sake; it was time to accept that his insufficiency to love her back was not her responsibility. It was another loss they would have to deal with. Whatever answers she hoped Nelson might provide would have to come from somewhere else.

~~~

Albert Saunders death was unexpected. He was physically fit, mentally sharp and enjoyed life. The last time Nelson saw his father he was in good spirits—very good spirits; he was plastered.

The following morning, shortly after midnight Albert ran his car into a phone pole at sixty miles an hour, six blocks from the family estate. His death was ruled instantaneous; he was not wearing a seatbelt.

His sons surmised there could only be one reason their dad would be sneaking out at that time of night. That possibility became a headline in the following morning's newspaper; one of his lady friends had come forward, putting their queries to rest on the front page.

Albert was seventy six years old when he died and had embraced life fully; if there was a glitch it would have been his choice of a mate. Without Albert's presence to serve as a restraint Ethel, was loosed to become the shrill, domineering woman they knew she was, but had enjoyed respites from because of him. Ethel's reaction to her sudden widowhood could only be described as narcissistic tunnel vision. Her mourning seemed scripted for whoever her audience was at the time. One by one, her friends began to distance from her, unnerved to see her self-destructing.

Four months after Albert's funeral, Ethel's maid found her lying unconscious on the floor of her dressing room; she'd suffered a stroke. The maid called Nelson at work, hysterical, asking him what to do. Annoyed, Nelson told her to stay with his mother and that he would make the 911 call himself.

The hospital called to ask him who had the power of attorney to sign Ethel's admittance papers; something he hadn't thought about and couldn't avoid. When he got to the hospital he avoided seeing her by prolonging the paper signing; hiding afterward in the visitor's lounge.

When the doctor on call located him, he asked Nelson if he had any questions about his mother's condition. Too quickly, it became apparent that he had none, so, after telling a distracted Nelson he could see her, the doctor walked away, shaking his head.

Reluctantly, Nelson took the elevator to the ICU. At the nurses' station, he stopped to ask where her room was; one of them pointed to a room directly across from them. He approached it, and although dimly lit, he could tell she was hooked up to numerous machines that were all blinking and beeping as required. She looked like a corpse, and he hoped if the same thing ever happened to him, he would die instantly.

He glanced behind him, aware that he was being watched, which was causing him to feel obligated to go inside. Hesitating, he opened the door, looked behind him again, and then closed it, making sure it shut behind him. Even from the doorway it was apparent that the left side of her face was paralyzed. Her mouth was hanging open, and drool had accumulated in the corner and was about to roll onto her chin. Nelson shuddered—repulsed.

"I hate you." The words popped out with no premeditation, but once they were out, his mission became making sure she heard him.

He walked closer, so he could be heard over the noise of the machines. This time he took his time, standing over her, and then leaning forward until his face almost touched hers. He looked into her vacant eyes and said it again, only this time much louder, "I hate you." Now he could leave; he was sure she'd heard him.

He turned, crashing into Lindsay who had been standing right behind him; he was so intent on his mission he hadn't heard her come in. He shoved past her, escaping to the elevator and outside the hospital.

Although they never spoke of that day afterward, what she witnessed shook Lindsay to her core. Only God could bring light to the darkness that dwelled inside her husband; it was more than she was equipped to fix alone. She reminded herself that she'd said the words "for better or for worse" and meant them.

That would be the last time Ethel would see her son.

CHAPTER 15

When Max returned to Portland, Jiminy Cricket was already there, waiting for him. After enduring a rather long lecture from the cricket, Max assured him that it was his intention to marry the girl. Two weekends later Max flew into the Oakland Airport, rented a car, and drove to Petaluma with an engagement ring in his carry-on.

He stood waiting outside her apartment wondering if he should have called to warn her he was coming. After a few minutes, Aura appeared at the door, wrapped in a towel, with dripping wet hair, having left a wet trail of footprints behind her on the floor. She stood in the doorway as though she expected him; Max decided later she probably already knew he was coming, with that being her job and all. Whatever he'd prepared to say was utterly lost to the vision standing in front of him.

Apparently she also suffered from a lack of words, because instead of attempting any small talk she dropped the towel.

Oh, oh! I'm going to be in trouble with the Cricket again, he thought, panicking. He bent over and picked the towel up off the floor, handing it back to her while desperately trying to retain eye-contact, deciding that what happened next would be the test—what would Aura do when she discovered he was a nice boy?

Nothing seemed to faze her. She took the offered towel, turned, and walked back to her bathroom, dragging it behind her on the floor. Max stood in the open doorway, unable to move.

Before closing the bathroom door, she said over her shoulder, "You might as well shut the door and come in."

He was sweating, but he'd resisted a whopping temptation.

Jiminy would be proud.

~~~

Max spent the night on her sofa. The following morning they drove to Las Vegas and got married. Aura's name, as it was listed on their marriage certificate, was Laura; Laura Ann Wilson, to be exact.

She explained to Max how Aura became her stage name. One day she was doodling on a napkin at the coffee shop, and realized that if she dropped the "L" from Laura her name became Aura, and that was who she became from then on. She decided she would also drop her last name, inspired by Cher, whose notoriety was partly due to her only having one the one name. So, when she hung her first psychic shingle, on the chance she should become famous—it read "Aura". She giggled when she told him the story, because she knew it made her seem naïve and unsophisticated. But, Max loved it. That event was nineteen long years ago. She hadn't become famous, and she now believed her recent restlessness was due, in part, to the feeling deep down, that her life had a larger plan. And, for the foreseeable future, that plan would be making Max Zimmerman a happy man. It was like the song in The Sound of Music; "Somewhere in her wicked, miserable past she must have done something good", to have been given a second chance at life. She wasn't sure how that fit with Karma, but she believed it to be true.

Fate had reserved Max for her. She didn't deserve him; she knew that was true. What was also true was that, by some divine providence, her wicked, miserable past had somehow been overlooked. Later she would credit the prayers of her grandmother for guiding her through her lostness.

~~~

It took Laura Zimmerman exactly one week after saying "I do" to pull her no longer messy life together. She closed down her Marin County life—destination, Portland, Oregon. Nearly everything she owned she gave away. Her slip covered and repainted shabby chic furniture was offered to a shelter for battered women, along with most of her clothes; she gave her Pilate's instructor everything else that related to her psychic life.

Last of all, she boxed up her grandmother's vintage pottery, the amethyst geode, and her dishes; shipping them off to Portland, along with some Depression glass she had begun collecting.

When she stepped off the plane at the Portland International Airport, Max was waiting for her with an armload of roses in one arm, and an eight week old yellow lab puppy in the other. For anyone watching them, the bar had been raised several notches for how a man should treat a woman.

Then Max kissed her. 'Only in the movies' was the real world for one extremely lucky woman. Laura had come home.

CHAPTER 16

It was quickly concluded that Ethel's stroke, while serious, was not life threatening. She was moved from ICU to a private room where she remained for two weeks. It became apparent that she was not making any progress, so her doctors offered the family the choice of moving her into either a rehab facility or to a nursing home that was equipped to do rehab.

It took Nelson and Ned all of five minutes over the phone to make their decision. There was a singularly lovely nursing home in the country in Connecticut, not terribly far from where Nelson and Lindsay lived that had a rehab facility on site. It was as expensive and as luxurious as nursing homes went, but the expense staved off any residual guilt either of them carried for knowing they would not be going to visit her.

Lindsay, being Lindsay, exclaimed, "How lovely! She'll be close enough for me to be able to visit her often!" And, she did. Every Tuesday and Friday, rain or shine, Lindsay went to the nursing home to visit her mother-in-law.

What she found was the same each visit; Ethel lying flat on her back, staring at the ceiling through blank eyes; deliberately remote and zombie like. The doctors explained that it was physically possible for her to move her head, but apparently it was her choice to lie stiff and unmoving with even her eyes fixed and rigid. Undeterred, Lindsay would brush her hair, powder her face, put lipstick on her, and file and paint her nails. Ethel had always taken extreme pride in her appearance.

After a few weeks of establishing her regimen with Ethel, Lindsay had drawn an audience. Two other older ladies, who did not have anyone who visited them, began appearing in the room to watch while Lindsay, as they put it "fixed 'er up". One day Lindsay asked if they would like for her to do their nails also. Their unabashed delight afterward cinched them both a weekly manicure. It wasn't long before she was taking them out for an occasional lunch and helping them with some of their errands. Her kindness evolved into two unlikely but appreciated friendships.

Ethel had become her captive audience. Lindsay wisely realized that the years of Ethel's dislike of her could not be erased immediately. Instead, she took the opportunity to minister to her as a divine appointment. What Ethel would never have accepted from her when she had her wits about her, she had no choice but to accept from her now. Lindsay wondered if it might be a sin to be secretly enjoying imagining Ethel's frustration to be at her mercy, but, if Lindsay had an operational Gift of the Spirit it was that she was merciful. Her enjoyment was balanced by her profound grief to see her mother-in-law so diminished.

Although Ethel had some paralysis on her left side, she could have been rehabilitated to some level of quality of life, but she simply refused to do anything to help the process along. Her physical therapists couldn't get Ethel to cooperate enough to do more than to sit her in a chair when her bed was being changed.

Ethel refused to use her right arm to feed herself and would clamp her jaw shut when the nurses tried to feed her, so to get nourishment into her the doctor explained they would be forced to revert back to a feeding tube. They explained that refusing to eat, often accompanied the depression that followed a stroke. The stroke victim preferring death than to being handicapped, but Lindsay insisted on allowing her more time to see if she could persuade Ethel to eat.

During the 'Let's all try to get Ethel to eat experiment', Lindsay headed to the nursing home immediately after dropping the kids off at school, so she could use her own gift of persuasion on Ethel. After a couple days of attempting to coax the mediocre institutional food between Ethel's pursed lips only to have it spit out, Lindsay left the home, drove back into town to her favorite bakery, and returned with an assortment of desserts that she knew Ethel loved. She lined the desserts in a row on her tray, holding them up where Ethel could see them, and describing what they were to her; apricot scones, Key Lime pie, Banana Crème pie. Ethel opened her mouth.

From then on Lindsay would bring along a selection of pastries and desserts whenever she came to visit, with enough to share with their inevitable guests. Was she to miss a visit she would walk through the door of Ethel's room to the warm welcome of her mother-in-law staring at the ceiling and shaking her good fist in the air.

That was Lindsay's signal that love would find a way.

Ethel missed her.

∾∾∾

Since conversing was impossible, Lindsay concluded that one way to spend quality time with Ethel would be to read to her. She had no idea what it was Ethel read for pleasure, so one afternoon she drove to the family estate on Long Island, looking for clues. The first place she looked was Albert's library, housing his collection of first-edition books that covered a broad range of masculine topics. It was dark and musty, giving off the aroma of old books and pipe tobacco; definitely a man-cave. Its walls contained nothing that reflected Ethel's refined tastes.

Finding nothing of interest, Lindsay went upstairs to Ethel's bedroom suite to see if it might offer some clues. Much to her surprise, Ethel's refined tastes had not influenced her reading at all—she enjoyed racy romance novels. In her sitting room, Lindsay discovered a cabinet overflowing with tawdry paperbacks; their covers exhibiting partially clad women being taken away by force by handsome, but twisted, captors. Even the back matter was PG13.

It was, at least, a starting point. The following Tuesday Lindsay's reading program began... "Garth Dexter threw her to the ground, ripping her blouse to her waist..." It was a world of fantasy she hadn't known existed. Her always present audience of two appeared to be equally shocked, but neither was offended enough to miss a reading.

After wading through several of the torrid novels, and doing some selective editing, Lindsay decided they all sounded predictably the same; what she needed to do was transition Ethel from the romance novels to something more meaningful.

She shared all of this with Maryellen who knew their family's dynamics. She thought the reading dilemma was hilarious and suggested Lindsay look into a series of books that were written in a similar format, but with Christian messages—books that wouldn't steam up her reading glasses.

So, taking Maryellen's advice, Lindsay transitioned Ethel to the new books, relieved that she could enjoy the stories with her.

One afternoon, while she was reading to Ethel, she looked over and saw that her head was turned sideways—for the first time Ethel was watching her. Her face was expressionless, but her eyes weren't. Rather than overreact and ruin the moment, Lindsay reached over, gently resting her hand on Ethel's arm. "I love you, Mom," she whispered, continuing to read as though nothing out of the ordinary had happened.

A tear slipped out of Ethel's eye, down her cheek, and onto her pillow.

Yes, love would win.

CHAPTER 17

Jeremy started a pot of coffee before waking Caleb to prepare him for a day out with his grandma. He wasn't sure he was ready to relinquish him, but Rebecca needed healthy dose of her grandbaby; with the house being a crime scene she hadn't been around him since before Lenette's death. He didn't doubt that a change of scenery would be beneficial for the baby, also.

During the night, a cold front had moved through bringing with it some much needed rain; the change in the weather felt cleansing—Jeremy thought he would enjoy hosing out the inside of the house if he could achieve the same result.

He poured some coffee, switched on the morning news, and settled into his recliner with the intention of giving his mind something to chew on besides it's obsession with Lenette's death. The headlines renewed the reality of what her concerns about the country were; how a new world order seemed to be rising like a Phoenix out of the desert. The references to it being possible were no longer subtle; even coming from the secular media. The newspaper and the news channels had moved on to other and more recent headlines. The world was still spinning and had taken no notice his had collapsed; it was as if her death had never happened.

His reverie was interrupted by the phone's ringing. He checked the caller-id. When he saw that it was Lindsay, he took a deep breath and answered. "Hi, Lindsay, I'm so very sorry..." He stopped before he choked up. When she heard his voice she began to cry. Jeremy realized this wasn't the time to bring up anything serious. The call was mercifully short, although, when they were ready to hang up, Lindsay lowered her voice, telling Jeremy, "We need to talk, but I can't do it over the phone."

"I know," he answered, "we will have to figure out another way"; wondering how they could manage it. The memorial service was the following week; perhaps they could find a few moments then. Both were relieved when the call ended. After hanging up Jeremy thought the house seemed, if possible, emptier, and extremely quiet.

~~~

He had run out of excuses for not going through the briefcase. Since he'd risked spending a decade or two in prison by hiding it, it surprised him that he had to force himself to go through it.

Maybe in the daylight he would be able to keep his thoughts focused—rather than having them wander over the dozens of imaginary sinister subplots that were waiting to lure him. The daylight might help eliminate the fear that someone was lurking outside the window, well, unless some hired goon had him in the sites of some long-range rifle—but, there he went again, preparing to chase another disturbing subplot.

Focus, Jeremy! This was a priority and time was his enemy. First he removed Lenette's laptop, putting it out of sight in the bottom drawer of his desk where he'd hidden her iPhone. Next he removed one of the notebooks. Three phone numbers were scribbled in pencil in the inside cover. Several pages had been torn out, leaving behind fringes of the torn paper still caught inside the spiral.

His hands were sweating inside the latex gloves. He looked out the window; it was still raining. He was pretty sure neither the police nor her killer could know he had her briefcase, both hopefully assuming the other one had it. But, pretty sure wasn't sure at all.

But, one disturbing subplot surfaced during his mental dialogue that hadn't occurred to him before; how would he ever get the briefcase into the right hands without incriminating himself?

CHAPTER 18

There were two times in Nelson's life he recalled being careless—no, make that three times. There was the night he told his mother he hated her; he still had trouble believing he'd succumbed to such spontaneous cruelty—that was a low, even for him; his justification for it was that she deserved it, so it had to be her fault. The second time was the night of his verbal slip at Basso's; that he blamed on drinking too much Scotch and Jeremy's blabbering. The third, and most recent, was forgetting his briefcase. There was no excuse for that one—even odder to him was how all three happened fairly recently.

I'm losing it, he thought. He knew the dinner conversation at Basso's would have fallen through one of Lindsay's mental cracks had he not reinforced it by his forgetting the briefcase later. No amount of badgering from Lenette had ever provoked more than a "Whatever are you talking about, Lenette?" from Lindsay and would be followed by a quick-step change of subject.

Lindsay did what she could do to avoid listening to Lenette's endless Chicken Little speculations about what Lenette thought was happening in their country. To give Lenette some credit, she rarely pushed any of her opinions on Lindsay because she knew it might upset her.

Lindsay's going through his briefcase was puzzling and totally out of character for her. He was completely baffled at what might have prompted her to do it.

~~~

It was a warm spring afternoon. Lindsay was sitting in their sunroom writing thank you notes to her sorority sisters who had helped her with their annual philanthropic gala. "Finally!" she exclaimed when she finished addressing the last one. With dismay, she realized she was out of postage stamps.

Mailing the notes could have waited until the next day, but Lindsay was fixated on putting a year's worth of frustration behind her. The economy had made the event an ordeal; the torch was thankfully passed to a new chairman who had grand illusions about how she could improve upon Lindsay's committee's fiasco. Her closure would be dropping them off at the post office. She was already going through brochures for the trip they would be taking at the same time next year so she wouldn't have to attend. It was ironic that it was the one event they attended each year that Nelson enjoyed.

After searching through her desk, purse, and junk drawer with no success, she was on her way back to the sunroom when she passed Nelson's office. His briefcase was sitting upright on top of his desk—he must have forgotten it. She knew Nelson would have stamps; it was a similar fetish as his making sure there was no less than a half tank of gas in his car at all times. She flipped it open without giving it a second thought.

Lying on the top of the neatly arranged folders was a memo labeled "**Top Secret**". When asked, Nelson was never specific about exactly it was he or his company did, but his recent jumpiness at any inquiry whatsoever had heightened her curiosity. This opportunity was just too tempting, and he would never have to know.

She undid the paper clip and removed the memo's cover page, exposing multiple copies of what appeared to be images of some kind of currency; money she had never seen before. In the subject line was typed the words "Proposed Currency for the NWO". Her heart began to race; it had to stand for New World Order. She recalled a conversation with Lenette about that exact subject—now she wished she'd listened.

Sitting down at his desk, she studied the images carefully, trying to keep her hands steady. The second page showed close-ups of the notes that were highlighted in bright yellow; the highlights imposed over some of the symbols on the bills. There were also some notes in the margins that seemed to be written in some kind of shorthand or code. She searched in Nelson's desk for a pair of his reading glasses, wishing the copies were clearer.

Could these possibly have something to do with Nelson's comment to Jeremy at dinner? She wondered. She closed her eyes trying to remember their conversation.

~~~

Jeremy had promised Lenette one last hurrah before the baby arrived. Lindsay hadn't seen Lenette pregnant, so it was a no-brainer that Lenette would choose New York for their trip. The twins quickly organized a shopping day, with dinner with their husbands that evening. Jeremy objected to the trip at first, but Lenette's whining won in the end. "It's only two days, and we'll be with family, Jeremy. The worst thing that can happen is the baby's birth certificate will have New York City on it." Jeremy finally gave in after calling a doctor near where they were staying, satisfied they would be minutes away from the best care possible.

Reluctantly, and only because Lenette insisted, Jeremy called Nelson to ask him for suggestions about where to meet for dinner; a necessary precaution since Nelson habitually sulked through dinners out if they weren't to his liking. Nelson recommended Mario Batali's restaurant, Babbo's, saying he could get them a reservation on short notice. Jeremy was impressed.

The evening got off to a painful start. Nelson was never one for small talk, nor was he a good listener; added to that he was already way ahead of everyone on alcohol consumption. Lindsay was giving Lenette decorating suggestions for their new house, leaving the men out of their loop, so to fill the dead air Jeremy started talking politics, mistakenly thinking he and Nelson were on the same page.

He began by paralleling what he saw as the government's deliberate weakening of the economy as the first of a strategic series of events designed to implode the country, drawing analogies from his own business to make his points.

Nelson's silence inspired Jeremy to continue talking, expounding on his belief there was some sort of coup coming before the next election that would become the catalyst for the government to declare an emergency state and seize power. He touted Cloward and Pivin's plan to orchestrate a financial collapse, adding a quote from a Rod Larson show for emphasis. Nelson drained his glass in a few gulps and waived to their waiter for another one; his agitation was waving like a red flag.

Jeremy remained oblivious to Nelson's heightened agitation and plunged in deeper still. He mentioned how Lenette recorded the Rod Larsen show every afternoon for them to watch together later, telling him how Rod was suggesting that people be prepared for the worst, hoping it was too extreme to be possible.

Nelson sneered at the second mention of Rod Larson, but Jeremy had moved on to the subject of food storage, announcing, "We had our architect design a secret storeroom in the new house, so we can stock up on supplies."

"Why the hell would you do that?" For the first time, Nelson looked directly at him.

"We wanted to have a safe place to store some extra food, non-perishables, batteries, a compressor, water; in case there's an emergency—you know—stuff you can barter. And, we keep a stash of money in there, also."

"But, why would you do that? Will you have homing pigeons, too?"

Nelson's usually monotone voice had reached a new pitch.

Jeremy laughed, "Now, that's one good idea, Nelson. I'm going to write that on my list next to smoke signals." He waited for Nelson to laugh, but, undeterred, pressed ahead, "We're stashing cash and some gold coins. We want some money that isn't in the banks. Larson thinks they will all be nationalized at some point. You, of all people, should know that will mean there will be runs on them."

Nelson sniped, "So you think you have it figured out. Forget it, Jeremy. Hide your money if it makes your wife feel better, but it will all be worthless as a commodity—even the gold. We're way ahead of you."

The women had ceased talking at some point during Jeremy's dissertation, maybe it was the high frequency of Nelson's voice that caught their attention, but the men's conversation now had their undivided attention. Everything Jeremy said was new to Lindsay, and with dismay she saw Nelson was upset.

Ignoring her bulging belly Lenette leaned toward Nelson, "What in blazes does that mean, Nelson? That sounded like a threat. How could you possibly know that? Is your company part of it? I've seen their website. Does this have something to do with a one world government?"

Jeremy was speechless. Nelson's comment had gone in one ear and flown out the other. He was trying to remember what it was he'd said that provoked him. Nelson's response was a surprise since Jeremy hadn't thought he was listening, anyhow.

Lenette was one of those talented people who could listen to more than one conversation at a time and remember them both later. But, despite her probing, that exchange was to be the end of it. Nelson ignored Lenette's questions and Lindsay tried to salvage what remained of the evening by changing the subject and raising her glass to toast Jeremy and Lenette. Nelson receded into himself and ordered another drink.

Jeremy didn't have many vices, but he was secretly wishing he smoked. This would be the perfect time to go outside and light up.

The following week Lenette went into early labor. They never spoke of it to each other again.

CHAPTER 19

Rod Larson's interview with Eleanor Crosby concluded with enough decent material for two shows; perhaps even three if he added some dialog of his own. Eleanor had a self-imposed discipline to keep her opinions to herself, but when it became clear she and Rod's philosophies were the same she dropped her guard. Likewise, Rod was rarely interested in listening to someone else's opinions; he'd been cornered too often and forced to listen to opinions that couldn't be backed up. For Rod, such opining was what he called "opinions without works"; if someone could show him something they had done to affect a change in behalf of their opinion, he might listen. It was a given when someone like Eleanor had an opinion about something it was educated and could be evaluated by the litmus test of experience.

He presumed nothing regarding his own destiny. His approach to making sense of what was happening was based on a combination of the study of history as it related to the issues, combined with logic, cynicism, and detective work. He believed that one generation would be alive to face the critical mass of man's greed and narcissism that would so weaken the world's systems they would self-destruct, ushering in the close of the age.

The scripture that best fit the mantle he'd assumed was John 21:18—when Christ said to Peter, "*I tell you the truth, when you were young, you were able to do as you liked; you dressed yourself and went wherever you wanted to go. But when you are old, you will stretch out your hands, and others will dress you and take you where you don't want to go.*" Ego had long ago been put aside—he was compelled forward without reason.

There were so many weakened areas in the fabric of American society it was impossible to put a finger on just one and say with authority "This is the one thing that will cause our demise." But the one single thing Rod felt was the most egregious was what had taken place in the area of education.

He believed that the indoctrination of the youth in the schools, hand in hand with the erosion of the Judeo-Christian ethic, was the crack in the foundation that would allow the rest to cave in.

~~~

Victoria Larson's futile fight against Outcome Based Education, once his bane, had become his inspiration.

After becoming concerned about some of the changes she noticed were taking place in the public schools she became an active member of a faith-based organization, having identified with their pro-family stand on the cultural issues. What she learned prompted her to invest what amounted to a part time job into the organization in an attempt to educate her friends and church family hoping to arm them with information and inspire them to get their rears off their pews and become involved in the schools and the offices of the State Boards of Education. The enemy was Outcome Based Education.

Vicky spoke out, mailed newsletters, lobbied, and showed up unexpectedly at her district's curriculum meetings—sounding the alarm wherever she went. Although she had never spoken publicly before she assumed the mantle of "Well, somebody needs to do it..." she began speaking in homes, church basements, donated office spaces, and on rare occasions, from a few offered pulpits. It didn't matter if her audience was two or two hundred; she believed that one day the seeds she planted would take root and bear fruit.

After a year of badgering her own pastor, who she and her husband considered a close friend, he reluctantly agreed she could hold one of her meetings on a Tuesday evening at the church—unofficially (whatever that meant). On the Sunday prior to the event her husband leaned over, pointing out that Tuesday's event had made it into the church bulletin. She read it and smiled at him, delighted. Her smile turned into a scowl when he turned the bulletin over she saw that there was a disclaimer printed on the bottom of the back page. She threw it away, wishing later she'd framed it instead. Over the years, she realized those experiences were her badges of honor she'd earned for standing up for her beliefs.

What she was discovering in her research was an underlying NEA & OBE agenda that was blood curdling. After obtaining copies of several years of National Education Association convention notes she became convinced that OBE was a social experiment that would soon be introduced to the American classrooms.

"Our teachers are being held hostage by the teacher's union, trading their ethics for benefits and tenure in support of a predatory agenda that wants to take ownership of the minds of our children." she said, speaking at a state leadership meeting.

About that time states, one by one, had begun shifting public schools over and into the system at tremendous cost to the taxpayer, even though no evidence could be offered it had been tried or found effective. Their own literature stated, "OBE schools are expected to become success based rather than selection oriented by establishing the instructional management procedures and delivery conditions which enable all students to learn and demonstrate those skills necessary for continued success." What the OBE salespeople weren't telling parents was that success for all children meant success in demonstrating only the dumbed-down outcomes that the slowest learners in the class can attain.

The tragic outcome of OBE proved to be that its successes would rest in educational mediocrity rather than excellence. A bitter irony was that Outcome Based Education had been tried in the 1970's by a professor named Benjamin Bloom, in the Chicago school system, only he named it "Mastery Learning", or ML. It was essentially the prototype of OBE. It was a colossal failure and ended up being abandoned in disgrace. The illiteracy rate had become a national scandal with test scores having dropped to an appalling low.

One of Bloom's now infamous quotes was, "the purpose of education is to change the thoughts, feelings, and actions of students." Had anyone else made such a claim it might not be noteworthy, but, in the context of Bloom's other writings; it was a declaration of indoctrination, pure and simple.

Bloom further believed education should focus on the mastery of subjects and the promotion of higher forms of thinking, rather than a utilitarian approach to what he called simply transferring facts. He called fact-transfer and information-recall "the lowest level of training" rather than true and meaningful personal development.

So, the Chicago model of ML was renamed and subsequently sold to the American public as Outcome Based Education. The OBE model further offered no method of accountability to students, parents, teachers, or even taxpayers. What made it a compelling sell to parents were the failing public school systems. State Boards of Education seized the day to implement and restructure; again, with no restrictions to the cost.

Parents, whose children were already products of the failing public schools, became frogs in the agenda's kettle. A few got it, like Rod's mother, but even with the clout of a nationally recognized group behind her, she could never rile up enough people to stop it at the state level. The unionization of the system created a loyalty to it that, in essence, had purchased the educators. Khrushchev once said the Communist theology could take over America without ever firing a shot. Communists understood the concept of indoctrination. Secular Humanism was now in its third generational rotation.

Rod and his sisters were jerked out of the public school system immediately after his mother uncovered yet another troubling aspect of the new curriculum. Tucked between the lines of the Social Sciences curriculum was a broadened approach to sex education. The girls in one room and boys in another philosophy had been exchanged for co-ed classes that began in first grade, and no topic would remain sacred as long as the language describing it was clinical. The traditional family was dumbed down as old-fashioned.

It amused Rod that his own shyness with girls had lasted through college—he was convinced it was a direct result of his mother having spared him large doses of forced intimacy in mixed classes. Yeah, Victoria Larson! She was something else then—and still was. After her kids were grown she took her show on the road and became a popular speaker for grass roots movements across the country.

Rod owed her for having taught him not to take anything at face value, but instead to question everything and to keep on questioning even after you got the answer you wanted. The minds of the nation's children had been kidnapped with their parent's standing right outside the door.

~~~

Rod decided that assumption was a theory, rather than a word. Eight different meanings were credited to the word assumption—the key one, in Rod's mind, was "to take something for granted". If that could be accomplished—if a populace, for example, would simply roll over, and it was taken for granted that the status quo could maintain itself, at some given point they would also assume what they had taken for granted—or, put differently, what had gradually been changed or reformed right under their noses.

Therefore, Rod reasoned, unless that same populace could be reeducated, and reclaimed their initiative to question the status quo, they would assume everything was still going to end up okay because they had been taught to believe that was true!

His prayer was that a God inspired Reformation would sweep across the land and turn things around before the pendulum had swung too far. In a letter from Thomas Jefferson to William Smith, Jefferson wrote, "Lethargy is the forerunner of death to public liberty." The founders had an understanding of the degree of commitment it would take to maintain freedom for the new Republic. The implication—that the pursuit of happiness would take constant vigilance.

Based on her own experience Eleanor cautioned Rod not to assume his audience was where he was because of his own quest to know. The question remained of how to instill the same relentless seeking in those who didn't exhibit an ear to hear while there was still time.

Before the program was aired, he did some personal spiritual introspection. She'd confirmed his worst fear—Lukewarm gets spit out.

CHAPTER 20

One thing Laura would never adjust to was living on top of an earthquake fault. The floor moving beneath her feet was not one of her favorite sensations, and when she recognized what was happening she ran outside with her puppy in tow, that they named, quite appropriately, Burger.

Once outside, she spotted other neighbors who were waving at each other with the now familiar "You don't think this is the big one, do you?" look on their faces. The woman from the house next door approached her, "I'm so embarrassed I haven't been over to meet you—I'm Dana. Why don't you come over for a cup of coffee? I was about to fix some when my house started shaking!"

They both laughed at how funny that sounded. Laura was thrilled at the invitation.

~~~

Laura's and Max's home was located in Hillsboro, one of the nicer suburbs in the Portland area. When Max moved to Portland he bought a condo in the Pearl District, and while he enjoyed it, the area was hip, and he wasn't. He soon realized that being close to the action was not an asset to his painting.

His condo was located near the waterfront. When he purchased it, the area was generating large gains in appreciation, in relatively short turn-around times. Once he made up his mind to sell, it sold quickly and with a nice profit.

Max's intention in moving to the suburbs was to have privacy, so he made little effort meeting his neighbors. The house he bought was in the Craftsman style and might have seemed masculine except for the artwork displayed throughout the house. There were two artists in particular whose work he liked enough to purchase. One was Vicky Montesinos and the other Colleen Ross.

Both artists painted in bright hues; Ross painted voluptuous women of a past era, romantic and mysterious. Montesinos painted voluptuous flowers, large and equally mysterious, there being a resonant chord of voluptuous in their interpretations that was hard to miss.

Only two of his own works were on his walls. One was of a little boy who was sitting by a stream with his arm looped around the neck of his black lab. Max had painted it by memory; it was a recollection of the last family outing with his little brother who died of leukemia when Max was ten. The other painting was the one he painted after meeting Aura. It hung over his fireplace.

~~~

The first time Laura saw the painting was from the vantage point of Max's arms when he carried her across the threshold. For Max, it all made sense now—to have a real home to share with a wife, and he hoped, a family.

Laura's breath caught in her throat when she saw it. While not a frontal view of her, Laura immediately recognized who it was—the statuesque back of a woman, pensive and lost in the moment with a bag of French fries folded opened next to her. To think that while she was daydreaming he had been standing behind her already invested.

She put both of her arms around his neck and hugged him, her tears baptizing the moment. Her wicked, miserable past was no more; the painting memorialized the day she'd given herself permission to dare to live. And, as for Max, he could not have imagined her reception to his labor for love being more meaningful. That was her gift to him.

Both of their destinies had been divinely crossed, and neither of them doubted it for a moment. For Laura, entering the house was like walking into the pages of a decorating magazine. The open floor plan sprawled, with large open rooms and walls of windows across the back of the house to capture the view of the woods and mountains in the distance. Max would always remember her expressions the first time she wandered through the house, trailing her fingertips over the surfaces and trying to take it all in; that this would be where she would live and be protected.

"It's as much your house as mine, Laura." He told her. "I think it might be a bit masculine. If you don't like it, we can change whatever you don't like." But, she loved everything about the house. While it would be fun to add her touches to it, at that moment she couldn't imagine what they might be; two months earlier she'd thought her life was at a dead end. She hoped she would never have to move again.

~~~

The kitchen was large and contained all of the bells and whistles a real cook would insist upon, one of which was a six burner gas range named after a wolf. Laura renamed it Apollon, telling Max that the burners reminded her of fiery chariot wheels.

That the stove intimidated her was noteworthy, because her only previous experience with cooking was programming a Microwave. Most mornings, after Max left for work, she would sit with her coffee on the granite counter opposite the stove, staring it down.

Their Sub-Zero side-by-side refrigerator and freezer took up what would have been a whole wall in the kitchen in her apartment; beside it were double-ovens. *What will I ever do with two ovens,* she wondered? Even the microwave was intimidating; she anticipated having to read the manual to boil water.

Max assured her that he would do the cooking, but she was determined to learn to cook for him. She had no excuses not to—she had plenty of time and a dream kitchen; the only problem was that she had never successfully boiled an egg.

~~~

Laura discovered that Dana Tracey was warm, funny, and gregarious; and she liked her instantly. After giving Laura a tour of her ultra-modern home, they spent the rest of the morning outside on Dana's patio eating processed cheese curls out of the bag and drinking hazelnut coffee. Dana had few pretenses, and it was evident that she was confident enough not to care what anyone else thought, and she liked to talk. Since Laura was anything but confident, she was an excellent listener, plus she didn't think that she had much to offer in a conversation. Like Max, Dana was instantly mesmerized by Laura. There was something childlike and sweet about her that made Dana feel protective of her.

Laura was thrilled to have a friend. She was sure that Dana could be trusted, sensing a depth of spirit in her that was rare and a gift to be embraced.

CHAPTER 22

Were Nelson found to be involved in the country's implosion at a top level, now, that would be something. Lenette wondered if she could somehow manage to convince him of the consequences to his immediate family were that true. Nelson worked for one of the largest banking and security firms in the world; that put him in the epicenter of the financial end of the conspiracy.

Right under our noses, she thought. *It has been happening right under our noses for decades.*

She sat at Jeremy's desk for most of the night staring at the faxes and praying for Lindsay. Her sister's call could only have occurred if Lindsay found herself so far out of her comfort zone that she was forced to react and Lenette feared she might never find her way back. Lindsay's had deliberately insulated herself from extraneous conflict; she had enough on her plate coping with her marriage.

Are you afraid of him? Lenette wondered, trying to imagine what it must be like to live with Nelson. She knew her twin well enough to know that Lindsay was also experiencing a sleepless night. *Oh, I hope you covered your tracks, girl!* It was unnerving to think that Lindsay might have, inadvertently, put them both in Nelson's sites.

Lindsay's love was the kind that covered a multitude of sins, which, by definition, also qualified her as an enabler. Nelson was brooding and sullen—remote. He had little to do with his children and what the family had once described as stoic now seemed sneaky and secretive—his drinking was no secret. Everyone made adjustments for Nelson, but Nelson didn't have to.

Lindsay's passivity had always perplexed Lenette; she would never have put up with the emotional neglect Lindsay did. It wasn't Nelson's money that kept Lindsay in the marriage, nor was it because she feared losing the children—Nelson wouldn't know what to do with them if he got them. Two years earlier, when Lindsay asked Jeremy and Lenette to be their children's guardians were something were to happen to her, Nelson signed off without a fight.

Only once did Lenette broach the subject of a separation from him with Lindsay, who was horrified, and told Lenette how offensive her suggestion was. "Lenette, I'm in this for better or for worse. I took a vow, for Pete's sake! I will not argue with anyone who may have observed that my marriage is different, but I am not unhappy. There is a purpose for us being together, and whatever it is, I am not going to miss it."

Lindsay doesn't want to miss what His purpose is, Lenette had mused afterward. *God help me to have one tenth of Lindsay's faith.*

And, that prayer was answered. Lindsay's faith became a standard that caused Lenette to seek to redefine her own. She realized how in all of her own going and doing she had left out the Helper who knew the end from the beginning. Whatever the end was, it would not come as a surprise to him.

Okay, she thought, *Tomorrow morning I have an appointment; with God, and, then I'll call my sister.*

CHAPTER 22

It was impossible for Rod to ignore the threats that were an occupational hazard of his chosen profession. The virulent hostility contained in some of them obliterated any remaining doubt how his career had put his family on a dangerous path. Moving his family somewhere secure was no longer optional. Friends of the Larson's had been warning Rod that it was time to protect his family's safety. Reluctantly, Jenna agreed with them. As much as they didn't want to admit it, it was time.

Based on very specific security requirements, few properties were available that met their criteria. But, when their realtor drove them up the drive through the sprawling grounds and they saw the intriguing house, better than meeting their needs, it satisfied what it was they wanted for their family; even though its location would require Rod spending a few days a week in the city each week preparing for his show.

The primary house looked like an oversized bungalow, with gables and leaded glass windows and covered porches on three sides of the house. It wasn't old, but was designed to look it. Jenna was sure it was patterned after Teddy Roosevelt's home at Oyster Bay.

The compound was spread out over thirty acres of mostly forested land. The entire property had been fenced by the previous celebrity owner who became concerned over his own family's security after a stalker was caught following their teenage daughter. There were four cabin-sized houses on either side of the driveway shouting distance from the big house, but not visible to it. The original owner's built them, preferring their staff live within the compound.

Before Rod would move his family into the house, he contracted for a second fence to be installed several hundred yards inside the first one. Between the first and second fences was installed some decidedly elaborate, customized security; not land mines exactly, but that was the idea. They were customized traps that were placed randomly and would trip if walked over, sounding an alarm. They weren't explosive, but the consequence of tripping one would be adrenalin producing at the very least. The security team said the goal was *cardiac 'arrest'*...the pun was intended.

Although Rod initially resisted, he took the recommendation that individual companies be used for each separate component of required surveillance, with each consecutive layer unaware of what the other layer did.

When their neighbors found out who had bought the property, they petitioned the city in an attempt to get the city council to prevent the Larson's from moving in. Needless to say, the security buffers wouldn't be necessary to keep their neighbors away.

Rod knew he wasn't being paranoid—he was just grimly realistic. The deeper he dug into the cistern of betrayal once called "The Government for and by the people" it heightened his awareness of the high price he and Jenna would inevitably be called upon to pay; and he did believe it was inevitable. While he hated it for his family; thankfully Jenna felt as strongly as he did about what he was doing. The founding fathers were called to forsake all and did so; freedom had never come cheap.

The media had some sport when it was disclosed that the Larson's intended to homeschool their kids, but that was a foregone conclusion for Rod and Jenna. Going forward, they would be who influenced the minds of their children; not the NEA. So, for the time being, their children were safe and insulated.

~~~

In a convoluted way, Rod had his mother to thank for meeting Jenna. She had been married once before; the Larson's oldest daughter was Jenna's child from her first marriage. Whenever she was asked to share her story, she closed with a phrase that summed up what she learned firsthand. "Without guidance and accountability we are doomed to follow the path of folly to its bitter end."

For her, the 'bitter end' part was literal. One afternoon, shortly after the birth of her little girl, Jenna took the baby to the thrift store to buy her some baby clothes, leaving her husband home alone working in the garage—something he did a lot—he was cooking meth. There was an explosion, and everything they owned, including him, were obliterated with the exception of the car Jenna was driving.

When she drove up to their rental house later, not only was everything she owned, or loved, gone, but additionally, and without allowing her a moment to process what had happened, she was arrested and forced to watch while her baby girl was driven away by two women from the social services.

With her one phone call, Jenna called her family for help. Her father's reaction, with some very audible coaching from her mother, was to inform her how she'd burned her bridges with them by getting herself knocked-up and dragging the family name through the mud. He said they wanted nothing to do with her. Jenna learned much later, during counseling, how many of her poor choices were prompted because of her subconscious desire to distance from her contentious family.

Jenna's appointed counsel explained the extenuating nature of Jenna's poor choices to the court, offering a plea for the judge to "Please give the girl a break." The judge's advice to Jenna was to "go home, grow up, and don't get married again until you have your head on straight." Good advice—if you had a home.

When Jenna signed herself out of jail, she was handed a sack containing her personal belongings and informed that she would have to provide the court with proof of employment and a living address before she could get her baby back. She almost fainted; she had nowhere to go, and no one to turn to.

Her attorney knew of a woman who would help her who was a former prostitute who had 'come to Jesus' and ran a safe home for women who were brought to her from off the streets; women who were trying to escape that lifestyle and wanting help finding new way to live. Clara Brown was a large black woman who strong as a wrestler, and had a heart of pure gold. She offered the terrified women professional counseling, Bible study, job training, and room and board if they agreed to abide by her rules—in writing. Otherwise, they would be asked to leave. "One lousy attitude is like mold in an apple" she told them, "so if I taste any mold I'm gonna spit you right out." No one doubted it for a minute. It was humbling, but Jenna submitted—in writing; it was her only option.

While there, it was mandatory for Jenna to attend counseling sessions; her counselor was Leslie Phillips, who was one of the certified counselors who volunteered at the shelter. After a few weeks of observing Jenna, she took her aside after noticing she was clear headed and had taken responsibility for her choices. Leslie recognized her potential and offered to spend some private time with her, also noting that she truly was a victim of several layers of misguided people who had influenced her.

Three months after Jenna arrived at The House Leslie asked her if she would like to work for her as her receptionist. With Leslie's help of a loan for the security deposit, Jenna rented a small apartment of her own and started her first real job. And, she got her baby back.

~~~

It was her fourteenth day on the job when Jenna met Rod Larson who had breezed in for his monthly maintenance session with her boss. Jenna was a new face to him, so while waiting for Leslie he flirted shamelessly, compulsively telling her the short version of his story and why he was there. His self-deprecating humor took her by surprise; Jenna laughed so hard at his colorful descriptions that Leslie was forced to step out of a session to ask if they would hold it down.

Rod's anger issues stemmed from resentment he'd developed for his mother's cause-driven involvements, down to and including her removing him and his sisters from public school and subsequently home schooling them. Of course, at the time Rod was a less than stellar student, claimed his teachers sucked, and blamed his lack of studying on too many distractions in study hall—he wasn't exactly motivated by the system. One casualty resulting from the switch was that he lost his audience since class clown was his best subject. He had never thought of his mother as creative, but she pulled out the stops when issuing ultimatums to reduce his clowning in class, which became another feather in his hat of resentment.

His mother, along with several other moms who also home schooled, formed a co-op. Each mother took a day each week to teach, or took over a subject they were equipped to teach, or did both. It took the first year to get the bumps smoothed out, but it worked. The kids had interaction with other kids and the moms didn't feel as overwhelmed with the process, which was the main reason for burn-out with homeschooling.

Rod's grades improved significantly, despite volumes of vocalized dissention aimed at making sure his mother knew she'd ruined his life and had "messed with his brain"; Rod had a futuristic approach about not accepting responsibility. Looking back, he realized that the person he was now and the values he stood for was a debt he owed her, but the process of getting to that realization had taken some time with a patient counselor to figure out.

Once Leslie helped him get to the core of his need to assess blame rather than take responsibility for his actions he saw how that pattern of behavior had affected him. Once he recognized the pattern he was determined to break out of it and do something productive with the rest of his life. Up until then he had a pathetic history of job turnover, which, of course, he blamed on his employers. Thanks to Leslie, his mother finally got the apology she deserved. Years later he saw how her selfless tenacity had been driven by her concern for him and his sisters.

He stuck with his maintenance program, partly because Leslie strongly urged him to and partly because his therapy was like taking a college course in psychology. He asked if she would compile a list of various writings by people in her field, books, lectures on DVD, and practical lessons from the scriptures to help him understand the war that was constantly being waged between the soul and the spirit, and took place in the brain.

Leslie didn't push the spiritual part because she knew that some of her clients wouldn't stay in the program because of it, believing her calling was to sow subtle seeds in her patients that would take root later. But, Rod recognized that living up to his spiritual potential would enhance everything else; the side benefit would be to understand the psychologies that motivated others—for good or bad.

For months, Jenna held on to her original impression that Rod wasn't her type. The most unsettling thing for her was Rod's alarmingly openness about his issues, since she guarded hers carefully. But after dating him for a few months, observing his perseverance to work through the things in his own life that needed fixing, and watching him fall in love with her little girl, she knew she'd found a keeper.

After a year of celibate dating, followed by several months of couple-counseling, they were married by a Justice of the Peace in Leslie's office on a Friday afternoon. Rod's family joined them, and Jenna's refused to come.

~~~

While they purposely left their past behind them a media hungry for any tawdry tidbit they could find to discredit Rod was able to dig up enough about their former lives to distort and fabricate endless sordid articles about them, with additional titillating details embellished in the tabloids.

The press was merciless with Jenna in particular, finding it easy to build on the very accessible public record of her life before Rod. But, the Larson's were rock solid in what they believed and confident in God's ability to lead them through whatever came. Jenna longed for normalcy, but one night at dinner Leslie, who remained a close friend, reminded her how normal, for everyone, was relative to their current circumstances; for some reason, that helped.

So, from his ignoble beginning, Rod Larson spiraled his way to the top and with his success came all of the trappings—fame, money, tall fences, a mine-field around his home, live-in armed security, constant surveillance, and hate mail...every aspect of their life was continually under a microscope from two extremely opposite sides.

Therefore, even if it appeared paranoid, everyone, including their maintenance people, was rotated on a timely basis. The swimming pool was maintained by the security people who lived on-site, as was the barn and surrounding acreage. No matter how much the Larsen's liked them; plumbers, gardeners, electricians, cleaning people; all were rotated on a timely basis. Jenna finally put her foot down on changing housekeepers, after having to retrain new ones every other month.

The subject of needing a nanny came up when Rod wanted Jenna to accompany him on one of his trips. A young woman named Tilly was soon added to the household to help with the children. She was a member of their church, and they knew she could be trusted with what was most precious to them. She moved into their home and was treated like family.

If someone else hadn't already coined the phrase *It Takes a Village*, they would have.

CHAPTER 23

Jeremy had been coasting on the reprieve the delayed memorial service offered to justify his staying home from work. The time helped him sort through his game plan while avoiding the overly-solicitous attention he knew would be coming. What hadn't immediately occurred to him was how he would need a full-time housekeeper once he returned to work.

He toyed briefly with putting the house on the market, but after talking to his attorney, he concluded it was impractical on several levels. First, who would buy it with its recent history? Secondly, with the economy the way it was it was upside-down in value. Thirdly, even were someone interested, they probably couldn't get a jumbo loan. Fourthly, it would take too much of his time. Fifthly, a friend who worked in real estate told him that people were generally superstitious about buying a house that someone died in. Sixth, he needed to regain some continuity in his life and for his young son and moving would be a significant adjustment. Each reason, by itself, was compelling; six was convincing.

He would have to deal with mental reruns, and hope that, in time, it would get better. And, each successive day proved he had resilience he wasn't aware of until a few short weeks ago. As much as he hated to give up his privacy totally, there was only one possible solution, and that was to convince his mother-in-law, Rebecca Kennedy, to move into the house him and Caleb.

While Rebecca personality was pleasant enough, Jeremy would, if pressed, have to admit how at one time he had thought of her as dowdy. The twins didn't resemble her, but that could partly be blamed on her looking like someone who got caught in a time warp from the fifties; her hair, clothes, and even the colloquialisms she used when speaking all dated her; plus an extra thirty or forty pounds.

In short, when he thought about it, living with Rebecca would be like moving a plump version of the Betty White character from *The Golden Girls* into the house. Rebecca exhibited a mental airiness that would have made her a great flower child, along with a simple way of viewing things. She exhibited little curiosity about things outside her immediate world—

and in that way Lindsay did resemble her. When she spoke about current events, she displayed a superficial understanding of what was going on in the culture, but would state it in a way that was endearing because the listener could tell that being deep was relative.

Putting all that aside, she was a terrific grandma. When Lindsay and Nelson had their first child, Lindsay said her mother was the ideal babysitter because she could become childlike in a split second. The arrangement wouldn't be terrific for dinner conversation, but Jeremy knew this wasn't about him.

~~~

Jeremy was pouring himself a cup of coffee when the doorbell rang. It was still early— about 7:30 a.m. Glass doors were a complication of living in a contemporary house because there was no way to see who was outside without being seen by them. Two detectives were standing on the front porch; Jeremy recognized them both from the other day. He took a deep breath before opening the door.

Immediately, one of them asked, "Mr. Dobson, could we ask a favor?"

"Ah, sure; I suppose." Jeremy felt weird and couldn't breathe out.

"We owe you an apology...uh, for the inconvenience."

"Well, okay. You guys work early..." Is that all? Jeremy thought, feeling better.

"Well..." *Deep subject*..."Well...we, ah, need to impound your wife's car. Do you mind if we take a look at it?"

"Why?" Jeremy said, feeling weird again.

"Well, uh, we didn't search it—yours either. We've been going over the evidence and remembered we don't have either a computer or a cell phone. She must've had them. Right...?"

"Yes, she had both." The feeling graduated from weird to debilitating.

"Well, that's why we're here. ...mind if we look at it?"

The apprehension of that day was returning..."No, go right ahead; why don't you follow me and come through the house?"

"You haven't moved the car then?"

"...haven't even thought about it..."

"...or take anything out of it?"

"No. I haven't touched it." *Well, I haven't!* Jeremy was rationalizing now.

"Great. Come on." He motioned to his sidekick.

Jeremy held the door open for them, walking ahead of them to the back hall, remembering to grab the keys off a hook for them. After they were in the garage he stood on the other side of the door with his knees buckling, and his stomach sending signals that he was going to be sick, hoping he wouldn't feel like hurling whenever he got nervous for the rest of his life.

But, he knew his reaction wasn't nerves. *What if they figure out I have her briefcase? Maybe this is a setup.* He looked around the kitchen realizing how careless he'd become with leaving things lying out in the open.

Inside the bathroom, he splashed cold water on his face. Maybe it was only the lighting; could his face actually look that red? His urge to vomit passed.

There was a knock on the garage door. The detective who did all the talking looked was as pale as Jeremy was red. "...you want to sit down?" The officer asked Jeremy, motioning with his thumb towards the kitchen.

"Do I need to?" Jeremy asked him.

"Yeah, you need to."

"Okay." Jeremy reluctantly agreed. *Oh boy.* He was tasting stomach acid. The detective added, "I need to sit down, too. Do you mind?"

Jeremy welcomed the opportunity to sit down. His legs felt like soggy noodles. He motioned toward the bar stools where they all three sat down. After a long pause, the officer said, "Sir, there's good news and there's bad."

"Okay?" Jeremy felt his heart rate continue to race.

The detective stared at Jeremy, swallowed hard, and said "The good news is that no one moved the car." He waited a moment for that to sink in. "—the bad news is if one of us had we'd all be dead. I hate to be the one to tell you, but the car was rigged to blow up."

"What?" Jeremy gasped.

"Son, it appears somebody wanted your wife dead really bad. If we'd started the car without checking it, we'd be dead—you, me, all of us. I can't say for sure, maybe the car was fooled with after she died, to get you, but we're thinking it was done before. That might explain the car your neighbor said he saw parked on your street that day.

"Our theory is" he gestured with his thumb to his buddy, "that when the babysitter didn't show up for work it messed up their plan."

"How's that?" Jeremy asked.

"It messed it up because your wife stayed home; shooting her might not have been their first choice. My guess is they wanted to make sure the sitter didn't show up, and mess it up again by finding her, so they killed her, too." He paused to give Jeremy a moment to process.

That seemed plausible to Jeremy. So someone had been in the house, or at least in the garage. And to whoever was behind it, their baby would have simply been collateral damage—and Melissa; either way she would have died. If the house and everything in it blew up, a teeny tiny microchip would have been literally "the straw in the haystack" since no one else would be looking for it.

It was too much information—he couldn't process it. He stood to his feet, lurching for the bathroom but not making it in time. In mid-lurch, she remembered he was wearing his new tan kakis'.

In a moment's time, he saw himself in a line-up, looking across the sterile gray room into a fake mirror. On the other side of the mirror, a detective was asking people he couldn't see if they recognized anyone in the line-up.

"Yes, I'd know him anywhere." One said. He's the one with the coffee stains on his pants."

"Good enough!" The detective turns to a waiting officer, "Cuff him, and take him downstairs."

Jeremy wondered if he'd be puking in his mug shot. But, the grim news aside, his having her computer was once again a moot point.

CHAPTER 24

Eleanor was hidden from view, obscured behind a curtain where she could hear the golden voice from out front singing, "*then face to face...in all of His glory*"...

Tonight the message within the song accosted her—*soon; very soon; it could be soon. Who could be ready, really? How could anyone truly be prepared to face Almighty God? The world thumbs their noses at the message—scoffing*, she thought

They will be eating, drinking, and giving in marriage...as in the days of Noah...so will it be...at his coming. The world would continue with the business of living; only it was living outside of covenant, outside of grace...

No man could know the day or the hour, but a promise was given to the faithful, to those who knew him in his word, and the promise was that they would know the season, not the hour...

There was little room left for doubt that the signs were there; laid out like the bold print in a headline. But, out of the nearly eighty percent of Americans who claimed to be Christians, she was grimly aware that most were not only unprepared for his return, but many were oblivious to his coming back at all.

~~~

One by one, her relatives had made it their mission to be sure Eleanor was aware of their corporate opinion that they did not share her views. None of them, other than Candy and her family had ever attended one of her meetings or heard her speak. If they'd read her books, they'd been successful at resisting the impulse to let her know it.

Not being able to reach her family was heartbreaking, but she refused to lose faith. She found consolation in how even Christ could identify with her deep grief for them. Isaiah the prophet labeled the promised Messiah as "rejected of men". Out of everything Christ's death represented it was comforting to Eleanor that the pain that accompanied rejection was so crucial to the Father that the scriptures mentioned it specifically two thousand years before Christ died.

The warnings in the third chapter of Revelation had dire implications for the modern day church— the last of the seven warnings to the churches, how a believer would be better off to be hot or cold than be lukewarm; those were the people she targeted her message to reach.

One prophetic red flag, for those who believed as she did, was watching the pressure being put on Israel to give up her land, divide the Holy City, and forced to enter into treaties that would compromise her more. It astounded her how biblically astute people could ignore the history of that covenant land—that it belonged to Israel? The scriptures were clear that the Jew was, is, and would always be "The Apple of God's eye". By divine providence, the land was theirs; deeded to them by God from the time of Abraham. The Romans renamed Israel and Judea, calling it Palestine in 135 B.C. That fact had seemingly slipped thought one of history's cracks. But, the answer wasn't that difficult; it wasn't taught— even in seminaries. It took two generations for facts to become fiction.

Whenever his contested return took place wasn't the point; her message was a warning for the church to prepare and nothing more. And, further confirmation was that it dovetailed with what Rod Larson was warning, with the difference that Rod was invoking a call to arms; only his weapon was to educate his audience by getting them mentally fit with an arsenal of facts, and stirring their faith to stand up for their principles. It would be impossible to win the fight without having an understanding of the enemy. That was why, by all appearances, the wrong side was winning. They'd done the homework, while the sleeping giant hadn't and figured out that a giant could be bound and gagged, even killed, while asleep in his bed; or on his couch.

Eleanor liked Rod. He understood this was not a battle waged in the flesh. What the nation was fighting was insidious; like an infection festering out of sight, its contamination spreading through the organism of democracy—perhaps fatally, and it was taking place incrementally. Rod only confirmed what she already knew—it was like a wound that was septic. By virtue of how toxic the infection was, by necessity, the cure would be drastic.

The prophet, Hosea, prophesied, "*My people perish for lack of knowledge.*" For sixty years, Hosea tried to wake up God's people; to get them to heed his warnings. Prophets were raised up for a season, and Eleanor wondered if Rod Larson might just be who God had chosen to usher this one in. Deep down, Eleanor was convinced that the generation who would be last was the one she was calling to arms.

Lost in thought, Eleanor was startled by a tap on the shoulder. A security guard gestured toward the stage, letting her know the audience was waiting for her. She jumped to her feet and shook herself alert wondering how long she'd been daydreaming. How ironic for her not to be ready. She smoothed her skirt. Ready, set—she stepped out walking briskly toward the podium.

Silence—the audience was at rapt attention. Stepping into the spotlight she turned toward them repeating the phrase she'd used to open every meeting since God sent her on this mission.

She could feel it in her bones. In a strong voice she declared, "The time is short"...

CHAPTER 25

Laura had ants; tiny uninvited guests that were invading her kitchen. She swatted them, rinsed them down the disposal, sprayed them, put out bait, tried different bait, sucked them into the vacuum, and stored everything she suspected of being sweet in sealed Rubbermaid bins—and still, when she turned on the coffee the next morning there they were again—the seemingly endless succession of dark invaders—mocking her.

"I curse you, little army." she threatened, faking a German accent. "I vill vin."

Max concluded that he would be sorry when Laura's battle with the ants ended. The sight of his pajama-clad wife furiously intent on their annihilation was a sight to behold.

Finally, Laura gave up. No matter what she'd try the next day they reappeared so, as she put it, "I'm callin' in the big guns."

At the exterminator's instruction, she and Max emptied out the pantry, the cabinets, and anywhere else they had seen the little vermin, so the bug man could spray and put down bait of his own. He solved their ant problem—he used different bait than Laura did. He explained how what he used tasted sweet, but was in reality, poison. It attracted the ants, so they would tell their ant friends, inviting them to partake of the sweet feast, and in turn share it with the queen. When the queen died the remaining ants would leave in search of a new queen. Their purpose was to serve.

~~~

Max wanted to invite their neighbors over for dinner.

"Why can't we just go out?" Laura asked. *He knows I can't cook!* She thought, frustrated.

"Because, they've had us over twice, and we offered to have them over the next time. It doesn't have to be fancy."

"Max, you know I can't cook!' She was almost crying.

Max caved, "Ok, this time we'll go out, but next time we're having them over! Wasn't it nice to eat at their house with no crowds or noise?"

She nodded her head sheepishly; he'd made his point. The last time they went out to dinner it was Laura who complained about the restaurant chatter and how she hated yelling over it to be heard.

The next afternoon Max surprised her with a new laptop computer after it dawned on him that she didn't have one. She feigned delight because she didn't want to admit she'd never used one; it was humbling enough to have been caught reading the microwave manual before using it.

Once Max had left for work, she darted across the yard to Dana's with her new computer under her arm. "Dana, do you know how to work one of these things?" she asked. After asking the question for the third time, Dana realized her friend honestly didn't know what to do with it. They spent the morning setting it up; giving her computer a name (Aura), and a password (anthill). She was officially auraZ@aol.com.

Is that cool, or what? Laura thought excitedly.

Proudly, she carried her laptop home and placed it on her planning desk with the lid raised so she could tell when an email came in. She wondered how long it would take for her to get one. While she was waiting for the World-Wide-Web to locate her, she grabbed her remote to see what was on TV. She sailed past something that looked intriguing, so she sailed back.

A provocatively dressed woman was preparing a pasta salad. *Hmmmmmm...*Laura thought. *It doesn't look that hard.* She grabbed a notebook and a pen to take some notes. She was sure it was something she could do. When the show ended the perky show host, with knife skills that equaled her impressive cleavage, said, "...and you will find this recipe and more from The Foodie Channel at www.thefoodiechannel.com."

Wow! she thought, sitting down in front of her computer, as the new power it gave her began to dawn on her. She typed the address into the line at the top where it said http://. She waited for it to load—nothing. She waited some more—still nothing.

She called Dana.

"You did what? Oh, Laura, just push 'enter'."

Laura was pretty sure she could hear Dana laughing when she hung up.

Laura pushed enter.

The cooking page sprang to life before her eyes. She recognized the woman from the TV show leaning over a different plated pasta dish than on the show and smiling at the camera; this time Laura noticed her gleaming white teeth. She decided the chef was a role model on more than one level. Next to the picture was a button that read, "Click here for today's recipe". She cautiously moved the little arrow, clicked, and voila!— there it was in living color—her recipe! And, not only the recipe but a series of pictures that showed the evolving stages of preparation complete with a grocery list.

The recipe called for a rotisserie chicken from the grocery store, so she only had to use Abaddon to cook the pasta. After two tries, she got that part down after letting the cooked pasta sit in the hot water too long not realizing it would dissolve. The second time she was ready.

According to the recipe the prep time took twenty-five minutes. It took Laura four hours, but she was including going to the store and cooking the pasta twice. So what! Max wouldn't believe it. She could cook!

She changed into fresh clothes, remembering that sex appeal was a key ingredient to the meal's success, stepping outside to watch for Max. When she saw his car, she ran inside.

"Do you notice anything different?" she asked when he walked in.

How do I get around that? He wondered; then he noticed that her computer was open.

"You're using your computer!" He said, trying to calculate his odds of being right.

That was all she needed! She took the mail from him, escorting him to the nicely set table. "Dinner will be served shortly, sir." she said, draping his napkin over his lap. He had no idea what had gone into that evening's meal, although he could guess. She sat across from him at dinner watching while he ate; when he asked for seconds she knew she'd found her passion—Laura Zimmerman could cook!

~~~

They ate their dinner early because Laura couldn't wait. After dinner, Max turned the TV on to watch the news. Typically, they didn't watch television that time of day; but Laura had been following the murder of the young mother, who was killed in her home, and her memorial service had taken place that morning. It was the lead story on the news.

A female reporter was interviewing Lenette Dobson's pastor. What moved Laura was how he appeared to know the woman who died, and genuinely cared about her.

Laura's only experience with death was when her grandmother died, and she rarely allowed herself to think about it. Before meeting Max, had she died there was no one who would have missed her. She'd had nightmares about what would happen to her body if she died. One of her clients was a nurse, who told her that unclaimed bodies were often donated for science. That added another layer to her paranoia. In her mind, had she died before meeting Max, it would have been as if she didn't exist.

~~~

Laura was adopted by a couple who couldn't conceive, had money, and could afford to pay for the care and keeping of a young pregnant girl who would be willing, for the price of her care and keeping, to them her baby. That part went smoothly. Laura's birth mother collected her money and was never heard from again.

What hadn't gone smoothly was her adoptive parent's marriage. They divorced when she was three, and in the process they also divorced her. For whatever reason, neither parent sufficiently bonded with her, and neither wanted custody of her after the divorce was final. It was her maternal grandmother who offered to take her. Once the divorce was final, her father ceased to visit altogether, and visits from her mother were at first infrequent and tapered off to rare.

Years later, after she'd gone through some counseling Laura saw that while her Grandmother loved her fiercely she had developed some deep rejection issues. Rejection issues weren't uncommon for an adopted child, even those placed in a good home. Laura felt rejected on several levels that had harmed her immeasurably.

Grandma Laura was a Christian and Laura grew up hearing Bible stories and going to with her to church. But, by the time she was in high school Laura rejected her grandmother's beliefs feeling disassociated from a God who she felt hadn't bonded with her either.

While attending a junior college, many of her new friends were exploring the New Age Movement. That belief system was a perfect fit for Laura who immediately went to work locating her inner child. Her embracing that philosophy over Christianity broke her grandmother's heart, which was an unintended consequence, but she knew her grandmother prayed for her and that thought comforted Laura on some level. She did believe in prayer—in her own way.

After her grandmother was diagnosed with cancer, and subsequently died, Laura's adopted mother swept in like the Wicked Witch of the West, claiming her mother's meager inheritance for herself. Grandma Laura did not have a will, having naively assumed Laura would automatically become her beneficiary.

Laura refused to fight over her grandmother's things. In a week's time, her mother arranged for her grandmother's cremation, had an estate sale, and listed her house with a realtor. It was a whirlwind and had the same effect on Laura emotionally that the aftermath of a tornado would have had physically; her life was decimated. There was no memorial service for her grandmother, and Laura's mother never mentioned what happened to her ashes.

Her mother vanished into thin air as quickly as she swept in. Once she was gone, Laura realized she didn't even have her phone number; she couldn't imagine feeling more empty.

Laura ended up moving to California, having hitched a ride with a friend who was leaving for Berkeley. After exploring the area, Petaluma felt right to her; it was further outside of San Francisco where the rents were cheaper, and the setting was more rural, and the laid-back atmosphere appealed to her. She worked at a coffee shop on 2nd Street, where she found meeting people easy. She began doing psychic readings on the side.

Much to her surprise, she soon found that she could live on what she made doing the readings. Most of her customers paid her in cash so, in her mind, it was hers to keep; reporting it or paying taxes were neither a moral or ethical issue for her.

That part of her life had seemed simple; empty, but simple. But, she had enough psychic success to choose a stage name and dream of a happy ending.

~~~

The coverage of Lenette Dobson's memorial service ended with a teaser for the Rod Larson show that seized Max's attention. "Economies collapsing—unprecedented growing debt—Rumors of war and threats of terror—Environmental disasters. We have answers to your questions and questions for your answers, all on today's show..."

Neither Max nor Laura watched the program, partly because the opening commentary sounded negative to them, although had Max heard some of his coworkers talking about watching it, saying they never missed it. So, Max did have some idea who Rod Larson was. He had a legitimate excuse for being out of touch with world events—his recent preoccupation with his new bride needed no explanation. But, reality had intruded. The last election put dynamics in play that were hard to ignore; the teaser brought him back to reality and brought the reality into his home.

Rod opened the show conversationally, explaining that tonight's program was not live, but was previously prerecorded. He urged his audience to record the program, reminding them that it had the potential to change people's lives—if they'd let it.

He chose a quote by George Orwell to set the stage for what was coming, "During times of universal deceit, telling the truth becomes a revolutionary act."

~~~

Max listened; fixated and fascinated. For every event on the planet, cultural or natural, that Rod Larson brought up Eleanor Crosby tossed a

Biblical parallel back at him. Back and forth they went, covering natural phenomena—in the sky and below the sky—disease, wars, earthquakes, man-made environmental disasters, discrimination, wars and rumors of wars, terrorism, and the progressive agenda that was moving mankind towards the prophesied New World Order.

Laura, who usually flipped through food magazines while Max watched the news, was listening intently. She was clearly upset.

"Are you okay?" Max asked.

"My Grandma believed that." She told him.

"Believed what?"

"She believed in a world government that will one day control everything and everyone. She said the Bible predicted it."

"What do you believe?" Max asked her.

"I don't know, but she believed that I would be alive to see it happen."

For the first time, they didn't know what to say to one another.

The next morning Laura went shopping and bought them each a Bible.

CHAPTER 26

Bob Murphy never took on clients who might tarnish his carefully polished reputation. He prided himself on his impeccable instincts, and he was superstitious about them. If his gut told him not to engage, he didn't; no matter how much money was involved.

If he was ever mistaken, nobody knew but him.

He briefly worked for the CIA, in the International Division, best described by their own website as "The Ultimate International Career – The CIA's Clandestine Service is the front-line source of clandestine information on critical international developments, from terrorism and weapons of mass destruction to military and political issues. The mission requires clandestine service officers to live and work overseas, making a true commitment to the Agency. It is more than just a job – it's a way of life that challenges the deepest resources of personal intelligence, self-reliance and responsibility. National Clandestine Service Officers are individuals with varied backgrounds and life experiences, professional and educational histories, language capabilities, and other elements that allow us to meet our mission's critical objectives."

He passed all their criteria; intellectual, polygraph, blood work, urine analysis, background checks, psychological evaluations, memory analysis, and physicals—actually, he sailed through them. He was a quick study and quickly learned new languages. He was told by one of his superiors "Many are called, but few are chosen." He was issued security clearance and with it the title of Operations Officer.

As an operation's officer, he served on the front lines of the human intelligence collection business. He recruited for them and handled different sources of foreign intelligence. He had the skills and disciplines to determine the relationships that resulted in high-value intelligence from clandestine sources, plus the aptitude and instinct for both work and the stress that accompanied it. But, after his first lengthy overseas assignment and after meeting his wife on a trip home to the States, he knew it wasn't the career of a lifetime. He also realized he wasn't cut out to take orders.

His resignation was accepted without comment, but Bob accepted if he were in anybody's radar, it was theirs. It was a business of secrets, and he knew some. He hadn't thought of that particular side effect when he took the job, and it only crossed his mind briefly when he left.

~~~

Bob was the consummate networker. He kept meticulous lists of the people he had met and worked with while in the CIA—not the covert part, but a network of people who crossed his path in the process. That was the base he used to build his business.

He lived in D.C. for a year, but soon realized that having his office in Washington, D.C. was too conspicuous a return address no matter how subtle his business model. He and his wife spent several months visiting different cities across the country before choosing to office his firm in Portland, Oregon.

He liked the idea of its remoteness, although it was a booming growth area. The climate was temperate, and since he was a boater having both the Willamette and Colombia rivers converging there with access to the Pacific made the package sweeter.

His wife was in love with the area after their first visit. The city was sophisticated and upscale, with gorgeous views and lots to do. She grew test roses, so when their realtor informed her Portland was considered the Rose Capital of the United States Bob knew it was a win-win for them both. They found a house with a mountain view in Beaverton, and he began looking for an office. In a matter of months, he had more work than he could handle alone.

CHAPTER 27

After securing his lot, Jeremy began interviewing architects who specialized in contemporary design, with some out of the box thinking. Lenette was adamant about two specific details—their home would have a secret storage room and a suite of rooms for her mother.

A thoughtfully designed suite was built for Rebecca, behind the garage; designed for her to have privacy and still be part of the family. The apartment had its own entrance to the pool and back yard, with a fenced area where Rebecca could garden.

Her wing had a living and dining area, and a small, but fully equipped kitchen that overlooked the pool. French pocket doors opened from the main room into a bedroom with a sitting area, and a bath. It was larger, and nicer, than where she was living, but nothing they said could convince her to move in with them. So, even after much cajoling by Lenette, Rebecca refused to move into it. Her initial response after seeing the space was "How nice of you to think of me, but I'm perfectly happy where I am."

Looking back on the coincidences, Jeremy saw God's providence leading in nearly every decision he and Lenette made over the last few years, with each one having ripple effects that continued into the present.

First coincidence: The apartment was waiting for Rebecca.

Second coincidence: Rebecca hadn't moved in.

Third coincidence: They had to hire an outside babysitter.

Fourth coincidence: That babysitter ended up dead, and Rebecca was alive. (Jeremy wasn't sure, but that might be five coincidences.)

And, all she had to do was to move in.

~~~

Caleb was happy, and while Jeremy celebrated that, it bothered him. He commented about it to Rebecca one evening after dinner. Her answer was thoughtful, "Oh Jeremy, children don't have memories from when they are as small as Caleb. It's a gift if you think about it. If Lenette walked through the door he might remember her, but it would be vague.

"Babies live for the moment. When the twins were Caleb's age, I went with Lyle on a business trip; we were gone a week. When we got home I expected for it to be the same, but they acted like they'd never seen me before. I might as well have been a stranger. It took a week for them to forgive me.

"Every passing day she's gone she is fading—even for us; I have trouble picturing her sometimes. But, it has to be that way for a young child; there's no way to explain to him what happened to his mommy."

While that sounded reasonable, it hurt.

She added, "One thing you need to consider is how much love both of you poured into him. A secure baby is a happy baby."

Caleb was in his high chair, frantically sucking on a teething biscuit, subsequently pounding it into pulp on his tray, jabbering, and spitting—fully enjoying his new found creativity. Jeremy wet a rag to wipe the goo from his face—who knows? Perhaps something about it jogged a memory, or Caleb's reaction was as uncomplicated as the feel of the cool rag on his face that triggered it, but his jabbering of random syllables suddenly came out a clear, "Mama."

Jeremy took a step back and looked at him. Caleb smiled up at him, and once again, out came, "Mama?" only this time it sounded vaguely questioning. Then he looked around the kitchen, toward the back door, and back to Jeremy, saying "Mamamamamama". The moment ended with him holding his arms out to Jeremy saying the word over and over, and crying.

Jeremy picked him up, holding him close. The platitude he had so resented sprung out of him, "There, there, it will be all right." Both Grandma Rebecca and Jeremy teared up knowing that "all right" could never be perfect.

Could I have willed this on you, little fella? He wondered, thinking about his conversation with Rebecca a few moments earlier.

Briefly he felt guilty, but then a thought popped into his mind suggesting to him how perhaps this was a gift, not for Caleb, but for him. God had allowed him to see how Lenette's memory did reside in Caleb's little spirit; how he did miss her, and that she would always be there. One day Jeremy would tell Caleb this story and how much his mommy loved him.

Tenderly, he carried the baby upstairs and lay down beside him on their bed. Caleb reached out to touch his face with one hand while he gave in to sleep—his eyelashes still damp from tears. Jeremy couldn't wipe them away, not wanting to disturb the moment; wanting to believe Lenette was watching.

Finally, he fell asleep, too.

~~~

After the drop-in visit from the police, Jeremy put his confiscated evidence in the secret storeroom—another detail he realized he'd neglected to mention to the authorities. It was time to give his investigating another try. He checked all of the doors and closed the blinds before getting it out of the room; then he did some deep breathing exercises. No nausea—yet.

Methodically, he put everything inside it out on the desk in front of him. The shock of finding the gun had worn off after obsessing about it for twenty-two hours straight, but he had another adrenalin rush when he realized that it was loaded. With moderately shaking hands, he put the gun in his wall safe, pushing it toward the back. It was unnerving to think he'd been sleeping with a stranger because, in ways, he was beginning to feel like it.

He opened the second blue notebook. Tucked inside the front cover was a small envelope he hadn't noticed the first time. Inside the envelope was a handwritten note, along with a tiny manila envelope; seemingly empty. A nine digit number was scribbled on the envelope; it matched one of the three numbers written in the notebook.

The note read, "Your guess was an educated one; they are being manufactured currently—by the billions. And, yes to your insights about the plan. Remember, I will not be calling you under any circumstances. If you call me, use the enclosed number. Be careful, and don't tell anyone you have this. N." Wow, Jeremy thought, realizing he was part of the "anyone" Nelson was referring to.

He shook the little envelope and heard a faint rattle. When he tipped it over a tiny, greyish tube fell into his palm. He knew what it was; it was a micro-chip.

What he was holding in his hand was what conspiracy theorists went crazy speculating about. Their propaganda was how every living human at some point would be required to have one. Of course, anyone daring to admit they believed their theory would be ridiculed, but, without the public involved or demanding answers, the plan could be implemented, without any kind of organized uprising to stop it.

Jeremy's pastor once said that he had been watching the evolution of the chip, and correctly predicted it would be promoted for medical record keeping, animal tracking, and even child tracking. Of course, at the time Jeremy thought he'd gone off the deep end.

Details for the implementation were written into the fine print; deep inside one of the bills that had been ramrodded through Congress after the last election. Were there to be an emergency that required martial law, people wouldn't think twice about receiving one.

    God. What in God's name was Lenette involved in? His mind was racing.

CHAPTER 28

Rod Larson reached across the linen clad table, tapping the rim of his glass against Jenna's. "Happy anniversary, you lucky woman you." he said, smiling at her.

"Same to you, you lucky man." she said, returning the smile.

"You have no idea how grateful I am to have you." He added, knowing there was no way to convey how he felt without turning the evening from celebratory to heavy.

But, Jenna did know. He told her often, "I think I have a pretty good idea." She answered, a bit more soberly than she would have liked.

Leaning back, he gazed at her from across the candlelit table, thinking to himself how utterly lovely she was. And, part of what made her so beautiful was that she was unaware of it.

He turned to glance around the room, brought back to reality by the two neighboring tables that were occupied by their security detail who were deliberately conspicuous, watching everything and everyone—on the lookout for anything out of the norm.

This lifestyle had become their normal. Living 24/7 with the ever present security precautions was a constant reminder there were those who could harm them at any time. Actual death threats were no longer uncommon.

"Hi, guys," Rod said, "Don't mind us." They grinned at him. While there was no denying it was awkward, they did their best not to intrude; but somehow the Larson's always managed to make it all seem weirdly normal.

Jenna laughed at how ridiculous it was to try to pretend they were alone. She leaned over, pointing out some entrée's they'd tried before, suggesting several to them; good food was a perk when working for the Larson's. The evening was relaxed and pleasant—convivial even; Rod made every effort to keep it light.

The reaction to his television special was intense and had overwhelmed his staff with responses—mostly favorable. The inundation of emails, faxes, packages, and letters that each potentially contained a lead, tip, or information that all needed to be read and sorted through. It was laborious, but they'd reported some pretty riveting stuff had come in.

With the good came the bad and the ugly. By now, many of the sources of vitriol were predictable—they hated Rod, and he hated them back. It was a push and shove sort of gamesmanship, with an undercurrent of pure menace. Most days he could blow it off, except for those rare occasions when some of the menace managed to seep through a crack in his armor. Rod didn't scare easily, except when it came to his family—that was his crack.

After an enjoyable dinner, the entourage enjoyed Banana's Foster for dessert, prepared tableside with a flourish by their waitress.

When their waitress returned to give Rod the check her demeanor was different. "Mr. Larson, I have something for you, but I'm not sure what to do with it. I-I wasn't sure you'd want it, but I told them I'd give it to you." Her speech was disjointed, and she was speaking so softly Rod had to ask her to repeat herself to hear her.

Rod nervously glanced around the restaurant, demanding, "Them who? What kind of something?" He didn't whisper, nor was he smiling.

Her fingers trembled when she held out a small square of paper. "Do you want it?" She asked.

"Who gave it to you?"

"They're gone."

"Who's gone?"

"There were two men and an older woman; they were sitting over there…" she pointed to a table across from them that was being cleared. "When he paid for their dinner, he asked me to give you this. I took it, and then they left."

Reluctantly, he took it from her. His instincts assured him that she wasn't the problem; just a poor single mom who got caught in the middle of something. "It's okay; you did the right thing." He reassured her, sensing her fear.

She almost fainted from relief.

"Do you have surveillance camera's?" he asked.

She looked around, her eyes nervously scanning the ceiling, pointing to one over the front door. "We do; kind of. The cameras look real, but they're fake. My boss put them up to scare bad people away."

Rod sighed. *Wouldn't you know?*

"Do you think you'd recognize any of them if you saw them again?" Rod asked.

"I-I think so."

He handed her his card. "If they ever return I need you to call this number immediately" he handed her his business card, "Tell whoever answers it was me who told you to call, and why—tell them who you are and where you work. We will compensate you if you help us." He took back the card, printing his personal email on the back. "If you learn anything less urgent, contact me by email."

"I will." She looked worried again. "Will I lose my job over this?"

"No, of course you won't." Rod forced a smile. "You've been an exceptional waitress. We will ask for you the next time we eat here."

She returned the smile; hers was both tentative and grateful. When she left, everyone leaned in to see what was in the note. Rod unfolded the two by two inch piece of paper, and a separate, loose piece of paper floated to the floor. The folded cover was blank.

What the other piece said was, "Poof".

"What does that mean, Rod?" asked Jenna, wide-eyed.

Rod hesitated before answering, "I think it means that if we think we're safe away from our home it's an illusion."

Soberly, the security people nodded. Up until today they had been watching for anything out of the norm; now they would be required to watch for what appeared normal, as well.

They made a pact between them that no one would harm the Larson's on their watch. The job was harder when you respected who you worked for.

CHAPTER 29

Bob Murphy's assistant buzzed to tell him his client had arrived. He looked up from the paperwork that was spread across his desk and checked his watch; his client was five minutes early.

He was young, Bob wasn't expecting that. He was pleasant looking, not terribly tall, blonde, and blue-eyed, with a ruddy complexion; his style was casual; it was also evident that he was in extremely good shape. Bob admired the disciplines of the fit. Good first impression, young man, he thought.

He stood up and walked around the desk, holding out his hand. His guest took it, shaking it firmly. "I'm Jeremy Dobson," he said. *A good handshake,* Bob thought. Another test passed—Bob mistrusted people who gave him insipid handshakes. He liked this guy.

Jeremy was relieved. After his phone conversation with Bob Murphy, he wasn't sure what to expect, but standing across from him, he knew it was the right firm.

Bob had gone overboard explaining how his firm wasn't in any way a detective agency. Jeremy followed suit, finally getting the message across that what he wanted were specialists in researching data and if the job required a private investigator he would pay them to hire one. Jeremy was decidedly cautious about sharing any pertinent details before they met in person; they both agreed that was the only way to ascertain if the firm and project were a fit.

Although Bob was aware of the tragic death of the young wife and activist, he hadn't become a groupie; neither Jeremy's face nor name rang a bell. He asked him to sit down, gesturing toward a chrome and glass table and chairs by the window. His assistant buzzed again, asking if they wanted coffee and when Bob wanted her to bring their lunch.

On the table, between them, were two embossed leather folders. Bob slid one of them across the table to Jeremy. "With my compliments, whether we have a deal or not." Jeremy was impressed; he noticed his initials were embossed on the lower right hand corner at the bottom. He was mentally taking notes, so he would remember to make the same gesture for his clients.

He had a briefcase with him, but it was his and was mostly for show; all that was in it was a newspaper, a folder of news clippings for Bob, along with a DVD. Lenette's briefcase, along with her laptop and cell phone, was hidden in the secret storage room.

Jeremy opened the briefcase and handed Bob what he'd brought, plus a picture of Lenette and Caleb. Bob looked at the picture, and back at Jeremy, puzzled. "I know," Jeremy said, recognizing the look, "we could be brother and sister. I'll never know for sure who our baby looks like."

Bob browsed through the newspaper articles, taking his time. Jeremy nervously doodled in his new leather folder.

The lunch was first class; thin sliced roast beef, onion, tomato sandwiches on fresh pretzel bread. There were several salads to try, and homemade potato chips. Bob jokingly told Jeremy if he finished his lunch he could have dessert, holding out a plate of doily sized chocolate-chip cookies. Bob Murphy fed his clients well. His fees were hefty, but, after a meeting with him, they left feeling indulged. A few days before Christmas, they would receive coupons for two at a day spa.

Bob popped the DVD into a small television on a credenza behind him while Jeremy fidgeted, tired of the endless replays that would again remind him again how his life had imploded. When the video was over, Bob looked at him, visibly moved. "I'm sorry—truly sorry. I want to help you."

Jeremy was stunned, fully expecting to have to do a hard sell. *Wait until this guy sees what I didn't bring,* he thought.

The deal was struck. Bob laid out the terms, "I will need ten thousand dollars, non- refundable, paid today. I will take a personal check, but we won't start working on the case until it clears. The research will cost you three hundred dollars per hour; due the end of each month. We get an additional twenty-five thousand at the end, if we get the job done. If you change your mind, the initial deposit isn't refundable."

Jeremy thanked God he wasn't poor. He felt better knowing he had some help; perhaps his baby would have a daddy for a while.

~~~

Jeremy took a late afternoon flight home, praying for no delays. Before boarding the plane, he called Rebecca. She answered, informing him that she was giving Caleb his bath; explaining that he was having a sleep-over at his grandma's. Jeremy could hear him jabbering in the background, and wondered if all babies were as noisy.

"Is there anything else?" Rebecca asked.

"No. I'll fill you in when I get home. Thanks, Mom. Love ya." For the first time, he felt like maybe things could be fine again; not wonderful, perhaps never great, but he would take fine over how he'd been feeling in a heartbeat. It felt as though an immense weight had been lifted from him.

Jeremy wandered around the airport looking for something decent to eat, wishing he'd thought to ask Bob for a doggie bag. He settled for a pizza in the food court, finding an empty booth near a television. The Rod Larson show was on.

All he caught was only the last twenty minutes of the show, but it was enough to make the hair on his arms stand on end. It seemed surreal; realizing how Lenette put her life on the line to stop what seemed inevitable. Was it possible what Rod was suggesting could be how it ended; with the USA brought to her knees by a small, but determined, bunch of progressives, led by diabolical and largely invisible orchestrators, who were blatantly willing to steamroll over the majority?

He felt the weight crushing down on him again, and in light of the larger picture, it felt heavier. He wondered how heavy it felt for Lenette before she died.

~~~

On the plane ride home, Jeremy's mind drifted back to a few months before Caleb was born. He had arrived home early from work one Friday afternoon, forced to park his car down the street from their house. Their driveway was filled with cars, with more parked up and down both sides of the street. The only plausible explanation he could think of was her friends had surprised her with a baby shower, knowing she was housebound, protecting her hard-won pregnancy.

Inside, he found Lenette, sitting with her feet propped up, sitting in his recliner; the obvious director of a well-orchestrated event.

"Hi, Jeremy, grab some poster board." The person yelling at him was someone from their Sunday school class who was lying on his stomach on the floor, drawing. He was the only person out of the thirty or more people there that Jeremy recognized. Rectangles of poster board were spread over every flat surface on the lower level of the house; that explained the craft paper wrapped parcels he'd been walking by in the garage for the last week. His guests were making signs. **Honk if I'm paying for your mortgage—Give me liberty, not debt—Don't tread on me—Liberty is all the stimulus we need.**

He looked up to see Lenette, watching him. She was shameless, but, for once, she had the grace to look worried. *Well, she should look worried,* he thought. He'd surprised her by coming home early, or he might never have had a clue what she was up to. He tried to look stern, but after passing another sign which read, **I've been porked**, he lost it.

"You are incorrigible, Lenette." He scolded. "I think this is the behind the scenes part that I missed when I was staring at your behind the first time I saw you. That was very distracting."

She was watching his face, aware that he was annoyed. "Well, that is very true. So, I guess you can't act too shocked since it was obvious I already had a mission."

"No," he answered, "but I may have to lean you over the hood of my car and spank you later. I'll check with your doctor first, though."

She giggled, thinking of the expression on her doctor's face were Jeremy to call with that request.

Lenette explained how in her boredom she had been watching more cable TV; blaming it for her heightened aggravation. "Jeremy, I know this looks bad..." she feigned a contrite look, "but, people have to wake up. There is some serious stuff going on—some really bad stuff." It was Rod Larson's show that inspired her to become an activist from home. So, she sent out a mass email to local friends and acquaintances after contacting one of the original organizers for the meet-up groups that began on the east coast. Lenette's email took on a life of its own, after it continued to be forwarded to other frustrated people, who also passed it on.

The sign waving they were preparing for would be the first of several local events that were intended to be both informative, and a vehicle for change. Three hundred RSVPS' had been called in, and the list was growing daily. Lenette was not one to think small; she was hoping for a thousand.

After forming a skeleton committee to help her, she called a local art supply store and ordered poster board cut to size, directing them to deliver the bundles to the house, along with markers, pens, and a hundred blue and red baseball caps. She pointed to a vase on the piano, stuffed with five and ten dollar bills. "Everyone chipped in for the signs. But, I gave them each a hat; I signed and dated them, so we would remember today." she said proudly. None of them could have imagined how priceless, a year later, those mementoes would become.

Jeremy was trying not to take her leaving him out personally. Lenette read his mind. "I wanted to tell you, Jeremy, I really did. You were so preoccupied with your next implosion I couldn't find the right time. It wasn't something I could communicate in five minutes; I knew I'd have to do a sell-job on you. Sorry." She feigned a contrite look.

"So, when were you going to tell me?" Jeremy asked her, trying to keep his voice conversational. He realized people had stopped what they were doing to listen.

"Oh, I was going to tell you before next week—before the sign waving, for sure." She reached behind the recliner and pulled out a sign that read, Stop the spending...Or we're going to implode.

"This one's for you. I made it up myself." She offered, grinning like a little kid who just won the Science Fair. "We're giving an award for the best sign. Of course, mine can't win, but it deserves merit for the most fitting sign. I wish I could be there—there will be TV coverage and everything."

"I think we need to talk about this later." Jeremy said, feeling slightly queasy.

His instincts were rightly telling him this was not all going to be fun and games.

CHAPTER 30

Eleanor had been neglecting her emails. "I'm too old for this", she scolded her reflection that was staring back at her from her computer screen, rubbing her temples and vowing she would catch up before it became impossible to get through them all.

She mourned the days when the postman personally delivered the bundles of letters to her door, and that was the extent of her mail. It took time to open each one, but each letter retained some sense of individuality. She wasn't sure why the stacks of letters seemed less intimidating than the emails; perhaps because they were easier for her to sort through mentally, opening them one at a time, and knowing it would be twenty-four more hours before the postman brought more.

While she analyzed her plight, three different emails popped up. Ouch! That took her inbox count to over six hundred emails, and that was after her new, expensive spam program had been uploaded, guaranteed to stop junk mail from getting through.

One by one, she began opening them; flagging some as valuable, while saving others for what practical information they contained; most were deleted. She noticed one that had come in a few days earlier. Subject: From Rod Larson—open immediately. She was now perched on the edge of her seat.

Dear Eleanor.

I hope this finds you well—and safe. I will keep this brief. Things have begun to escalate since we last   met that make me want to press forward with the next program. Some of what we covered seems prophetic in light of some what's been happening. If you say yes, I'll send a private plane for you. Wear what you wore last time. It needs to look like the same taping session. The ratings from the first show were so high the network agreed to give us two hours if we can fill the time slot.

Yours, Rod

Eleanor printed it off. Her answer was immediate. "Let's roll."

~~~

Four days later she and Candy waited for Rod in the same room as before. The door opened, but instead of Rod, a woman walked in.

"I'm Jenna—Rod's wife." She smiled at them, adding, "Rod will be her in a few minutes; he had to take an unexpected phone call."

Eleanor and Candy stood up, with Eleanor stepping forward to embrace the young woman.

"I can't believe I finally get to meet you," Jenna Larson said. "I have been in one of your studies for years."

Eleanor was touched. It was a blessing to think that she was solid in her faith and strong in spirit; Rod needed that behind the scenes. Eleanor called her devotee's "Troopers" if they lasted more than three years in her studies.

Jenna Larson was petite, but appeared to be athletic. Her ash blonde hair was unpretentiously pulled back with a twisty, and while she was attractive, it was her eyes that were captivating; they were large and cat-like, giving her an air of perpetual curiosity. Her attire was casual; she had on an oversized black silk blouse over blue jeans, belted with a silver chain, and black high-heeled boots; her only jewelry was a cross. Eleanor appreciated that no attempt had been made to impress her.

Rod came in a moment later—looking worried and all business. "Shall we sit?" He asked. Pointing to some refreshments on a table near the door, he offered, "May I get you ladies anything? We have time to visit a bit before we tape."

Eleanor knew not to eat unless her stomach was literally growling before a taping. "No, thank you." Eleanor said. "But, would a doggie bag be an option? By then we'll both be starving because Candy won't eat if I don't."

"Consider it done." Rod agreed. He knew the dangers of eating prior to a taping, also.

He and Jenna quickly filled them in, explaining how recent events had put a greater urgency on what they felt they were called to do. At different times in their discussion, they stopped to pray, shaking their heads at the enormity of what was taking place. The world truly was groaning for its Savior.

They quickly moved through the amazing continuum of natural disasters, increasing terror threats, the unrest spilling into the streets, the overlapping economic concerns, and how each was being propagandized by the media, and the bizarre reactions coming from the country's government. It was all working together to inspire more government regulations that were signed into law during Congress's summer recess by Presidential Order—circumventing any representation "Of and by the people", although the people didn't seem to be concerned. The Presidential Order was delivered with the warning that any single event could trigger a state of emergency, giving the government reason to declare martial order, cancelling the pending elections.

Eleanor put a spiritual commentary on the heavy news they were digesting, reminding them, "We cannot become faint of heart, in spite of what we see happening. Whether we are wrong or right about where this is heading, we will praise him and stay focused. And, praising him may be the last thing we get to do. I don't want to be right because of what it means to the human species who aren't ready, but I am not going to quit warning the people, because either way, the alarm must be sounded.

"By observation, our enemies can rely on the Body of Christ gathering in a circle to shoot at each other."

Rod held up his left hand for her to slow her down. He was writing furiously, taking notes.

Eleanor continued, "Christ deliberately placed himself in the epicenter of the political and religious corruption of his day.

"The Priesthood was intended by God to be the people's liaison to him, the way Christ's ministry is to the Body of Christ. Instead, because the power corrupted them—absolutely corrupted them—the people were left spiritually insipid, sickly in spirit and soul, physically and financially broken, and all because they didn't know who Jehovah God was or what was theirs by Covenant.

"Had the priests been properly expounding the prophetic scriptures, the Jews would, on their own, have been able to discern who the Christ would be. It is no wonder God put a stern warning about adding to or subtracting from His word at the end of The Revelations! To be accurate, that mandate didn't originate at the end of Revelations—God gave the same warning to his people in the book of Deuteronomy."

Jenna spoke up, "I've never heard anyone say that before, Eleanor. Where Is that?"

"It is in the fourth chapter—I'm pretty sure it's the second verse. It's crucial to read it in the context of the whole chapter. That chapter warns the Jews how they were to live after they entered the Promised Land; it is about their being Covenant people; it's warning for them to keep their end of the Covenant by obeying the Lord. "

She paused, "The Church was to have been the watchman on the wall, the voice in the wilderness, the prophetic voice that spoke out of both warning and blessing, announcing "The time is at hand" to both the church and the culture. That's why we haven't had prophets as such. The church, with the gifts of the spirit and the work, was to be able both collectively and individually, to discern what was taking place.

"It won't matter if we are wrong about the timing, should the Lord tarry for a while more. His tarrying may even be the result of prayers for His mercy to allow mankind more time; being prepared is about being wholly his—wholly owned by him.

"We've awakened some, and there will be more who will join us. Should this only be a wake-up call to the church the torch must be passed to those next in line, and hopefully, at the very least, parents will see their responsibility to teach and train their children in the word. God allows times like these to make his people take their Christian role-modeling seriously, and show the next generation what to be watchful for.

"We are not alone in speaking out. We speak in the tradition of the evangelists, and preachers, who are still mocked by the church's elites... The worldwide harvest that will take place just before he appears will be staggering in numbers, but there will be cost attached for those who come in. Time has run out on country club Christianity."

She paused, "I know these are strong opinions on my part; I apologize if I have overstepped."

"Eleanor, no you have not overstepped." Rod assured her. "I just wish the cameras were rolling." Rod continued writing notes, seeing a personal, prophetic component of one of his favorite quotes by Albert Einstein, "The more I learn, the more I realize I don't know." He couldn't believe how far in over his head he felt at the moment.

Eleanor was studying the framed quote by C.S. Lewis hanging on the wall above him; ""Experience is a brutal teacher, but you learn. My God, do you learn."

~~~

Later that afternoon the Larsons headed home; they were in the back of a specially fitted SUV, complete with a driver who was part of their security detail. The most recent adjustment forced on them was the warning that it was no longer wise for them to be driving alone. It was, perhaps, the most difficult realization for both of them, because it represented not only another vestige of their personal freedom, but what little spontaneity they retained, as well. Nearly all of their independence had now been sacrificed to the cause.

A few weeks prior, dead birds had begun showing up in their yard. A single bird was found in the yard the first day, two the next, the third day a half dozen more were found. The birds had been poisoned. Their security detail surmised the perpetrator knew the odds were that some of the birds would find their way onto the Larson's yard, delivering a message.

"Those pesky environmentalist hypocrites", Rod muttered, once they were told the incidents were not coincidental. Next, one by one, their barn cats began dying; possibly from eating the sick birds. It was intrusive, and a warning of worse things to come; only this time it involved their children.

Rod bent forward and caught his head in his hands. Every pent-up emotion he'd been bottling inside found its release while Jenna watched, helpless and unnerved. She let him cry uninterrupted, knowing his tears were neither selfish nor self-indulgent; he was crying for the unprepared masses—those he hadn't been able to reach.

Finally, she spoke, "Rod, you're the bravest man I know—you may be the bravest man in America. We don't view the present darkness through the same lens the world does. It makes me think of the Bible verse, 'The first shall be last, and the last shall be first'. Those who went first are watching us now from the bleachers of Heaven, cheering us on...

"I don't want you to worry about me. I'm not afraid—no matter what. We were chosen for this time, and God will give us the strength to face whatever comes."

Rod wiped his eyes. "I can't explain what just happened, Jenna; it was unstoppable. What Eleanor said earlier crystallized a lot of my own thoughts. The nice guys finish last—it shouldn't be that way, but the clock is running out.

"The nice guys assumed too much. We assumed the school system retained the same values we did, so we got lazy teaching those values to our kids—the way our grandparents and parents did. We assumed the same with our churches, because we believed our youth groups were instilling the faith of our fathers into our kids, and not some watered down version of the gospel. And what happened...again, parents quit doing it at home.

"We assumed when our leaders put their hands on the Bible to take an oath of office, they meant it—that the Book they put their hand on meant as much to them a to us. We didn't ask enough questions, and we didn't question the answers we got. We accepted their pat answers, and we assumed they were truthful—and why? Because if they weren't, then what the hell were we supposed to do?

"We assumed we were indispensable, viable participants in the democratic system—but never expendable. Our leaders can spit in our faces now because, behind the scenes, a deal's been struck—they've been promised something to be complicit. We ASSUMED...!

"And who do they consider is expendable...? It's the dreamers, the thinkers, the doers, the risk takers— the middle class—the ones who dared believe that nothing was impossible.

"A middle class won't exist in a New World Order—it can't. The middle class represents the dreamers who reach for the stars, or instead they charter a rocket. We are the only system holding the door open for people do that. The playing field, by necessity, will be leveled for those who would undo us to take control. When we play our last card it won't matter which one we were holding because they have the Aces—the deck is stacked."

"Rod, I've never heard you sound this futile before..." Jenna responded, troubled.

"It's not futility, Jenna. I'm seeing things from a different vantage point. It will play out the way it has to. The Bible predicts how it will be before his coming, so it shouldn't be a surprise. We are possibly the 'few are chosen' generation. Just think what it would be like if the whole church were ready? I believe this time of upheaval is to judge the church; to warn us to buy the oil...to be ready.

"Being ready in the end comes down to each and every individual; it's a warning to get our priorities straight. Our own church started Sunday the early services, so people could get out for an early T–time."

"I was part of that committee, Rod." Jenna reminded him.

"Sorry!" he grimaced, and went on, "Jenna, think of the spiritual role models who died to give us the freedom to worship! Those who went before us would spend entire Sunday's in church! When worship became prioritized by "Let's go to church early, and get it out of the way, so we can play golf" someone has to wonder how that fits with God's standards of readiness.

"Each of us is called to be fishers of men; and, you are right, the last will be first; does that make sense?"

She nodded soberly. It did.

"He means us, Jenna! Our generation! We may be the ones who get to close this age out! How do we convince the unprepared that the peril isn't simply communism or socialism? Somebody has to show them how they're being led like sheep to the slaughter on false promises—and how in the end freedom may be lost?" He put his face on his hands again.

"Jenna, I see them in my sleep at night. Weren't most of the prophets killed?"

"Pretty much..." She answered, gravely.

CHAPTER 31

After much deliberation, Nelson concluded the only place that made sense to do the dirty deed was in a car. From home he called a cab to take him to Hertz rental, where he rented an Eclipse. He nervously watched his rear view mirror while he wound through the countryside, finally ending up in a remote area in Connecticut. He was sure he wasn't followed, at least by land. Of course, as long as he had the chip, they had him.

Surveillance had been stepped up for anyone who was part of bringing down the financial systems. The U.S. wasn't alone; it was every government in the civilized world willing to sell out their populace was involved. The strategy for the third world was easy; they wouldn't know what, when, or how it happened. When the effects of it reached them, the wailing of the already affected masses would be reduced to a whimper; there would be no one able to help them.

In the beginning, when he was climbing the ladder, when he signed on to be part of the fraternity of the selected survivors, he was able to emotionally distance from what the real agenda was—how they viewed the coming revolution as a means of eliminating those deemed disposable by the new system.

He had never even considered his own expendability, but that was in the beginning. It wasn't like he offered them anything of significant value; he was, in a way, a glorified go-fer. But, in order to pull it off, there were tens of thousands of people like him, all positioned to do their part on different rungs of the collective ladder. At the top, only a few made the rules for those beneath them.

Darwin's theory, "The Survival of the Fittest", accounted for a gradual genetic reprogramming of species adapting to survive, but a manufactured survival could only be accomplished when those in power had the power to declare that they were the fit, and systemically rid the world of the unfit.

When each incremental level of commitment presented itself, it was gradual; so much so, there were times he'd grown impatient for things to move along faster. In the beginning, when he was totally in sync with them, the redistribution of wealth for the common good was a no-brainer—just so it wasn't his wealth. Those toward the top of the ladder never gave a thought to a reduced standard of living.

Hidden in various bills Congress had passed in their short, but efficient, reign since the last election were so many controls on the populace heads would be spinning...if they knew. His company was positioned to make billions. But, the media kept the public distracted, knowing they could count on its historically short memory.

The nationalizing of the small banks had to happen; the regulations demanded by the OCC had cast a devouring shadow over them while the news efficiently watered down anything that threatened to make the dozing masses sit up and take notice. The public ate up the propaganda the media fed them like birds gobbling up birdseed. He questioned how the spirit of a true journalist could be convinced to trade a legitimate investigative story for ratings; it was an anomaly—but with few exceptions, the media had become complicit.

Some days there was a thread of hope to hang on to, but most days he accepted it would be him who was found hanging, and it wouldn't be by a thread. He had nothing to lose by blowing the whistle; the question was who to blow it at since they were all lying in the same bed.

But, above all else, he had to protect his family, and that was the spoiler—they were their secret weapon to keep him compliant. When he'd signed on he never once considered there might be risk for Lindsay or the children, if anything, he believed they would be safer because of what he did. The ability to control those who had sold their souls to the company store was because they were promised a safety net. For Nelson, it was because he believed his family could never be expendable.

Perhaps what he was about to do would exorcise his demons...

~~~

How different things might be now if he and Lindsay could have just moved away, and started a life of their own, somewhere away from his family. They'd talked about it, but at the time, his warped idea of family honor had kept him on the narrow Saunders path. Guilt—his ever present companion—the damned if you do, damned if you don't, choke-hold his mother used to manipulate him; the need to know the right people; to use the right people; to step over the right people, and, now, for him, to be forced to look back and see how perverted your loyalties were.

His soul's sovereignty had always been for sale, and he had no one to blame but him. When his membership in his fraternity propelled him, gradually polluting his thinking until he no longer knew what truth was, it was because he'd had the grandest of awakenings—that it was all relative.

There were three in Nelson's pledge class selected to rise to the top. The secrets, oaths, hidden agendas; at the time they seemed almost harmless— like a game, but each time he'd consented he'd given away another piece of his belief in moral excellence.

Looking back, he could see his promotions upward seemed too easy; and, at the time, he took full credit. Later, he would blame his mother for pulling strings, but deep down he'd always known she wasn't a factor at all, but became a convenient excuse; his goal to escape her distracted him from seeing how he was trading his own ethics for someone else's. He wondered if, in the end, there was only one sin—the sin of rationalization. He was proficient at it.

It was pointless to revisit it all since there was no going back; or unless it could help him to fix things. He could only hope that in some eternal moment, where forgiveness might be offered, he could look back, knowing he'd gone out with a bang for the right reasons.

He remembered a quote by Benjamin Franklin; "Three can keep a secret if two of them are dead." He laughed out loud at the thought.

~~~

He spread a folded bath towel on the seat. His monogram, NAS, was face up. "Nelson", he mocked himself, "You are class all the way."

Beside him was a newly purchased Red Cross medicine chest. In it was a retractable exacto-knife, a bottle of rubbing alcohol, bandages, and a half-full bottle of scotch, among other items of less importance at the minute. He'd found a partly used tube of Neosporin in the children's bathroom that was in the glove box.

He probed his right hand with his forefinger. The chip was closer to the surface than he remembered, but he was thinner now. "Here's to the New World Order," he said, raising the scotch bottle, following the toast with a swig. "Let's see if you thought of this..."

Obviously, they thought of it, because when he accepted it he was warned that were it removed a fatal dose of lithium would be released. He'd neglected to look up 'Death by Lithium...'

At a certain level, each and every family employed by Levy & Sinclair was required to participate in a mandatory identification process— accepting a microchip that would be inserted in their right hand or their just above the hairline; not to comply meant instant dismissal. He'd neglected to ask if that meant they would be fired or dismissed permanently, as in a mysterious death by natural causes. It could be assumed that people at his level knew too much.

The timing of the scheduled identification process was the week of his mother's stroke. Lindsay was dutifully occupied with his mother, so she and the children were given a pass. Apparently, someone failed to log their failure to report into the computer, because his family had never been rescheduled.

He took the exacto-knife out of the medicine chest, pressing the lever to release the blade. He couldn't resist touching the tip of it with his forefinger, to prepare himself for the pain. *Ouch!—Okay, it hurts.* He dipped the knife into the rubbing alcohol and laid it on the towel.

He took another swig of the Scotch, but that was all. He screwed the lid back on the bottle and tossed it on the floor in the backseat. He needed to be mentally steady—after all, he wasn't a surgeon. He poured some of the rubbing alcohol on a square of gauze and vigorously rubbed the back of his right hand.

Nelson's left hand began shaking. *Just be careful*, he thought, trying to steady himself. *Slow and steady wins the race*, he told himself. *Otherwise, you're dead*. If the thing burst there was no Plan B; he'd just rot in the rental car until somebody found him.

Judas Iscariot wanted to fix things once he knew it was all going south, he thought. Maybe *I'm not too late. Maybe there is redemption for someone who traded their soul.*

He put his right hand on the towel, pressing it flat. The chip was inserted between his second and third finger; he traced it with his finger one more time to be sure. He could feel it; now to get it out without releasing the lithium.

"God." He said it involuntarily. His whole body shuddered, but there was no going back now.

He put the tip of the knife next to where the chip was applying pressure until it disappeared into his flesh. It hurt, but not as much as he'd been dreading. Now he was afraid he might pass out at the sight of his own blood. Slowly, he drew the knife toward him, watching a slit open. It bled out—he quickly removed the blade to see what he was doing, grabbing some more gauze putting pressure on the wound; he remembered getting a badge for doing something like it in Boy Scouts. He remembered, too late, something about using a tourniquet...

When the bleeding was under control, he reinserted the blade, enlarging the opening some more. The pain had become an annoyance. The opening was, give or take, an inch long. He was bleeding like a pig, but he was finished and still conscious. Stitches might be in order, but he'd settle for a battle scar.

He swabbed the cut, spreading it apart with his fingers. The small, silver colored chip was exposed, but now he needed something or someone to help him get it out. Then, almost as a reflex, he put his mouth over the cut, sucking until he felt it on his tongue.

It was out. And, the best part was that he hadn't died—yet.

~~~

Before returning the rental car, he drove by the drop box at the Post Office, wanting to catch the last pickup. He jotted a note to Lenette and put the chip in a small manila envelope; he put it and his note inside a larger one. It would go out that afternoon. For less than a half dollar, something that no doubt cost billions of taxpayer dollars to research and manufacture would be winging its way across the country.

This didn't exonerate him, but inexplicably his head felt clear for the first time in a long time.

Now it was up to Lenette—perhaps she could fix what he couldn't...

At the time he wasn't thinking about Big Brother being in the envelope with the chip.

CHAPTER 32

Bob stuck his head through the conference room door, trying to get Max's attention, motioning for him to join him. When Max realized what he wanted he resisted a sudden urge to bolt for the exit door. *Cut that out,* he told himself. Later he would call that a premonition.

~~~

Max was never included in client meetings, so he wondered what was up. Two of the firm's top research analysts were sitting across from the client. Max thought he was experiencing a déjà vu, certain he'd seen him before.

"Max Zimmerman—Jeremy Dobson," Bob said. They shook hands.

"Jeremy, Max is our legal counsel. I've asked him to join us to cover our legal bases. We can't be too careful—if we're ever called to testify all we can do is to plead The Fifth. Right Max?" He looked at Max, laughing nervously, but no one else followed suit. He added, "The lips of everyone in this room are sealed— understood?"

Jeremy nodded, thinking he meant him. He was thinking how Bob might as well get it all out on the table; it might alleviate the endless Ping-Pong game in his head. He hadn't thought about pleading The Fifth before.

"Max..." Bob proceeded to explain the details of the case and Jeremy had compromised himself. "I don't' need to tell you this is sensitive information, and nothing is to be discussed outside of this office. Since you and I haven't discussed this prior to this meeting, I want to be sure we're on the same page." Max nodded, shocked on every level about what he'd just heard. What Bob hadn't communicated specifically, was how he'd compromised every man in the meeting by taking the case in the first place—*too late now,* he thought.

"Man, I am so sorry, Jeremy," Max told him after he'd been filled in. He remembered him now, and the beautiful blonde woman who was his wife. He was trying to imagine how Jeremy was functional.

"Thanks. I think the numbness is wearing off. It hurts more now; I didn't feel much for a while," Jeremy answered. "Thanks for not saying, 'I know how you feel'; every time I hear it, I vow I'll slug who says it next—so, I'm glad it wasn't you."

"Me, too." said Max, unsure how anyone could say such a thing.

~~~

Max left the conference room two hours later, and what he'd heard was numbing.

Apparently everyone but him was aware of the shift in policies that were moving the country towards the world government. He was glad he and Laura started watching the Rod Larson show a few weeks before, or he would be close to clueless. The irony was that he was a walking Thesaurus for trivia.

He realized how, between his work, painting, and Laura, he hadn't been paying any attention to world events; only catching the news in bits and pieces. He'd judged a couple of the guys at work as being pretty radical—now radical had a perspective.

While Laura might come across as a bit of a lightweight, what took him by surprise was her tenacity to dig in and study when presented with something intriguing to her—as in her desire to learn to cook. In three weeks' time, she had progressed from pasta salad to pasta primavera. She told Max that, if he didn't mind, she was going to learn everything there was to learn about pasta before she moved on to something else. He could tell his pants were tighter, but he didn't have the heart to ask if pasta could become a side dish.

To his surprise, one day when he walked into the kitchen after work, fettuccini strands were draped over every lateral plane in the house—drying. Laura had made pasta from scratch.

My woman! he thought.

She was standing in the middle of the kitchen—a vision of loveliness covered in flour. She beamed when he said he didn't think most people ever attempted to make pasta for themselves. *Who knew?* Max offered to make a salad to go with the fettuccini.

Within that same period of time, she'd figured out how to 'Google' on her computer. It started harmlessly enough, with her Googling different cooking techniques and recipes, and doing some online shopping.

She'd been taking notes during the Rod Larson shows, listing the names, groups, and other details of what the day's subject was, to check out later. In the mornings, she Googled them one by one, following up by sorting through the links she discovered, and noting what she thought were pertinent. "Ask lots of questions & Question the answers" was written on the front of her notebook. She hadn't opened a magazine for weeks.

~~~

At night, before bed, Laura began reading the bible out loud to Max. She began with the book of John because that was what the lady in the bookstore suggested when Laura told her neither of them had read a bible before.

And so she began..."Max, I'm reading from the Book of John: In the beginning was the Word...Max, did you realize the Word was God?"

"I never gave it much thought."

"What that means is that Jesus was the Word."

"Huh?"

"That's what it says. 'In the beginning was the Word and the Word was with God, and the Word was God, and all things were made by Him.' Did you know that all things were made by him?" She asked.

"Him who?"

"Jesus! Max, are you listening? Jesus is who John is writing about!"

"No, I didn't know that."

"Yes, Max, it's true. When he says the Word became flesh he is talking about Jesus."

"Well, that settles it for me."

"...for me, too."

Ask lots of questions, and question the answers...

~~~

What made no sense to Max was how the authorities could have dropped the ball with locating Lenette's computer. Somebody was clearly asleep at the wheel not to have turned over every rock to find it; especially in the context of her being executed—presumably for what Murphy's Law was now in possession of. Perhaps it was because there were so many agencies involved. But, still, it didn't make sense, unless...

The one thing that it bought was time—for Jeremy. But, Jeremy's dilemma would be the immense political and personal backlash that was bound to come on the chance it was made public—otherwise why take the risk? Lenette Dobson trespassed where few dared to go.

He had to give her credit; she did it from her home on a Mac. And, whatever it was she was on to, it was necessarily big—the price she paid was her life.

Only two months ago Max would have reacted decidedly differently; perhaps he would have thought it might be fun to be involved on a case at this level of intrigue. But, without the additional and unsolicited confirmation Bob's new client unknowingly provided, Max wished he could escape to an island with Laura for a belated and extended honeymoon.

He was agitated, again, and feeling the urge to bolt, except he trusted Bob's instincts. They were impeccable.

Max had no issue with not telling Laura; he didn't want to bring any of it into their home. At the moment, he was wishing he hadn't bought her a computer.

CHAPTER 33

What Lenette could not have known when the microchip arrived in her mailbox, was it was both a state of the art monitoring device, insidiously designed to program behavior. By then she should have known enough to handle it like a hot potato. And, perhaps she had—she was but hours away from handing it over to someone who could unravel what she could not.

Unwittingly, waking or sleeping, Nelson was owned once he accepted the chip; it had been monitoring his every minute since. "Did they withhold that part of the deal; or did I somehow miss it?" He asked Lenette the last time she saw him. "The devil's in the details, isn't he?"

Lenette nodded; she knew the answer to the question. The scriptures said that would be true at the end.

Nelson explained how the chip was designed to self-destruct if someone attempted to remove it; that event releasing a lethal dose of lithium. Was he alive because he sucked it out rather than touching it with anything metal...? Or, might the warning have been a scare tactic to insure people wouldn't attempt to remove them? Damn; everything was a scare tactic. How did any of them function at all; scared out of their wits day and night?

Kicking himself would be Nelson's unrelenting preoccupation for forgetting his briefcase on his desk that Monday. When he opened it later, and realized what was on top, his stomach sank; the orders were to destroy the copies of the new currency after the meeting. He was preparing to do just that when he noticed the fax transfer sheet.

It was a given that Lindsay would have involved Lenette in what she found if for no other reason than for her to explain it to her. Now he would have to pretend he wasn't aware she found it.

With each passing day, it was increasingly evident to him that he had lost her trust. The tiny remnant of intimacy that remained between them was now gone. Lindsay had become as remote as he was. Death was not the worst thing that could happen.

~~~

His unexpected relationship with Lenette began after the infamous dinner.

Several weeks after the baby was born Lenette put in a call to Nelson at his office. The first time she called, he declined her call. Peeved, Lenette called back, insisting that it was an emergency; his secretary put her through again. Reluctantly Nelson took the call, listening long enough to realize Lenette's intention was to quiz him; he cut her off saying was late for a meeting.

She dug in and called him back a third time. Nelson resigned himself to the fact that she wasn't going to leave him alone until after they talked. He returned the call from a pay phone down the street.

He knew precisely what it was she wanted. He was the flypaper, and she was the fly, and there was no other option but to meet. There was no safe way to communicate unless it was in person. While that seemed extreme, what they had to discuss was too serious to trust to the air waves; he knew something about random surveillance, and he didn't feel particularly lucky. After that day, they communicated with disposable phones purchased with cash from obscure places.

For three months, he fed her information; information he hoped would somehow save Lindsay—a reverse blackmail of sorts. Perhaps, if he could convince them, were it to become necessary, their security was compromised in another way, then he might still hold some cards, a few cards—a card.

The last time he spoke to Lenette she suspected that she was being watched; she described it as little things at first, like catching a driver's eye in her rearview mirror, or seeing someone she had seen before in line at the coffee shop who coincidently left when she did, clicks on the phone and compromised reception—nothing overt; just a creepy feeling she couldn't shake off. But, the incidents seemed to be gaining momentum.

If she told Jeremy it would open up a Pandora's Box of questions, so she didn't. He would kill her with his bare hands if he had any idea how deep in she was. And, she now she could see how she had not been careful covering her tracks in the beginning. But, Nelson knew, and it worried him.

Nelson and Lenette agreed that neither Jeremy nor Lindsay could know they were playing spy tag—covert took on a whole new meaning when even their spouses might be compromised by what they couldn't know. Nelson was worried for her, and with compelling reason. Lenette was being careful now, but she had been reckless before she understood the rules.

Lenette and Lindsay never kept secrets from each other; the only thing that made the lying plausible now was because Lenette believed she was saving her twin from something much worse. What was that phrase again...a slippery slope? She was on it and stepping carefully; one misstep and she could be sliding down with nothing to grab hold of—no, it was worse than that—with no one to grab hold of.

Nelson either. They were trying to save their families, their country; or at the very least, buy time for either, praying they would not lose everything.

They agreed to risk a meeting. Lenette told Jeremy she was meeting Lindsay for a quick overnight in Boston, so she could see the baby; that meant she would have to bring him with her, but she had no choice. Jeremy objected, but, in the end, she won. "Girl power," she called it when she and Lindsay were trying to arrange one of their girl weekends. By the time they were all together again, Jeremy wouldn't remember Lindsay saw him.

Lindsay would assume Nelson was spending the night in the city, which he routinely did; they rarely talked during the week. It would be statistically improbable for Jeremy or Lindsay to call each other.

CHAPTER 34

"Max, did you know about this?"

"Did I know about what?'

"I can't explain it. You need to see it for yourself." Her tone sounded serious, and that wasn't like her.

Max finished shaving and sat on the bed next to her. Laura was in bed with her laptop open on her lap. Without trying to explain further, she turned the computer around so the screen was facing him.

1773 - Mayer Amschel Rothschild assembles twelve of his most influential friends and convinces them that if they all pool their resources together, they can rule the world. This meeting takes place in Frankfurt, Germany. Rothschild also informs his friends that he has found the perfect candidate, an individual of incredible intellect and ingenuity, to lead the organization he has planned - Adam Weishaupt.

May 1, 1776 - Adam Weishaupt (code named Spartacus) establishes a secret society called the Order of the Illuminati. Weishaupt is the Professor of Canon Law at the University of Ingolstadt in Bavaria, part of Germany. [This date, May Day, is to become highly significant to the Soviet Communists. They held festive military parades on this day.] The Illuminati seek to establish a New World Order. Their objectives are as follows:

1. Abolition of all ordered governments
2. Abolition of private property
3. Abolition of inheritance
4. Abolition of patriotism
5. Abolition of the family
6. Abolition of religion
7. Creation of a world government

She backed up a page to show him the search she was working on. "Max, this website takes me up to just a few years ago; there is another one with the same information that brings it up to the last election."

She pointed to the results for her search, two billion possible hits for the search term New World Order. "I've followed up on thirty seven, do you think I'll finish?" She was teasing, but she wasn't smiling. She added, "If I type in the term One World Government there are almost eighty six million search results; some are duplicates, but many aren't, and it changes every day. That's what's weird about it; some that I look at one day and go back to the next are gone, with a disclaimer that no such website exists."

Laura opened her notebook to show him some of the other websites she had looked at and had written down. "How come we didn't know about any of this?" she asked him.

When he finished reading, he said, "It must have been all around us, Laura. If what we are finding out was dismissed as a conspiracy theory, which is what most people think, they've adopted a mindset that dismisses this as rightwing wing craziness. As for me, I simply denied it could be possible, and no facts stuck because I wasn't even curious. Obviously, even your grandmother heard about it somewhere."

"Yes, she heard about it in her church, and I thought she was crazy. I refused to listen to her about any of it. I think she was trying to warn me; it was all she talked about."

He noticed there was a long list of website links copied by hand into her notebook. "Do you know how to bookmark on your computer?" he asked.

"What's a bookmark?"

"It's how you can store what you've been looking at online, so you can go back to it again later. Here, let me show you." He punched a few keys.

"Wow, that's so easy." She said.

"Well, it is easy, but if your computer ever crashes you can lose them, but we can do a back-up later. You might write down the significant ones, but this will help you keep a record of what you've done. See, I've given this a file name New World Order."

"Show me how you did that."

"Okay. Let's make a file called 'Pasta'."

"Wow."

~~~

When Max settled in at work, he started doing some research of his own.

Soon he had bookmarked several credible looking sites, avoiding the ones with skulls and crossbones or leaping flames on the title page.

He started with Wikipedia: "Prior to the early 1990s, New World

Order conspiracies were limited to two American countercultures, primarily the militantly anti-government right, and secondarily fundamentalist Christians concerned with the end-time emergence of the Anti-Christ Skeptics, such as Michael Barkun and Chip Berlet, who expressed concern that the right-wing conspiracy theories about a New World Order have now not only been embraced by many left-wing conspiracy theorists but have seeped into popular culture, thereby inaugurating an unrivaled period of people actively preparing for apocalyptic, millenarian scenarios in the United States of the late 20th and early 21st centuries. Political scientists warn that this mass hysteria may not only fuel lone-wolf terrorism but have effects on American political life, such as the far right wooing the far left into joining a revolutionary Third Position movement capable of subverting the established political powers."

Next he found 'educate-yourself.org'. After reading the introduction page, he was sweating. What struck him in particular was something written in 1992 by Dr. John Coleman, "In 1992, Dr John Coleman published Conspirators' Hierarchy: The Story of the Committee of 300. With laudable scholarship and meticulous research, Dr Coleman identifies the players and carefully details the Illuminati agenda of worldwide domination and control. On page 161 of the Conspirators Hierarchy, Dr Coleman accurately summarizes the intent and purpose of the Committee of 300 as follows; "A One World Government and one-unit monetary system, under permanent non-elected hereditary oligarchs who self-select from among their numbers in the form of a feudal system, as it was in the Middle Ages. In this One World entity, population will be limited by restrictions on the number of children per family, diseases, wars, famines, until 1 billion people who are useful to the ruling class, in areas which will be strictly and clearly defined, remain as the total world population.

There will be no middle class, only rulers and the servants. All laws will be uniform under a legal system of world courts practicing the same unified code of laws, backed up by a One World Government police force and a One World unified military to enforce laws in all former countries where no national boundaries shall exist. The system will be on the basis of a welfare state; those who are obedient and subservient to the One World Government will be rewarded with the means to live; those who are rebellious will be starved to death, or be declared outlaws, becoming a target for anyone who wishes to kill them. Privately owned firearms or weapons of any kind will be prohibited."

By lunch time, he'd read enough to question why there wasn't a daily update by each of the news outlets explaining how the world government was advancing. One point of interest from a few months earlier was an article by Mihir Bose titled "India bats its way up the new world order", talking about the shifting of world power from the West to the East.

The labeling of those on the right as hysterical had been successful, and it stuck. Those crazy Christians—they were the perfect foil. It was like what was done to the Jews throughout history; only now it was the Christian's turn. They were being marginalized and discredited, with the facts becoming clouded in the process. It had been working. He could see how they had used the tactic successfully on various issues, hoping to engage with them in the marginalizing; even winning over other professed Christians.

Another site caught his eye.

Signs of the coming World Government

The move to create a New World Order (NWO) probably started in America during the early 1900's. Significant milestones are:

- 1935: a NWO symbol appears on the back of the US dollar bill
- 1940: H. G. Wells publishes a book titled, The New World Order
  - 1945: UN is founded
  - 1948: World Council of Churches (WCC) is formed
  - 1954: Bilderberg Group is formed
  - 1957: EEC is formed under The Treaties of Rome
  - 1973: Trilateral Commission is formed
  - 1974: Universal Product Code (UPC) introduced in retail stores
  - 1990: George H. W. Bush spoke on Toward a New World Order
  - 1995: World Trade Organization (WTO) formed
  - 2002: American FDA approved the VeriChip (human implanted microchip for electronic ID)

The last entry seemed to be pulsing on the screen.

He was anxious—it was the kind of anxious that ruins your appetite with the potential of changing your sleep habits. Max called it "nervous plus". Going forward, there would be no way to separate him from what was over the top TMI, and he knew it. His gut was telling him things were going to get ugly. Bob had taken on the big guys, only he didn't know it yet—or was in denial.

Laura fixed him some leftover pasta. The pasta and Laura settled both his stomach and his head. She had been Googling pasta dishes. His eye rested on the words grilled shrimp. Perhaps they were entering a new phase of culinary experimentation. Since Laura and the range remained at odds, he guessed he would be doing the grilling.

"Max?"

"Yes, Honey."

"That Eleanor Crosby, the woman on the Rod Larson show..."

"Yes..."

"Well, she's going to be in Seattle next month. You keep saying we need to get away. What do you think about going to hear her in person?"

"I'm not sure..."

"Well, Dana said she'll go with me if you don't want to."

That was the last thing Max wanted—he didn't want Laura out of his sight, much less away. "I didn't say I wouldn't go, I just said I want to think about it."

"Well, think fast, Maxwell. I'm Googling hotels. I need to know if I need a king-sized bed or twin beds." She flashed him a smile, followed by a wink.

Driving back to work Max decided Laura was either the master manipulator of all time, or simply gifted in a unique way; only he already knew she was gifted.

They were going to Seattle.

He decided he would make the trip their honeymoon.

~~~

Back at work he punched "VeriChip" into his search bar.

An article in the World Net Daily popped up.

"LIFE WITH BIG BROTHER"
Deal forged to equip VeriChip with GPS
Deal forged to equip VeriChip with global positioning satellite
Posted: December 23, 2004
1:00 am Eastern
© 2010 WorldNetDaily.com

Setting the stage for controversial tracking technology, the satellite telecommunications company *ORBCOMM* has signed an agreement with VeriChip Corp., maker of the world's first implantable radio frequency identification microchip. VeriChip, a subsidiary of Applied Digital, will work with ORBCOMM to develop and market new military, security and health-care applications in the U.S. and around the world, the company said.

As *World Net Daily reported*, Applied Digital has created and successfully field-tested a prototype of an implant for humans with GPS, or global positioning satellite, technology.

Once inserted into a human, it can be tracked by GPS technology and the information relayed wirelessly to the Internet, where an individual's location, movements and vital signs can be stored in a database for future reference.

"ORBCOMM's relationship with VeriChip provides yet another new and important industry that will use the ORBCOMM satellite system and its ground infrastructure network to transmit messages globally," ORBCOMM CEO Jerry Eisenberg said.

Initially, after privacy concerns and verbal protests over *marketing the technology* for *government use*, Applied backed away from public discussion about such implants and the possibility of using them to usher in a cashless society.

In addition, to quell *privacy concerns*, the company *issued numerous denials*, stating it had no plans for implants.

When WND reported in April 2002 that the company planned such implant technology, Applied Digital spokesman Matthew Cossolotto accused WND of *intentionally printing falsehoods*.

Less than three weeks later, however, the company issued a *press release* announcing that it was accelerating development on a GPS implant.

The article showed a picture of a man sitting in front of a large computer screen with the caption: Satellites monitored 24 hours a day from ORBCOMM's Network Control Center in Dulles, Va. (photo courtesy: ORBCOMM)

The next site provided something he found chilling; the former Speaker of the House was on the VeriChip board.

He supposed that he had to see it for himself. And, there it was in bold print, confirming the fears of many. The VeriChip was in the works in one form or another since 2002 and had been approved by the FDA. He did a search on the VeriChip and found over eight hundred thousand possible hits.

It was too close for comfort; way too close.

Max decided he wanted to skip the gourmet lunch Bob catered in for his team. He wasn't hungry, and he needed a break from his self-imposed obsession that had made his head spin. He wished he could talk to Laura about their new client; it seemed like more than a coincidence how her findings on Google paralleled the Dobson case.

He wondered who was influencing who.

~~~

"What exactly do you think you're doing?"

Max jumped at the sound of Bob Murphy's voice. "Hey, you startled me!" He said defensively. Bob was standing behind him. Max had been so engrossed that Bob walked into his office without him even noticing.

"I asked you a question." Bob was unusually curt.

"I'm not sure. Well, actually it was my wife that inspired me. She Googles everything, and it is amazing what she comes up with. I thought if I did some poking I could get my head around what Jeremy's wife may have been on to—so I decided to do some of my own research." He handed a file folder of print-outs to Bob.

"Would you mind telling me where the chip that Dobson brought is now?" Max asked him, curious to hear Bob's answer.

"...in my office."

"It's in your office?" He was incredulous.

"Yes, Max. I repeat—it's-in-my-office!" Bob sounded edgy.

"Do you think we should tell the team about this? I mean, perhaps it isn't one that's fully loaded, but it could be. How will we know? Obviously someone knows we have it. This article is old. It says that they are being programmed to do all sorts of stuff. Wait until you see what their potential is."

Bob didn't comment. He wasn't sure about anything these days.

"Bob, what I'm accessing on the internet is basically public knowledge. Is it possible there's a lot more information under wraps? If our security is tight, wouldn't theirs have to be better?"

For once Bob didn't have a ready answer. And, he knew he should have one; he should have taken more time to consider taking on this job. How could he have not realized the potential for disaster when Jeremy Dobson told him what he wanted them to do—and admitted the evidence was stolen?

He grabbed the file out of Max's hands, turned abruptly, marching into his office, slamming the door behind him leaving Max alone with his thoughts—and they weren't good. He'd never seen Bob look worried before. That in itself was unnerving.

He glanced at his watch, wishing it was time to go home.

CHAPTER 35

Eleanor was preparing for her meeting in Seattle.

The Seattle event would be the second to the last event she would hold. She didn't have a plan for what would happen after New York, but God left her little room for doubt that it would be her last meeting. She began to write down some thoughts; she wrote as though she was writing her audience a letter.

Dear ones,

The time is short.

The Bible gives us many clues about how we will know it is the close of the age. Bear in mind the world does not end; that is not what the scriptures say. The King of Heaven will return to rule and reign, and he will do it from the Holy City. At that time, the earth will be restored to how it was meant to be; the way it was in Eden in the beginning.

But for the moment, we need to be sober, vigilant, and to be prepared. I am here to remind you to get ready, and you are here because you have questions about the events that we see taking place and try to discern what they mean; because you want to know how to prepare for what is to come.

The time is short, and there is much work to be done.

The Scriptures give many examples of signs that should warn us of the coming end of the age. Six such signs are given by Jesus, two characteristics are given by Paul, and eleven other occurrences are given by the prophets, who prophesied about events that would occur prior to or soon after the end of the age.

While we are also told in scripture that we will not know the time of the End of the Age, God obviously wanted us to be alert to the signals that would occur around us. As some Christian Churches are sucked into the interfaith movement, and other churches go into isolation, perhaps God knew it would take a few significant signs to wake us up, and remind us that we have work to do. We are approaching the end of the age; not the end of the world.

Unfortunately, many Christians take the verses that we won't know the time of his coming to mean they should ignore any and all scripture that might warn us of this time of tribulation. Others have fallen into the trap of fearing being labeled a conspiracy theorist should they display an interest in the Biblical prophecies about our future on Earth. My philosophy is actually quite straightforward. God included it in the Bible and, since God is all knowing, we should presume that it is something we should be aware of and study along with the rest of His Word.

God tells us in Isaiah 46:9-10, *"For I am God, and there is no other. For I am God, and there is none like me, declaring the end from the beginning, and from ancient time's things that are not yet done ... "*

And in Isaiah 34:16 he says, *"Search from the book of the Lord and read -'Not one of these [prophecies] shall fail; not one shall lack her mate..."*

Next, I am going to ask you to distrust everything I have told you. When you leave today, make it your goal to try to prove me wrong.

I believe that the Holy Spirit will show you into the truth. Ask him to do that. I seek truth, and if you are seeking the same, the Lord will confirm to each of us what is true. Individually, we have an obligation to guard each other against error, and I am no exception. Eternity is knocking at the door, and what we must be committed to, is following what is true. It is time people unite, and not create division.

Now let's see what Jesus has to say about the days that will lead up to His return.

Mat 24:3-9 (NIV) *As Jesus was sitting on the Mount of Olives; the disciples came to him privately. "Tell us," they said, "when will this happen, and what will be the sign of your coming and of the end of the age?" Jesus answered: "Watch out that no one deceives you. For many will come in my name, claiming, 'I am the Christ,' and will deceive many. You will hear of wars and rumors of wars, but see to it that you are not alarmed. Such things must happen, but the end is still to come. Nation will rise against nation, and kingdom against kingdom. There will be famines and earthquakes in various places. All these are the beginning of birth pains. Then you will be handed over to be persecuted and put to death, and you will be hated by all nations because of me."*

C.S. Lewis wrote: "God will invade. But I wonder whether people who ask God to interfere openly and directly in our world quite realize what it will be like when He does. When that happens, it is the end of the world. When the author walks on to the stage, the play is over.

"God is going to invade, all right, but what benefit is it to say you are on His side then, when you see the whole natural universe melting away like a dream and something else - something it never entered your head to conceive - comes crashing in; something so beautiful to some of us and so terrible to others that none of us will have any choices left? For this time, it will be God without disguise; something so overwhelming that it will strike either irresistible love or irresistible horror into every creature. It will be too late then to choose your side. That will not be the time to choose; it will be the time when we discover which side we truly have chosen, whether we realized it before or not.

"Now, today, this moment, is our chance to prepare and share the gift of Christ's redemption with others. I believe that God, in His mercy, is holding back His judgment to give us that chance. That is a gift of his longsuffering towards us and will not go on forever. I believe the choice becomes clearer with each passing hour."

She paused from her writing, the C.S. Lewis quote seeming prophetic in light of what was happing worldwide. Interesting, she thought.

Normally she would not have prepared any notes, much less write out most of her talk, although every meeting was taped and could be transcribed into written form. But, this time she was giving her audience a summary of her what she said, so they could dig through the scriptures for truth.

"Question until you get the answers. And when you get them, question again." She quoted out loud, thinking of her friend.

The longer she lived the more questions she had.

CHAPTER 36

Lindsay was being stalked. Even though she recognized it, she was still terrified. Fear met her everywhere, but it wasn't a rational fear; for her it was worse because nothing seemed rational anymore, and because of it, she was losing the battle inside her head.

Fearful imaginations pursued Lindsay day and night, upending everything she relied on for security. Something terrible had happened that was too far gone to fix. And worse, she was sure that her husband was involved. She prayed, but even that seemed futile to her; the implications were unimaginable. Day and night, night and day, the thoughts came. She knew what they said was true. *You are next, Lindsay; then Jeremy, and then your kids. You can't protect them because you'll already be dead.*

She kicked herself for not having made copies of what she'd sent Lenette. *How could I have been that stupid? What would life be like now if I hadn't noticed his briefcase? What if I hadn't needed stamps or been compelled to get those stupid notes in the mail? Could Nelson somehow know I saw the documents?* She told herself *No!* But she was tortured because there was no way for her to know for sure.

Fear had not come alone; guilt was also stalking her—awake, asleep, day in and day out, taunting her, "It was you who killed your sister, Lindsay. It might as well be you who pulled the trigger." And Lindsay believed it.

She was watching the children playing in the yard—chasing each other around in circles, playing some form of Tag. Suddenly, one of them sprinted up close to one of the others in the game, tapping him on the shoulder, and quickly dashing away, yelling over her shoulder, while running like mad in the opposite direction, "You're it!" Very briefly, the new aggressor looked confused, and then, after gathering his wits, began chasing the next victim.

The dynamics of the game changed with those words; the one being chased was now doing the chasing. The mental picture gave her a sudden chill...

What if I hadn't faxed those papers to Lenette? Her brain screamed. But she already knew the answer—it was as clear as day to her—Lenette would still be alive.

Lindsay, you're 'it', she thought.

~~~

The sound of Maryellen's minivan honking from the driveway jolted Lindsay back to reality. She told the babysitter she was leaving and ran outside, grateful for her mind to have the opportunity to saturate in something hopeful. Today was their Eleanor Crosby Bible study.

"You look awful."...words from a friend; words only a true friend could say to you and not have to be forgiven for.

"You don't; you look great. Let's talk about you instead of me, okay?" Lindsay stuck her tongue out at her friend, trying to smile and failing.

Maryellen reached over to touch her friend's arm. "Are you alright? Be honest—and, you know me too well; let's do talk about me..."

Her comment made Lindsay laugh, and it was a welcome sound to them both. Maryellen was the most sincere, honest, and kindhearted person Lindsay had ever known...and also the funniest. Lindsay sighed, wishing she could share her fears with her. But, she loved her far too much to draw her into the web of intrigue that was sucking her family into its sticky embrace. "No, I'm not okay, but I don't want to talk about it."

Sensing she was close to tears, Maryellen let it go. She knew that her manner came across pushy, but Lindsay had accepted that about her long ago. She would talk to her about it when she was ready.

They arrived at the study and took two chairs toward the back of the room. Heads turned to check out who had come in; they had missed the coffee and fellowship time, not that either of them cared.

This was the ninth week of Eleanor Crosby's study on "The Book of the Revelations of Jesus Christ".

The group's facilitator, Susan Green, walked to the podium. "Let's pray," she said. "Lord God, I thank you for each woman here, brought here today because you arranged it. Enlarge our spirits to receive what you have to say to us. Amen."

Maryellen looked up and playfully nudged Lindsay, saying, "The time is short..." quoting Eleanor Crosby's signature motto. Lindsay turned as white as chalk.

~~~

"Before we begin our study," Susan said, "I have good news to share, and I have bad news." She had their attention.

"First, I want to remind you that in November Eleanor Crosby is scheduled to hold her last event in New York City at Madison Square Garden. That is only four months away." She waited for the hum of voices to stop. "I spoke with her niece last evening. It will indeed be her last event. Her long-standing bible studies are being given advanced notice, so we can get our tickets early. I have already reserved a block of rooms at the Marriott Hotel on Times Square for out group. The meetings are free, but the group rate at the Marriot will cover meals and transportation if you don't want to take a car." She gave them a few seconds to process the information, before adding, "I think we need to call this 'Be there or be square'." It took a moment, but her pun earned a deserved groan.

She concluded, "Eleanor's retiring from speaking is the bad news, so we got that out of the way first. She wanted me to assure you that she is well, and the word for her to quit came from the Holy Spirit. The good news is that the event will be simulcast in one hundred and fifty different cities around the country and more overseas. Those of us who have been involved in her studies over the years have been asked to get the word out; starting immediately. She wants us to agree in prayer for millions worldwide to turn out for this event "And, the best news is that her studies will go on."

Maryellen leaned over, "I think we should go to New York, don't you?" Lindsay was too tired to argue; she agreed.

Susan began again, ignoring the buzz..."I think we need to read this week's lesson in its entirety before we begin; would one of you please do the honor?"

A voice from somewhere in front began to read, *"Revelation 13: And the dragon stood on the shore of the sea. And I saw a beast coming out of the sea. He had ten horns and seven heads, with ten crowns on his horns, and on each head a blasphemous name. The beast I saw resembled a leopard, but had feet like those of a bear and a mouth like that of a lion. The dragon gave the beast his power and his throne and great authority. One of the heads of the beast seemed to have had a fatal wound, but the fatal wound had been healed. The whole world was astonished and followed the beast. Men worshiped the dragon because he had given authority to the beast, and they also worshiped the beast and asked, "Who is like the beast? Who can make war against him?"*

The beast was given a mouth to utter proud words and blasphemies and to exercise his authority for forty-two months. He opened his mouth to blaspheme God, and to slander his name and his dwelling place and those who live in heaven. He was given power to make war against the saints and to conquer them. And he was given authority over every tribe, people, language and nation. All inhabitants of the earth will worship the beast—all whose names have not been written in the book of life belonging to the Lamb that was slain from the creation of the world. He who has an ear let him hear. If anyone is to go into captivity, into captivity he will go. If anyone is to be killed with the sword, with the sword he will be killed. This calls for patient endurance and faithfulness on the part of the saints. Then I saw another beast, coming out of the earth. He had two horns like a lamb, but he spoke like a dragon. He exercised all the authority of the first beast on his behalf, and made the earth and its inhabitants worship the first beast, whose fatal wound had been healed. And he performed great and miraculous signs, even causing fire to come down from heaven to earth in full view of men. Because of the signs he was given power to do on behalf of the first beast, he deceived the inhabitants of the earth. He ordered them to set up an image in honor of the beast that was wounded by the sword and yet lived. He was given power to give breath to the image of the first beast, so that it could speak and cause all who refused to worship the image to be killed. He also forced everyone, small and great, rich and poor, free and slave, to receive a mark on his right hand or on his forehead, so that no one could buy or sell unless he had the mark, which is the name of the beast or the number of his name. This calls for wisdom. If anyone has insight, let him calculate the number of the beast, for it is the number 666."

Lindsay leaned over to Maryellen; she was trembling. "I think I am going to be sick." She whispered. "Don't come with me. I want to be by myself."

Maryellen let her go, resisting the impulse to follow her. In the end, she acknowledged that everyone's journey was singular.

CHAPTER 37

Bob Murphy stayed late at the office, needing time alone to think. He was watching the sun setting over the Tualatin Mountains; he'd forgotten how beautiful the sunsets were from his office; watching while the colors changed from the rose and yellow afterglow into shades of lavender and deep purple. *Night comes next;* he thought.

His mood was somber. He had been taking a personal inventory; his life experiences were extraordinary—he had an MBA from Amherst, a judicial internship, acceptance into the CIA foreign program, three years living in the Middle East, his gorgeous wife, his own plane, boats, travel, all the expensive toys, and having established one of the top three research consulting firms in the country—they had no kids, but that had been a mutual decision. A family would have tied them down, and up until today he had believed his best years were still ahead of him. He was not someone with a long bucket list.

He tried to think of someone he could trust to help him; one of his contacts in the FBI or the CIA. But, no—they would distance instantly, and perhaps, once they knew what was in his possession—what his research team was pursuing—they would compromise him even more. There was no doubt—they would because they had to. That part wasn't even in the small print.

Unwittingly, Jeremy Dobson had set him up in as perfect a scenario as any legitimate could hope for. Governments toppled because of set-ups this brilliant but never accidentally. Dobson had, with a handshake, turned something over to him that compromised Bob's firm, his team, everyone who worked for him—their lives and their families' lives. Bob relied on his instincts, and he was never wrong—until now. He hadn't seen this one coming.

Everything he had ever worked for was compromised because of one little glass chip; its origin a mystery, but the origin, he knew, would lead them to Big Brother. But, too late for that—Big Brother already knew about the chip; he knew who had it, and he knew precisely where it was.

This was no science fiction movie; it was the real deal.

"Big Brother's watching you," he said to himself out loud, grimacing, and looking around.

He glanced at his cell phone, wondering at what its true capability might be. It wasn't something he, or anyone else, had given much thought to until recently. To think that the public had been paying to carry something around that, very likely, had the capability to keep track of just about everything they said and did. All that, and they say it kills brain cells, too. He thought.

Kids today grew up with them; they had no memory of what life was like when you didn't carry one. People on welfare got them—they were being supplied by the government at taxpayer expense. He wondered why that fact hadn't troubled him before now.

Big Brother was already watching, and when the world woke up it would be too late. The thought struck him funny; he and his wife had gone to bed with theirs for years, and when they got up in the morning they were the first things they grabbed—before a cup of coffee.

One thing Bob understood was that everything was disposable for the higher good. No individual retained value once the system was compromised. It was historically true of all governments, but this existed above governments, and to use the current administrations overused platitude, it was "too big to fail".

The inner circles of secret keepers knew who was expendable were the plan threatened. They wouldn't fail, because they would be who chose who would rise and who would fall. The ebb and flow and rise and fall had been happening for hundreds of years, waiting for everything to be perfectly positioned for the necessary, and final, catastrophe that would bring everything else down with it. And, they were patient...

His cell phone rang, interrupting his downward spiral of thoughts. It was his wife. "Hi, Martha... Sorry I didn't call to let you know I'd be late... I didn't mean to worry you... No, I haven't eaten... That would be great... I love you, too." God, he hoped she was out of the loop.

The people at the top would be hardened, calculating, and merciless; either they had something in their grey matter that made them unique in that way, or they were lacking the compassion gene. It was a different, controlled kind of ruthlessness. That's why he'd gotten out.

It had always seemed surreal, at the level of espionage he'd operated in, how you could look someone straight in the eye, lie to them, assuming that everything they said to you was as likely a lie, still accepting that you both were invested in the idea you could walk away, each having gained something. The best part of the experience was walking away— literally walking away. Some didn't.

The chip residing in his desk drawer was sophisticated and tied into a very intricate network. He knew there would be an immediate reaction on the master computer system once the GPS zoned in, and his firm's name popped up. Anyone who left the CIA after being in clandestine operations would forever be retained as a Hot File. He would be presumed guilty immediately; he would be assumed as dangerous because he knew how it worked...

He had heard a story once—in a sermon if he remembered right—it had been presented in the context of swimming near a drain. In its original context, the analogy was directed towards ones spiritual life, but it fit. The idea was to stay outside of the gravitational pull of the drain; otherwise it would slowly seduce you into its pull—if you didn't remain alert you would be drawn in without realizing it.

It never occurred to him that he might one day have to save himself, much less anyone else. But, he could feel the downward pull of the vortex and its pull had become irresistible.

He didn't think a lifejacket would make any difference at that point. He didn't have one.

CHAPTER 38

For Jeremy, the grim fact remained, that no matter how things ultimately fell out, he would still have enormous legal and moral culpability. Chances were, he could craft some story about finding it, how he found it, and what was or wasn't in it when he found it. Worst yet, whatever excuses he came up with would be lies. So, even if in the beginning, they believed an intruder took it when they rigged Lenette's car, the chip would lead them back to him. Of course, he hoped that when that time came he would tell the truth, but who'd believe anyone could be that stupid?

They would believe him or not, but, explaining how it got to Bob Murphy would be what nailed him. Every layer of fabrication threatened to take him further down a path that fully compromised his belief system. He wondered how litigators could live with all of the rationalized subtleties of what percentage of doctored truth equaled a lie. Without Bob Murphy on his side Jeremy might never find out what was behind Lenette's death. Perhaps that is why the case was handled so sloppily. Could it be possible they had figured out he withheld the evidence? But, he already knew the answer. He was a little fish. Killing him or Lindsay would serve no purpose other than to draw more attention to Lenette's murder. Nelson either; he might just disappear. They were all little fish. Jeremy surmised they would wait to do something extravagant.

When he wasn't obsessing over the what if's, he realized that, for the first time since Lenette's death, it seemed he might have a future. The sluggish, futile dragging himself through each day had changed. Once he handed Lenette's briefcase over to Bob Murphy, he no longer felt alone in trying to figure out who was behind her death. It was comforting to know if something happened to him Bob would be vigilant to work even harder to solve the mystery.

The exchange with Bob Murphy had been accomplished by transferring the briefcase and its contents from one latex gloved hand to the other. The briefcase may not have been hermetically sealed, but neither it, nor the items inside, had been compromised by anyone else's fingerprints but his. When he left for the airport, their lab was already at work testing for anything that might provide a trail to the killer.

~~~

After a few uncomfortable days back at work Jeremy surprised everybody by telling them to take Friday afternoon off, insisting that when they returned to work on Monday he wanted to be treated normally. For some reason, it worked. The following Monday felt as though a cloud had lifted for all concerned.

Jeremy's pastor had offered Jeremy as much time as he needed to talk through what he had experienced, sensing that Jeremy needed a listening ear, and another perspective to cope with his emotional apathy. He simply listened, allowing Jeremy to be vulnerable about his lack of emotions, helping Jeremy prepare for a possible outpouring of delayed grief later.

Rebecca, also, had her good and bad days. When she experienced a bad day, like Jeremy, she just plowed through. After the move, she confessed to Jeremy that moving into the house had been the hardest thing she had ever done in her life. Although she had no attachments to where she had been living, taking Lenette's place in the household seemed wrong to her, and she worried that every single thing she did would remind her that it should be her daughter doing it instead of her. But, what she found instead was that as the days passed there was an intimacy with Lenette's memory because she could walk in her footprints and could appreciate the joys of each day for her; it was an unexpected communion.

For her and Jeremy both the cherub baby was the gift that got them through. His halo of blonde hair and bright blue eyes were credited to his mommy—there could be no more arguments about whose gene pool had won. Rebecca was, however, adamant that he favored his daddy in his temperament.

Caleb was fussy about being clean and having things in order. He did not like to be messy nor did he have any tolerance for dirty diapers or dirty hands. He also had preferences in how she fed him; which bowl, which cup, which spoon. Rebecca was laughing one day after she had to totally reapproach mealtime with the right combination of utensils. She told Jeremy that Lenette and Lindsay had no problem eating off the floor. Not so, Caleb!

The baby's disposition was happy. Caleb rarely cried. He was a vocal baby, with an infectious giggle, and he found a lot to giggle about. Jeremy and Rebecca forged a bond because of him, sharing in caring for his needs before their own while helping each other with their loss by speaking often of Lenette with no apology.

Somewhere, in the back of his mind, Jeremy tucked away his

concerns over what was inside the brief case; sometimes able to go a day without thinking about it. He didn't know if that was normal or not. When the thoughts surfaced again he figured it was likely he would be told in therapy later that his pushing the thoughts aside was some kind of deferment—a denial of sorts; an attempt to push the realities of what Lenette had involved herself back—a denial that there might be someone still lurking outside—perhaps right outside.

CHAPTER 39

"Laura, what did you spend your money on?" Max asked her one evening after dinner.

"You mean, like, yesterday?"

"No. What did you spend it on before we got married?"

"Me."

"What does that mean?"

"It means that I spent it on myself. Why are you asking me that?" She was feeling defensive.

"But, on what?" Max asked her, again.

"I don't understand what you're asking me. Why does it matter?"

Max pressed her for an answer. "I'm asking you what you spent your money on. You came here with two boxes of pottery, some dishes, and workout clothes. And, you said most of the pottery was left to you by your grandmother. You didn't own a car or a computer, you lived in a partly furnished apartment, and you had no savings."

"Oh."

"So, can I ask you what you made in a year?" He softened his tone, sensing he was upsetting her.

"I don't know."

"But, how could you not know?"

"I just spent it. It would come in and I'd spend it. I didn't keep lists."

"What do you mean by "lists"?

"Well, you know, like who would pay me what. It didn't matter. I would only spend money if I had it. If I didn't have it I couldn't spend it, could I? I was paid in cash, so I kept my money in an envelope."

"You kept it in an envelope?" He asked, incredulous. "And you are telling me that you have no idea at all what you made?"

"Huh?"

"You didn't report your income or pay any taxes?"

"No. I never got a bill."

"Didn't you wonder about that?"

"No. Why should I?"

"And, you didn't think anything at all about ever owing the government any money?"

"No. I thought that was only for rich people."

CHAPTER 40

Daily, multiple bags of mail were delivered to Rod Larson's office; the amount of mail markedly increased because of the two-hour special with Eleanor Crosby. Rod's staff was overwhelmed at the continuum of emails, not to mention what continued to come in on Twitter and Facebook.

Each piece of mail would need to be opened because of the valuable tips and information some contained, others were supportive, or voiced concern for Rod and his family, and there would always be the ones that were septic. When he thought about the information lifeline his show had become for so many, he realized that he and Eleanor weren't the only ones who felt like they were walking a plank over a sea of sharks.

One evening, he took a bag of mail home for Jenna, who said she felt left out when he told her about the volume of mail that was coming in. "Oh isn't this exciting?" She exclaimed to their children when he entered the house, dragging the bag behind him with exaggerated drama.

He and Jenna retired to their bedroom early, with the mail bag that Rod promptly emptied on their bed. Jenna put on her pajamas preparing for a late night of mail sorting with Rod positioned across from her in his arm chair. His feet were resting on the ottoman with his iPad in his lap, informing her that while she opened mail he would be going over his bullet points for his program the following day.

Jenna scolded him, "Rod, for the hundredth time, I don't like it when you call them 'bullet points'." *One for Jenna*, he though, amused.

She began tearing into the mail; "Rod, listen to this. 'Rod, our family prays for you every night. Thank God for what you are doing. We know you pray a price for it.'"

She read through several before interrupting him again. "Here's another good one, 'Whoa! Enough already! My brain hurts! You're doing a great job, man! P.S. I think people should stock up on batteries; they could be worth more than currency if things go down—pass that on!'"

"Not a bad idea," Rod agreed.

"Yeah, I think a barn full of extra-soft Charmin makes sense for us." Jenna grinned at him; Rod was extremely particular about his toilet paper.

She continued reading, "Dear Mr. Larson, I thank you for helping us to see the other side of the story. We record all of your shows and invite our neighbors over to watch them later. Slowly, they're coming around. It isn't much, but it is a whole lot more than we were doing a year ago."

Another said, "Rod, I used to be open to listening to all kinds of different opinions from people. I thought I was being tolerant. Now, I ask people for their resume when they start with the liberal bull. When they ask what I mean by that I tell them, "I want to know what you have done on behalf of your opinions". If they don't have any scars to show me for standing up for their beliefs, as far as I'm concerned their opinion is only talk. If they can prove they stuck their necks out to defend them, I'll listen. It's like the verse, 'Faith without works is dead.' Who needs a dead opinion? Those people have a surprise coming, and you are waking some of them up. Thanks for what you do!"

Jenna piped in, "Rod, that's a great idea. You should challenge people to do that on the show next week—put that in your bullet points."

"Don't call them "bullet points", he retorted.

She ignored him and read another one, "Dear Rod, I never took any interest in politics before. I'm a Christian; my church is apolitical, so I'm actually discouraged from actively participating in politics. There is a trend towards what my minister is calling "The Emergent Church". The concept is for everyone to be ultimately tolerant and embracing of all beliefs, including accepting there are many paths to God, but still retaining being Christian. (Does that even make sense?) My pastor is for it, but I don't feel good about it. Please address this on your show. Could that be the trend Ms. Crosby calls the apostate church? Is there something else I should be watching for?"

"Wow, Rod. That is a scary thought." Jenna said. "It sounds scarier when you hear about it from someone who's caught up in it happening to them."

Rod reached for his bible, turning to Second Timothy 4:3, "*For the time will come when they will not endure sound doctrine, but according to their own desires, because they have itching ears, they will heap up for themselves teachers, and they will turn their ears away from the truth, and to be turned aside to fables.*'

"Jenna, that's the reason I've devoted so much air time for Eleanor's interviews. The viewer who wrote that has an advantage because she's been warned and is waking up to the agenda. People like her will sound the alarm to others.

"If we are in the last days we need to be ready. If we are wrong about what is currently happening, heck, we still need to be ready! Either way, God is using some of us to call the alarm, so there must be a reason.

And, instead of losing viewers, we have increased our viewing audience by nearly 30 percent since the first interview with Eleanor.

"I think the media's spinning information and covering up much of it has caused more people to question the difference between truth and fiction. If our viewers are an indication, people are screaming for us to give them the tools to decipher between what they hear, or suspect, for themselves. I can only take them so far in one hour each day.

"There is a great quote from Daniel Webster I wrote in my Bible." He flipped to the front page, "'If religious literature is not widely circulated among the masses in this country, I do not know what is going to become of us as a nation. If truth be not diffused, error will be; if God and His Word are not known and received, the devil and his works will gain the ascendancy; if the evangelical volume does not reach every hamlet, the pages of a corrupt and licentious literature will; if the power of the gospel is not felt throughout the length and breadth of the land, anarchy and misrule, degradation and misery, corruption and darkness, will reign without mitigation or end.'"

"Do you remember how Eleanor showed us how if you chart all of the verses in the New Testament about the coming of Christ, beginning in the Gospels and reading through Revelation, how each time his coming is mentioned the immediacy increases? In the beginning, Jesus is giving signs of when he'll come, Paul's letters warn of his coming, but in the third chapter of Revelation Jesus tells John, 'I stand at the door and knock...' the verb is in the imperative. The second application of that chapter is God's warning of the church of the end of times. If that is us, then he is on the other side of the door, and we'd better be ready. Or, for those who aren't convinced his return is soon they have no excuse for not preparing their children to know the signs. One generation will play this thing out, and the torch will be passed. The stage is being set."

Jenna was quiet for a moment. "Rod, we need to pray for this country. We don't pray enough."

They both got on their knees beside the bed. Rod began, reciting the nation's anthem out loud.

O! Say can you see by the dawn's early light,
what so proudly we hailed at the twilight's last gleaming,
whose broad stripes and bright stars through the perilous fight,
o'er the ramparts we watched, were so gallantly streaming.
And the rockets' red glare, the bombs bursting in air,
Gave proof through the night that our flag was still there;
O! Say does that Star - Spangled Banner yet wave,
o'er the land of the free and the home of the brave?
O! Thus be it ever, when freemen shall stand

Between their loved home and the war's desolation!
Blest with victory and peace, may the heav'n rescued land
Praise the Power that hath made and preserved us a nation.
Then conquer us must, when our cause it is just,
and this be our motto: "In God is our trust."
And the Star - Spangled Banner in triumph shall wave
o'er the land of the free and the home of the brave!
Together, they prayed for their country and for those God was rising
up for the last days.

"Jenna, we follow Christ's banner no matter where it leads."

She nodded solemnly, "No matter where..."

"If something happens you'll know where to find me."

"If something happens I will probably be joining you shortly."

He kissed her, admiring her stalwart faith. They held each other tight. They firmly believed every time they held each other was a gift. Rod knew too much to think otherwise.

CHAPTER 41

Nelson was putting things in order; his urgency prompted by the flood of communications that had started coming into their office from seemingly everywhere on the globe. The top brass had been summoned for an emergency meeting in Brussels, and the meeting was rumored as BIG. The list of those attending included past and present world leaders, top executives in select industries, media moguls, and names that only a scant few would recognize because their influence was silent but ultimately powerful. Something significant was going down.

The World Health Organization, or FEMA, would issue the order when it was time to bring out the hibernating micro-chips, although that wouldn't happen immediately. The printed currency was printed, and waiting for distribution. It was intended to be a psychological tool, intended to move the masses past the initial panic of the changes that were coming. Everything, including all buying and selling, would ultimately be monitored by the chip, making currency obsolete. And, for those who would oppose, the indoctrination camps were set up and ready.

By now all of the small local banks had been swallowed up into the larger ones. One by one their obituaries had been listed in the Friday papers, their epitaphs buried on the back pages—it could never have been accomplished without a complicit media. Only people in the industry were keeping track of them now; the public had lost interest.

Things like class warfare, border issues, growing unemployment, war in the Middle East, unrest in the streets, the threat of terrorism, increasing attacks on the Christian right—those were the stories the media used to keep the public off track. The issues of cutting welfare and losing so-called entitlements had their desired effect, increasing racial tensions and stirring up unrest with the nation's youth. That was assisted by Mother Nature, who'd thrown in some natural disasters of her own that added credibility to the environmental frenzy, also serving as a distraction. All of it together made it necessary for more controls to be imposed on the populace—more regulations that were accepted without a whimper, except but by a few.

Each distraction worked to provide a smoke screen while the banks were gradually, and for all practical purposes, being nationalized, and the large banks were already positioned under the giant umbrella of The World Bank. It was a pity for the owners of small banks. When the housing market crashed the first time small, local banks were weighed down with large percentages of bad loans that had resulted in foreclosures, and those resulted from the loans they had been pressured to extend to a consumer who would ultimately be unable to repay their debt—creating the bubble. The OCC issued reprimand letters to the troubled banks with exhaustive lists of demands they were expected to meet in order to have their ratings restored. The regulators swarmed all over them.

Because of all of the losses on their balance sheets, capital infusions by their investors were required. If the capital couldn't be raised a bank was sold, or seized. The banks and their stockholders screamed "Hidden Agenda", which was, of course, denied. The little guys were being sucked dry while the big guys got the bailouts and rewarded themselves at the expense of the taxpayer. The recession's second dip sealed their fate.

Companies like Levy and Sinclair all got bailouts—big ones, and the guys at the top got obscene bonus's. It was decreed they were "Too big to fail". Having friends in high places paid off, but there was a price—they were now part of the plan.

There was a price tag; going along made them complicit.

In the beginning, the local bank closings were news, spurred on because the public wanted a scapegoat. Bankers were stereotyped as whores who had gotten rich off the backs of the workers. So the small banks took the brunt of it because they were the face that made banking personal, so it took the attention away from the larger institutions. That was important, because the small banks sold the papers, and, in the end, it was GMAC, Wells Fargo, Bank of America, or someone else who held it, and they were faceless. The bailouts quickly ceased to merit front page status of the financial section, with "out of sight out of mind" being their goal, and the evening news focused on the news of the day.

The public remained in denial by choice. Judgment day was deferred by an illusion; the balloon mortgage rates came due, and the mortgagee's couldn't pay. The small banks got the used goods back; their burned creditors blamed them for their lowered credit scores, and for lending them the money in the first place. It was the proverbial "passing of the devalued buck" from every side.

From the other end, the regulators upped the percentage levels of the capital the banks were required to have on hand. Many couldn't raise the necessary capital; which forced them to be taken over or closed. Of course, the capital put in by the owners and investors was sucked into a black hole, leaving them no way to recover it. Fortunes were lost, but only a few took notice, outside of those affected. If anything, the public had been programmed to have no sympathy for the greedy bankers.

Regulators further demanded the smaller institutions write down their commercial real estate loans to cut back their exposure. No bank could survive without doing commercial loans. The plan was insidious; when the collateral was liquidated, every loan on their books would be undermined.

Thomas Jefferson said, foreseeing a day when corrupt large banks controlled the wealth, "I believe that banking institutions are more dangerous to our liberties than standing armies. If the American people ever allow private banks to control the issue of their currency, first by inflation, then by deflation, the banks and corporations that will grow up around the banks will deprive the people of all property - until their children wake-up homeless on the continent their fathers conquered."

The smaller, independent banks had no power, but once were the lifeline to small towns, and communities, except now, large and faceless institutions were sitting on the nation's money. The irony became the inability for the average person to get a loan while being taunted with the historically low interest rates.

If Nelson thought about it too much it overwhelmed him. The only hopeful part of it was that his reawakened conscience might indicate he had a soul—lost perhaps, but a soul nonetheless.

He finished printing off copies of his "To Whom It May Concern letters." One he would put in his desk at home, along with the code to his safe and a key to his safety deposit box. When the dominoes fell, he knew the safety deposit boxes would become inaccessible; for safe measure, he put a substantial amount of gold coins in their safe, although he doubted they would be worth much. Another irony was how Jeremy and Lenette ad got it right; batteries and water purifiers would be worth more in the end because they could be traded. *The homing pigeons were my idea,* he thought wryly.

Through tears, he wrote personal letters to each of his children, wishing he had the guts to say what he was writing in person; the letters were a grim reminder of how he barely knew them. In his letter to Lindsay, he asked for her to ask his mother to forgive him. A man of stronger character would do it face to face, but his feelings were complicated by both regret and remorse; there were days he still thought he hated her.

One day, should he survive, perhaps he could pay someone to help him work through his issues. Left to himself, he wouldn't know where to begin.

CHAPTER 42

Candy tentatively tapped her fingernails on her aunt's bedroom door. She had something exciting to tell her.

There was no need to be tentative. "Candy, I'm awake!" her aunt answered.

"Now how did you know it was me?" Candy poked her head through the door with a big smile on her face. Eleanor was propped in up in bed, with her Bible lying open on her lap. Candy should have known; her aunt's sustenance was not food. She sat a cup of brew down on her aunt's bedside table and handed her an email that had arrived from her mother during the night. After briefly glancing at it, Eleanor took off her glasses, handing the letter back to Candy "Would you mind reading it to me?" she asked, leaning back into her pillows.

Candy sat down on the edge of the bed to read it.

Dear Candy,

We have both left a trail of voicemails (which we both hate!), so, instead, I'm writing because I want Eleanor to have it. I miss talking to you, but I know you are doing something beneficial for the Kingdom.

When I told the family about Eleanor appearing on the Rod Larson Show they were livid that she would even consider being on his show. I actually screened my phone calls for a while to avoid listening to their ranting's. Of course, much of their reaction was because of their strong feelings about Rod Larsen. I got an email from your Uncle Ed that I could only read in bits and pieces; what he said was so upsetting to me.

Anyhow, that was before the show aired. (I told your dad I was going to go to a remote island after it was over. He agreed, saying we might as well be alone on an island already since we no longer have friends or a social life.) After the program, I heard nothing from anyone—nothing; not one phone call, not even from your brothers who are never timid about telling me what they think.

THE GOOD NEWS IS THAT EVERYONE IS GOING TO BE AT THE EVENT IN SEATTLE. The show woke them up!!

They are all hooked on Rod Larson's show now, every last one of them, and they feel guilty for giving Eleanor such a hard time for so long. They asked me if I would write her for them and ask if she will accept their apology. (I know the answer to that!) Eleanor...it's a miracle! Remember when we started claiming verses for the salvation of our family all those years ago? He is faithful!!

Candy, don't forget whose daughter you are - DNA-wise. Please do call me when you have a chance.

Love to you both,

Mom & Phyllis

P.S. Eleanor, I'm sure you'll be hearing from them in person. They just wanted me to break the ice!!

Candy looked at her aunt who was predictably teary. Unexpectedly Eleanor held up her right hand.

"Girl, give me a high five. The reunion just got better!"

CHAPTER 43

The car was packed and ready to roll—the Zimmerman's were leaving for Seattle. Laura was beside herself with excitement. Max had taken three days off, plus the weekend; the trip was going to be their honeymoon!

The weekend before the trip, Max took Laura to South Waterfront, an area of shops, galleries, restaurants, live music, and entertainment—a favorite spot for tourists. It was a perfect evening. "There is something so festive about being near a waterfront!" She told him while they were strolling along the river. "Doesn't this remind you of when we met?"

When they drove home, the car was brimming with shopping bags full of things for Laura to take with her on their trip. The evening was fun and romantic, with Laura disappearing behind a curtain, and then twirling out dressed in a new combination of clothes and accessories, and Max giving her a thumb's up, or thumbs down, to signal his preference.

Everyone had the same comment. "Doesn't this remind you of the movie *Pretty Woman*?" Laura had no idea what they meant, not having yet seen the movie, but she could tell it was a good thing.

When they arrived home, she draped her new clothes over the backs of the sofa, chairs, and hung some from the doorways, her new shoes and boots she lined up on the kitchen counter.

"I don't want to go to sleep in case I wake up, and this was a dream." she said to Max.

The same thought occurred to Max most evenings.

~~~

The evening before they left for Seattle, Laura walked Burger over to Dana's. "He's going to sleep with us." Dana teased her. "Be prepared, you may not get him back." Laura hugged her friend, thankful for Dana's willingness to share herself with her.

The only thing on the Zimmerman's agenda in Seattle, besides each other, was the Eleanor Crosby event on Saturday afternoon. Since they were in no hurry to get there, Max suggested they drive the long way, along scenic back roads in the mountains. Laura packed a picnic basket, and they brought along their hiking boots, in case they wanted to do some exploring. Laura had never been on a real vacation, and she was beyond excited.

Max couldn't wait to get on the road, but his reasons weren't all as uplifting as being with Laura. He couldn't get away from Bob Murphy's dark side fast enough; he had never seen him like this before. It both worried and scared him—he was sure it had something to do with the Dobson case. Max got uneasy just thinking about it.

But, Enough of that! He told himself, turning off his cell phone and putting it in the glove box.

"Carpe Diem", he said out loud.

"Carpe Diem", she echoed. "What is that? Is that a fish? You didn't say we were going fishing."

Max turned to look at her, laughing, until he realized she wasn't kidding.

"No, Laura. No, we're not going fishing. I already caught want I wanted."

CHAPTER 44

Bob was at his desk, staring at the fingerprint analysis on the Dobson case. The only fingerprints in it were hers, with the exception of Jeremy's that were on the outside—well, and except for one other partial set; those belonged to Nelson Saunders. There was a trace amount of blood on the small manila envelope that the chip was mailed in; running a DNA test would clear that up, but it would be Saunders blood.

He had one of his analysts look up Nelson Saunders. He was a big-wig with Levy and Sinclair, the securities firm; he was also Jeremy Dobson's brother-in-law. Bob wondered he and Lenette Dobson had an affair.

He checked his notes. Lenette Dobson was into some pretty heavy activism; her laptop history indicated she was in communication with some high-level sources. How she had worked her way up and through the system that high he couldn't imagine. But, her persistence had paid off; he recognized some of the names and was impressed.

Millions of people used Google and any one of them would be able to access the same information Lenette Dobson found. Even if they connected with someone willing to cough up some inside information, that, by itself, wouldn't put them on a hit list. But, the internet had its risks. His firm didn't use Google; they had safer methods that insured their anonymity, and that weren't suspected of being in bed with the government.

Another part of the puzzle was the means of her execution. It wasn't characteristic for a government agency to be so blatant—to draw so much attention to it. Consummate professionals would have set it up to look like an accident; it was astonishing how many people simply died of natural causes, asleep beside their wives or husbands in their own beds, or out jogging, if the government wanted them dead. The government had too many resources at their disposal to chance it would get messy. Either they were desperate to stop something or his woman's death was a warning—to Nelson, perhaps? It made him wonder about the seeming urgency;

Lenette Dobson was not some high level spy.

So, that brought it back to Lindsay; back to that night in the restaurant and back to Nelson's retort to Jeremy.

"We're way ahead of you." Bob said, out loud to himself. The implication was Nelson meant his firm. *No*, Bob reasoned, *it has to be bigger than that*.

The media continued to put out a wide range of conspiracy theories of their own to keep the issue confused in hopes the public get bored with it, tuning it out entirely. Even though Bob had not connected all of the dots he was pretty sure he'd figured out most of the players.

His time working in the Middle East put him in the center of a tapestry of deceit. The tapestry would ultimately be wrapped around Israel with the hope of her extinction. Everyone hated Israel—let the Muslims be the fall guy for taking them out. He viewed the hatred of the Jews as irrational at best. But, irrational or not, there was no doubt they were hated. They should thank their lucky stars for the extremely vocal fundamental Christians who continued sticking their necks out for them— even the U.S. government was bailing.

He could only guess what the plan might be for the Jews worldwide who would remain after Israel got nuked; they would have to be dealt with. There was only one other scenario, and that was if Israel could be deceived and bought into some plan that offered them peace and they fell for it; well, that would buy them time, and they would be fools to walk away from it. But, anti-Semitism was alive and well, and their total annihilation was the preoccupation of the militant Muslims.

Bob's wife called it a spiritual war and said that the Bible was clear about who would win. "The Jews are the apple of God's eye." She told him. "God will protect them." She believed that.

Whatever, Bob thought. He stayed out of her way whenever her Bible study and end-time talk began. He loved her, he would even go to church with her on occasion, and he never objected when she wanted to give money to some Christian organization. But, her belief system was light years from his own, so all he asked of her was for her not to preach to him. Her beliefs were her convictions, and he gave her credit for that; she'd never wavered from them, even with his perpetual cynicism. *I'm a loving husband and a good citizen. God would have to have a pretty sizeable chip on His shoulder if people like me can't get in*, Bob rationalized. His arguments had only worked to make her dig in deeper.

"I'll call Nelson myself," he thought. Perhaps, if Nelson would agree to talk to him, he could peel that layer away and some of it would make sense.

~~~

Bob's call to Nelson confirmed some things. He wished he could call the team together and brainstorm, but Max was out of the office until Tuesday. He didn't want to carry it around in his head by himself all weekend, although he knew he had no choice. He could tell that Max knew something; he was acting differently. Amazingly, the others seemed oblivious to the risk they'd taken on.

Previously, when he talked to Lindsay Saunders, she told him that when she found the copies of the currency how they related back to a conversation Nelson and Jeremy had the previous autumn with her dead sister and Jeremy. It was the confirmation that the fax's represented that scared her. She told him that rather than intending to involve Lenette in something, she rather hoped that Lenette could calm her fears.

He regretted his call to Lindsay. It was clear that before his call she hadn't known Nelson knew what she'd done; Bob could tell by her reaction that she was afraid of him.

OK, he thought, *so Nelson sends Lenette the chip through the mail. Was it because she was going to pass it along to someone else...but, who? So, she ends up with it in her briefcase—but why was it in her briefcase...? Certainly it wasn't for safekeeping or she would have hidden it somewhere more secure; she was delivering it to someone. Where was she going with it the day she was shot? Carrying that chip around like that was risky.*

At one time, it was rumored the public would be barcoded, but the chip was better; once they figured out they could use it to track people it was only matter of time. It would be either FEMA or the World Health Organization that would get the job of making it happen. Bob knew the concept of programming individuals was not as far-fetched as people might think; he knew the CIA was the best place to test their potential.

He thought of a quote by Shakespeare he'd recently read, "...man, proud man, dressed in a little brief authority, most ignorant of what he's most assured..."

~~~

Bob needed a break. Maybe he could convince Martha to go boating; they both could use a change of scene. He walked over to the window to watch his people coming and going in the parking lot below. He loved how so many people were on his payroll—how they depended on him. He took satisfaction knowing that when they endorsed the backs of their checks every two weeks they had him to thank—well, and vice versa. He had a fantastic crew. He was an excellent boss.

He looked through the glass window into the outer office. His secretary caught his eye, flashing him a wide smile. He winked at her. He liked Suzie. She didn't take him seriously, but she took her job seriously.

She kept him balanced.

Suddenly, he saw her smile turn to quizzical. Her eyes widened; one hand grasping at the front of her blouse. It was then that she went limp, falling forward, and toppling across her desk like a rag doll. Bob saw several other people falling at the same time...

He moved to help them, but suddenly he couldn't breathe; it was as though his lungs were exploding—he grabbed at his own throat...

His last thought before hitting the floor was, "Hell..."

CHAPTER 45

In the beginning, before Candy became her aunt's assistant, she had spent time waiting on God to confirm to her what she should do next with her life. Every job opportunity she'd pursued after college felt wrong. But, crawling around in the back of her mind was the ever present thought that her aunt needed her.

Contrary to what either her family or the public might think, living with Eleanor Crosby was anything but boring. Once they came to an agreement Candy was swept up into a whirlwind of activity from the moment she set foot in her aunt's townhome—even their downtime was anything but boring.

When Candy first approached her Eleanor was hesitant, not wanting to assume responsibility for interrupting Candy's life. But, Candy convinced Eleanor that it was she who wanted her life interrupted—explaining how polluted she felt after watching her friends, and in particular Christian friends, who one by one had morally caved to the pressures of a culture that justified self-gratification. She watched them giving in to it, never with any sense of apology, but instead offering their defensive rationalizations of how the Judeo-Christian ethic needed to be flexible to the culture.

Candy credited her Aunt Eleanor for provoking her to live her life as if the Lord could return at any moment. Eleanor warned her, "His coming is the hope that purifies, Candy. It is what keeps us clean as believers! I wish that someone would have thrown to me when I was a captive to the culture. Once you've crossed over the line to the secular side willingly, your moral compass has been compromised. It is usually a long, disappointing, and sometimes futile road to find your way out if God isn't part of it." What gave Eleanor credibility was that she called a spade a spade and refused to whitewash the story of her own journey toward grace.

Candy could talk to Eleanor about anything. The family retained the idea that Eleanor was a prude; that she thought she was better than they were. *What a loss for them*, Candy thought; glad that she knew the real

Eleanor; she was the least judgmental person Candy knew.

She loved her job and felt especially valuable in the weeks that preceded a meeting. It was her responsibility to make sure Eleanor could shut herself away to prepare. After she came to live with Eleanor Candy couldn't imagine how she was able to be prepared before she signed on.

Once Seattle was behind them, it was to Madison Square Garden— and the spiritual battle of a lifetime.

CHAPTER 46

Prior to leaving Max told his secretary to pretend he was leaving the country. Absolutely nothing was going spoil his and Laura's long overdue honeymoon.

Laura had never experienced the drive to Seattle, so Max took his time, stopping at the scenic outlooks, convincing other travelers to take their picture, and snacking on the assortment of cheeses, fruits, crackers, and sweets Laura packed for them.

Max checked his phone one last time for message, shut it off with some fanfare, and placed it in the glove box. Thursdays were normally slow, and Friday was a down day, so he knew his secretary would only interrupt him in case of a real emergency.

Max's surprise for Laura was a suite at the Four Seasons Hotel. When the busboy opened the door, Laura clapped her hands together like an excited child. "Max, you are tooooo good to me!"

He swept her up in his arms, announcing that their honeymoon had officially begun, and that he hoped she was ready.

"Oh, I'm ready, big boy." she said with her lips on his neck.

Max tipped the Bus Boy asking him to skip the commercial. The Bus Boy was relieved when Mr. Zimmerman remembered the tip.

~~~

When Bob found out where they were going he made dinner reservations for them at Dahliah's restaurant, one of his and Martha's favorites. They'd never given them a wedding gift, so it was their treat to the newlyweds. The dinner was extraordinary; particularly since they'd worked up a healthy appetite.

Laura declined a drink, but asked if she could have a sip of Max's wine. "Mmmmmm...that's really nice." She told him. "If you want I'll order a bottle," he offered, raising his hand to get their waiter's attention.

She reached across the table, touching his hand with her fingers and shaking her head from side to side. "I won't be drinking any wine for a while." He looked at her quizzically. She was smiling.

He leaned towards her. "Laura...does this mean what I hope it means?"

"Well, if you are hoping I'm going to tell you that we're going to have a baby next spring, then you would be correct." At last it was out; she'd been waiting to tell him for weeks.

Max burst out with a loud "Yahoo!"

Suddenly she looked serious; "Max, that was why I didn't want you to buy me all those new clothes, but it would have ruined the surprise if I'd told you then!"

"Laura, we will just go shopping for more!" He and Laura were going to have a baby! Finally, everything in his life was going in the right direction.

CHAPTER 47

Caleb grinned down at his daddy, watching his exaggerated wince when a dollop of drool landed on his eyelid. Jeremy was lying on his back on the floor holding Caleb above him, playing High into the Sky—Caleb's new and favorite game. "You got me again!" Jeremy laughed, and the baby squealed back at him.

Jeremy watched while another drool bomb formed on Caleb's lips. He was beginning to wiggle and kick; his overt body language, along with some tell-tale grunting told his daddy it was time for another ride. Jeremy was looking forward to a relaxing weekend at home.

Rebecca entered the room and sat down on the sofa near where "the boys", as she called them, were playing

"Jeremy?"

"Yes."

"What's the name of the man who owns the firm you took Lenette's things to—the firm in Portland?"

Jeremy winced again, only this time it was from his regret at making her his accomplice when he told her about the briefcase. *What can I say?* He thought to himself. *It was a weak moment.*

"His name's Bob Murphy."

"You're sure? His name's Bob Murphy?"

"Yes? Why are you asking?" The bad feeling had joined them.

"He's dead." She blurted it out, not knowing how to couch it.

He turned so he could see her face. *Surely she's mistaken; how could she know?* He thought. "What did you just say?" She had his attention.

"Jeremy, he's dead. You need to turn on the television—it's all I can find on the news. Not only him, but everybody else who worked for him, too; over a hundred people."

"How, how is that possible?" Jeremy found himself stammering, feeling the adrenalin rush that was a precursor to nausea.

"Jeremy, I have a really bad feeling about this. What if this has something to do with Lenette?"

"Don't say that.' he snapped. She had to be wrong.

"I'm trying not to be scared, but they are saying one hundred and ten people just died in a mysterious manner, and it's the same firm you hired to figure out what that stuff in the briefcase meant. You and Caleb would both be dead, too, if you'd started Lenette's car. Are we going to be next? Never mind my not being scared—it's way too late for that."

"Mom, okay, I'll admit it; I'm scared, too—terrified, if you really want to know. I don't think it's wise for us to call the police and we probably should be taking walks to talk each other from now on. Reason number one is that I think the last people I could trust were just wiped out." Reason number two is, he paused for effect, "we don't currently have anyone we can call to watch the baby when we go in for our mug shots." Rebecca couldn't help but smile. She was a sucker for dry humor.

The grim news for Jeremy was no matter how things ultimately fell out he was most likely going to end up behind bars, so he may as well ride it out until the end. That would be the best case scenario; if he went to jail he wouldn't be dead. There was no getting around it— the cat would be out of the bag now for sure, once they discovered what Bob had and saw where it came from.

Bob Murphy was dead because of him. So much for rationalizing that he would go to the slammer a happy man if he got his answers. He knew he had just run into a dead end—literally. There would be no more answers.

Before leaving the room, Rebecca squatted down to look directly into Jeremy's eyes, saying in all seriousness, "Jeremy, I want you to buy me a gun."

"Good idea, Mom", he said knowing that arguing with her would be useless. "Get on the internet, do some research and then we'll get you a gun. Just beware; I won't register anything."

"Okie-dokie." She stood up. "I'm going to fix supper now. I feel better."

She handed Jeremy the remote before heading to the kitchen.

He could hear her humming while she put the finishing touches on their dinner. To think he had been concerned life with Rebecca would be boring.

CHAPTER 48

Lindsay and Nelson were watching the news in bed. He couldn't believe she hadn't banished him from the bedroom long before.

"...the White House is denying this was a terrorist attack. White House spokesman, Samuel Burns, said it was apparently a grudge-related incident. 'Mr. Murphy appears to have had made some enemies.' He is quoted as saying." They went on to speculate about Bob Murphy's time serving in the CIA.

A picture of Bob Murphy flashed across the screen. Nelson sat straight up when he recognized the face; he'd looked him up after they spoke earlier. He couldn't breathe. *I just talked to him. That's who has Lenette's briefcase. Bob Murphy has the chip.* Wherever the chip went, death followed.

Lindsay had begun tearing tiny pieces of paper off a page of the magazine she was reading. She turned to look at Nelson. "Nelson, you look funny. Did you know him?" If he looked funny, she sounded funny.

"No. I think I may have known of him. I didn't know him personally." He lied, trying to appear calm. She let out a sigh of relief.

The news continued, "...one hundred and ten people died today of mysterious causes..."

"Give me a break," Nelson blurted into the air, "suspicious causes...they were either gassed or poisoned."

"Nelson?" Lindsay chose her words carefully, not wanting to give away her own connection to Bob Murphy. "Nelson, you know more about things like this than I do—who would have the nerve to undertake something involving so many people? Won't every law enforcement agency in the country will be on this?" She hid her hands under the covers to hide their shaking.

"We can hope." Nelson answered; his voice flat.

Every agency in the world could be called in, but he knew their presence would only be to create a giant diversion away from whoever had set it up. He didn't dare look at her, or he might lose it and say too much.

Whatever hopeful thoughts Nelson tendered, wishing there might be a way to deflect attention from his family, would never return to cheer him again. Dread closed in on him, and the feeling was suffocating. He accepted that there was nowhere to go—nowhere any of them would be safe. It was the proverbial, "You can run, but you can't hide scenario." *So, why run?* He thought.

In the morning, he would transfer funds into an escrow account for his mother's nursing home expenses. He was no hero—it was her money anyhow. But, doing so would insure the transition would be smoother for her. That was another piece of the coming world order he avoided thinking about; what their plan was for the aged. The one thing that could be relied on; he knew that whatever happened to any of them would be quick, not as in merciful, but, quick, as in efficient. Even if he wouldn't be there with them, he had comfort knowing where his family would be.

I need to talk to Jeremy—fast. He must be panic stricken. He thought. Time, it appeared, had run out. He got out of bed and went downstairs to his office, locking himself in to avoid any more questions from Lindsay. He knew falling asleep would be the impossible dream going forward.

CHAPTER 49

The Murphy's Law campus was swarming with every brand of law enforcement, further sensationalized by the rainbow of flashing lights emanating from the ebb and flow of emergency vehicles. Whatever toxin was used would be elusive to pin point; the air had been tested, and tested clean; there were only some trace chemicals in the bodies—within the normal range. The agent used was one hundred percent lethal.

A local reporter was doggedly determined to land the first interview, sticking her mike in front of any face in the crowd pausing long enough for her to accomplish it. She hated it, but the only way to be promoted in television media was to be obnoxiously persistent. She was the first reporter on the scene, and her goal was to land the interview that would make her career...

Ben Cross, the chief of police, made the mistake of pausing to hitch up his pants, allowing himself to get trapped. She stuck out her microphone, optimistic that he might open up.

Get that thing away from me. He was trying to project his thoughts, and failing.

She cleared her throat and put on a concerned face for the camera, "Excuse me, Sir, would you please say your name for our viewers?"

"Ben Cross."

She persisted, "Has there been a motive established for such a horrendous crime?"

"No."

She could tell this wasn't going to be a slam-dunk. "Sir, is there anything else you would like to say to our viewers?"

His first thought was, *How about if you leave me alone before I hack you to pieces?* He settled on, "Not right now—please excuse me." Before she could ask him anything else, he had turned and walked away.

She turned and looked into the camera to assure her audience, "Well, as you can see, our law enforcement is hard at work..."

That would be the best interview anyone would get for a while. The networks would have a heyday digging into a story that had so many rabbit trails to chase—and they would chase them until another catastrophe occurred that the potential to titillate their viewers, and bump their ratings again. But, unless a tsunami hit the west coast, this one had the makings of a long run.

Dazed and bewildered relatives of the deceased began to arrive, with police personnel guiding them through the growing mass of reporters, toward a taped-off waiting area, from where they could be summoned to identify their family members. They might as well be inside a fishbowl with the growing presence of reporters circling them like sharks—snapping candid's while hollering insensitive questions at whoever they were closest to. By morning, the news outlets would have located the names and addresses of the bereaved, and camping in their front yards, looking for a few people who would be willing to sell their integrity for some quick cash and a moment in the sun.

Bob Murphy had played in the big leagues. The media would have a lot to work with once they looked up his resume.

The hearses came and went; returning and leaving again, delivering more identified bodies to the morgue; the process was expedited by it being a clean crime scene. The police chief shook his head, thankful they hadn't used machine guns; killing this many people took some finesse. He wanted no part of it—he knew some of the people; he had to remind himself it was all part of the job.

Ben liked Bob Murphy; he was one of the good guys. Bob had been willing to meet with him a few times when Ben hit a snag in a case. Ben had never thanked him. Not really. He'd paid for his beer—that was all.

CHAPTER 50

Maryellen offered Lindsay a frosty glass of cold lemonade. She took it, holding it against her cheek; the feeling of the cool glass against her warm skin brought with it a flood of memories. They were sitting at the end of the dock at the Kennedy family's lake house, watching the children swimming in the clear, blue-green water.

Lenette's death usurped their annual summer outing, so they decided to take advantage of a stretch of Indian summer and a school holiday, to get away for a long weekend. Maryellen's daughter was the same age as Lindsay's middle child, and the children had all grown up together; they were like cousins. Their moms had anticipated that their tolerance for the cold water would betray them; they could see their lips were already tinged with blue. Sun-warmed towels, cookies, and lemonade were waiting for when their chattering teeth compelled them to get out on their own.

Lindsay's father's request had been for the lake house to be kept within the family. His wish was honored, although it got little use, and suffered neglect because of it. Lindsay and Lenette had used it for two weeks every summer, and occasionally Lindsay would drive up with girlfriends for some girl time, but no one else in the family had been there since Lindsay's father passed away, other than Rebecca; who went one time and said it was emotionally too hard for her; she'd never been back.

The occasion of Lenette's memorial service was the first time the whole family had been together in over four years, with the exception of Nelson who didn't want to go. Lindsay wondered what the catalyst would be for them to gather again; perhaps Lenette's death would serve as a wake-up call in more ways than one. While they gave each other assurances they would make the effort to see each other more often, there was not enough enthusiasm to assure any of them when it might happen. She wondered if this same fracturing was true of other families besides hers.

When Rebecca moved to be near Lenette, the family dynamics

changed. Lindsay couldn't blame her for going; while she loved having her mother nearby, the reality was she didn't see her often. Everything about her mother drove Nelson crazy, and Rebecca knew it, so when Lenette and Jeremy said they wanted her near them, she jumped at it. She told Lindsay her life had been too predictable, and how she was ready for an adventure; after all, she could always move back if she hated it. Lenette's rationalization for moving her close to them was her desire to be a catalyst for the family since they lived centrally. But, unfortunately, her priority didn't transfer to her siblings. As with so many things recently, it was clear now that God had his hand in settling Rebecca near Jeremy.

Lindsay closed her eyes, picturing her and Lenette running down the dock with their brothers chasing them; she could hear her mother laughing before the water closed over her—their dad was already waiting for them in the water. The memory seemed so long ago now; when summers seemed endless, and time was not a taskmaster. The images were hauntingly clear. She could feel tears forming, while she watched her children playing together; she prayed they would learn from her mistakes and remain close when they were older. In the urgency of the day by day, she had neglected what was important. She needed to work harder to bring her extended family together; especially now.

~~~

Once the trip was planned, Maryellen insisted on doing the driving. Before she'd turned her minivan onto the interstate, Lindsay had fallen asleep, drifting into one of those heavy and enveloping slumbers that would be hard to come out of later. Maryellen could tell she wasn't sleeping well; the dark circles under her eyes enhanced her perpetual sadness.

Whatever was on Lindsay's mind had changed her from a Pollyanna spirited optimist to someone quite the opposite. Maryellen was sure it was more complicated than Lenette's passing alone—it was eating her alive; she was bone thin.

Mourning had brought with it a heaviness of spirit that Maryellen could sense by osmosis. *Oh God*, she prayed, *Change my friend back to the way she was. Let this time away be a time of refreshment for her*. She thought of the Psalm that said, *"As the deer pants for water, so my soul pants for Thee, O' God."* That was the refreshment she was praying for Lindsay; whatever was troubling her friend, only the Master Fixer could fix. Perhaps Maryellen could break through the wall Lindsay was erecting before it got any thicker. She hoped so.

For supper, they fed the kids Kraft Macaroni and Cheese, hot dogs, potatoes, pickles, and carrot sticks, laughing at how fast the food disappeared. Part of the fun of being at the lake was breaking the rules; there would be a lot of carbs and sugar consumed over the next forty-eight hours, by all of them.

In the main bedroom was a stone fireplace; Lindsay built a fire while Maryellen put *Sleepless in Seattle* in the DVD player. They turned on the movie, nestling into the soft featherbed with a bowl of popcorn between them. "Nelson calls this the ultimate Chick Flick." Lindsay commented.

"Russ said the same thing, but he always gets defensive when he cries at the ending." She laughed at the memory. "How many times have you watched it?"

Lindsay also laughed; Russ had a reputation for being a softie. She answered Maryellen, "At least ten times—maybe twice that. For me, it's like eating a bowl of mashed potatoes on a rainy day. Have you ever done anything like that?"

"Not that, exactly... Give me fresh out-of-the-oven peanut butter cookies—only I eat the cookies for dessert after I finish the potatoes." Maryellen replied, with a straight face. Lindsay decided a friend like Maryellen was better than comfort food.

With some persistence on Maryellen's part, Lindsay acknowledged she had been neglecting herself. "Lindsay? Is there anything you want to talk about? You know I would never say anything to anyone."

"I know, but if I tell you, I'll have to shoot you. It's that bad."

"Funny!"

"I wish I was joking." She thought of what happened to Bob Murphy and wondered if she'd endangered Maryellen by inviting her to go to the lake with her.

"That's what the news keeps implying. The Enquirer said she had an affair with some spy, which I know is ridiculous."

Lindsay changed the subject; she had not read any of the stories in the tabloids. "Can you feel it?"

"Feel what?"

"The atmosphere—it seems different. Doesn't it feel heavy to you?" She asked. "Remember how, in the months following 9/11, we had a sense of hope? It was our president who rallied us, he spoke of prayer—and God; it was so healing for our country. Even after having our breath sucked out of us by what happened, we could breathe—his instilling hope for our future as a country was like infusing the air with oxygen. We all pulled together for a common good; there was a sense of renewed faith and pride in being American."

Lindsay agreed, "For me, it's the difference of having hope or not having it. Who could have dreamed our country could become so fractionalized a little over a decade later? Can you imagine wading through everything that has happened since the towers fell without faith?"

Maryellen nodded, "No, I can't. But, wouldn't you think there would be more people asking questions about what's really going on? My neighbors are hostile to any discussion about God or faith; and they're rabid about politics. This politically correct stuff has gone way too far."

They were quiet for a few minutes, each one reflecting. Lindsay spoke up next, "Maryellen, we have to remember that it isn't the people who are the problem. We are living through a spiritual war of unprecedented dimensions—its Ephesians Chapter Six playing itself out in real time; *"For we are not fighting against flesh-and-blood enemies, but against evil rulers and authorities of the unseen world, against mighty powers in this dark world, and against evil spirits in the heavenly places."*

Again, they were quiet, trying to digest what that meant to them, personally.

Maryellen spoke up, "Lately I've been noticing their eyes..."

"Whose eyes?" Lindsay asked.

"Our leaders; our elected officials; the ones who seem to want to suppress us and steal our liberties..."

"I don't know what you mean." Lindsay said.

"Lindsay, you can see it in their eyes. It's not their faces; there's plenty of expression there—but, it's their eyes. It's like looking at dead people—they're cold and vacant. Remember the movie where the kid said, 'I see dead people'? We look at people on the surface, forgetting how if they are opposed to what God's word tells us, they can't be one of us—they can't be trusted, because they oppose the things of God. Jesus said, 'He who isn't with me is against me'."

Lindsay hoped Maryellen was watching *Sleepless in Seattle* and not her. "Whatever their agenda is, they are committed to it. When the Health Care Bill came out right after the last election, and it was over two thousand pages long, I remember Lenette asking me who I thought had written it, and when. She said it was impossible for that bill to have been written from November to January. That troubled me, because not one person admitted to having read it, or even said they intended to read it, so they passed it with...pun intended...'blind eyes'.

"Wouldn't Lenette just love it if she knew I was talking politics with you? She would have said she'd lived a full life!" The idea tickled her, because it was true. And she knew Lenette would have taken full credit for it.

Maryellen laughed in agreement. She and Lenette had enjoyed some lively debates on some issues when they were together. She added, "Russ thinks they've been promised something; that they couldn't be so brazen if they didn't believe they and their families would be okay once it's all done and over with. They've been bought out by whoever is pulling the strings at the top and, mark my words; many of them will be betrayed before it is over. Russ says they're puppets."

Lindsay sighed, "How weird you would say that. Yesterday I looked through one of my old Bible studies from Eleanor Crosby. Her commentary points out how we have all been too hung up on legalistic terms; like the use of the word Antichrist or the number 666. She said being dogmatic often blinds us to the deeper meaning. What she said was how the word antichrist implies a larger application...in reality, it means anti-Christian, and it covers everyone who opposes the Gospel of Christ. Did you ever think of it that way?"

Maryellen nodded. She remembered it from the study. "We are seeing it all around us, and the vice that will squeeze the true Christ followers will be used in the name of 'tolerance'.

"Yes! She says it will be more subtle than someone just standing up and saying he's against Jesus. Instead, a religion will emerge that uses Christ's name, but denies the absolutes of his word. Millions are being led into error because they haven't taken the time to study, and know for themselves what the word teaches. In the end, it might be our neighbors, or even our families that will turn against those who believe in the inerrant word; and they will do it in the name of intolerance. Don't forget, the bible says all but the very elect will be deceived."

Maryellen broke in, "That would make it possible for a world leader who is anti-Christian to be accepted. He will be the antichrist, but he probably won't call himself that. The public sentiment is going that way—not anti-Christian if you embrace the broader view, that all paths lead to God, but if you believe the sign on the narrow road that says *One way only*—we are the ones will have to be dealt with. The ones on the broad way will stand with the rest against those of us who can't take a detour."

Lindsay broke in, "Yes, that is exactly what I was reading yesterday. Eleanor believes those of us who are still here, who believe in the narrow way, are, by virtue of the Holy Spirit, hold back God's judgment. When the church is removed there will be nothing left to hold back the tide of evil."

Maryellen sat straight up, "Isn't that scary, Lindsay? We need to talk to our kids, and explain what is happening, and prepare them—so the culture can't seduce them."

"Yes, I like it! We'll begin tomorrow. We'll make it fun for them, so it won't seem as scary—and interesting. If we begin while we're here, it will help them remember what they learned." Lenette responded, affirmatively. "I need that, myself. I forget it is a spiritual war by focusing on individuals, forgetting who it is we are really at war with. We've come full circle, haven't we? We're back to Ephesians Six, *"we wrestle not against flesh and blood..."* Lindsay's voice broke at the end; her thoughts immediately turning to Nelson.

CHAPTER 51

It was an untypically hot autumn afternoon. A rather full-figured woman looked around, before feeding quarters into a pay phone in the Barnes & Noble Bookstore parking lot. She was wearing a tan blazer, black slacks, and an evidently new pair of bright white Nike running shoes. Her hair was curly and dark; partly hidden by a baseball cap. She also had on a pair of black Chanel sunglasses, similar to the ones Jackie Kennedy made famous in the 60's; she was currently wondering if Jackie's cheeks sweat where the glasses rubbed on them like hers did. Beside her was a stroller, with a sweaty, sleeping baby inside.

Rebecca Kennedy wasn't sure if Jeremy would be proud of her, or annoyed. "When in doubt keep your mouth shut", was her motto—something she wasn't good at. The sunglasses were Lenette's, but the wig was hers; purchased on the internet. She felt confident that if there were security cameras in the parking lot she could not be recognized.

Jeremy wasn't the only one to think of latex gloves; she'd bought some of her own, and used them when she went through Lenette's brief case before Jeremy took it to Portland.

She checked the palm of her hand before punching another phone number into the phone. She'd copied the numbers that were written in Lenette's notebook onto her hand, so she wouldn't lose them. The first two numbers were dead ends; she felt her heart rate going up when she realized the third number was ringing.

She couldn't believe her ears when she heard the voice that answered on the other end. It was Nelson's!

"Oh my God...! Nelson, is that you?"

"Who is this?" He demanded, sounding wary.

"It's Rebecca Kennedy—your mother-in-law. I'm not at all surprised you don't recognize my voice." She immediately regretted her compulsion to zing him, so she added, "Are you okay?"

She could sense panic in his voice. "Why are you calling me? How did you get this number? Where are you calling from?" Nelson demanded, sounding very stern.

Rebecca pulled her wits together. She took a deep breath, "One question at a time, Nelson. I'm at a payphone. Can you talk?"

"I don't think it matters—I'd be afraid to put it off. But, how on earth did you get this number? Lenette's the only one who had it." Now his voice was flat.

"She wrote down in something, and I wanted to know who it belonged to; I figured it might help us figure out who killed her." She'd zinged him on that one; but that time he had it coming. When he didn't respond, she added, "Since I have you on the phone, you and Jeremy need to talk. What should I tell him?"

He paused for a long minute, "Tell Jeremy I agree; we do need to talk. Rebecca, you need to buy prepaid cell phones for both you and Jeremy. And, whatever you do—pay in cash. Don't buy them locally or more than two at a time because there are camera's everywhere and who knows who's watching at this point." He wasn't asking a question. He also didn't realize Rebecca was in disguise.

"Ask Jeremy to call me tomorrow. If I don't answer, have him keep trying. If he can't reach me, it may be too late. I am not sure what might tip the scale. I won't call until he has a safe number and, after tomorrow, you won't be able to reach me on this phone; I can't believe I still have it.

"And for the record, I didn't kill Lenette."

The phone clicked, and he was gone.

Rebecca Kennedy pushed the stroller through the parking lot on her way to the bus stop. She took off her sunglasses, wiping the sweat off he cheeks with her hand. She looked around to see if she was being followed.

She reached inside her pocket, patting her pistol. The gun belonged to Lenette; she'd found it in the safe and it was loaded.

Rebecca was a spy.

~~~

Three days later Nelson and Jeremy met at a lounge, in a cheap hotel near O'Hair Airport. Jeremy flew into Chicago, Nelson drove; that seemed safer to Nelson than both of them arriving by plane at the same time.

Jeremy had arranged a meeting with a client to make the trip appear legitimate. Since he had a built-in alibi, he wasn't trying to cover his tracks. Nelson phoned in sick. The benefit of having cut the chip out was he was no longer a moving target. Seeing Jeremy would be his final act of penance—after that he just wanted it over.

They shook hands, staring at each other. It was a déjà vu feeling for them both; partly because when they'd seen each other before, they had no clue about who the other was. Impulsively, Jeremy reached out and embraced him. He recognized that Nelson was working out his redemption. *God save this man*, he prayed.

"Jeremy, I can't tell you how sorry I am." Nelson broke down. "I was one of the bad guys—still am in a way. The night at the restaurant I didn't even question whose side I was on. But, you have to believe me; I would never have done anything to hurt Lenette."

"I know that, Nelson." Jeremy didn't waste any time before changing the subject, "Where did the chip come from?"

Nelson stuck out his hand. Jeremy stared at the pale line where Nelson had cut himself; he shuddered; thinking about any kind of self-inflicted pain made him queasy. "You've crossed over to the other side now, Nelson. Personally, I think we're both going to end up dead, but if the worst happens I'd rather be dead on the right side."

"Why is that comforting?" Nelson asked him.

Jeremy nodded his agreement. "Funny, but it is. Now let's get to work; we have miles to go before we sleep."

Nelson grimaced; he got the pun.

Nelson explained, in as much detail as he knew, what he believed was about to take place; some of it soon. Then, he began speculating on what the larger plan's strategy was. "Call it educated speculation, or pure fantasy, but the sleeping giant woke up too late."

Jeremy rolled his eyes. "So, you think he's awake? I don't; I think he's still napping, and I'm worried he's not as big a giant as we thought he was."

Nelson agreed. "Best case is he's finally stirring. I think he's plenty big; he's just out of shape. The problem is the coincidences have become too many to ignore, and he won't have time to get in shape to take this on. While he was asleep, the noose of the New World Order was looped around his neck."

Jeremy reached in his pocket for some Rolaids. "So you think Lenette knew this?"

"Lenette got too close—she was proactive and all it took was one lucky break for her to cross over from being one harmless nut into someone who got too close to the real truth; at that point she would need to be monitored.

"The government has started keeping lists of people they have labeled as terrorists; a while ago the president signed an executive order that allows people to be selectively assassinated if the government deems them dangerous; they have kill lists of people they are watching. A jury of one's peers is a thing of the past." For Jeremy, that news hit too close to home.

"Jeremy, if you knew the degree of monitoring of civilian's already taking place it would shock you. There is no doubt that every citizen is being monitored randomly. There's been a recurring rumor the government will be using drones to monitor our own citizens; let me tell you, it's more than a rumor. There are sites prepared for them to launch from all over the country. I believe they have been selectively monitoring for some time. Lenette put a lot of the pieces together, and the chip may have been the last piece she needed. She knew the public was already being monitored via their cell phones and GPS devices, possibly aided by the drones, but you can leave a cell phone behind, buy one, or rent a car. The next step would have to be, by necessity, personally invasive."

"So, you think the chip was the final piece of the puzzle and that she was about to do something that made it necessary to kill her?" Jeremy asked.

"I'm can only guess what the catalyst was, but her having the chip would have tipped the scale. She hinted to me that she was in contact with someone powerful who'd agreed to meet with her. Somehow their communications must have triggered a reaction that forced a response. For example, the radical left wants the Tea Party movement stopped, and we know Lenette left a trail there. That was one of the triggers that got people using the internet to get a lot of information into people's hands. I never would have thought the Rod Larson show could have pushed so many buttons. So, once the cost of being involved is too high, they are counting on a majority of people putting their heads between their legs again; her elimination served multiple purposes. Fear is a powerful motivator." He paused for a moment, reflecting. "But, one thing I know for a fact; Lindsay didn't know a thing before that night in New York. Had we not gotten into that conversation at dinner, I doubt she would have even thought twice about what she faxed to Lenette.

Jeremy interrupted, "Nelson, we both know it wasn't the faxes that got Lenette targeted; they were only confirmation that she was on the right track. I did some Googling on my own and found pictures of the money everywhere; thousands of places, including sources on YouTube that explain what the different symbols mean. They've been playing with the new currency for decades. Can you imagine the number of people who have to be involved behind the scenes; who kept this information under wraps over the years?"

Nelson broke in, "Yes, I have some idea about how many people are involved, and the numbers are staggering. About the leaking of the images—I think they wanted the conspiracy theorists to run with the currency thing. That way they could be labeled wackos and the public would distance from them. Obviously, there was some risk doing that, but it paid off."

Nelson added, "Jeremy, at every G20 Summit the currency is discussed; that part is no secret and we have known about the leaks. The New World Order is happening, and most of it hasn't been done with as much cloak and dagger as most people think. The information is out there and generations of elitists have kept the dream moving forward.

"Those, like Lenette, who become suspicious and do some due diligence, start digging and don't always have to dig that far. It's just that we—they—know how to make those people on the right look like radical nutcases. If they aren't marked for some mysterious elimination, they are marked and then targeted to undermine their credibility; even their followers will back away from them. Either way, they're marked."

"So, what might she have known?" Jeremy leaned forward looking intently at Nelson.

"She specifically asked me what I knew about a chip having been developed to monitor the world population. If she told anyone else what she knew they would have dismissed her as crazy, but what she figured out was right on; so, I dug mine out and sent it to her." He looked sheepish; saying it out loud sounded much weirder than when he thought about it.

"She wanted proof, and I had it. We both surmised that the chip in my hand was far superior to any of the other ones that are being used commercially."

"What do you mean?" Jeremy leaned forward.

Nelson leaned toward him, also; lowering his voice. "The chip has the capacity to listen, and to program a person's thinking. All I know is that I began thinking differently since the day after it came out."

"You're kidding me!" Jeremy was incredulous.

"I wish I was. It was like a fog lifted. I realized that even my limbs had felt weighty; perhaps it was a pseudo depression or something like that, but whatever it was affected me physiologically as well as mentally." Without realizing it, Nelson had begun to rub the scar where the chip once was.

"Take it one step further, Nelson. The damn thing has to be the reason why all those people in Bob Murphy's office died; that's why he's dead."

"Jeremy, people have known about the potential of the chip in theory. 'They' wanted the public to get used to the idea. It's been used for veterinary purposes for years, in the military, prisons, and for health records, etc. The Health Care debate had brought it out in the open again.

"People are already adjusting to the idea of their personal and vital information being accessible; you'd have to live on an island not to know about it! By the time they need to implant it, people will be ready and willing to line up—and I think we're there. There'll be very little resistance by the time it's mandated. This might hit too close to home for you, but they may already be inserting them into infants in some hospitals."

"God." Jeremy was pale, thinking of Caleb.

Nelson added, "No, not Caleb—military hospitals first, where there's more control and the mindset's more accepting. He's one super-cute baby, by the way."

He continued, "Lenette had the chip in her possession and she died. You had it, and you got rid of it, but they know it was you who transported it to Portland. Bob Murphy became involved, and now he's dead. I'm truly surprised I'm still alive, and the only reason I can think of is I'm related to Lenette, and there are still some honest reporters around who might manage to connect the dots."

Jeremy looked surprised, but added, "Well, if that's true, maybe they think I know more than I do, also. That may be cheap life insurance for me, since I don't know anything. Nelson, might we assume my every move is being watched?"

They both glanced around the room. They were thinking the bartender looked suspicious.

Nelson nodded affirmatively, which was not a comfort to Jeremy, who said, "Never in my wildest dreams did I think I would live to see anything like what is happening. Where is Spiderman when you need him?"

"He's one of them now, Jeremy." Nelson said, seriously, "I heard he recently changed sides."

They stood up, ready to move on. "Jeremy, will you at least let me buy you dinner?" Jeremy could tell it was important to him; he answered, "Of course, but I'm buying."

Nelson's face showed his gratitude that Jeremy would share a meal with him. "Accepted, brother."

Hailing a cab, they asked the driver if he would drive them downtown via Lake Shore Drive. They both leaned back, lost in their own thoughts. Inside the darkened bar, they'd all but forgot it was still light outside. The afternoon was sunny and windy; a typical early fall day in Chicago. It was the kind of day that might deceive one into thinking that all was right with the world.

Jeremy looked over at Nelson, studying him. It was amazing, but he looked better now than he had in a long time. He was extremely thin, but the brooding, secretive demeanor had been replaced by a tentative, resigned countenance. He realized he hadn't had a drink.

Jeremy was at peace. He knew where he was going and was prepared to face that possibility—he hoped with dignity. His wife was waiting there for him. God, he knew with certainty, would watch over his baby. Rebecca, he hoped, would be safe, too—if he wasn't around to protect her, he trusted that God would send someone else who could keep her out of trouble.

~~~

They had skipped lunch, so by the time they were finished hashing things over, they were starving. Jeremy suggested a bar & grill that was near downtown, on the river, where they each ordered steaks, and every side dish listed on the menu. While they ate, they reminisced, talking about when they'd met their wives and each other.

Jeremy reminded Nelson how the girls would use their maiden name, Kennedy, to get them into places most people could not. Nelson shared a story about how he and Lindsay went to D.C. one weekend, wanting to go to a play at Kennedy Center. When they arrived the tickets were sold out. He described how Lindsay (yes Lindsay!) took out her driver's license, asking the women at the desk if she realized who she was. The woman snatched the license out of her hand and disappeared with it, returning momentarily with two security guards. Nelson told Jeremy he'd kissed his career good-bye that night; before it started—arrested for impersonating a Kennedy.

One of the guards asked them to "Please, follow us..." Since they were in possession of Lindsay's license, there was no point in running for it. The story ended with them being led to the front of the theater, and offered seats in the second row; accompanied by a profuse apology. The seats were complimentary.

After they were seated Lindsay poked Nelson's arm, pointing to someone a few seats down in the front row. "Isn't that Ted?" She asked him, leaning forward and waving like they were long lost friends. Ted returned the wave. "The only one she didn't fool was my mother." Nelson added, with a straight face. That struck them both funny—they laughed 'til they cried.

When the meal was over, the waiter came to the table with the check. Nelson reached out and grabbed it from him. Jeremy exclaimed, "Nelson!"

Nelson's responded, "So, I lied."

"You?" Jeremy asked him, with a straight face.

That set them off again; laughing so hard the other patrons couldn't help but stare. The laughter felt good, cleansing. It was a release of pressure for them both; for those watching, they would never guess both men were expecting to be executed.

When Jeremy was describing the evening to Rebecca later, he told her the evening with Nelson was like having found a Krugerrand in a manure pile.

~~~

They both knew it was unlikely they would see each other again, or as Jeremy put it, "On this side..."

"Jeremy," Nelson said before they parted, "I blame myself for what happened to Lenette. I should have known sending her the chip would put her in danger—but she insisted that she had a plan. Something told me that I shouldn't send it—if I had even waited a day I wouldn't have."

"Maybe she's the lucky one, Nelson; maybe she's the lucky one. We can't second guess one single detail in any of this. Things happen for a reason, if you love God." When it was time to leave, they embraced one last time; for both of them, letting go was difficult.

"Until we meet again, Nelson; you know the way." Jeremy looked into his eyes, "Promise me."

Nelson nodded, but he couldn't promise; he wasn't convinced it could be possible.

CHAPTER 52

When Dana heard Max's car pulling into the driveway, she burst through the front door and ran down the porch steps toward the car, with Burger at her heels, hollering, "I've been trying to call you the entire weekend; why didn't you call me? Something terrible has happened." They could tell that she'd been crying. "Max, it could have been you!"

"What could have been me?" he answered, feeling defensive.

"You don't know? Oh, I didn't want to be the one to tell you." Now she was crying. "Max, it's horrible. Let's go inside first; you need to sit down."

Laura looked confused. Max already knew that something life-altering had taken place. They followed Dana into their family room where the TV was turned on to one of the cable networks. Before they could sit down Burger demanded to be acknowledged; his life hadn't changed.

Dana was staring at them in disbelief. "How can it be possible you don't know anything? It's the only thing that's been on the news since last Friday night."

Max was becoming impatient. "Dana, please just tell us. What the hell's going on?"

Dana muted the TV. "There's no easy way to tell you..." But, before elaborating she turned to Laura, knowing the news would burst her bubble and change her life. "Laura, I am so sorry—I know you wanted to bring your honeymoon home with you..." She trailed off again, turning back to Max, "It is the worst thing imaginable. Every employee of Murphy's Law is dead with three exceptions; one of the secretaries who worked on the first floor, who had a doctor's appointment, the guy the firm used as a courier, who was delivering something—plus you. There were also some clients who were there for meetings." She waited for him to process what she'd said. "I'm surprised they didn't have you picked up, or something, although I did see a police car here on Saturday. I'm sure they'll want to question you as soon as possible. I hope not, but you could be a suspect."

Suddenly Bob Murphy's face took up the screen. Max stared at the television, too stunned to speak. "Bob? He's dead, too?" Max asked, incredulous.

Dana nodded, crying again. She knew Martha Murphy from a Bible Study she was in, and had always found it endearing how her face would light up whenever she spoke of her husband. She nodded, "Yes, he's dead, too."

It was obvious they needed time to digest her news. "I made some tuna salad and put it in your refrigerator, and some bagels and chips on the counter. If you need anything just call." Dana all but bolted for the door, clearly overcome.

Laura escaped into the kitchen, leaving Max alone with his thoughts. All she knew was that if they hadn't gone to Seattle to hear Eleanor Crosby, Max would be listed among the dead. God, truly, controlled their destinies.

She thought of her grandmother, thanking God for prayers that she believed were still following her.

CHAPTER 53

With the Seattle meeting behind her, Eleanor found it necessary to look forward; out and beyond the meeting in New York. She wanted to make certain Candy was thinking through every option for her future, rather than staying with her out of either habit or loyalty. What she didn't want was for something happen to her that would put Candy in the position to become her caretaker.

Eleanor's ministry had financially blessed her, but she chose to live simply, giving much of her money away. Her ever evolving ministry had gradually taken over most of the living areas of her modest townhome, with the overflow of what came to her through the mail, but wasn't urgent. Since she and Candy didn't entertain, they'd allowed the overflow to occur, but it was now to the point that Eleanor decided it was affecting her concentration. Before the Seattle meeting, they made a pact to making getting organized a priority when they got home.

Practically, it would be helpful for both of them to prepare for the possibility of Candy moving on; they didn't talk about it, but it was like a cloud hanging over them both. Eleanor couldn't be sure what her own restlessness of spirit was about, but she wanted to make sure that all of her bases were covered in case something was to happen to her, and setting Candy free was one of them.

~~~

Eleanor and Candy were sitting in the middle of the living floor, with a tray of crispy fried chicken, and assorted side dishes, between them. They felt silly; their giddiness prompted by their leaving greasy fingerprints on everything they were touching. It was nothing less than ridiculous how, since neither of them ever ate finger food, they chose the one night they were preparing to get organized to do it.

Candy passed her aunt a manila file folder, complete with her greasy thumbprint on the front. Eleanor pressed her thumb under Candy's, so now both of their signatures were on it. Eleanor decided she wanted to cut the fingerprints out of the folder later, and frame them; seeing them together had the same effect on her as seeing a baby's footprint on a birth certificate; it legitimized their pairing.

Candy stood up, surveying the room. She leaned down and took hold of two over-stuffed black trash bags. "...it's better, don't you think?" she asked Eleanor, dragging the bags behind her. "I'm going to put these by the back door. What can I bring you?"

Eleanor called after her, "How about a washrag?"

Eleanor could see some light at the end of the tunnel. The living room had been nearly impassable before, and now might pass as very cluttered.

Is this me? She thought. *I used to be tidy. I'm still tidy in my head!* Once again, the persistent thought returned—the time is short.

"Oh, God. I'm not ready to go yet!" She blurted it out, hoping Candy couldn't hear her. Eleanor couldn't shake the sense of finality that pursued her of late.

Candy returned a few minutes later, bringing two Dove Bars with her. She handed one to Eleanor, who unwrapped it and tapped it against Candy's... "Here's to Jesus." she said. Candy echoed, "Here's to Jesus—may his appearing be soon."

Those words calmed Eleanor's restless heart.

∼∼∼

The previous spring Candy had set up a Facebook account for her aunt. Eleanor hated everything about it. When she first began using it, and read some of the perpetual narcissistic comments, she couldn't help but think how it punctuated the apathy of so many people in the church, who spent hours devouring mental candy, and never picked up a newspaper or news journal, much less their bible.

"Julie...is drinking coffee" "Lou...is looking at a fantastic butt" "Sarah...loves the Lord and hopes he's tolerant". She read them out loud to Candy, who had braced herself for the inevitability that Eleanor wouldn't be able to keep her reactions to herself.

"Candy, how do we wake these people up?" To Eleanor it was serious.

It took some doing, but Candy managed to set it up, so that Eleanor's Facebook name was, "The time is short"; the phrase would precede whatever her thought for the day was.

Today's missive was, "The time is short... so stop playing games..."

She had no more posted it when one of her cousin's names popped up, offering her a stray colt in one of the endless, mindless games that were all too available on the internet; further evidence for Eleanor of how so many were wandering in a wasteland of mental lightheadedness.

She typed in another one... "The time is short...the harvest is ripe, and the laborers are few." She posted it. She waited. She didn't have to wait long; only seconds later up popped an offer from someone wanting to share some golden apples, and another who needed a home for a homeless panda.

God help us, she thought—our country is bankrupt, we can't control our borders, race relations may take generations to rebuild, we're heading toward socialism, and Ginny found a pretend stray colt and now she needs pretend lumber to build a pretend pen for it.

God, help me to help them, she prayed.

After Facebook, she would move on to Tweets. It had the makings of a long morning.

~~~

The following morning Candy scanned everything of value, uploading video files on Eleanor's website, and posting more on YouTube—she predicted thousands of hits by the weekend. Eleanor was thrilled when Candy told her how quickly people would access and share the videos. "I'm encouraged. At least some people use their computers for eternity." Eleanor voiced her despair to her niece.

Candy agreed, saying, "Wasting time is hard for me; I feel guilty taking a bubble bath."

"Candy, don't get me wrong, I believe God wants us to take time for ourselves. That's why he created Sunday; to re-create. The word recreation' is about becoming renewed. I believe these games are as seductive and addictive as porn. If Satan can steal our brains and thoughts away from being productive, he has stolen our fruit. Each individual will give account for what we did for him on the earth—golden apples won't cut it.

"Taking a bath is a whole different thing than giving your time away for no purpose. Satan doesn't care if we take a bubble bath or not; he might even fear us if we used part of that time to meditate or pray. But, mark my words, he's overjoyed when people spend time looking down some cyberspace bunny hole, sending invitations for friends and family to join them on their way down the hole.

"The bride who is invited through the door is anointed; it is the anointing she was told to seek; you can't share that oil or buy it; it is of the Spirit and he is jealous towards those who seek him. Read the verses about the ten virgins and tell me if you don't think the bridegroom doesn't sound insulted when half of them aren't ready.

"I think another twist to that verse is that every one of them is asleep when he comes. I don't believe it is the same kind of sleep for all ten of them. God gives rest to his beloved--that's a whole lot different than snoozing on the job.

"I think the five who were ready were resting after a hard day's work—the other five were asleep at the wheel." She took a breath, realizing she was preaching again.

"Candy, the time is short—I feel it in my bones. Don't you think we should take a bubble bath while there's time?"

CHAPTER 54

Laura was lying on her back in bed, with both hands resting on her stomach. It calmed her to focus on the blessing of their baby; her eyes were closed, but she wasn't asleep. Max was lying on his side looking at her. It calmed him to watch her.

The phone rang, startling them both. Max sat up, looking past Laura to the caller ID. "Laura, it's the police station."

"Well then, I think one of us should answer it, don't you?" Laura said, forcing herself to remain calm for him.

"Yeah...I guess." He reached over her to grab the phone before it could ring again. "Hello?" She watched his expression change from inquisitive to one of concern. "Give me an hour." He said. When the call ended he threw the phone across the room, clearly agitated. His life had been spared but changed irreparably.

Laura got up and started for the kitchen. "Let me make the coffee, Max. Take your time; it isn't good if you allow your nerves to take charge. You won't be keeping the people who died waiting, only the police."

"I have a good alibi for Friday." He winked at her.

She smiled. "Yes, you do; I'll vouch for every minute."

"I love you, Laura." Max said it, trying to imagine how superficial his life must have been a year ago.

"Me too...now, quit borrowing trouble by worrying. It's perfectly obvious why they need to talk to you. And, we both need to start asking God for wisdom, because we're going to need a lot of it."

For one brief, shining moment, they had lived in Camelot.

~~~

Laura asked Max if he wanted her to go along, but he said no. The time in the car would be the only chance he would have to think, and he needed that time. His brain was on high alert, and he knew there was no way to slow it down.

One thing that helped his frame of mind was that he knew some of the officers and detectives; the firm occasionally engaged them to offer their input. The police had been helpful in supplying some boots on the ground information that assisted with their research, so knowing some of their first names, on a small level, helped his comfort level.

The police chief, Ben Cross, was outside, smoking a cigarette. Max took the bull by the horns and walked up to him, thinking he could test the waters; he watched his eyes carefully, "Hi, Ben. Been busy?" He said, trying to be light.

"Hey, Max. Can you believe how lucky you are you weren't at work on Friday? Where were you, anyhow? We tried to find you after you didn't call us back. Your neighbor told us where you were, and why, or we would have gone after you."

"Yeah, we were in Seattle. We went up to hear Eleanor Crosby, and I decided to make it our honeymoon, since we hadn't had one. We didn't want interruptions." He ignored the reference to him not calling, adding, "We didn't even know about it. Our neighbor told us when we got home last night."

Ben winked at him, "Well, that makes sense—I get the no interruption part. How was the Crosby thing?"

"Good. It was good. Scary, but good..."

"Scary? How was it scary? Maybe I don't know who she is..."

"If you don't know her by name you may know her by The Prophetess; she is pretty well known. It was about how the crazy stuff that's going on ties into Bible prophecy. We bought the DVD's; some friends are coming over to watch them with us next weekend. You're invited, if you want to come."

"Naaah—my job's scary enough."

Max laughed dutifully; he could tell Ben was uncomfortable with the subject. "Ben, what's going down is white knuckle stuff. I wouldn't have believed any of it three months ago, but I'm not so sure now."

Ben looked away, breaking eye contact—suddenly a wall had gone up. Now he was all business. "Follow me into my office; let's get your statement down and see what's next. I need to question you, and for the record, you're not a suspect."

Something had undoubtedly changed. It was subtle, but Max recognized a red flag when he saw one.

~~~

Max took a break to call home. "Laura, it looks as though I'm going to be awhile."

She could hear the tension in his voice. "Like, how long? Are you okay?"

"I'm fine. They want me to go over to the office, and identify some things. I can pick dinner up on my way home, if you want. I don't want you to leave the house today, okay?" He knew she had to be stir-crazy, but it wouldn't be wise for her to leave.

He heard her sighing. "You're scaring me. Is it okay if I to go to Dana's?"

"Don't be scared and if you want to go to Dana's, go. I just don't want you to be driving around until we've had a chance to talk."

"Well, I'm scared, but I was already scared before you left this morning."

"Laura, I'm so very sorry, and if misery loves company, I'm as scared as you are. Now, go get one of the DVDS's we bought at the Crosby thing, and take it with you to Dana's. Keep your head there, okay?"

"Okay..."

"And, Laura?" Max's tone had changed.

"What?"

"Don't say anything to Dana she wouldn't already know from the news."

~~~

Ben drove Max to the office building that up until a few weeks earlier had been the ideal work environment. The parking lot was guarded by an arsenal of law enforcement. Max let them in using his palm print; they took the elevator to the third floor.

He'd already seen the pictures of the crime scene at the station, but walking into the building in real time was horrifying. White chalk outlines of his dead coworkers were everywhere; each outline had the victims' names scribbled inside. These were people he knew, and liked, and now they were all dead. He felt woozy—reality hitting him full force.

He walked by his own office, trying to remember what was in his file. He was pretty sure the NWO file was at home. Max knew, in his gut, he would be living there for days to come. Ben made a point of saying they would be going through everything, so apparently the investigation would be painstakingly thorough, and they would be watching him closely; his behavior would be scrutinized through a microscope.

Ben turned on a recorder. "Okay, Max. Let's start with Bob. Give me everything you know." They were sitting in the conference room; the only 'clean room' in the building, meaning no one had died there.

"There isn't a lot to tell you, Ben. I didn't know him socially. I went to their home one time after an art show and installed a portrait they bought from me. He offered me a job when he learned I was an attorney.

"At work he was a straight arrow. His ethics were stellar, and his reputation was impeccable; he was very generous if you worked hard. I was never involved in a conversation with anyone who worked for him who ever thought of leaving. And, Bob rarely let anybody go, either; one of his gifts was bringing out the best in people." He paused, it hit him that not one shred of what he'd enjoyed at Murphy's Law remained. His voice broke when he added, "It was the perfect job. He gave us the freedom to do our job our way, as long as we knew our limits. He was great to work for because he commanded the kind of respect that made his crew want to please him..."

Ben cleared his throat, uncomfortable with Max's show of emotion. "You said precisely what all of the wives said. By the way, it's interesting there were no women on the team..."

"I never thought about it. I think if a woman could have added to what we do—er, did— he would have hired her. He wasn't like that."

"What about clients? Can you think of anyone who seemed suspicious...or who might have a motive or a grudge?"

Max's training as an attorney kicked in...don't hesitate or clear your throat, watch your eye contact—look right at him, don't say 'um', just keep going...he knew that Ben would be watching him for any signs that he was hiding something.

"I wasn't on that part of the team. I was the corporate attorney; it was my job to be intimidating."

Ben laughed. "I'll tell you what; I'll remember that if I ever need an attorney, although I might need some referrals from anyone who could testify that you can be intimidating." He laughed at his own joke. "Do you think you'll throw your hat in the ring again?"

Max had thrown him off, at least for the moment.

~~~

When Laura heard the garage door open, she met Max at the door with a tall glass of iced tea. He drank most of it in a few gulps, asking how she knew he was thirsty.

"I'm gifted that way. You know that!" she answered.

She was gifted; no argument there.

Compliments of Dana, their dinner was waiting for them on the counter. Max noticed meat loaf, scalloped potatoes, and a salad; it looked appetizing, but it wasn't really dinner without pasta.

After they had eaten he suggested they go a walk. Without explaining, he put his cell phone in a drawer while she got Burger on his leash. Once they were well away from the house he said, "Just listen to me; we don't have a ton of time.

"Laura, I need for you to know some things. Do you remember the woman who was murdered a few months ago—the one with the baby—"

"Of course I remember her. Her murder was a big deal. We watched her memorial service on TV; remember?" she said, stopping and turning so she could look at him.

He nodded affirmatively and took a deep breath, feeling a weird sense of betrayal to be sharing what was supposed to be confidential. "I wasn't supposed to talk to you about the case, but Bob is dead, and everything has changed. I think you need to know what the murders may be about, and how it involves me."

"Okay..." she said hesitantly. "Why did you mention that woman?"

"Laura, the man—the husband of the dead woman—his name is Jeremy Dobson. Well, ah, he called Bob some weeks ago to ask if our firm could help him find his wife's murderer. He wanted us to take a look at some items that might be clues; some things he should have given to the police, but didn't." He knew he was rushing, but he had to get it out. "She was involved in some of the protests that..."

"You mean like the Tea Parties?" She interrupted.

"Yes, like the Tea Parties; only he called them 'meet-up groups'. She was an organizer in one of the groups and was putting out a lot of political information online. Anyhow, she was doing some investigating about what she believed to be a larger conspiracy to undo our country—maybe the world..."

"You mean like what Eleanor Crosby talked about?"

"Well, yes. I suppose it could all be one and the same."

"How many plots to take over the world are there?" She asked him, growing impatient.

"Obviously, two would be too many..." Max appreciated how Laura operated in the gift of keeping things simple.

"Back to the Dobson's; a few weeks ago Bob called me into one of the team's meetings. Normally I wouldn't have a clue about what was going on until it went to court and he needed me to testify, but Bob knew he'd bent the rules this time and wanted a legal opinion. I knew immediately that we were in pretty deep." He said it, remembering how his first impulse was to run like mad in the other direction.

"What Jeremy brought us was a briefcase—his wife's briefcase. He found it after she was murdered and hid it from the police; basically he withheld evidence from them, which, for the record, is a felony. Bob took it knowingly, if you know what I mean; he knew better, and everyone he involved became an accomplice. What Dobson brought us is very likely the reason why everyone was killed."

"Oh, my, Max, shouldn't you have told Bob not to do that?" She didn't want to sound argumentative but she hoped that everything they talked about for weeks to come wouldn't be centered on what had happened.

"I found out after he'd already signed on. I wasn't part of the decision, and normally wouldn't have been involved, except Bob figured out too late that he was in over his head. My not being there on Friday has to have created a problem for whoever is behind this; truthfully, I don't understand why Jeremy Dobson is still alive; unless they think he didn't know anything, or what he does know could lead them somewhere else. Or, he might have interrupted his own execution by coming up here and involving us."

Laura interrupted him, "Max, I don't want to know anything more."

"Okay. I wasn't going to tell you the specifics, anyhow. But, I will write it all down and hide it somewhere safe should something happen to me."

"MAX!"

"I am so very sorry, Laura. We both have our fear to share for a while and help each other through this. And, we need to get a plan together for what to do if we think we are in danger. As Eleanor Crosby said, we need to be ready—for anything."

Laura began to cry, but he continued anyway—he had no choice.

"If you see anybody lurking around the house it will be the police. They want to put us on 24/7 surveillance indefinitely. Tomorrow morning they are coming over to sweep the house to make sure there are no listening devices hidden; they'll check our cars, too. They'll put a device on our phones that we can trip if a call seems suspicious.

"But, neither of us should say anything incriminating to each other on the phones; we need to save what we have to say for when we're away from the house. They will go to a lot of effort to make it appear they are helping us—and we will have to go along. At this point, trust no one."

They were almost home. "Oh, as a precaution, I don't want you to use your cell phone except for the little stuff; it would look odd to them if we didn't use them at all. When you aren't using it, just stick it in a drawer. And, whatever you do, don't talk about any of this to Dana. We don't want her assumed guilty by association."

Their lives had taken an abrupt turn, and he hated it for them both. "Laura, this isn't going to be easy for either of us." He paused, and added, "The funerals begin next weekend."

CHAPTER 55

Lindsay pulled the side chair up close beside Ethel's bed, to feed her a cookie. She could feel Ethel's eyes on her; expectant about what pleasure Lindsay had brought for her this time. Lindsay shut the door to ward off visitors; today she needed time alone with Ethel.

Ethel seemed so small now, and fragile; the once larger than life, five foot seven woman, weighed only ninety eight pounds. Her nurse told Lindsay they all would be convinced she'd made up her mind to starve herself, except for how she always seemed hungry when Lindsay came. Lindsay knew her feeding Ethel was a love language for them both. They bonded in the tender moments when they shared communion over a cookie or dessert.

No matter what was on Lindsay's mind, in the time it took her to get from her home to the nursing home she offered it to the Lord before seeing Ethel, even if it meant sitting in the car for ten or fifteen minutes making sure her own spirit was calm so that she brought nothing into Ethel's room besides compassion. She had relatively short time to spend with Ethel, so it was essential that she not seem preoccupied.

She broke off a small piece of the freshly baked sugar cookie, holding it out to Ethel who opened her mouth and closed her eyes simultaneously, savoring the moment and making it last.

Today Lindsay had trouble staying focused; her thoughts kept returning to when she and Nelson first met. Oh, how she'd loved him then; finding the tender and gentle man who hid behind a self-imposed shell of cynicism and distrust. And it wasn't one-sided; he was crazy in love with her, as well. How was it possible they could have become a silent partnership of two people who now coexisted with no surviving sense of intimacy any level?

Is it too late to reach him? She wondered. *Where would I even begin? How would I start?* But, as impossible as it all seemed, she trusted that God would reach him before it was all over; she didn't want to be in Heaven without him. She'd broken through his hard shell once, and she believed with God's help, she could do it again. *Nothing is impossible*, she reminded herself.

She startled when she heard Ethel clearing her throat, wondering how long she'd been daydreaming. She could tell that Ethel was watching her closely, her forehead furrowing when she noticed Lindsay's eyes tearing up.

Lindsay put her hand over Ethel's, squeezing it. "I'm okay, Mom. I was just thinking back over the years. Some of it makes me sad, but I'm okay." She brushed away a tear.

Ethel looked at her more intensely now, "Nel...nel...nel...?" making an exceedingly rare attempt to speak.

"Nelson?" Lindsay asked.

Ethel nodded.

"Yes, Nelson does make me sad; he's been different lately. After Lenette's death, I noticed he seemed different. He is more withdrawn now than he ever was—but it isn't all bad; recently he doesn't seem to be as career-driven, or as one dimensional as before; he's calmer.

"We don't talk about it. I have tried to get him to open up, but when I try he withdraws." She sighed, "I wish I could say Nelson's fine, but he isn't." She added, "He seems sadder, too."

Ethel nodded, trying to tell Lindsay she understood. She hadn't seen Nelson for six years and, it was impossible for her not to remember how the last time she saw him, he told her that he hated her. Now, she accepted that much of it was her fault, and wished she could repent to him. Adding to her guilt was remembering how she once hated Lindsay. Was that woman me? She wondered. How could I have been blind to the prize Lindsay is? She could feel tears forming in her own eyes.

Lindsay tried to smile at her. "Well, aren't we a fine pair? Pretty funny, how we figured out how connect without speaking, isn't it? Who would have thought it possible?"

Ethel's heart went out to her. She knew without any explanation that Lindsay's marriage was empty. Even before her stroke she'd seen Nelson becoming more introverted and gloomy. While Nelson's father was career driven he had a rounded personality—perhaps too rounded in some ways, but rounded all the same. They'd enjoyed some enjoyable times together despite the obvious clashes of their personalities.

Nothing about Nelson seemed rounded as far back as she could remember, and she blamed herself—he couldn't hate her more than she hated herself. With Lindsay's help, she'd come to realize recriminating served no purpose. Prayer was the one thing she could still do, and she had plenty of time to pray.

Lindsay fed her the last morsel of the cookie before gathering her things to go. "I promise I'll come back in two days."

Ethel nodded, smiling her crooked smile.

Oh, love—love had indeed found a way. *Nothing is impossible,* Lindsay thought. *Praise His wonderful Name!*

~~~

Lindsay returned two days later, and based on what she had told Ethel earlier, she felt the urgency to push through to what she feared was the inevitable ending, wanting to prepare her for the worst.

First she took the time to read to her—they'd gone from reading the torrid romance novels to Christian fiction. Lately, she'd begun reading from Eleanor Crosby's most recent book, *He's at the Door.*

She'd brought with her the makeshift elements for communion. Makeshift or not, there was power in the basic elements that had the ability to transport their spirits when they remembered that the One who had suffered so horribly himself, and was now risen and standing court for them in the heavens.

Ethel listened intently while Lindsay explained to her how Lenette's murder was tied into something very sinister. With halting words, she tried to prepare Ethel for the time she wouldn't be able to come, and she knew that the time to prepare her would soon run out.

"Mom, I don't want to scare you, but if I don't come for a while it won't be my choice. There are things going on in the world that can't be stopped, and as odd as it might sound, they directly affect me. I wouldn't mention any of this if it weren't important for you to know what could happen ahead of time." She took Ethel's hand in hers. "You will need to pray for me if that happens; and for Nelson—for his soul. What we know by faith is if the whole world appears out of control, our God reigns supreme in Heaven. We have read the end of the book, and it's a happy ending." Lindsay forced a smile.

Ethel's eyes opened wide; she understood and was convinced of everything Lindsay was saying to her. She watched TV and understood that the United States of America was in serious trouble and on the verge of collapse.

When Ethel was young she was never outwardly patriotic, but it wasn't because of any contempt for her country. Her generation had taken it for granted that the American Dream would remain as enduring as the heavens. They lived that dream, and raised their sons and daughters to expect it as their rite of passage. *Could it be possible the opportunities they took for granted might be heading for extinction?* she wondered.

Lindsay spread a white cloth napkin on the tray table at her bedside. On it, she placed two plastic cups, a soft tortilla, and some grape juice. "Sorry about the tortilla, it was all I had at home," She smiled. "At least it is unleavened! Aren't we blessed we aren't legalistic?"

Ethel returned the smile, nodding and thinking how pleased God must be to know his Son's death would be remembered today, and not put off because of some legality; how the communion could be celebrated by two women who shared the mystery of his grace in relationship.

"Mom, shall we pray...?" Ethel nodded, wiggling her fingers; her signal for Lindsay to hold her hand.

"Our Father, which art in heaven..." She prayed for both of them, watching her mother-in-law, whose eyes were closed, but her lips moved while she mouthed the words being prayed.

Then Lindsay took the bread, breaking it in pieces...

"This is my body, broken for you..." She put a piece of bread on Ethel's tongue, watching while Ethel chewed it slowly. She partook next. Some miracles might seem more tangible, but none could be more profound than how their hearts had been melded through His Son's sacrifice.

She poured juice into the plastic cups, holding Ethel's head, so she could drink hers, saying, "This is my blood; drink ye all of it."

So the visit would end on a lighter note, Lindsay told her a Maryellen story. Maryellen sometimes came with her, so Ethel was able to appreciate how her antics often got her into trouble.

"Now, Mom", she said, after reminding her again of her fear she might not be returning soon, "I don't need to ask you not to repeat what I told you today, do I?" Ethel was delighted at the joke, and they both laughed while Lindsay prepared to leave.

But, when it was time for her to go Ethel refused to let go of her hand, sensing the prophetic in Lindsay's carefully chosen words.

CHAPTER 56

Jeremy promised Rebecca he would buy her a new car after she moved in with him. It would have seemed logical for her to have Lenette's Lexus, but it was still impounded and the police were making no promises about when Jeremy would be getting it back. Jeremy had issues with Rebecca's Toyota because it was small, not well-rated for safety; and it had already been in to the dealer for two recalls.

Rebecca had never owned a brand new car. During her married life, her husband would drive a car for several years for business. When it was time to replace it, he would unceremoniously hand her the keys to his old car, after which she would drive him to the dealership to pick up his new one.

While the transition wasn't accomplished with much flair, it was still exciting for the family to pile into Russell's 'new', previously owned—not used, car, and acknowledge Rebecca's moving up into his old one. Rebecca hadn't minded.

So, first thing one Saturday morning, Jeremy, Rebecca, and Caleb set out to find a car for Grandma.

Rebecca was standing firm on wanting a minivan. Jeremy tried to talk her out of it, but she'd been online and had a folder full of printed off brochures of different models to show him. Jeremy was glad they were starting early.

"Jeremy, I need to haul things," she announced.

"Like what?"

"...mostly flowers and plants—dirt, manure; things like that; well, and maybe I'll load up on some commodities."

Jeremy chose not to argue with her, remembering Lenette evidenced a similar tenacity of thought. If Rebecca wanted a minivan, she would get a minivan. He refrained from mentioning how they had moved most of her belongings in her previous apartment to her new one in the back of his Escalade in three trips.

The purchase had become such a process he was wishing he'd

surprised her, but her excitement was endearing, considering she'd never been car-shopping before in her life. By the time they'd made the rounds of car lots, Jeremy was exhausted, but, it was worth every arduous minute for him to see Rebecca's expression when the salesman handed her the keys.

What she finally chose was a Ford Escape. Her only objection to the salesman was, "What do you mean it doesn't tow?" What helped the decision along were the heights of the mini vans, and the practicality of her having to climb in and out with Caleb, to put him in his car seat. After driving the Escape, she told Jeremy she'd fallen in love. "Jeremy I love it, and don't you love the name?" She lowered her voice, moving in close to Jeremy so the salesman couldn't hear her. "You know...*escape*—like we might have to?"

Jeremy nodded, knowing she wouldn't leave it alone until he agreed with her. Before their quest began, she'd insisted that she wouldn't even look at a car manufactured by General Motors. Being immersed in her spy mode Rebecca's mind was made up that she would not own a car manufactured by a company who'd been bailed out by the government, on the chance they were installing tracking devices in them. He knew there was no point trying to talk her out of that one; she was already on a mission for him to trade in his Escalade. He was thankful they didn't own GE appliances, or he might have to replace them to satisfy Rebecca's increasing paranoia.

Jeremy wondered where this Rebecca had hidden for so many years.

Lenette, I hope you're watching!

~~~

The car shopping event ended up being so entertaining Jeremy couldn't resist calling Lindsay to describe the day to her. Lindsay found the story amusing, marveling at how the strange pairing of Jeremy and her mother had ended up being such a remarkable blessing for them both. She told Jeremy she hadn't known this Rebecca Kennedy either.

It was time to get to the business at hand. Even though months had passed they had yet to talk about the details surrounding Lenette's death. "Jeremy?"

"Yes, Lindsay."

"You saw the faxes, then?" She asked.

"Yes, I saw them."

"Do you think they had something to do with Lenette's death?"

"No I don't," he crossed his fingers. "It was something else; something else she found. I can't tell you what, but it wasn't the faxes."

"You're sure?" She didn't sound convinced.

"Lindsay, if you go online and search some topic like New World Order Currency you will find thousands of hits. I don't understand it, but someone has been leaking similar currency images to the public for decades. So, even if Nelson had pictures of the real deal, it wouldn't have been enough of a reason for them to kill Lenette. You have to believe me."

She started crying; he hoped with relief.

"So you don't think Nelson had something to do with her murder? But, if he somehow figured out it was me who sent them, he might have had to..."

"Lindsay, no, I absolutely don't. And neither do the police or don't you think they would have questioned him by now; or you?" He hoped he sounded adamant.

"Oh, Jeremy; of course...you're right! Oh, thank God! I am so relieved! Somehow, I thought..." she trailed off without revealing what she was thinking.

"Lindsay, listen to me; we know some weird things are going on, so keep your eyes and ears open. The faxes are but a small piece of a much larger puzzle.

"Nelson works for people who are a part of an agenda to institute a world order of rule—that much we know. The agenda isn't new and will go forward one way or another; I think we have come to a place of critical mass. The ones who are in control are patient, and they're organized—this has been the goal of a wide range of people who normally function like oil and water. For some reason, they have been able to homogenize their different agendas for one purpose. It would be interesting to be able to stick around and see how fast it will take them to fractionalize afterward and start eating each other." He waited for what he'd said to sink in.

"We know Nelson works with them in some upper echelon capacity, and that's why the copies of the currency were in his briefcase. If Nelson hadn't been so wasted at dinner that night, he wouldn't have reacted the way he did to me.

"Sinclair & Levy are only one of the players. Nelson knows things he can't talk about, and secrets put people at risk simply for knowing them. He may be every bit as frightened as we are. The one thing I can say without a doubt is Nelson would never hurt Lenette. He may be in danger himself; you need to be prepared for that."

"Oh, Jeremy—it never occurred to me that he could be a good guy." Her relief was evident.

"Lenette was the only person who could have read something into Nelson's comment—she put herself in danger without Nelson's or your help. I believe she was in over her head before she ever saw the faxes— you, more than anyone, know she wasn't afraid to push buttons. This thing is bigger than we are, and we all need to be ready for what may...

"I think the time is shorter than we think." What Jeremy told her reminded her of her last bible study and meetings that were coming up in New York. She was thankful Maryellen took the bull by the horns and had made their reservations early.

"Thanks, Jeremy." He could hear the relief in her voice. "I think I'll sleep better tonight." And, for the first time in months she was feeling hungry.

CHAPTER 57

Max felt like his life had been switched with someone else's; either that or he'd been selected for the starring role in some never before aired episode of the Twilight Zone, only it wasn't fiction. What brought him back to reality each evening was driving his car into his garage, knowing Laura was waiting for him inside.

For over a week, he'd reported in at the police station by 8:00 a.m. Every inch of Bob's property had been declared part of the ongoing investigation, and Max feared things could go on this way for months. He'd overheard someone say that Bob's widow had moved to a hotel while they went through their home the same way. *Poor Martha,* he thought, trying to imagine having every aspect of one's life devastated.

The toxicology reports had been run and run again. The Chief's prediction was what killed them was an airborne agent, probably a gas distributed through the HVAC system. Max had heard enough from a couple of one-sided phone conversations to be able to piece together how they thought it might be an agent meant for gas warfare, and quite possibly stolen.

Max believed the toxin was likely created specifically for the purpose it was used for. One of the details that made it intriguing was how it had left no side effects whatsoever—most gasses blistered skin, nasal passages, lungs, etc. Whatever this was, it was deadly, efficient, and impossible to detect.

Max feigned boredom, pretending to be reading on his Kindle, but playing Angry Birds instead. He hoped his presence would be forgotten, making him unobtrusive, like a fly on the wall. His training as a lawyer had made him an astute observer of human nature, and he was sure if he played his cards right there would be a time when they would relax and let something slip.

He desperately wanted to talk to Jeremy Dobson, but if Jeremy's phones were tapped any call that was initiated from the Portland area would point back at Max.

For the moment, he and Laura had ceased to Google anything that could indict either of them later. Since the New World Order's plan was new to him, Max probed his memory for any validation of what he had learned versus what had occurred.

He wished he'd taken notes the day Bob had him sit in on the meeting with Dobson. He relied on Bob's practice of taping his meetings, so he hadn't bothered. He wondered if Bob had the foresight not to leave a trail, or if a tape would show up. If there was a tape it would be incriminating.

Even should he manage to get access to Bob's office before they went through it, he couldn't move the chip; it was the red herring—and thankfully the red herring had never been in his position.

Dear God! Was it possible something so evil had been concocted it could make the pursuit of happiness vanish for millions around the globe? He wondered.

He remembered something his father told him shortly before he passed away. He told him, "Notice, Max, that a fascist government cannot tolerate a middle class. That class would have to be dealt with before this nation could become truly socialist. They will have to break it; our economic underpinnings will have to be compromised. It won't be pretty, nor will it be reversible. The middle class is what makes our nation strong—vibrant, and it makes this country the envy of the world. The average man can reach for the sky in America; even an immigrant arrives here with the hope of changing his family's lives for generations to come. They come to America because they see an opportunity here. So, while you can, reach for it."

He realized the irony in what his father told him. The headline in the paper two days ago was how the middle class was shrinking. He wished he'd questioned his dad about why he believed that, only at the time Max thought he was being negative.

The masses would soon be aware that the sky they'd been reaching for was only vapor.

∿∿∿

When he got home that afternoon the shades were drawn, and the house was dark.

"Laura?" He tried not to panic.

He heard a whispered "Shhhh" coming from the living room.

"Where are you?" He whispered back.

"Over here."

He followed her voice, finding her sitting in the corner on the floor, with Burger curled up next to her.

"Max, I need to go to the bathroom, but I was afraid to go."

"Did something happen?"

She started to crawl towards the bathroom. "Wait—I'm going to go now that you're here. I'll be right back."

Max sat down by the dog. "Sorry, fella. This isn't what you signed on for, is it?"

The dog rested his head on Max's leg, closing his eyes. Max wished he could be a dog. It would be gratifying to live for the moment, and not have to worry about what was going to happen tomorrow.

Laura crawled back, nudging a pillow from the bedroom along in front of her.

"Laura…"

"Shhhh! Max, I'm asking you to be quiet!" She continued to whisper, emphasizing her point by putting her forefinger over her lips. "I know we're being watched, and I think we're being listened to, too."

"What makes you think that?" He asked.

Shhhhh! "The people the police sent to guard us—well, they're acting weird. Wouldn't you think they should be watching the area around the house?"

"Yes."

"They aren't. They're watching the house all right, only they're watching me with it! And, I've been watching them back. I needed to go to the store earlier, so I went outside to ask if I could go. The one guy said, "Fine", that I could go. When I came inside I looked back and he was talking on his cell phone gesturing toward the house. Then, after I left and turned the corner at the end of our street, a silver car pulled out from somewhere and started following me; the driver was a woman. She followed me to the store, but she passed by me when I parked. Then, on my way home, I noticed her behind me again, and she was talking on her cell phone. By then I was convinced she was following me. Max, I think she was warning someone here that I was on my way home.

"When I got back, our bedroom door was open—like, it was ajar. I always shut it so Burger can't go in and I specifically remember shutting it, because when I was in the garage I decided to check to be sure; it was shut. Max, I'm positive they were inside our house."

"Laura…" But, before he could continue she interrupted him, "Shhhh! Max! How do I get you to lower your voice?"

"Okay!" he whispered. "Laura, later tonight I'll check for listening devices. I know what to look for. It would make sense they would want to eavesdrop in our bedroom, but remember, if I remove them it will tip them off, so we will just have to live with it. Now, I'm going to say your name you are going to say 'Oh, sorry I didn't hear you, I was napping'. Then I'm going to say, 'It's Friday night, let's go out for dinner'. If they are going to following us, at least it won't be boring."

She smiled at him, relieved. She knew that Max was concerned she was alone too much, and right now she agreed with him.

He leaned over, so he could whisper right into her ear. "Laura, we're going to have a nice weekend. When we talk at home we'll talk about general things like the weather or the news, but if we need to talk about something private we'll go for a walk or take a shower together." She smiled, whispering back, "I don't think we'll be talking."

"Me either; that was a test. I wanted to see if you were paying attention."

"Did I pass?" she asked, to which he gave her thumbs up.

"We may be living like this for a while, but, we can do it. Now, turn on some lights, and do what I said..."

He called out, "LAURA!"

"Hi, Max!" Sorry! I was napping..."

"Well, let's get you out of here and do something fun. How about Sushi for dinner and then let's rent a movie?"

"What movie?"

"*Catch Me if You Can* sounds good." He said, trying to be funny.

"No it does not." She frowned at him, clearly, not in the mood for jesting.

"Then let's go for a walk, eat out afterward, and you choose the movie.

"Come on, Burger! We're going for a walk."

Max placed his cell phone in the desk drawer, motioning Laura do the same. What they needed to talk about was not for anyone's ears but theirs.

CHAPTER 58

The second the door shut after him, Jeremy heard Rebecca's voice calling out, "Daddy! Hurry! We have a surprise for you!"

Caleb was sitting on the great room floor, playing with some rubber blocks. Rebecca plopped down beside him, coaxing, "Let's show your daddy what a big boy you are!" His pudgy hands reached up over his head at the words "big boy"

"Sit down over there, Daddy." She demanded, playfully—gesturing for Jeremy to sit down in a spot a few feet away from where they were sitting. Jeremy saw a flash of Lenette in her expression.

"Now what are my two favorite people up to?" he asked, immediately noticing the appreciative look Rebecca gave him after he said it. He meant it; he thanked God every day that she was with them, never expecting the blessing it would be for both of them.

After Jeremy sat down she pulled Caleb to his feet, pointing him towards Jeremy. Caleb took three steps before getting so excited that he threw himself into his daddy's waiting arms. For a moment, everything was perfect.

After celebrating Caleb's new milestone a few more times, Rebecca excused herself to finish preparing dinner. Since he had a few minutes to kill before eating, Jeremy decided to go through his mail. He set a pile of bills aside for later, amazed how fast a month rolled around based on the billing cycle, pitching everything else, with the exception of one other piece of mail—it was a note-sized envelope addressed in a woman's hand. He turned it over and saw that it was sealed with wax. Adding to the intrigue, there was no return address—it was then he noticed the postmark; Portland, Oregon. He felt his stomach reacting—he hated the feeling; it was always a harbinger of something bad. *Here we go again*, he thought. He glanced at Rebecca, who was stirring gravy, thinking, *and I knew it was too good to last.*

Willing his hands to stay steady he opened the envelope; sure that it did not contain a thank you.

God, he thought, *God.* In the end, he was all there was. Whatever was lurking in the shadows was not greater than who was watching over him and his family. *Jeremy quit being a wimp. Enough of this!* He told himself.

He took a deep breath, unfolding the letter. It was from Max Zimmerman, dated three days before.

Dear Jeremy,

I would have called you, but that would be dangerous for us both. In case you don't remember who I am, I was the corporate counsel for Bob Murphy. My wife and I are being watched. I don't know who to trust anymore; I probably don't trust anyone. Tomorrow I will take this letter to the police station and put it with their mail. If the seal is broken, you can guess what that means. Sorry! Sounds paranoid, but for the moment, the shoe fits.

By now you've figured out that Bob's having the chip put him on somebody's radar. Bob was with the CIA a long time ago. He told me once that one reason he chose to keep a low profile was not to give them any reason to watch him too closely because they knew Bob had sources at his disposal that most people don't. I'm sorry if I'm the first one to point this out, but we are all walking time bombs. I can hear my clock ticking since I am sure they assumed I would be at work that day.

Your wife discovered some vulnerability in the plan. Whoever she was meeting must have been powerful enough they had to keep them apart. Too bad; now we'll never know. Forgive me for delivering what I know cannot be pleasant news, and for the rambling. I probably think I am only confirming what you already knew. Be careful. Until we meet again,

God speed. Max Zimmerman

Enclosed with the letter was a folded advertisement of an Eleanor Crosby event taking place in New York City in November, with "We hope to be there," scribbled on the bottom in the margin. He was sure Lindsay had mentioned the meeting in a previous conversation.

Jeremy's head was exploding. He tried to reel his thoughts in, while saying a prayer for the Zimmerman's. It hit him with premature remorse that if something happened to them, he would be, at least partially, responsible for their deaths.

"Jeremy?" Rebecca was talking to him. "Jeremy, are you okay?"

"I'm fine; Mom, just hungry. Dinner smells great!" When he said it, his stomach offered up more indicators of a betrayal.

"Well, then, I say 'Let's eat'!" Rebecca announced; strapping Caleb into his high chair.

Jeremy joined them. "You know who Eleanor Crosby is, don't you?"

She nodded affirmatively.

"Check on a meeting she's having in New York City in a few weeks, would you? I think we need to be there."

CHAPTER 59

From their first meeting, Eleanor and Jenna Larson formed an immediate bond. Jenna was raised in a setting of acute dysfunction, so she cherished the interest the older woman took in her. Eleanor loved her at first sight, and felt that, for the second time in her life, God had given her a true spiritual child.

Jenna and Rod took a risk, and asked if Eleanor and Candy would consider having dinner at their home the night before the Madison Square Garden event. Respecting her well-documented practice of prayer and isolation before she spoke, they fully expected to be turned down, so when Eleanor accepted the invitation, they were ecstatic. In spite of the somberness, they all took the opportunity of being together as a cause for celebration.

They all sensed the imminence of time running out; her event seemed like a catalyst for whatever else was 'out there'. Eleanor would take nothing for granted in the time left to her. The invitation from the Larson's offered her the opportunity to encourage them; something she knew they needed. She couldn't imagine how Rod managed to appear so calm, knowing the mental and spiritual warfare he dealt with every day. The vitriol aimed at him was unprecedented, vicious, and its intensity seemed to be increasing—and it was coming from high places. They all understood that the stakes were extremely high.

She surfaced from her fasting and preparation long enough to get updates about the pending legislation on Hate Speech, hoping it wouldn't affect her meeting. The bill was described as "any speech intended to foster hatred against individuals, or groups, based on race, religion, gender, sexual preference, place of national origin, or other improper classification." Although she knew it had not yet passed both houses, once it did, the reality of what it imposed on a free people was sobering; another pending clarification of the First Amendment was intended to further isolate Christians as intolerant.

Like many other bills passed in recent history, while the polling showed that the country remained overwhelmingly against them, it was probable they would be passed by some procedural bait and switch. The week before this bill was introduced, a high ranking member of Congress referred to Rod Larson by name on the Sunday morning talk shows, labeling him as divisive, and dangerous. Unless you watched his programs, and knew who he was, he was convincing. Rod was a gift-giver with his over-the-top rhetoric, that when taken out of context, made him look equally 'out of context'.

Ironically, the opposing side's rhetoric was harsher, targeting the grass-roots groups who had organized for the purpose of protesting a runaway government. The Speaker of the House was calling for an emergency session of the Senate, promising they would not leave the Senate Chamber until they bill was passed. The Speaker further promised how "hate speech would be a criminal offense and worthy of the most severe punishment; with fines assessed, licenses revoked, and if necessary criminal charges would be brought against anyone refusing to comply."

"This can no longer be tolerated..." the President was quoted as saying, at a press conference earlier that week, also promising a quick passage of the bill.

Eleanor commented to Candy, "Does that appear to be a stacked deck to you?"

Candy could only nod. It had become difficult for her to look forward very far.

~~~

The morning news confirmed that the House of Representatives had the votes to push the legislation through, guaranteeing that it would be on the President's desk by the weekend.

The noose was tied, ready, and dangling from the Progressive's branch; its purpose to intimidate and still its detractors. They're setting things up for a sacrifice, Eleanor thought. It will be something that will satisfy those on the side of the public debate who are crying for blood, and the same offering will suffice to make those who were already afraid compliant.

Although she had not heard her own name mentioned, she had caught part of a commentary that talked about a "gathering of fundamentalist Christians" that was soon taking place in New York City, also referring to the "millions across the globe" who were registered for the same event. Apparently that meant she was getting a pass.

It didn't take a lot of imagination to be able to picture how the public's irrational fear of fundamentalist Christians could be manipulated to trigger something significant that could wind up being the public lynching the fear mongers cried for. Pilate washed his hands in a similar scenario.

Those who had become the apostate church distanced, and even sided with those who had convinced them "sold out Christ followers" were radical, fanatics...extreme—funny that kind of enthusiasm was tolerated at a baseball game, but not in church. Tolerance was now mandated for all faiths, except for those who refused to abandon the plumb line of God's word. The grey areas of doctrine had shrunk to almost nothing, leaving the nominal Christian with a choice; and the choice that remained was to be either hot, or cold.

Eleanor murmured the Constitution's Preamble, reminding herself how honorable men had sacrificed so others could enjoy it's benefits, "We the People of the United States, in Order to form a more perfect Union, establish Justice, insure domestic Tranquility, provide for the common defense, promote the general Welfare and secure the Blessings of Liberty to ourselves and our Posterity, do ordain and establish this Constitution for the United States of America."

She prayed, "Dear God, give me the strength to accomplish whatever lies ahead... ".

~~~

The days before the event passed quickly. Eleanor didn't have one thing on her agenda beyond it, nor did Candy. It would seem strange to have the luxury of time, only it hardly seemed a luxury to Eleanor, who panicked whenever she thought of it.

Rod sent a car for his dinner guests, who were staying at a hotel near Times Square. Jenna had been working on the dinner for two days, wanting it to be memorable. Before they ate Rod jokingly told them that Jenna's being the cook insured the food wasn't poisoned; while funny, it hit too close to home for Jenna, who glared at him, handing him a saucer with a dab of the main course on it, with the request he taste it before she served it to their guests. He ate it without hesitation.

When Eleanor saw the sizeable acreage they lived on she couldn't help but wonder how many security people must be wandering around at any one time, making sure Rod and his family were safe. She decided she was glad she didn't know.

Every effort was made to insure evening would be informal and relaxing for everyone. While Jenna was finishing the last minute preparations, Rod and the children took Eleanor and Candy on a tour of the grounds and the stable. It had been awhile since Eleanor had been around children; particularly well behaved ones. It touched her how quickly they befriended her, with each one talking over the other, to tell her something about themselves.

After telling Rod how impressed she was with them, she

commented, "Do you remember what Carl Sandberg said about children?"

He didn't. "No. You've got me on that one, Eleanor."

"He said 'Children are God's opinion the world must go on'."

"I like that." Rod said. "I like it a lot." He turned to look at them and got choked up. It was an extra heavy load when your convictions and choices were compelling your entire family down the one-way road you had chosen to take. He cleared his throat, trying not to let his emotions get the best of him; his faith in the world going on was being sorely tested.

~~~

A bell rang; it was Jenna announcing it was time to eat. The table was set in a glassed-in area off the kitchen that overlooked the back yard, pool, and barn; now all shrouded in the deepening shadows of twilight.

The assembly included Tilly, the children's nanny. Before eating, they took hands, and Rod blessed the meal, "God, Abba, we approach your throne humbly tonight. Especially bless Eleanor and Candy. We are awed to be part of those you set aside, somewhere in eternity, to be part of the events we see taking place around us. While we watch with horror and awe, we are expectant for what we know you are doing in the midst of this darkness. I speak 'Shalom' over each of us. Bless our conversation, our time, and this food. We affirm our meal sanctified by your word. Bless and keep us all. And, bless and keep our beautiful land. "In Jesus name, Amen."

"Thank you, Rod. That was beautiful; we thank him for you, also." Eleanor told him, with Candy nodding her agreement.

Jenna excused herself to get the salad course, with their oldest daughter helping her. Eleanor was touched by the obvious effort Jenna had put into the preparations. The salad was delicious; a bed of butter lettuce covered with strawberries, kiwi, oranges, with sliced almonds.

Eleanor asked Jenna, "There is something unusual in the dressing; is it Lavender?"

Jenna was delighted that she'd noticed. "Oh, yes. I love to use it in my salad dressings and in sauces. When we moved here, I discovered a huge bed of lavender in the back by the barn. I didn't want to waste it, so I've been finding different ways to use it. It's nice for a bath, too; I'll give you some before you leave."

At the mention of bathing, Eleanor winked at Candy, who was already looking at her, smiling. They savored each course, and each other; holding at bay the issues that would inevitably come up later. The food and fellowship were delicious.

On the window ledges, on the floor, and on the table candles cast a flickering light, each from inside its own unique ceramic or glass holders. Rod bragged about how Jenna collected things that had to do with light. He explained, "She has sun catchers in most of our windows; it's like a rainbow is in our house every day."

"I am not the least bit creative." Eleanor commented, "Jenna, if you don't mind I am going to steal your idea about the sun catchers. You might not remember the Pollyanna books, but she hung prisms in the window of an invalid woman she visited; Mrs. Snow, I believe. She took them off the woman's chandelier and hung them. I tried it once, but it didn't go over so hot with my mother! I think I may have washed a lot of dishes for trying it."

They all laughed. Trying to imagine the child version of Eleanor standing on her mother's dining room table, removing prisms, was both comical and endearing.

"My friends say I'm hard to buy for. Now I have something I can say I want!" she said, delighted.

"Well then, I want to be the first person to give you one," offered Jenna, suggesting Eleanor select one before they left.

"What a lovely gesture, Jenna." Eleanor commented. "I will, and it will be treasured."

"You catch the light, you know," Jenna told her, sincerely.

"Oh, do you think so? I'm going to hang on to your beautiful thought; my messages seem heavier over time."

Rod spoke up, "Boy, you and me both; we both bring heavy messages. But, as Jenna has pointed out recently, light only hurts the eyes of those who have been in the dark too long. Gradually, they will either adjust to the light or crawl back under their rocks where the darkness dwells. We've offered them an alternative.

"I go by the adage, 'It ain't heavy if it's the truth.'"

While what he said was true, it was also a reminder how both their messages contained eternal consequences that extended far beyond the issues at hand.

Jenna added, soberly, "Don't let him kid you—it's heavy."

~~~

When the meal was over, Tilly took the children upstairs, while the adults adjourned to the living room where a cozy fire had already been set in the fireplace.

Rod's demeanor had changed; his countenance had become more serious, somber— perhaps even troubled. Eleanor knew that he, like she, had made a tremendous effort not to bring the weight they were both carrying into the mealtime. He removed a white linen towel covering some objects on a table next to the bay window. The elements for communion had been set out.

"You may have wondered why I called this meeting..." He looked around, searching for a smile from one of them, and when none followed, he said, looking straight at Eleanor, "To quote someone far smarter than me, 'The time is short'...".

"What is it that you know?" Eleanor asked, never one to dance around unwelcome news.

"Not close to all of it, but I have pieced together enough to believe that our lives are about to be changed forever—and that it will happen imminently. Mark my word; by next week at this time nothing will remain the same.

"Nero played his fiddle while Rome burned. What we have politely called denial, is in reality apathy, and it is my opinion the church - meaning the organized church - bears the most accountability because they have excused it, and perhaps, even encouraged it. Mankind won't be judged by the deception but for its inability to judge deception by the truth." He paused, waiting to see if anyone else wanted to say something. When no one jumped in he continued.

"For most, accountability is the "A-word", and that mindset has been programmed into our culture. People view accountability as an infringement on their rights; it's been sucked out of the largest institutions down to the smallest; even the family unit has ceased to value the wisdom or faith of their parents and grandparents, much less respect it. Who will there be left to hold the banner high when half our youth have no memories of role models who exhibited what faith or ethics look like?" He paused; too emotional to continue. "Faith requires me to speak as though we have a future, but I fear there is no way to stop what is about to take place."

Again, he looked at Eleanor, "We gave it everything we had, but the pendulum has already swung too far."

"Rod, tell us what you do know, please. I think we can handle it." Eleanor spoke up, adding, "We have no choice but to handle it." Even while she spoke she looked around the room, trying to take in every detail and memorize each face, knowing that with every tick of the clock they were being obliged toward something that would require them to draw on every morsel of their individual faith.

Rod cleared his throat and continued, "I have an anonymous source who recently sat in on some of the closed door meetings regarding the Hate Speech Legislation." He made the quotation gestures with his fingers in the air when he said "hate speech".

"We, the United States of America, are the last bastion of any form of freedom of speech left on the planet. Europe has been all but silenced; even Australia and New Zealand are under new restrictions.

"I don't think fifty years ago anyone suspected the role the Muslims would play in the world order scenario. It wasn't until after 9/11 when they, I am speaking of those with the hidden agenda, seized the opportunity to use the terrorists as a shield to effect tolerance that benefited their purposes. Wouldn't it be fascinating to see how long it takes for the unholiest of all alliances to fall apart once the debris settles?"

"Back to topic—my source said that while we were able hold back the inevitable for a time, it was and is, inevitable. He told me at the time of our meeting many of our officials were being transported to secret bunkers to wait it all out; I don't know about you, but that has an ominous sound to me. We all believed that one generation would be alive to watch it all unfold—and, we, us, certainly have watched some pretty unbelievable stuff unfolding.

"The Hate Speech bill was the cherry on the sundae for them to have the power to move forward unrestricted. How ironic that the enemies of the State are the Christians, Jews, entrepreneurs, and Capitalists—The New World Order stands at the door." He paused again, knowing how weighty this sounded to his small audience.

"The leadership, the mythological "THEY", have been working on this plan for literally hundreds of years. Ironically, the leaders that we currently see as the players, who we assume are part of it, who have been deliberately assigned to play out their roles out in the open, are the puppets for the real string pullers. The unrest and dissension that are behind this more restricted environment is being underwritten by uber-wealthy leftists.

"About a year ago we found another source; or rather it was she found who found us—let's just say we found each other. She said she could provide proof that the NWO had developed something capable of controlling the world's population. What she had was a microchip that came from the highest level; one that had literally been removed from someone— she was told by a person in a position to know, that billions of them have been manufactured, and stored for implementation. She was going to hand it over for us to have analyzed—but she never showed. We jumped through all of her hoops, the time and place; everything—and then she didn't show. But, I believe she was on to something..." he trailed off...thinking.

"If we could have taken it to our experts, if they could have dissected it, then we would have had the tangible piece of evidence we needed to slow down their machine. Whatever she has might be the missing piece of the puzzle—or a curse..."

He stopped mid-sentence; the realization hitting him like a brick. How could he have missed it? She hadn't stood them up—and that could only mean that what she had in her possession was so vital to what would happen next she had to be eliminated. It also meant they knew who she was delivering it to.

~~~

Rod gave the elements for communion to each one, explaining that the word 'Eucharist' in Greek meant 'thanksgiving'. "Think of it," he said. "Christ initiated this ultimate act of thankfulness just moments before he was betrayed. Those are big shoes to fill."

The scripture he chose was from Paul's letter to the Colossians, "I am glad when I suffer for you in my body, for I am participating in the sufferings of Christ that continue for His Body.

"We may seem insignificant in the vast numbers of the many God called; but significant in the numbers of those he chose from the foundation of the world to hold His banner high at the end."

How fitting Rod would have the foresight to know how meaningful remembering Christ's last supper before his death would be for the five people, who were perhaps celebrating it for the last time, as a free people.

CHAPTER 60

Eleanor ran her hands across her skirt, smoothing it. Again, she was waiting for their car to arrive; she wasn't nervous, but instead felt expectant—in an anxious way. She was never one to reveal much emotion, but she decided that she had now experienced firsthand what the word *tremulous* meant.

Overnight, all of the signs of a crackdown were now visible; the streets were emptied of traffic, stores fronts were closed, with some being boarded up, guarded by the National Guard, who Eleanor was told were called in to prevent looting. Foot traffic was sparse, if at all. The media called it a "high alert" terrorist threat, but the hard to miss irony was how anyone who was registered to attend the Crosby meetings could attend.

The police, although their increasing presence had been downplayed, suddenly seemed to be everywhere—it was happening exactly how Rod predicted. The networks were still broadcasting, but it was the anchors that were doing the reporting, and it seemed scripted. There had been no 'man on the street' reports for two days. Some cable stations were *temporarily* off the air. The lack of news had a tranquilizing effect, but that would be temporary. But, it would keep a lid on people being called to participate in organized riots, or protests; until they spontaneously took place because of panic.

She stood up, unable to sit still any longer. She walked across the room, and pulled the window treatments aside to look outside. Unexpectedly, someone in a window across from hers moved, too quickly, from sight. They were being watched. Her reaction was to quote scripture. *I will not fear; what can man do to me. You are my strength and my shield, O'Lord. You are my defense.* She looked down to the street below; it was eerily empty.

Eleanor checked her computer and cell phone to see if they were working, recalling that Rod believed at some point communications would cease.

She sensed Candy's presence; she was standing beside her with a cup of brew, pretending, as best she could that things weren't drastically different than before. "I've got your brew, Auntie. Are you okay?" Eleanor knew Candy was concerned for her. Neither of them had slept well, although she blamed her own lack of sleep on the second helping of apple cobbler she'd eaten at the Larson's the night before.

"I'm better than okay, thank you, dearest." she said, hoping she sounded braver than she felt. "And, how are you doing? Have you called your mom yet?" She tried to keep her voice light.

"I did. She sends her love. Uncle Fred's there with his family; they're spending the weekend at Mom and Dad's."

She lowered her voice, as if someone else might be listening, "I spoke to Dad, too. He asked me not to tell you this, but I didn't promise..." She held up two crossed fingers for Eleanor's benefit. "Dad is pretty worried; I guess it's almost as spooky there as here. He swears he saw a black helicopter yesterday." Candy emphasized *swears* because her father was a conspiracy novel fanatic and always on the lookout for anything that smacked of being conspiratorial. Neither could resist smiling, both thinking how smug he must be feeling at the moment. They knew that even if things got ugly he would take pride in getting in an "I told you so" to his family of scoffers.

"Mom's more optimistic; she thinks this will blow over. She's hoping you'll come out and stay with them for a while, now that you'll have more time."

"I think a reunion is likely," Eleanor answered her; but she wasn't thinking in Seattle.

They heard someone in the hallway clearing his throat; alerting them that it was time. "Onward Christian Soldiers," Eleanor said. "It's now or never, Candy. Be on the alert-be aware of everything." She didn't want to upset her; aware that Candy's over-solicitousness was due to her own apprehension, but it was essential they retain everything they saw or heard. The more ominous the darkening landscape looked was only the backdrop for the final act of the King of Kings.

Two armed men, dressed in black, escorted them to a car—it was a black SUV that, Eleanor saw with dismay, had darkened privacy windows; now they couldn't see outside.

"Aren't you scared at all?" Candy whispered. Suddenly, her face showed alarm. "I-I-I think I just saw a tank." she said, pointing forward toward the windshield, lowering her voice still more, "Something enormous just went across that intersection. Do you think...?" She looked at her aunt for reaction.

Eleanor willed herself to remain calm; for both of them. She wanted her response to refocus her niece on the importance of God's sovereignty and how they were chosen for this hour. "Candy, we are living through historic times. Sadly, I don't think those who are in charge will allow history to be recorded accurately, if it is recorded at all. That's why we need to be able to recall as much as we can later, with God's help. Our God is on His throne, and he knows the end from the beginning." For emphasis, she added, "None of this is a surprise to him, so that means he's got us covered."

~~~

While they were being processed, Eleanor noticed there were piles of purses, coats, and jackets that had been confiscated; a chorus of ring tones drew her attention to cardboard boxes filled with cell phones lining a hallway. It was sobering to see how people had willingly sacrificed their civil rights to be there. The lack of any attempt at organization was testimony to them never being returned to their rightful owners.

The lines to enter the building stretched down the street and disappeared around the corner; there were armed police positioned every few yards along the sidewalks. Some asked why and were told it was for their protection, but their presence was intimidating. Unknown to those who were waiting, recent news reports confirmed that armies who were gathered to the north of Israel were now on the move southward. The world would soon be in turmoil.

Eleanor pictured Rod, sitting in his studio, holding tightly to his very near the surface emotions, trying to frame the right words around the stark message he was recording. And, with God's blessing, he could post it before the internet went down; his living legacy as a purveyor of truth could still go out to tens of thousands.

Rod, she knew, did not expect to see another tomorrow. Dear Jenna would be sitting inside The Garden with Tilly, and their kids; her and Rod's decision to be separated was witness to their faith, even while knowing they would not see each other again. But, in truth, every person present had to put their fears aside to come.

When Rod and Jenna walked their guests to the car after dinner, he remarked how every good-bye should be treated their last. His last whispered words to Eleanor were, "It's dire, Eleanor. Please take every precaution..." They stood in the driveway staring into each other's eyes—breaking away was difficult. Neither said the words "good-bye"; they both accepted they wouldn't see each other again.

~~~

Before going inside, and knowing this might be the last time they would see each other that day, or ever, Candy and Eleanor lingered in the car, hoping for a few minutes to themselves before, as Eleanor succinctly put it, "All hell breaks loose."

First, she said, "Candy, I want us to say the Lord's Prayer together." She reached over and took her niece's small hands in hers while they prayed the Lord's own words, "Our Father, who art in heaven, hallowed be thy Name. Thy Kingdom come, Thy will be done, on earth as it is in Heaven. Give us each day our daily bread, and forgive us our trespasses, as we forgive those who trespass against us. And, lead us, not into temptation, but deliver us from evil. For thine is the Kingdom, the Power and the Glory forever and ever. Amen."

Eleanor's voice was husky, "Dearest girl, I don't want to alarm you, but should we become separated, I want to say again how much I love and treasure you. I can't imagine loving my own flesh and blood child more than I do you."

Candy, also, took the opportunity to say what her aunt meant to her; both of them stopping before their emotions incapacitated them.

"Because of Him", Eleanor said with Candy nodding her agreement. The few seconds of calm were over; now to, Eleanor quoted, "face the music"

~~~

When their car pulled away from the hotel, several police cars pulled out from side streets to escort them. The second they were escorted inside the arena, the head of The Garden's security pulled Eleanor aside to inform her that the setup had been changed by police order. The reason offered was that it was for her security. So, instead of the podium being at the far end, the way she was accustomed to, the new arrangement required her to speak from a stage that was already set up in the middle of the arena. By necessity, lights were trained on it from all sides; it would not be the darkened atmosphere she preferred. Their excuse was lame; she already felt like a goldfish in a fishbowl. So much for security; now she was a target from all sides.

Eleanor wasn't happy about it, but the setting reminded her that what they were engaged in was a contest. The Holy Spirit was her defense, and her protector. She could do this.

Most people might be thrown off by the unexpected changes, but Eleanor was not. It was her cameramen who were thrown off, madly scrambling to pull off the simulcast professionally.

~~~

It was time.

In spite of every obstacle that had presented itself to prevent their being there, the auditorium was packed to capacity, with people who couldn't find seats standing around the perimeter. No one was turned away.

The soprano walked to the center of the stage—the signal that it was time to begin. She took an extra moment—trying to maintain her composure, also shaken by the last- minute changes. She took her cues from Eleanor who, if anything, seemed serene.

Taking a deep breath, she began to sing, her voice was clear, and strong...

"The sky shall unfold
Preparing His entrance
The stars shall applaud Him
With thunders of praise
The sweet light in His eyes, shall enhance those awaiting
And we shall behold Him, then face to face
O we shall behold Him, we shall behold Him
Face to face in all of His glory
O we shall behold Him, yes we shall behold Him
Face to face, our Savior and Lord
The angel will sound, the shout of His coming
And the sleeping shall rise, from there slumbering place
And those remaining, shall be changed in a moment
And we shall behold him, then face to face
We shall behold Him, o yes we shall behold Him
Face to face in all of His glory
We shall behold Him, face to face
Our Savior and Lord
We shall behold Him, our Savior and Lord
Savior and Lord!

Her voice trailed off... And, for the last time Eleanor waited to speak; hearing the words of the beloved song that had never failed to prepare her audience for what God was prompting her to say. The moment the soloist's voice faded, Eleanor rose to her feet. And, like every other time, she smoothed the wrinkles from her skirt. One last time, the ritual calmed her.

It was while she was making her way through the crowd toward the stage that she heard them...'Thunk, thunk, thunk...' It was the distant sound of rotator blades—helicopters; and a lot of them—their timing anything but a coincidence.

He would instruct her... *I can do all things...Jesus, we can do this...Father, watch over your sheep; not one sparrow falls to the ground without you noticing...every hair on every head in this auditorium is numbered...!*

The sound of the choppers grew louder and more invasive, now with the vibrations from their propellers felt as well as heard. The lights flickered on and off. The atmosphere also changed— the air was suddenly charged with static electricity; the hair on Eleanor's arms stood on end.

What began as a humming soon turned to a murmur, while the trapped audience reacted to the stimulus of the sounds of occupation. Every eye was trained towards Eleanor, who continued her gradual walk through the audience, toward the podium.

A bodyguard took her arm when she reached the stage, assisting her up the steps. Once on the stage she held her Bible out in front of her, looking at the Cross on its cover. She remembered the price her Lord paid for her to have the honor of offering him to others. The thought of martyrdom for the privilege of preaching the Gospel, while considered, had not seemed a real possibility before today—today it felt decidedly real.

There was more commotion, but the noise continued to emanate from outside the building. The air increasingly was becoming more static, and heavy, as though there was an approaching storm. Eleanor circled the lectern slowly, and deliberately, looking down and directly into the eyes of her audience, while also making eye-contact with the cameras. Now she understood why God had rearranged the layout; there was an intimacy with her audience she had not experienced before.

She was calm, divinely calm, and it transferred to the people who had ceased murmuring. She smiled at them, holding out her right hand, palm forward while continuing to circle the stage— beckoning them to *"Hush"*.

Inside the auditorium, there was total silence, broken only by the chaotic noises that were escalating outside; now the unmistakable wail of sirens could now be heard in the distance, gradually building in intensity. But, despite the disruption, every eye remained fixed on her; drawing strength from her. The undeniable miracle was the peace that prevailed in spite of the confusion.

The lights overhead flickered, and, again, she held out her hand— "Now hush", was its message.

One more time she circled the stage, looking into their eyes with her hand still held out in front of her; quiet prevailed.

She stepped up to the lectern and took a deep breath, before declaring for the last time, "My dear friends in Christ Jesus—the time is short. The auditorium went black...

~~~

It did not take the authorities long to get the emergency power running again; just a little over six hours. They had been warned to expect a world–wide blackout brought about by an Electro Magnetic Pulse. An EMP was a cunning weapon, designed to knock out the whole world's electrical grids with violent voltage surges. While something of this nature was rumored to be one of the catastrophic options used to gain control, it wasn't expected to take place so quickly. They were assured it would be a last resort.

The clean-up after an EMP would be exhaustive; some predictions said as long as seven years. Everything relying on electrical impulse would cease to function; anything depending on electricity of any kind on land, sea, or in the air would be rendered useless, along with all communications. Computers, televisions, phones—would all become obsolete in a moment's time. It was a man-made disaster of Biblical proportions. Only the planners would be prepared.

For the masses, it would be chaos and untold suffering. That it had happened early changed the plan somewhat, but the resulting mayhem, in the end, would make it easier to manipulate a reason for the resulting change in government.

∽∽∽

The officer in charge began shouting orders, aware something way beyond his control had taken place; fully expecting to be mobbed by the people trapped inside. What was happening wasn't in his job description, but his training overrode his fear. "Circle the building. Watch the doors. If they charge you, shoot to kill." Snipers, hidden behind barricades and on roof tops, waited impatiently for riots to break out.

The Crosby meetings had been a gift, with so many of the radical right assembled together, in pockets, around the globe; all individually searched beforehand, and willingly handing over whatever they were asked to give away.

∽∽∽

Inside the auditorium, it was as silent and dark as a tomb. The security guards had their flashlights in hand, fumbling to turn them on; one of the camera men yelled out that he had a battery pack and a floodlight. Somewhere in the vastness a voice shouted to no one, "You okay?", and someone else, sounding far away, shouted back, "Yeah, I think so…"

The cameraman fiddled with the floodlight, finally inserting the battery. He clicked it on, holding it overhead and scanning the room. "What the hell? Where did they all go?" He looked around; looking in vain for someone who could explain how, with the exception of a handful of people scattered around the huge theater, it was possible it was empty.

One of the security officers ran to an exit door, shoving it open to see what was happening on the outside. The building was now being rocked by explosions. When he stepped through the door to the outside, a sniper's bullet took him out.

Someone yelled at the shooter, "God Almighty! You just shot a cop! What are you, crazy?" The officer in charge turned to say something to his partner, but he had disappeared into thin air—one moment ago he was standing right behind him.

"Dear God, what's happening?" he cried out loud to no one.

There was a crash, followed by an explosion behind him—then two more. Helicopters were dropping like dead birds from the sky. The air was toxic and smoke-filled—he could barely see or breathe.

"God!" He yelled again, to no one in particular, looking around again for his partner. "Danny's gone...he's gone! He left his gun, his uniform...everything. What the...?"

~~~

Nelson was alone in his office at Levy & Sinclair—his despair was incapacitating. He decided he might as well make it easy for them; the events had run their course. He was living on borrowed time anyway.

I want it to be over, he thought. He was convinced that his still being alive was hell, and his eternal sentence would be reliving the last few months over, and over, and over, into eternity.

Lindsay was only a few miles away attending the meeting at The Garden. He couldn't help but wonder if she knew more than she'd let on; he knew from the literature she left lying around that her bible study told it like it was.

She was with Maryellen and the other women from their Bible study, and not at home alone with the kids. He knew she wouldn't have taken the children with her if she'd known. Taking the children was Maryellen's idea; she said this event would be like hearing Billy Graham for the last time—it was that big a deal. So, the kids were with their mom's and that was as it should be. His consolation was that his family was together. He was pretty sure Jeremy was there, too.

I sold out...for forty pieces of silver, and there's no way to return it! I've tried to make some things right, but now it was too late, and some things will never be made right. In the end, Judas hung himself because he couldn't find redemption. Another thought superimposed itself over that thought—"Nelson, Judas didn't ask me for it."

He rested his head on his desk, listening to the rhythmic ticking of the clock, the calming effect of the metronome suddenly overridden by the sound of helicopters. He looked up in time to see a chopper move across his field of vision outside his windows, and another, and another—he could see dozens of them, coming from all directions; it looked like a multitude of hornets.

It had begun.

The lights in his office flickered, and the air suddenly felt extremely thick and warm. He cried out, "Oh, Jesus, I am so sorry."

He began to weep; deep gut-wrenching sobs that wouldn't be stopped. In his despair, he pulled open his desk drawer, running his hand along the side to release the lever that would open the hidden compartment in the back. Impatiently, he pushed the pens and clutter out of the way. Where is it? It was in there the last time. It has to be here, he thought, frantically groping. His hand bumped against it—no, it was his gun. Distraught, he shoved it out of the way, groping from side to side, until his fingers finally closed around something small and square.

Then he heard voices; they were coming closer. So be it.

The lights went out, but the clock kept ticking...

~~~

They were surprised when they tested his door and found it unlocked.

A florid and heavyset man stood outside the door of Nelson's office, with his legs splayed, and gun raised. He was accompanied by one of the seniors of the firm. He was dressed in the dark navy uniform of the Levy & Sinclair security detail and perspiring profusely. "We're coming in Mr. Saunders—please don't do anything stupid."

No answer.

The air was crackling with static electricity, becoming uncommonly warm; the lights flickered off and on, and off again.

"Hey, what was that? Did you feel something?" He glanced at Mr. Edwards, pointing to the ceiling where the lights were out.

"Forget about the lights, you goon—you're on the clock. It's day time—we've got windows; you blind?"

The goon tried the door, pushing it open with his shoe; he stepped cautiously into the doorway. "It's unlocked," he said, before entering, as if surprised.

He leaned forward, looking around the space; his gun was raised and ready. "Mr. Edwards, there's no one here. I thought you said you saw him go in."

"He went in, you idiot. I saw him go in, and he hasn't come out."

"I'm sorry, Sir, but his office is empty."

"Oh, for Pete's sake, move over. I want to see for myself." He tried to push him aside.

The gunman reacted protectively by stepping ahead of his boss into the space, pointing his gun every which way, making sure the room was empty before allowing him to enter.

"No sir. It's empty. Is there some secret exit you didn't mention?"

"No, there isn't. Damn it, he's got to be here. I saw him go in with my own two eyes."

"Nope. All's that's here is a pile of clothes on his chair, and a Bible on his desk." He bent over, picking something up. "Oh, and what do you know; his Rolex was on the floor. Would you believe it; he left his Rolex." He held it out for Mr. Edwards to see.

"You said a Bible? Nelson?" He scanned the room; certain that Nelson could not have gotten away.

"Yeah—it's right here. It's one of those pocket Bibles like the Gideon's give away; they gave me one once." He bent over, "Look, his pens still inside it; he must have been reading something. Yeah, he's got a verse circled. John 3:16. I used to know that one when I was a kid. I learned it at church camp."

Mr. Edwards elbowed him aside to look for himself, "Don't bother quoting it! I want you to find him, you hear me? He can't have gotten far. And when you find him, get rid of him—without a trace—do you understand?"

"Yes, sir! Trust me—he's as good as dead."

~~~

The worldwide power outage was not caused by an EMP, although it provided a plausible explanation for the millions of missing men, women, and the world's population of children. It exempted anyone from having to come up with an explanation for what couldn't be explained.

The losses were incalculable, but grieving was a luxury; self-preservation became the preoccupation for the masses. The economies of the world had crumbled and the predicted anarchy erupted in places that were once called civilized; there was no food, and pestilence would kill still more, while wars broke out across the globe.

The pillars of the civilized world supported the rest. That they were strategically undermined had caused them to collapse; the vacuum created would soon become a cesspool.

In the end, a lie was easier to accept, for the desperate and grieving, than having to deal with the reality of what actually happened...

THE END

For this reason God sends them a powerful delusion so that they will believe the lie and so that all will be condemned who have not believed the truth but have delighted in wickedness.
2 Thessalonians 2: 11 & 12

~~~

Delusion: noun
• A deluding or being deluded
• A false belief or opinion
• (PSYCHIATRY) a false, persistent belief maintained in spite of evidence to the contrary
Delusional:
The state of being deluded
Delusion:
From Wikipedia: A delusion, in everyday language, is a fixed belief that is false, fanciful, or is derived from deception. Psychiatry defines the term more specifically as a belief that is pathological (the result of an illness or illness process). As in pathology, it is distinct from a belief based on false or incomplete information, dogma, stupidity, apperception, illusion, or other effects of perception.
In other words, delusion is a choice.

POSTSCRIPT
Thessalonians 2:1-13 (NASV)
Now we request you, brethren, with regard to the coming of our Lord Jesus Christ and our gathering together to Him, that you not be quickly shaken from your composure or are disturbed either by a spirit or a message or a letter as if from us, to the effect that the day of the Lord has come. Let no one in any way deceive you, for it will not come unless the apostasy comes first, and the man of lawlessness is revealed, the son of destruction, who opposes and exalts himself above every so-called god or object of worship, so that he takes his seat in the temple of God, displaying himself as being God. Do you not remember that while I was still with you, I was telling you these things? And you know what restrains him now, so that in his time he will be revealed. For the mystery of lawlessness is already at work; only he who now restrains will do so until he is taken out of the way. Then that lawless one will be revealed whom the Lord will slay with the breath of His mouth and bring to an end by the appearance of His coming; that is, the one whose coming is in accord with the activity of Satan, with all power and signs and false wonders, and with all the deception of wickedness for those who perish, because they did not receive the love of the truth so as to be saved. For this reason God will send upon them a deluding influence so that they will believe what is false,

in order that they all may be judged who did not believe the truth, but took pleasure in wickedness. But we should always give thanks to God for you, brethren beloved by the Lord, because God has chosen you from the beginning for salvation through sanctification by the Spirit and faith in the truth.

~~~

There are different schools of thought about when the Rapture of the Church will take place, or if it takes place at all. For the purposes of this book it happens, and I have placed it before the seven year Tribulation—the message to the believer, inarguably being—readiness. For the sake of argument, it would be my opinion that readiness takes on an even more heightened sense of alertness if one believes that God requires His Body to go through the seven years of Tribulation.

~~~

Luke 17: 22-27 (NIV)

"Just as it was in the days of Noah, so also will it be in the days of the Son of Man. People were eating, drinking, marrying, and being given in marriage up to the day Noah entered the ark. Then the flood came and destroyed them all."

"It was the same in the days of Lot. People ate and drank, bought and sold, planted and bought. But, the day Lot left Sodom, fire and sulfur rained down from heaven and destroyed everyone except the family that God had called out to escape His judgment."

"It will be just like this on the day the Son of Man is revealed. On that day no one who is on the roof of his house, with his goods inside, should go down to get them. Likewise, no one in the field should go back for anything. Remember Lot's wife! Whoever tries to keep his life will lose it, and whoever loses his life will preserve it. I tell you, on that night two people will be in one bed; one will be taken and the other left. Two women will be grinding grain together; one will be taken and the other left."

"Where, Lord?" they asked.

He replied, "Where there is a dead body, there the vultures will gather."

The time is short...

References

Hans   Brinker,   or   The   Silver   Skates   -
http://en.wikipedia.org/wiki/Hans_Brinker

Chapter 1
The Free Online dictionary

Chapter 2
We Shall Behold Him: music by Dottie Rambo; lyrics by Vicki Winins

Chapter 15
Song: *I Must Have Done Something Good,* from the movie "The Sound of Music".

Chapter 18
Cloward & Piven:
The strategy of forcing political change through orchestrated crisis; The "Cloward-Piven Strategy" seeks to hasten the fall of capitalism by overloading the government bureaucracy with a flood of impossible demands, thus pushing society into crisis and economic collapse. David Horowitz

Richard Cloward and Frances Fox Piven were two lifelong members of Democratic Socialists of America who taught sociology at Columbia University (Piven later went on to City University of New York). In a May 1966 Nation magazine article titled "The Weight of the Poor," they outlined their strategy, proposing to use grassroots radical organizations to push ever more strident demands for public services at all levels of government.

The result, they predicted, would be "a profound financial and political crisis" that would unleash "powerful forces ... for major economic reform at the national level."

They implemented the strategy by creating a succession of radical organizations, most notable among them the Association of Community Organizations for Reform Now (ACORN), with the help of veteran organizer Wade Rathke. Their crowning achievement was the "Motor Voter" act, signed into law by Bill Clinton in 1993 with Cloward and Piven standing behind him. November 23, 2009, Cloward-Piven Government: By James Simpson

http://en.wikipedia.org/wiki/Cloward%E2%80%93Piven_strategy

Chapter nineteen: Outcome-Based Education "What is wrong with Outcome-Based Education?" Phyllis Schlafly Report May 1993

Statement by Karen Hayes/Assoc. Director, Concerned Women for

America of Illinois (Given at Illinois Children's Mental Health Partnership Preliminary Plan Public Forum July 3, 2004 Chicago, Illinois) "There is no accountability attached to this plan whatsoever. Simply put, since social and emotional health is subjective in nature, it is impossible to judge the social and emotional health of the plan itself. We will not know in 10 years whether or not our children have been helped or harmed by such an overreaching state mental health intervention system."

Chapter 30
Deuteronomy 4:1 & 2: Now, Israel, hear the decrees and laws I am about to teach you. Follow them so that you may live and may go in and take possession of the land the Lord, the God of your ancestors, is giving you. 2 Do not add to what I command you and do not subtract from it, but keep the commands of the Lord your God that I give you. (NIV)

Chapter 34
New World order: search results on Bing as of the writing of this book is 1,240,000,000 possible hits. Google has over 2 billion. Those numbers change daily.

VeriChip: an injectable identification chip that can be inserted under the skin of a human being to provide biometric verification. VeriChip, manufactured by Applied Digital Solutions, is about the size of a grain of rice. It holds an identification number, an electromagnetic coil for transmitting data, and a tuning capacitor; the components are enclosed inside a silicon and glass container that is compatible with human tissue. The chip, which uses an RFID (wireless transmission) technology similar to the injectable ID chips used by animal shelters to tag pets, can be read by a proprietary scanner up to four feet away.

VeriChip was originally intended to function in much the same way a medical alert bracelet does by giving medical personnel life-saving information about a patient's history. It is now being used for security and automated data collection, as well as medical, purposes. Taken from the website: http://searchsecurity.techtarget.com/

To find more information about not taking the chip when required: http://www.noverichipinside.com/

1. The VeriChip can be hacked
2. Security researcher Jonathan Westhues has shown how easy it is to clone a VeriChip
3. VeriChip cloning demo online at http://cq.cx/verichip.pl
4. Eighteen employees in the Mexican Attorney General's office who use an implanted chip to enter a sensitive records room
5. Companies own literature indicates that chipped patients cannot

undergo an MRI if they're unconscious.

6. Digital Angel Corporation (formerly Destron Fearing) has been involved in the development and manufacture of livestock identification products since 1948.

7. The company admits that critical medical information linked to the chip could be unavailable in a real emergency.

8. Chipped patients might also have to wear a Medic Alert bracelet as a back-up in case the VeriChip database containing their critical medical information is unavailable

9. Physicians are told the product might not function in places where there are ambient radio transmissions--like ambulances

10. Verichip Waiver "Patient...is fully aware of any risks, complications, risks of loss, damage of any nature, and injury that may be associated with this registration. Patient waives all claims and releases any liability arising from this registration and acknowledges that no warranties of any kind have been made or will be made with respect to this registration. ALL WARRANTIES, WHETHER EXPRESS OR IMPLIED, HOWEVER ARISING, WHETHER BY OPERATION OF LAW OR OTHERWISE, INCLUDING BUT NOT LIMITED TO ANY IMPLIED WARRANTIES OF MECHANTABILITY AND FITNESS FOR A PARTICULAR PURPOSE ARE EXCLUDED AND WAIVED. IN NO EVENT SHALL THE COMPANY BE LIABLE TO PATIENT FOR ANY INCIDENTAL, SPECIAL OR CONSEQUENTIAL DAMAGES (INCLUDING LOST INCOME OR SAVINGS) ARISING FROM ANY CAUSE WHATSOEVER, EVEN IF ADVISED OF THEIR POSSIBILITY, REGARDLESS OF WHETHER SUCH DAMAGES ARE SOUGHT BASED ON BREACH OF CONTRACT, NEGLIGENCE, OR ANY OTHER LEGAL THEORY."

11. VeriChip Corporation tries to ease consumer fears by referring to the chip as being "about the size of a grain of rice."

12. Scott Silverman, Chairman of the Board of VeriChip Corporation, promoting the Verichip human tracking device as a way to identify immigrants and guest workers

13. Silverman has stated the Verichip "be used for enforcement purposes at the employer level." He added, "We have talked to many people in Washington about using it...."

14. Columbian President Alvaro Uribe. He reportedly told Senator Arlen Specter (R-PA) that he would consider having microchips implanted into Colombian workers before they are permitted to enter the United States to work on a seasonal basis.

15. Tommy Thompson, former Secretary of Health and Human Services joined the board of VeriChip Corporation after leaving his Bush administration cabinet post.

16. Tommy Thompson, former Secretary of Health and Human Services went on national television recommending that all Americans get chipped as a way to link to their medical records.

17. Tommy Thompson, former Secretary of Health and Human Services stated VeriChip could replace military dog tags, and a spokesman boasted that the company had been in talks with the Pentagon.

18. Privacy advocates warn that once people are numbered with a remotely readable RFID tag like the VeriChip, they can be tracked. Once they can be tracked, they can be monitored and controlled

19. Electrical hazards, MRI incompatibility, adverse tissue reaction, and migration of the implanted transponder are just a few of the potential risks associated with the Verichip ID implant device, according to an October 12, 2004 letter issued by the Food and Drug Administration (FDA).

20. Albrecht cites MRI incompatibility is perhaps the most serious issue. An MRI machine uses powerful magnetic fields coupled with pulsed radio frequency (RF) fields. According to the FDA's Primer on Medical Device Interactions with Magnetic Resonance Imaging Systems, "electrical currents may be induced in conductive metal implants" that can cause "potentially severe patient burns."

21. FDA letter also cites the risk of "compromised information security" among its concerns. The VeriChip ID implant, about the size of a grain of rice, uses radio waves to transmit medical and financial account information to reader devices. There is a risk that these transmissions could be intercepted and duplicated by others or that the devices could be used to track an individual's movements and location.

22. "Once you're chipped, you can be identified by doorway portal readers without your knowledge,"

23. News reports earlier this year indicated 160 employees in the Mexican Attorney General's Office had been implanted with Verichip RFID devices. New information indicates that only 18 individuals received the device

24. Among the potential problems the FDA identifies are: "adverse tissue reaction," "migration of the implanted transponder," "failure of implanted transponder," "electrical hazards" and "magnetic resonance imaging [MRI] incompatibility." Not to mention the nasty needle stick from the "inserter" used to inject it.

25. VeriChip-MRI incompatibility means that doctors will be unable to order this potentially life-saving diagnostic procedure for patients with VeriChip implants, unless the patient undergoes a surgical procedure to remove the VeriChip first.

26. VeriChip implant can be read whenever you pass through a doorway equipped with a special VeriChip "portal scanner"?

27. Under the FDA guidelines, the human implantable RFID Verichip was approved by default without testing at any level, as the Verichip was not considered a 'regulated medical device'.

28. The patent, No. # 7,116,230 combines RFID tagging

technology with a portable receiver to track the location of assets within a fixed setting, such as a building or warehouse

29. VeriChip's infant protection systems, with one-out-of-three Hospitals and Birthing Centers in the United States

30. VeriChip Corporation Signs 3-year, $750,000 Distribution Contract with iChip Corporation of South Africa

31. Derek Brandon Jacobs, one of the first people in the world to bear an identification microchip, died at 18 in a Florida motorcycle accident.

32. Verichip is lobbying the Pentagon to choose its RFID tags as a replacement for the famous metal dog tags for ALL USA military!

33. The company has gone on record to say that the implantable GPS-tracked chip could be worth a whopping $100 billion comprising 26 potential vertical markets. That sort of revenue by any company's standards is stupendous and would require a great part of the world's population to be 'chipped'.

34. Two hackers (Annalee Newitz and Jonathan Westhues) demonstrated that the chip named RFid (Radio Frequency Identification) could be easily scanned and cloned during their intervention in the 6th Hope Conference.

35. Newark's Horizon Blue Cross Blue Shield of New Jersey, the state's largest health insurer, is launching a two-year pilot program with Hackensack University Medical Center that will implant microchips in 280 Horizon members.

36. Four hospitals in the US Caribbean territory plan to begin using the Verichip patients who have significant health problems or illnesses that cause memory loss.

37. Verichip IPO will offer 4.3 million shares between $6.50 and $8.50 per share from underwriters Merriman Curhan Ford, C.E. Unterberg Towbin, and Kaufman Bros.

38. The company's chief scientist, Dr. Peter Zhou, who has gone onto record to say "Before there may have been resistance, but not anymore. People are getting used to implants; new century, new trend."

39. American Medical Association's (AMA) Council on Ethical and Judicial Affairs has adopted a policy stating that implantable radio frequency identification (RFID) devices may help to identify patients, thereby improving the safety and efficiency of patient care, and may be used to enable secure access to patient clinical information BUT "These devices may present physical risks to the patient," the report said. "Though they are removable, their small size allows them to migrate under the skin, making them potentially difficult to extract." [Verichip cherry picked the press release maintaining its leadership in deceiving the public.]

40. New Jersey has actually passed legislation that will require "smart gun" technology on all handguns sold, which would be three years

after the state attorney general certifies that "smart guns" are available on the market.

41. "In principle, a device of this type should never be forced on anybody," Scott Silverman has gone on record to say. Please view the Operation Lie and Deceive Verichip Style video before you accept shape shifting Scott's word as gospel.

42. Lawmakers in Indonesia's remote province of Papua have thrown their support behind a controversial bill requiring some HIV/AIDS patients to be implanted with microchips

43. Upon successful completion of the in vivo glucose-sensing RFID development program, this self-contained, implantable bio-sensing device will, for the first time, have the ability to measure glucose levels in the human body through an external scanner, thereby eliminating the need for diabetics to prick their fingers multiple times per day.

44. The glucose sensor is a promising example, combining a unique application of the technology and an extremely valuable market. While there is much more to do, development of the binding environment was a big step towards reaching that future."

45. VeriChip Corporation announced that its personal health record used in conjunction with its VeriMed Health Link system will be accessible through Microsoft(R) HealthVault(TM), an online platform designed to put consumers in control of their health information.

46. VeriChip Corp has been notified by NASDAQ that it is not in compliance with the listing requirements. NASDAQ said that for the past 30 consecutive business days prior to Oct. 16, its stock bid price closed below the minimum $1-a-share price requirement for continued listing.

47. In addition, the stock has not maintained a minimum market value of $5 million as required.

48. September — shortly after the first 90 or so Alzheimer's patients received its chips in Florida, Verichip came under fire when cancer was linked to embedded RFID chips

49. A Dutch prototype for an RFID embedded in a passport was hacked in two hours by a local TV station. Hackers could access fingerprint, photograph, and other data on the RFID tag, perfect for creating a cloned passport.

50. Successful hacks of the Exxon Mobile key fob, the VeriChip human RFID implant, the California State Capitol building access system, and the new RFID passports show how easy it is to skim and clone poorly protected RFID devices and compromise RFID-dependent security systems.

51. India, with the Health HiWay initiative of Apollo Hospitals and IBM, which connects 250 users across 75 providers. The goal is a centralized database of patient records across the country.

52. 100 million e-prescribing initiatives, supported by a consortium of IT biggies like Dell, Google and Microsoft

53. Xega is the name for Verichip in South America

54. State banning micro chipping Wisconsin and North Dakota California Missouri

55. To date, about 100 patients and caregivers with Alzheimer's Community Care have undergone successful RFID implants with another 100 expected to be implanted by February 2009.

56. UK Ministry of Justice is exploring the possibility of injecting prisoners in the back of the arm with radio frequency identification (RFID)

57. Every single Metropolitan police officer will be 'micro chipped' so top brass can monitor their movements on a Big Brother style tracking scheme, it can be revealed today.

58. UK Chipping According to respected industry magazine Police Review, the plan - which affects all 31,000 serving officers in the Met, including Sir Ian Blair - is set to replace the unreliable Airwave radio system currently used to help monitor officer's movements.

59. The new electronic tracking device - called the Automated Personal Location System (APLS) - means that officers will never be out of range of supervising officers.

60. VeriChip US military. According to the DC Examiner, the company is lobbying the Pentagon to choose its RFID tags as a replacement for the famous metal dog tags, making information like a person's name and complete medical record instantly available with the swipe of an RFID reader

61. The process developed by Somark involves a geometric array of micro-needles and a reusable applicator with a one-time-use ink capsule. Pydynowski said it takes five to 10 seconds to "stamp or tattoo" an animal, and there is no need to remove the fur. The ink remains in the dermal layer, and a reader can detect it from 4 feet away.

62. Digital Angel, the manufacturer of animal microchips, exclusively makes the Home Again microchip and is the sister company of VeriChip.

For additional information go to:
http://en.wikipedia.org/wiki/VeriChip
Recent developments on the potential damage of cell phones to human physiology: http://www.nowtheendbegins.com/blog/?p=9880

Chapter 40

The Emergent (emerging) church:

Definition: a label that has been used to refer to a particular subset of Christians who are rethinking Christianity against the backdrop of Postmodernism....Emerging Church groups have typically contained some or all of the following elements:

• Highly creative approaches to worship and spiritual reflection. This can involve everything from the use of contemporary music and films through to liturgy or other more ancient customs. ...

• A flexible approach to theology whereby individual differences in belief and morality are accepted within reason.

• A more holistic approach to the role of the church in society. This can mean anything from greater emphasis on fellowship in the structure of the group to a higher degree of emphasis on social action, community building or Christian outreach.

• A desire to re-analyze the Bible against the context into which it was written.... Psalm 119:11

More information available at: http://www.apologeticsindex.org/306-emerging-church-web-sites there are websites listed on this site that include arguments for, neutral, and against this ongoing trend. It is vital that Christians be aware of the movement and the dynamics that are in play.

Chapter 43
Google and the government:
http://www.americanthinker.com/2011/02/google_and_the_government.html

Chapter 52:
The Financial New World Order: Towards a Global Currency and World Government by Andrew Gavin Marshall www.globalresearch.ca (search term: Global Currency)

A recent article in the Financial Post stated that, "The danger in the present course is that if the world moves to a "super sovereign" reserve currency engineered by experts, such as the "UN Commission of Experts" led by Nobel laureate economist Joseph Stiglitz, we would give up the possibility of a spontaneous money order and financial harmony for a centrally planned order and the politicization of money. Such a regime change would endanger not only the future value of money but, more importantly, our freedom and prosperity."

Chapter 59:
The first amendment to the Constitution: The First Amendment (Amendment I) to the United States Constitution is part of the Bill of Rights. The amendment prohibits the making of any law respecting an establishment of religion, impeding the free exercise of religion, abridging the freedom of speech, infringing on the freedom of the press, interfering with the right to peaceably assemble or prohibiting the petitioning for a governmental redress of grievances.

Chapter 60:

An electromagnetic pulse (sometimes abbreviated EMP) is a burst of electromagnetic radiation. The abrupt pulse of electromagnetic radiation usually results from certain types of high energy explosions, especially a nuclear explosion, or from a suddenly fluctuating magnetic field. The resulting rapidly changing electric fields and magnetic fields may couple with electrical/electronic systems to produce damaging current and voltage surges.

In military terminology, a nuclear bomb detonated hundreds of miles above the Earth's surface is known as a high-altitude electromagnetic pulse (HEMP) device. Effects of a HEMP device depend on a very large number of factors, including the altitude of the detonation, energy yield, gamma ray output, interactions with the Earth's magnetic field, and electromagnetic shielding of targets.

http://en.wikipedia.org/wiki/Electromagnetic_pulse

~~~

John 3:16: For God so loved the world that he gave his only begotten son, so that whosoever believeth in him should not perish, but have everlasting life. KJV

Homework for the curious

End time
New World Order
One World Government
The Fabian Society
Freemasonry
Round table
Brave new world
Club of Rome
World Bank
Illuminati
Protocols of the Elders of Zion
International Monetary Fund
World Council of Church's
General Agreements on Tariffs & Trade (GATT)
World Health Organization
The United Nations
Council on Foreign Relations
World Federalist Movement
The Bilderberg Group
Population control
Mind control
Occultism
Mass surveillance
Fourth Reich
Alien Invasion
Postulated implementations
New Age
Open conspiracy
Skull & Bones Society
http://www.nypl.org/sites/default/files/archivalcollections/pdf/cwg.pdf
http://www.nypl.org/sites/default/files/archivalcollections/pdf/461.pdf

http://green-agenda.com/globalrevolution.html
http://www.missionislam.com/nwo/index.htm
http://forcingchange.wordpress.com/2011/07/12/one-world-one-money-the-quest-for-a-single-global-currency/
History of the New World Order Parts I & II
http://www.michaeljournal.org/nwo1.htm

A CHRONOLOGICAL HISTORY OF THE NEW WORLD ORDER
By D.L. Cuddy, Ph.D.

Arranged and Edited by John Loeffler

In the mainline media, those who adhere to the position that there is some kind of "conspiracy" pushing us towards a world government are virulently ridiculed. The standard attack maintains that the so-called "New World Order" is the product of turn-of-the-century, right-wing, bigoted, anti-Semitic racists acting in the tradition of the long-debunked Protocols of the Learned Elders of Zion, now promulgated by some Militias and other right-wing hate groups.

The historical record does not support that position to any large degree but it has become the mantra of the socialist left and their cronies, the media.

The term "New World Order" has been used thousands of times in this century by proponents in high places of federalized world government. Some of those involved in this collaboration to achieve world order have been Jewish. The preponderance is not, so it most definitely is not a Jewish agenda.

For years, leaders in education, industry, the media, banking, etc., have promoted those with the same Weltanschauung (world view) as theirs. Of course, someone might say that just because individuals promote their friends doesn't constitute a conspiracy. That's true in the usual sense. However, it does represent an "open conspiracy," as described by noted Fabian Socialist H.G. Wells in The Open Conspiracy: Blue Prints for a World Revolution (1928).

In 1913, prior to the passage of the Federal Reserve Act President Wilson's The New Freedom was published, in which he revealed:

"Since I entered politics, I have chiefly had men's views confided to me privately. Some of the biggest men in the U. S., in the field of commerce and manufacturing, are afraid of somebody, are afraid of something. They know that there is a power somewhere so organized, so subtle, so watchful, so interlocked, so complete, so pervasive, that they had better not speak above their breath when they speak in condemnation of it."

On November 21, 1933, President Franklin Roosevelt wrote a letter to Col. Edward Mendel House, President Woodrow Wilson's close advisor: "The real truth of the matter is, as you and I know that a financial element in the larger centers has owned the Government ever since the days of Andrew Jackson... "

That there is such a thing as a cabal of power brokers who control government behind the scenes has been detailed several times in this century by credible sources. Professor Carroll Quigley was Bill Clinton's mentor at Georgetown University. President Clinton has publicly paid

homage to the influence Professor Quigley had on his life. In Quigley's magnum opus Tragedy and Hope (1966), he states: "There does exist and has existed for a generation, an international ... network which operates, to some extent, in the way the radical right believes the Communists act. In fact, this network, which we may identify as the Round Table Groups, has no aversion to cooperating with the Communists, or any other groups and frequently does so. I know of the operations of this network because I have studied it for twenty years and was permitted for two years, in the early 1960s, to examine its papers and secret records. I have no aversion to it or to most of its aims and have, for much of my life, been close to it and too many of its instruments. I have objected, both in the past and recently, to a few of its policies... but in general my chief difference of opinion is that it wishes to remain unknown, and I believe its role in history is significant enough to be known."   The remainder of this article can be found at:
http://constitution.org/col/cuddy_nwo.htm

God bless you as you in your seeking.

Ask lots of questions, and question the answers!

From the Author

On September 10, 1991 I was in my car, listening to the radio. What caused me to pause at one particular radio station was a discussion about the Clarence Thomas hearings taking place in our Senate—the program was enlightening regarding some of the behind the scenes' dynamics of the hearings.

The program I paused on was Concerned Women for America moderated by Beverly LaHaye. I called for information about a chapter in my area, and there wasn't one in Kansas. Two weeks later I met with Kenda Bartlett, and together, we formed one.

The call I made that afternoon was life changing; I went from a desire to learn more about the issues affecting our culture, to becoming the bearer of the information I was learning to whomever I could get to stop to listen. My involvement evolved into lobbying on behalf of the family at a state and national level.

Once I realized the enormity of what we were taking on, I was reminded of the story Hans Brinker, or the Silver Skates. The book is remembered for popularizing the story of the little Dutch boy who noticed a leak coming from a hole in a dike; the dike was what held the ocean back from flooding his village. He put his finger in the hole and stood steadfast, saving his townsfolk. Similarly, like a chip in a windshield, our culture has a crack that is growing, and it won't be stopped without enlisting others to join us in the fight to keep it from growing larger.

What I realized later, and after much frustration, was that the information we were putting forth wasn't simply instructional, but it also required a response, making it preferable (for some) to distance from the information, rather than become accountable for knowing it.

This book is about now... right now... today... it is about seizing the moment. Perhaps, if we can, collectively, wake up enough people, we can save this once proud people, and magnificent land.

Thanks to the vision of Beverly LaHaye, who when disturbed by the changes she saw warping our culture, called together a group of women to join her over coffee to see how they might become a voice for change. Concerned Women for America was born out of her concern.

Invest yourself—that's what great people do. Liberty has never been without cost. Invest yourself while there is still time. Opinions are worth nothing without some sweat and tears behind them.

The experiences with CWA enlarged me, and what I learned was invaluable; I couldn't have written this book without them.

The time is short...

Fran Riedemann

About Fran Riedemann

Fran Riedemann and her husband, Ken, have raised five children and have eleven grandchildren. Her career includes working in the field of interior design and owning a fine arts & crafts gallery for twenty years in Overland Park, Ks. and another in Naples, Florida. She has been proactive in defending pro-family causes, including her time working with Concerned Women for America. After retiring from the gallery she now has time to explore her own creativity, still working as a designer and in art resale and acquisition. Most recently she began writing. "Implosion" is her third published book, joining "Joseph: the Heart of the Father" & "Beatrice Baker, Bringer of Joy".

The artwork of Colleen Ross and Vicky Montesinos is available through the author.

Contact Fran Riedemann
Website: www.considerthe source.org
Email: fran@considerthesource.org
Twitter: @authorFran

Made in the USA
Lexington, KY
27 May 2012